CO
RECEIVED
JUN 29 2017

OWL

and the

ELECTRIC

SAMURAI

'NO LONGER PROPERTY OF
SEATTLE PUBLIC LIBRARY

Volumes in Kristi Charish's Owl Series

Owl and the Japanese Circus
Owl and the City of Angels
Owl and the Electric Samurai
Owl and the Tiger Thieves (forthcoming)

OWL

and the

ELECTRIC SAMURAI

Kristi Charish

GALLERY BOOKS

New York   London   Toronto   Sydney   New Delhi

Gallery Books
An Imprint of Simon & Schuster, Inc.
1230 Avenue of the Americas
New York, NY 10020

This book is a work of fiction. Any references to historical events, real people, or real places are used fictitiously. Other names, characters, places, and events are products of the author's imagination, and any resemblance to actual events or places or persons, living or dead, is entirely coincidental.

Copyright © 2017 by Kristi Charish

All rights reserved, including the right to reproduce this book or portions thereof in any form whatsoever. For information address Gallery Books Subsidiary Rights Department, 1230 Avenue of the Americas, New York, NY 10020.

First Gallery Books trade paperback edition May 2017

GALLERY BOOKS and colophon are registered trademarks of Simon & Schuster, Inc.

For information about special discounts for bulk purchases, please contact Simon & Schuster Special Sales at 1-866-506-1949 or business@simonandschuster.com.

The Simon & Schuster Speakers Bureau can bring authors to your live event. For more information or to book an event contact the Simon & Schuster Speakers Bureau at 1-866-248-3049 or visit our website at www.simonspeakers.com.

Cover art by Fred Gambino

Manufactured in the United States of America

1 3 5 7 9 10 8 6 4 2

ISBN 978-1-5011-3973-4
ISBN 978-1-5011-3972-7 (ebook)

For my mother.
Don't worry, Mom, I didn't
write any of the family into the book.

OWL

and the
ELECTRIC
SAMURAI

1

NO GOOD DEED

4:00 p.m. Backpacker lodge, Fikkal, Nepal

Have you ever had a deep-seated feeling that the world is out to get you?

And I don't mean for doing something where you might actually deserve it: I mean the kind that happens *despite* your best intentions to be a good person, turn over a new leaf, and potentially make up for a possible—though clearly not intentional—slight you *may* have done others . . .

And even though you may be doing your damnedest to fix things, including crossing the globe twice in the last month, you could feel that the universe *still* decided it was going to tell you that you could royally fuck off?

You know, *that* kind of "out to get you" feeling?

Because from this side of the backpacker hostel picnic table, sitting across from my Nepal contact, Dev, that was pretty much the vibe I was getting. To be honest, it was the vibe I'd been getting all month, like gum getting tangled in your hair.

I placed my elbows on the worn wood of our table, tucked in a corner of the lodge bar, and gave my onetime classmate and on-again-off-again business associate, Dev Rai, my best "do not fuck with me right now" glare. It wasn't hard; I'd been wearing it an unprecedented amount this month. Add to that the noise from the evening influx of hikers arriving for the night in the small, foot-of-the-Himalayas-trek stopover town, Fikkal, and the incense the lodge was burning—which, while pleasant on its own, lost its charm when mixed with stale beer—well, let's just say my patience for playing games was at its end. Not that I'd had much to begin with.

"Dev, you have to give me something," I said.

He fixed his brown eyes on me, no longer smiling. "What is this I keep hearing about the IAA breathing down everyone's neck?"

Goddamn it. Rumors reach even the outback at the foot of the Himalayas. The juicier ones first—or in this case, the story of how my using World Quest to track down artifacts *may* have contributed to the IAA's recent upgraded interest in locating the game designers. Add to that the kind of scrutiny an open bounty brings to anyone and everyone who ever had contact with the prey. Like Dev . . .

He was pissed. Rightly so. But his glare was nowhere near as effective as mine. He might have had the rugged-mountain-tour-guide act down pat, complete with windburn and calloused hands, but his brown eyes were way too pretty to convey any sort of menace.

Mine, on the other hand? Consider it one of my unsung talents.

I leaned across the table. We might have been tucked under the stairs and out of the way, but as the lodge filled with trekkers coming down for evening beer and dinner, I only trusted our privacy so far. "It's not what it sounds like," I told him.

He threw out his hands as he sat back against the wall. "That's what you said last time!"

I'd kind of been hoping he wouldn't remember that, or at least not bring it up. Still, I didn't look away. "Dev, this time is different. I'm not here to steal something."

Dev's brow furrowed and his eyes narrowed. "Thievery? Is that what you're calling it now?"

I winced. Last time had been a Buddhist stone tablet documenting an extinct sect of the religion—one that had been a lot more friendly to the offense-as-the-best-defense way of thinking. It had dated back to the twelfth century and had been written by a monk exiled from Tibet for said offensive activities. Interesting note, my buyer had claimed to be part of a sect trying to rekindle the old, violent Buddhist flame. To each reenactment group their own, I had figured.

Unfortunately the IAA hadn't seen it that way. "Okay, the tablet wasn't one of my wisest moments, and yes, I should have mentioned the IAA wanted it kept buried—but this time I'm not in it for profit—"

Dev made a derisive noise over his beer. "And I'm trying to stay off the IAA's radar, not send out a homing beacon. And word has it that's exactly what helping you will almost certainly get me—And don't even try to justify Benji," he added when I opened my mouth to argue, "and the fact that the IAA is even looking for these two . . ." His expression darkened, though that might have been a trick of the sun setting outside.

Thank you, universe, for doing your damnedest to keep me in everyone's bad books. At least I know I can count on you for one thing. "Okay, first, that's not entirely my fault. I didn't design a game based on all the things the IAA wants kept secret." Like supernatural monsters, ancient magic artifacts, monsters . . . the monsters bear mentioning twice. "And second, like I keep telling you, the entire reason I'm here is I'm trying to *avert* a disaster this time, not cause one. For once, why can't any of you let me put my unique talent for pissing off the IAA to use? For once, that's all I'm asking here."

Dev shook his head. "And you trying to avert disaster worries me even more. Artifacts? That I can handle, but screwing the IAA?" He swore and finished off his bottle of Rato-Bhaat beer, depositing the empty bottle on the table with a hollow clatter. "I thought they were going to drag me off to one of their Siberian digs for helping you last time." Dev pursed his lips and sat back. "Besides, you're putting words in my mouth. At no point—any point—did I say I guided two guys who fit that description," he said, pointing at my phone, where I kept the IAA's bounty file.

"And I'm not an idiot. Anyone with any brains looking for real artifacts and sites in Nepal uses you—*I* use you. And I can't be the only one who figured they came this way. There are only so many places to look for Shangri-La."

That made him pause. I could see it in the way his eyes narrowed and the corner of his mouth twitched. I took a gamble and started to count off the Shangri-La candidates. "The Kunlun Mountains, Hunza Valley in Pakistan, Zhongdian in Yunnan, I even checked out the Muli Monastery in Sichuan, for crying out loud." I picked up my own empty Rato beer bottle and pointed the end at Dev. "The World Quest dynamic duo checked all those locations, I'm sure of it, and this is the last stop." The Kanchenjunga region of Nepal, where the Lepcha mountain people had been telling stories about a hidden valley of immortality for ages. Only unlike the other locations, no one knew where it was.

"Those same stories also tell of demons—yeti and rakshasa—guarding the mountain."

"And we both know those aren't the most far-fetched parts of those stories."

The dark look returned to Dev's face as he leaned in closer. "There are stories about a hidden valley at Everest as well."

"Yeah, and that's where I'm betting all the bounty hunters and mercenaries are right now, and when they figure out that all those stories about the valley being at Everest originated *this* side of the Himalayan range"— I shrugged—"it won't take them long to connect the dots to you."

His brow furrowed, and I noticed his eyes doing their own sweep of the nearby patrons in the bar. I might have been the first to take the Nepalese connection seriously, but Dev was smart. I was only the first of many.

Someone jostled our table, breaking our stalemate momentarily before offering us a rushed apology. The place was more crowded than it had been an hour ago. Come to think of it, it was more crowded than it had been last night. I frowned as a large man, European or American, walked by, headed for the bar. He stood out from the backpacker crowd—older, cleaner, and better dressed.

As the man disappeared into the bar lineup, I shook off my unsettled feeling and turned my attention back to Dev. The man who'd looked out of place hadn't been searching for anyone. He was probably just a pro climber or hiker trying to get off the beaten Everest track. My paranoia ran well on high, but it wasn't always right.

"Look, Dev, I can't guarantee the IAA isn't going to turn over every stone, including you, to find them, but I can guarantee you I'm the only one doing my damnedest to make sure the IAA never finds them. All I'm asking is where you took them. Then you don't have to lie when everyone else shows up. You can point them in my direction, and I'll do the rest."

I could see Dev's conviction to staying tight-lipped wavering, and I silently crossed my fingers and toes. Out of all the associates I'd had through my career as an antiquities thief, Dev was one of the few I could honestly say I respected. He'd taken a few archaeology classes with me and Nadya through an exchange program, and he'd completed a master's—not for research, mind you, but for his family's tour guide business back in Nepal. An actual archaeologist taking you through Nepalese and Tibetan heritage sites set them apart from other outfits . . . and the fact that it was a relatively open secret that he acted as personal guide for academics and treasure raiders alike looking for the real deal, well, that hadn't hurt business either.

The point was Dev was good, and he had ethics—limits to what he was willing to turn a blind eye to. He had a reputation for turning down the shadier, sleazier operations and heists, which was rare in my line of work. And deep down Dev knew that despite my fair share of personality faults, I didn't intentionally screw people over.

Honor amongst thieves . . . or accessories to thieves. Go figure.

Dev shook his head, sat back, and swore. "God help me, I can't believe I'm doing this. *Fine*, but get me another beer—and you're buying," he said, passing me his empty bottle.

"You won't regret it," I started.

He made a face. "I'm doing it as a favor to Nadya, not you. And tell her I said that. And you'll owe me more than beer!" he called after me as I took both our empty beer bottles in one hand and waved over my shoulder before pushing my way through the crowd.

Okay, maybe he didn't know deep down I was a good guy. I didn't care if it was my reputation or his still-lit crush on Nadya that was crumbling his convictions, so long as they crumbled.

The bartender barely glanced at me as I passed him the two empty bottles and a pile of rupees before holding up two fingers.

While I waited for him to retrieve the bottles from the cooler, my attention drifted to the two men beside me shouting at the bartender's back, demanding what was on tap. Get with the backpacker program. There were three beers, all in bottles.

I frowned as I took in their clothes—expensive and well-fitting mountain gear more suited to climbing than backpacking. All recently laundered, and, to top it off, I could smell their deodorant. South African from their accents, early thirties if I had to guess.

Two more people here today who didn't quite look or sound like they belonged . . .

My phone began to buzz in my jacket pocket just as the bartender returned with my pair of Rato-Bhaat beers. I balanced them under my arm as I headed back to our table so I could fumble my buzzing phone out. It was Rynn.

That didn't bode well. Rynn had figured it'd be another two days before he finished tracking down his contact, a recluse of a supernatural who lived off the trails, closer to the foot of Kanchenjunga. Rynn hoped she might be willing to shed some insight on the local Shangri-La legends. Between Rynn's supernatural contact and Dev, I'd hoped we could get a line on where the World Quest guys had vanished.

But if Rynn *was* calling me after only two days, well, he'd either found his contact early or stumbled into something that had worried him.

Like mercenaries making an inopportune appearance.

I caught Dev's attention and held up two fingers before taking up an empty space on the hostel stairs. Dev and I were friendly, but not so friendly that he needed to hear half my conversation with Rynn, which could involve a potential supernatural snafu.

Negotiating the beer, I balanced my phone between my shoulder and ear and answered.

"Rynn, please say it's good news."

There was a pause, and Rynn made a small sound as if he was weighing his words carefully. "Well, as you like to say, there is good news and bad news—"

"Good news," I said before Rynn could finish. Never leave things like that open to interpretation.

"Good news is I made contact with Talie, and she does have some information on Shambhala—Shangri-La. Not the location, mind you, but details I think will be useful. After some bargaining on my part, she's willing to part with them."

Details I didn't have already was good. They also could have waited until Rynn was back at the lodge. "What's the bad news?" I asked.

Rynn let out a breath. "The bad news is Talie's contacts in Kathmandu say that we are no longer the only ones looking. They've spotted mercenaries arriving in the city—and not just today, over the last week."

Shit. I glanced back to the bar, but the two out-of-place backpackers were gone. I did notice a table of men who, though dressed the part, were larger and more muscular than most of the people crammed in here.

One of them glanced in my direction and gave me a once-over before turning back to his conversation and beer. Oh I hoped there was an international climbing competition in town. . . .

"What?" I said, missing what Rynn said. I covered my free ear as best I could while not letting the beer bottles crash to the floor. I almost dropped the phone as someone jostled me on their way up the stairs to the rooms and dorms. I stepped closer to the wall, making myself as small as possible. "Look, Rynn—this isn't a good time to talk . . ."

I trailed off as I spotted another table of suspect backpackers, this time from their matching gear and stoic expressions. I turned toward the wall as one of them glanced up, scanning the room. "The patrons are getting awfully burly. I think I've got mercenaries—as in more than one group."

It was Rynn's turn to swear. "Add those to the group of Colombians I took care of on my way out, a group of Russians Talie's people spotted in Kathmandu a few days ago, that's at least four groups of serious mercenaries that have arrived in Nepal in the last twenty-four hours."

Four too many in my mind, and I didn't want to know the details of how Rynn had handled the Colombians, though I was fairly certain it involved his incubus brand of suggestion.

"One, two I could manage, but four?" Rynn didn't need to finish the sentence. If there was one thing I knew from working with him as Mr. Kurosawa's intern security head, it was that Rynn liked his risk assessment. I should know, I'd been the source of his professional stress on more than one occasion.

And if he was this worried, I should be running. "I'd say we've just about worn our welcome out in Nepal," I said.

"How much longer do you need, Alix?"

"Not much—another half hour. Look on the bright side, they can't be on to me. Otherwise they wouldn't be sitting here drinking beer."

There was a pause. "Describe them to me," Rynn said.

"Ah, they look like a pro ski or climbing team. Matching hiking gear, dark, neutral colors, keeping to themselves. At least one of them is South African," I added, as the two men from the bar joined the table, carrying more bottles.

"Get me a look," Rynn said.

I turned my camera on. Once I could see my own pretty face, unkempt blond hair shoved under my red flames hat, I inverted the camera so it was showing the picnic table full of burly men in tight-fitting Henleys. "Getting this?"

Rynn swore. "Alix, listen carefully. Get upstairs and pack our stuff. Now. They're serious."

"Relax, they haven't noticed me yet. They aren't even looking. Probably chasing the same World Quest leads I am." The World Quest duo had covered their tracks, but with enough effort I'd been able to chase their credit card and travel this far.

I glanced back to where Dev was waiting, frowning at me. I held up the beer and a single finger. In no way did telling him about the mercenaries go in my favor.

"No," Rynn continued. "I mean, yes they're mercenaries, but I recognize them. They're human, and call themselves the Zebras."

"Zebras? What kind of name for mercenaries is that?"

"The kind who specialize in supernaturals. Have you ever heard the saying 'Don't go looking for zebras when you find a hoofprint in Central Park'? It's a play on that—except these men specialize in finding the monsters, mostly extermination. We leave them alone since they tend to handle smaller problems, but if they're in Fikkal, a group of at least six, no less . . ." He let the thought trail off.

Shit. "Maybe a couple yeti stumbled into someone's yak farm?" I offered.

"If the Zebras were here for yeti, there'd only be two. There's no way they're here doing reconnaissance for the IAA bounty. They're looking for a powerful supernatural. Like an incubus."

Oh, that did not bode well for us. "Nepal is getting awfully crowded. I'd say we've worn out our welcome."

"Can you be ready in ten?"

I hedged my answer as I glanced back at Dev, who was outright glaring at me now. "Give me twenty."

"Make it fifteen. I'll meet you in the room—I want to avoid the South Africans. And Alix? Be careful." Rynn hung up, and I feigned checking my email as I headed back to Dev, stealing another glance at the table of Zebras to make certain they weren't watching me, all the while trying to calm my own nerves.

Okay, breath, Alix. They aren't even looking at you.

I slid back onto the bench and passed a frowning Dev his beer.

"What the hell took you so long?" he said.

"Phone call." I shook my head and gunned a few large gulps of my Rato-Bhaat beer, checking the Zebras once again.

Dev watched, a perplexed look crossing his features. Finally I put my beer down. This was not going to help my new leaf as a responsible antiquities contact. "Okay, do you want the good news or the bad news first?"

He swore. "Bad news," he said, then took a generous drink of his beer.

A man after my own heart. "Don't look now, but see the table with the six varsity wannabes at my seven o'clock?"

Dev swore, sat up, and started searching the crowd.

I leaned across the table and grabbed the front of his jacket, pulling him back down. "What about the statement 'Don't look now' did you not understand?" I whispered, although it came out sounding more like a hiss.

"I thought you said the mercenaries weren't following you," he whispered back.

"They aren't—and that's the good news. They have no idea I'm here or that I'm talking to you. As far as I can tell, they ended up here by complete chance." Or looking for Rynn, but I figured that was speculation Dev didn't need to hear right now.

He shook his head before laying it on the picnic table. "I should have listened to Benji. Vampires, mercenaries, the IAA, World Quest—Is there no one on the face of the planet you will not tell to fuck off?"

"Okay, I admit I did not act completely honorably with Benji. Wait a minute, how do you know about the vampires?" A little over a year ago I'd been retrieving an artifact from Ephesus, in Turkey, for a client. A sarcophagus, an old one, which my client, Alexander, unbeknownst to me at the time a vampire, had instructed me not to open.

Yeah, that hadn't gone well.

Dev lifted his head to glare at me. "I'm off the grid, not oblivious. Frying an ancient vampire in sunlight is the kind of story that gets around. And what did we say about bringing your personal brand of shit into my hometown?"

"Not intentional—"

"Like seriously, you're a walking disaster of bad luck." He frowned as he appraised me. "Are you sure you're not some supernatural bad luck demon?"

"No!" I cringed as I said it a little louder than I would have liked. "Of course not," I added in a quieter voice, checking to see that Dev's use of the word *supernatural* didn't catch undue attention.

I drew in a breath, held it, then started counting to five. Had I been screwed by my own cohort? Hell yes, and not just by Benji. But I didn't want to live my life with that as my excuse to act just as badly as everyone else.

Damn Rynn's pop psychology. I think I preferred it when I got to be the bad guy.

Okay, Owl, new leaf. A responsible leaf. Don't reduce yourself to insults. Keep the conversation factual, on topic, and, most importantly, civil.

"Dev, I have a plan for the mercenaries," I started, warning in my voice.

Dev snorted. "What? Leave bread crumbs to a goblin den and hope they don't come back?"

I clenched my teeth. "Will you knock it off for two seconds so I can explain? Jesus Christ, do you actually think before you speak, or do you just like to hear yourself? Or do you want them to start paying attention to us?"

It was all fine and well to follow Rynn's advice to keep things civil, but what the hell was I supposed to do when the other person didn't stop their own shit talking? It takes two, doesn't it?

Dev sat back and crossed his arms.

"This isn't some run-of-the-mill treasure quest, this is serious shit list IAA bounty money."

Dev still looked skeptical, so I added, "Put it this way. They offered me a get-out-of-jail pass and practically offered to give me my degree plus a clean slate. *Me*, their perennial scapegoat."

"Fuck," Dev said, his face turning ashen as the ramifications sunk in.

"They mean business. Even if you didn't have anything on the World

Quest duo, you need to get out of town. Which I would have told you a minute ago if you had listened."

It wasn't a closely guarded secret that Frank Caselback and Neil Chansky, the World Quest duos' real names, had been working on Shangri-La myths before they'd disappeared. Take that logic a step further: their disappearance had something to do with their research. Then take that a step further: there was only a handful of locations on the planet where Shangri-La was fabled to be. . . . "Eventually they were going to put two and two together, and start looking for the guides." And for the specialized sites in the Himalayas, the kind that attracted IAA attention, Dev was one of the best. He knew it and I knew it. "They're going to chase down everyone. And it's not just one group either, Dev—the bounty is big. At some point these guys are going to fire a brain cell or two and decide to start pooling resources." Or shoot at each other. I had no illusions about that being good for anyone. "For all I know they already have."

Dev finished off his second beer, taking a much more careful and measured look around. "What are they offering?" he asked.

Knowing the IAA, it depended on what they had on you. I shook my head. "Enough that, as soon as we are done here, you should run, preferably somewhere very warm without a 3G cellular network. I recommend the Cook Islands. They don't actually have street addresses, so it's next to impossible for anyone to find you—"

Dev grabbed my arm. "And if they *do* catch me?"

"Make something up—sell them what they want, take them where they want, do whatever they ask, just don't piss them off."

Dev let out a breath. "Jesus. All right, I'll tell you what I know, but I'm warning you, you might decide you were better off not knowing. Those guys disappeared . . . what? Three, four years ago? They were here in the off-season, I remember them because they needed a guide who wasn't afraid to go into yeti territory to look at a set of hillside ruins."

"Looking for Shangri-La," I said. That matched up with what traces I'd been able to find on their research.

But Dev shook his head. "That's where it gets weird. They weren't looking for Shangri-La. I mean, they knew about it, we talked about it on the trek into the hillsides, they knew as much about the local legends as I did, but that's not what they were here for. They were looking for something else. An old monastery," he said as he pulled his backpack—a dark red nylon number that made me wonder if he wasn't nervous about wearing it in front of a yak—onto the table.

Another sect of violent Buddhists? "They must have had a reason. Maybe they thought it was related to Shangri-La."

Dev shook his head and pulled out a package from inside his backpack, wrapped in brown and roughly the size of a book. "I thought so too," he said, and unwrapped a book, opening it carefully to where a cloth bookmark had been left before sliding it across the table. "That is what they were looking for."

It was a research journal, the kind I used to use—bound with leather, the pages grid lined. The page Dev had opened to was a collection of handwritten notes. They weren't on Shangri-La; I had no doubt the rest of the book was full of that, but Dev hadn't been right either.

I tapped the page. "This isn't a monastery, Dev. It's a temple, they were looking for a specific site of worship for the Dzo-nga, the Kanchenjunga Demon." A local deity of legend worshiped throughout the Kanchenjunga mountain region.

When multiple religions and ethnic tribes managed to agree on a single deity, it usually meant one thing. That it was real . . . and probably ate people.

Seriously, if you want to get humans to worship, you threaten to eat them. Has a much better track record than being nice.

It also wasn't completely off line with their research on Shangri-La either. The Dzo-nga was tasked in a number of legends with guarding the way to the valley of immortality. They were not to be mistaken with yeti; oh, they were real too . . . just way less exotic than the stories made them out to be . . . or maybe more. I guess it really depended on what you thought of goblin culture and politics expressed in the form of entrail finger painting with yak horns thrown in for good measure.

I scanned through the pages. Whatever the reason they'd been look-ing for the Dzo-nga temple, it hadn't been a wild-goose chase. They'd gone through a number of locations—ten in all, with Dev I assumed, between May 3 and May 15, 2011. After the fifteenth, though, they re-turned to site three, which they'd written off earlier. "What changed after the fifteenth of May?" I asked Dev.

"Avalanche—a small one, but it uncovered a section of caves that we gathered hadn't been opened for more than a century." He tapped the diagram, a series of pictures of caves from the outside and another series of diagrams of the inside, carefully grafted on the journal grids. I frowned at the series of pictographs—animals, a few characters, various symbols. Nothing I recognized, but they were carefully categorized along the side and then diagrammed to various locations in the cave.

I frowned at the research notes on the pictographs. The rest of their notes on the caves had been carefully laid out, but these . . . I squinted at the shorthand in the columns but couldn't make it out. Shit, it was in code.

I glanced back up at Dev. "Any idea what these are?" I asked him.

He spread his hands. "The diagrams? Most likely the Lepcha or early Buddhists left them. What they mean? Frank and Neil never told me what they suspected, though they spent days in those caves taking notes and pictures."

"What happened?" And how did Dev end up with the journal?

"That is where things get strange. We hiked into the mountains less than a week after the avalanche exposed the caves. We were three days in when I got a call. Another avalanche had occurred not too far from us, caught a dozen mountaineers and hikers. They needed help searching for survivors. I tried to get the two of them to return to a lower camp—the mountain was still dangerous, and you know how finicky goblin-yeti get when there's that kind of upheaval."

Goblins in general tended to blame humans for mishaps, but that was more their looking for an excuse to eat any stragglers they came across.

"After two days of helping survivors, I got a call from Neil in the early evening, badly garbled by bad reception, but I picked up the word *help*. I reached the caves by morning." He leaned across the table and lowered his voice. "There was *nothing left*."

"Are you telling me the yeti got them?" I struck that off as a possibility. First, there'd be no World Quest. Second, there'd have been remains. Very disturbing finger-paint-style remains . . .

"No, I'm saying there was nothing there. No equipment, no remains, no trace," he said as he leaned forward. "No *tracks*," he said, and let it sink in before continuing. "The only thing left was that book. Left by one of the altars to Dzo-nga. I never heard from them again."

So they had disappeared. "Do you think they found Shangri-La?"

Dev tsked. "What I'm saying is that they found *something* in those caves. As to what happened?" He shook his head. "I think some things in this world are worth not knowing." He flipped the pages back to a map, where the caves were marked, including latitude and longitude. They'd even printed out a picture and taped it to the page. "Regardless, I have no intention of returning. You want to trace their steps? Be my guest, but mark my words when I say it's a bad idea." Dev finished off my beer, having already finished his own.

I took my phone out and started to photograph the journal, but Dev stopped me before I could take any pictures. "Keep it."

"You're giving it to me?" *What was the catch?*

Dev stood. "You're damn straight I'm giving it to you. Like you said, someone is eventually going to tell the mercenaries I was the guide who last saw Frank and Neil." He nodded at the journal. "Better that's in your hands than mine."

I tucked the journal into my parka and stood as well. "Remember what I said about those off-the-grid islands."

He shouldered his backpack and nodded. "I'll take the advice under serious consideration, but only if you take this piece of advice to heart: my family has lived in these mountains for generations, as far back as we can trace our family tree. We have a different interpretation of the legends that account for the mystical valley than you Westerners do, and it is this: when people start disappearing, never to be seen or heard from again, only fools and small children are so quick to think they ended up in a magical paradise."

Coming from Dev, it wasn't advice I was going to take lightly. "Regardless of what they'd found, they have to still be alive."

Dev nodded, a sobering expression on his face. "Which raises the question, why has no one heard from them outside of that video game in four years? Like I said, there are some questions I am happy not knowing the answers to."

I took another look around the bar. The mercenaries were still ignoring us, but there was one man, a local guide, who was paying attention. I wondered how long it would be before the locals got paid enough to turn Dev over as the guy who handled the weird shit. Solidarity of a community is one thing, but if there's one thing I've learned over the years, it's that everyone has their price. "Dev, three o'clock. Yellow canvas parka, local-looking."

He shot a glance in that direction and swore.

"Let me guess, voted most likely in high school to sell his mother?" Or in this case sell Dev out to the mercenaries. He looked the type too . . . especially the way he was giving us the evil eye.

Dev swore. "No, aahhh, I might have hooked up with his girlfriend last night."

I did a double take. "Seriously? That does not look like the guy whose girlfriend you want to mess with."

Dev offered a sheepish shrug. "You won't mention that to Nadya, will you?"

I didn't think it was worth mentioning, seeing as Nadya wouldn't care. My paranoia made me check the room one last time before glancing down at my phone. Fifteen minutes had passed. I needed to be upstairs now. Dev offered me his hand. I took it. "Just be careful, all right?"

"I always am," Dev said, winking at me. I stood there and watched until he was out the door. No one seemed to notice him leave. Not even the mercenaries.

My turn to disappear. I headed up the stairs to the lodge rooms that ran the length of the second floor. God I hoped Dev kept his head down. I liked Dev—he might not have been a friend exactly, but he was something close. And how the hell did the IAA always manage to pit the entire archaeology community against each other? At some point, shouldn't we all figure out they were the bad guys and band together?

Only in fairy tales and comic books. In real life, you might actually get hurt. That scares people. It scares me.

On the way down the hall I passed two men who looked like they could be part of one of the mercenary outfits on their way down. They gave me a brief once-over, and I ignored them. It wasn't unusual for a petite woman to avoid the big, burly, dangerous-looking guys in a backpacker lodge.

When I reached my room at the end of the hall, I checked that the small piece of tape was untouched before checking the handle. Still locked. I fitted the heavy metal key in and carefully opened the door.

The glow the neon streetlights cast through the thin drapes was only enough to show the outlines of the small double bed tucked in the corner and the open closet. No movement, no strange scents.

I reached around the corner and flicked the light switch, watching from the doorway as the ceiling lamp sputtered before finally flickering on, bathing the already yellow-painted room in a buttery glow. Still nothing out of place. I stepped inside and locked the door behind me before checking the window, pushing aside the thin fuchsia and yellow patterned curtains.

Nothing. And no tampering on the windowsill.

I let out my breath. Half the time I didn't know if my paranoia was getting the better of me or if it was forcing me into a reasonable state of caution.

Not wanting to waste any more time, I fetched our backpacks from the closet and shoveled what extra clothing we'd unpacked inside. Now where the hell was Rynn?

A hand clamped around my waist, another over my mouth, smothering my yelp.

I was spun around, and it felt like for a moment my heart stopped as I looked up into the face of one of the most attractive men I had ever seen. A little taller than me, with close-cropped blond hair and a slim build, he was dressed in a dark fitted jacket that hugged all the right parts of his athletic frame and rivaled anything the mercenaries downstairs were wearing.

Rynn. Son of a bitch. He smiled wide, pleased with his own fucking joke. My surprise and relief at seeing him safe morphed to anger.

I opened my mouth to express how pissed I was, but before I could say anything his lips were on mine, fast and insistent. Rynn was a good kisser, and it took me a second to remember I was pissed off at him. I pushed him away. He was still grinning at me.

"Rynn!" I loud-whispered and smacked him on the shoulder for good measure. That only served to make him laugh. "For Christ's sake, there are mercenaries outside and you're *sneaking up on me*? You said we needed to leave fast!"

He let me go and lifted his hands in surrender, even trying to wipe the amusement off his face. It didn't do much, which as far as I was concerned meant he wasn't actually trying.

I'd known Rynn for a year and a half. He'd been my bartender in Tokyo before we'd ever hooked up, and he was one of the few people outside my circle of ex-archaeology grads and antiquities smugglers who'd known about the supernatural and my run-ins with them. More importantly, he'd believed me, which was likely on account of the fact that he himself was an incubus.

Don't get the wrong idea—the whole feeding-off-sex thing is seriously overplayed. They feed off attraction, but it's more passive than you'd expect.

He *was* attractive, but more importantly, there were some other useful powers incubi had beyond sex appeal. If you asked me, that was the lesser of the bunch, and only served to make feeding off the energy of people's attraction that much easier. Their real talents lay in the usual supernatural cadre—strength, longevity, quick reflexes—along with a couple of extra skills, namely the ability to heal damage and to sense what people were feeling. I figured that had evolved to help them get a leg up for feeding more than anything else, but it had other uses as well, namely persuasion—using emotions to manipulate people's thoughts. That was where their real power was. I'd seen Rynn do it a few times— had it done on me—and witnessing it happen always left me with chills.

And to think he got his kicks sneaking up on me. "Seriously, and you think *I* have bad timing?"

The corner of his mouth turned up in a smile. "I'm sorry. I couldn't resist. You walked right by me, Alix. Twice."

I closed my eyes. He'd been standing outside the window. It was open now, the summer air stirring the curtains and carrying in the smell of cooking and incense. "I didn't even hear you open it."

"I waited until you had your back turned and got busy with the back-packs. Check outside next time," he said, and, picking me up, moved me out of the way of the bags so he could give them a quick once-over.

"For someone who fifteen minutes ago sounded like we were in im-minent danger, you're in an awfully good mood."

He tossed the larger of the backpacks over his shoulder and handed me mine, the smaller, lighter one—mainly because it didn't have any weapons. I have a strict policy on weapons like guns and stakes. In my experience, it just gives the vampires something else to beat you with, and they take the stakes personally.

I could have pushed, but Rynn and I had both been under a lot of stress the last few weeks. If he was in a good enough mood to play, as opposed to worry about our backs, that had to mean we were ahead of the game for once, despite the fact that we were in a lodge full of mer-cenaries.

Rynn shook his head at me. "I checked when I came in—no perim-eter, no patrol, no trip wires, no sensors. They're not even looking for supernaturals. Sloppy if you ask me. The South Africans, the Zebras, know better in a place like Fikkal, and an IAA bounty like this is bound to attract some supernatural competition."

Mercenary-style work was something of a career choice in the supernatural communities—mostly to police each other, but freelancing for a supernatural-smelling job like this?

"Not that we're going out the front door," Rynn said. "I'm not that—" He stopped and turned his head to the side, as if listening. The playful mood vanished, and I waited and watched as he hit the light and placed his ear against the door.

I blinked as my eyes adjusted to the sparse neon lights. "What? What happened?" I whispered.

Rynn abandoned the door and, taking my arm, steered me back to the window. "It's my fault. I got too confident when there weren't any patrols or sensors."

"You said they weren't looking for us!"

"They weren't—aren't—but I spoke too soon when I assumed they weren't keeping their eyes out," Rynn said.

"Fuck." I peered at the space between the floorboards and the door where the light seeped through. I could have sworn I saw shadows moving underneath, the kinds caused by feet, but I'll be damned if I could hear anything.

Rynn stepped outside onto the ledge first, checking to make sure there really was no one there. Once he was certain it was safe, he held out his hand and motioned for me to join him.

I hesitated. I was a professional thief. Gallantry or whatever Rynn was going for was all well and good on paper, not in practice. I could crawl my own way out a window.

"I don't want them to hear us leaving," he mouthed more than whispered at me.

I let him lift me out. I'm stubborn, but I also knew I wasn't as silent as him.

He set me down on the thin ledge out of view of the window as the first clink of a lock pick sounded in the door.

Rynn tapped my shoulder and pointed down to the road two stories down.

"Please say we aren't jumping," I said. My ankle was still smarting from our last hurried exit out of New Delhi. There had been a misunderstanding about an artifact I'd been collecting for Mr. Kurosawa . . . and misconception that if they chased me, they might actually get it back. Rynn had vetoed my run through a crowded market, and we'd jumped off a building instead.

"Not twice in the same week," I said, shaking my head.

"Think of it more as falling to safety."

"Falling? No, *no* falling," I demanded. At least with jumping there was some modicum, some pretence, of control. "Shit!"

Rynn timed it so that he pushed me at the same moment the mercenaries kicked the door open.

If they heard me yelling on the way down, there wasn't much they could do about it. I didn't even see if they made it to the window.

We landed with a thud on a tarp. Me first, followed by Rynn, who managed to look more graceful than I did on account of the fact that he got to jump instead of fall. The "tarp" was in fact a jeep—a dilapidated orange jeep encrusted with fuchsia rhinestones done into flower patterns. It roared to life with a sputtering cough as soon as we landed, then started to pull forward.

As it tore down the road, the engine still protesting, I turned on Rynn. "You just pushed me out of a window!"

"Off a ledge. And it couldn't be avoided. Look, I'm sorry, but better your indignity than the mercenaries." Rynn swung himself off the tarp so he was balancing on the jeep rail.

I followed his lead but took the other side, ignoring Rynn's proffered hand. "We humans call that sorry, not sorry," I said. "And what the hell is wrong with climbing?"

"It's not fast enough," he said.

"It's plenty fast! I climb out of tight spots all the time." I swung into the seat of the moving jeep beside Rynn. It was a patchwork of colorful blankets that had been sewn and stretched over long-gone padded seats.

His jaw clenched. "And every time you end up having to run through a city chased by someone." He gave the metal railing of the jeep three hard taps. It picked up speed, making the potholes we went over more pronounced. "This way we skip the chase. Faster."

"I still think we could have climbed down and avoided tossing me onto a jeep canopy." I was a little amazed it had held up, to be honest . . . if there was one issue Rynn and I had in our relationship, it was our disagreement over acceptable work risks. Namely, risks that I considered acceptable, he labeled suicidal.

But I was still alive, so my methods couldn't have been that bad.

"Besides, couldn't you have done the . . . you know?" I waved my hand around my ear, my usual method to indicate Rynn's ability to manipulate people's minds, then grasped the railing as the jeep bounced over an exceptionally deep pothole.

"I doubt it. They've probably got chemical inhibitors in their systems."

"Whoa. Wait, they can do that?"

Rynn gave me a wry look as he dumped his pack into the back. I followed his lead. "I never kid about people with guns. Did you get what you needed?" I nodded and patted the book still tucked in my jacket.

As the jeep coughed and sputtered our retreat up the hill and out of the valley, I got a look out the back at the town fading behind us. I thought I saw a handful of men standing in the lantern-lit road, but with the potholes jostling the jeep I could have been mistaken. I didn't hear screams, sirens, or any other indication anyone was following us. Considering how fast we left, I figured they were still trying to determine what had happened.

I turned to Rynn, who was also watching our departure from Fikkal. "I can't believe for once it's you catching their attention and not me," I said.

"Well, there's a first time for everything. And like I said, these guys are good."

The ambient light vanished as we passed the town limits—Fikkal was a concentrated place and not that large. It didn't take you long to get out of town, and once you did, the lampposts were gone. Got to admit, after bouncing between large cities and Vegas over the past few weeks, I could appreciate actually seeing the night sky. And the stars . . . all of them, not just the big ones. The fact that the purveying scent of incense and frying foods was also fading, replaced by the clean scent of the mountain forests, was a bonus as well. Something else you didn't get in Vegas.

I turned to say something along those lines to Rynn, but he wasn't looking at me. He was leaning over the driver's seat.

Right, our driver. I wonder who Rynn had roped into getting us out of Dodge.

I frowned as I caught a bit of what Rynn said—lyrical-sounding and light, an awful lot like the language I liked to refer to as "supernatural common."

I shimmied up to the back of the front seat to get a look at our driver, a feat in itself, since we were out of Fikkal now and the potholes had gotten worse, not better, bouncing the jeep over the uneven side roads.

But as luck would have it, the moon was out, and during a stretch of smooth road I got a good look. He—no, make that a she—was a kid. Twelve at the most, and dressed in a fuchsia tunic and matching pants layered with a heavy orange sari also adorned with fuchsia rhinestones that matched the ones decorating the jeep.

She glanced at me for only a brief moment, but it was enough to get a good look at her beautiful and *very* childlike face. More importantly though, I got a look at her shining gold eyes.

"Oh hell no," I said before my filter could kick in. I'd been in a jeep with a childlike supernatural with eyes like that once before—an Apsara, or Balinese luck demon masquerading as a "kid" in Bali.

"Alix, meet Talie," Rynn said pleasantly.

Yeah. No. "When were you going to tell me a luck demon was driving the car?" I didn't bother lowering my voice. She knew what she was. "And I thought we agreed not to involve any other supernaturals?"

There was already enough of a mess that we'd waded into with the IAA, and now add to that the mercenaries. More supernaturals would make things more complicated, not less. Besides, I didn't have the best track record with supernaturals; Rynn was the exception, not the rule. I did my damnedest to keep them out of my business and work, not that that had been working for me lately. When the universe keeps throwing lemons at you, saying you won't make lemonade becomes pretty pointless.

For her part, Talie didn't bother acknowledging me.

"They prefer the term *Apsara*—and it's not exactly the same. Talie has influence over clouds and snow. Kato, as you called him, works with water."

"Same species, different gig, and that's a tangent."

Rynn's mouth twisted into a frown, the first hint at irritation. He wasn't a fan of me lumping all supernaturals into one column. The dangerous one. It wasn't exactly an easy habit to break, considering they were usually trying to kill me. "Completely different temperaments," he said. "Note, Talie hasn't told you never to come back. Yet."

Wait a minute . . . Talie? Taleju, the child goddess of Nepal, the one that was supposed to be reincarnated in the body of a girl every decade or so and forced to live in the guarded temple in Kathmandu?

We came to a stop, not for a sign but for a herd of yaks crossing the road. She caught me staring at her. "Aren't you supposed to be locked inside a palace in Kathmandu?" My filter was really taking a backseat to my curiosity tonight.

"Alix—" Rynn warned.

Yeah, like hell was I not asking. "The whole reincarnation thing? Is that a myth, or do, you know, are they"—I really didn't know of a delicate way to put it—"hosts?" Possession by a supernatural entity was rare, but it happened.

She ignored me and turned her attention back on Rynn. "I have a place you can hide, but it won't offer protection for long, not with their equipment. I'm lucky, but not even a luck demon is that lucky. If you are smart, you will leave."

Wait a minute. What if we didn't need to hole up for days? Dev's warnings be damned. I'd feel better looking into it now rather than later.

I leaned closer and raised my voice. "Look, what about evading them for a few hours? Like heading into some caves at the base of the mountains?" I asked Talie. "A few hours is all we'd need. I even have a location," I added, and patted my chest so Rynn would get the idea.

Talie gave me a measured once-over, her gold demon eyes shining in the moonlight. "Mountains this time of year have yeti. *But* I believe a few hours is the kind of luck I can arrange."

I pulled the journal out and opened it to the map of the cave's location. "Then this is where we're heading."

Talie glanced at the map, then pulled out a cell phone decorated in more pink and yellow rhinestones. "GPS," she said when she caught me staring. "I'm not a fan of driving these roads at night." She tapped in the coordinates and fixed the rhinestone-encrusted phone onto the dashboard on a cartoon cat holder. She then turned her attention back on the road and kicked the jeep, sputtering and coughing, into a higher gear, scattering the remaining yaks.

I sat back in the patchwork orange backseat and let out my breath. Now all I had to do was figure out how the cave disappeared Neil and Frank. Preferably without stumbling into being disappeared myself. . . .

My name is Alix Hiboux, better known as Owl, antiquities thief for hire.

Welcome to my life.

2

A LONG WALK THROUGH A SILENT FOREST

8:00 a.m. Somewhere in the foothills of Kanchenjunga, Nepal

It took us the better part of the night to reach the caves marked in Frank and Neil's journal. Despite the Apsara driving the jeep and the bumpy ride, I fell asleep. For one, I needed it, and two, I figured Rynn would wake me up if things took a turn. They didn't, and the first indication I had that we'd arrived was when the jeep ground to a loud, wrenching halt.

I wiped the sleep out of my eyes and shrugged a blanket off. At some point Rynn must have tossed it over me. Or maybe I'd done so in my sleep. You'd be amazed at how efficient my unconscious autopilot is. I can detach a hungry Mau from my pillow and hit him with his Nerf ball across the room without batting an eye.

I sat up from where I'd stretched out on the backseat, then peeked outside the jeep's colorful canvas.

The sun was bright and well over a cloudless horizon, making the fuchsia rhinestones twinkle right into my still sleepy eyes. I squinted against the light as I got a first look at our surroundings.

Well, it might be too bright, but it certainly was pretty out here. And quiet.

We were in the end of May, so Nepal was in the off-season. The trees, grasses, and brush were green with the beginning of summer, and the small river that ran through the picturesque valley before me was running heavy with snowmelt. Despite the veneer of summer, you could still see white in the surrounding mountains, and we were high enough into the foothills that the air was crisp with the scent of nearby snow.

If it hadn't been for the fact that the river meant we were at serious risk of being caught in an avalanche from the melting snow above us, it would have been downright idyllic.

Dev's warning about the mystical valley came roaring back: "*When people start disappearing, never to be seen or heard from again, only fools and small children are so quick to think they ended up in a magical paradise.*"

I spotted the caves a ways into the valley, partway up the mountain steps and obscured by the summer vegetation. There were a handful of them, but only one that was big enough for people to walk in comfortably.

I pulled the notebook out of my parka, opened to the page with the diagrams and photos of the cave Neil and Frank had been interested in, and held up the images for comparison. Beyond a few fallen boulders over the past four years and substantially less snow around the cave proper, thanks to a warmer-than-normal May, it matched.

If I had to guess, I'd put it at a couple kilometers into the valley, maybe two and a half to three when you took in the incline. With the river and moderate brush terrain it'd take us an hour or so to hike in, provided there wasn't an avalanche to contend with. Though truth be told, an avalanche was the least of my worries right now.

I tucked the journal back into my jacket. There wasn't any point worrying about the details of the cave until we got there, and if my suspicions about the valley's quiet nature were confirmed, I'd deal with it.

We'd deal with it. I kept forgetting that I was working *with* Rynn, not against him. There were some serious benefits to having a partner. I'd gotten a good night's sleep—or as good as was possible in the back of a suspect jeep over back roads. I *never* got a good night's sleep while working. And I hadn't had to panic about transportation.

It also meant I hadn't been in control of all the plans.

Though it was still a huge adjustment. I was used to working on my own.

I trusted Rynn with my life, but it was a weird learning curve.

And being thrown out of windows . . . then again, the ball was about to be well and good back in my court.

I stopped my perusal of the hillside as I picked up the scent—warm, light roasted, brewed strong. I glanced over to where Rynn was standing outside the jeep with his arms crossed, scanning the area. "Coffee?" Oh God, please say he'd made enough for two.

In answer, he passed me a Thermos. I grabbed it. "Oh, the universe doesn't hate me this morning." Another benefit to having a partner in my job—one who understood my deep-rooted love of caffeine.

"It's early. You haven't had a chance to offend the powers that be. Yet," he added, glancing once more at the picturesque valley at the foot of the mountain.

I guzzled half the Thermos, then passed it back to Rynn before I finished it all. Not human did not mean does not drink coffee. I'd learned that one the hard way.

Talie was ignoring us. She'd opened the hood to her jeep and was fiddling with the engine—or the parts that were jerry-rigged into an engine. Good thing we'd gotten out of Fikkal in the dark of night, otherwise I don't know if I'd have trusted the jeep not to burst into an all-engulfing flame, let alone survive the offtrack roads.

Benefits of being a luck demon, I supposed.

While Rynn finished off the coffee, I turned back to surveying the valley. With the exception of the odd curse from Talie and the whine of metal being wrenched against its will, the valley maintained its veil of silence. Considering the fresh water, greenery, and abundance of grass and nesting spots, I was acutely aware of what was missing.

"Do you two hear what I hear?"

Rynn and Talie both looked at me before turning their attention on the valley. After a moment, Rynn said, "I don't hear anything."

I nodded. No birds singing, no small animals that should be in the trees, no yaks taking advantage of the water and prime breeding ground. The warm weather hadn't only affected the snow. Goblins bred faster in warmer weather, and by all accounts the last few years had been mild. . . .

"You two should hurry up and do whatever it is you came here to do," Talie said from back under the hood, her high, feminine voice clashing with the ringing and clanging metal. She looked up at the sky. "I'll do my best working the tendrils of luck and fate to keep you safe as long as they continue to flow by like the river, but eventually they will stray."

I gave her a blank stare.

She rolled her eyes, looking very much a twelve-year-old, despite the fact that she was most definitely not. "Even I can't keep the yeti-goblins at bay forever. The clock is ticking."

Right. Time to take a long walk through a picturesque valley infested with goblins. "Let's get this over with," I said to Rynn, tossing my backpack over my shoulder. I set off along the river toward the cavern, keeping my eyes on the trees and rocks for any sign of yak skins and horns.

"You know, one of these days you need to learn firearms," Rynn said casually.

"You know my stance on guns and stakes."

"I said learn—as in I teach you. Not 'grab a gun and see if you can figure out the safety' before a vampire takes it from you. Besides, it's not always a vampire," Rynn continued. "Like today, for example—it's yeti-goblins."

I bit my tongue. He had a point. Whereas vampires, Nagas, and mummies specialized in getting creative with their modes of torture, not all species were that high on the intellect scale. Their thought process tended toward "can I eat it?" and "I should try to eat it anyways." Like slightly less intelligent versions of Captain in their priorities, minus the soft fur, occasionally pleasant disposition, and need to clean. I'd never had the pleasure of seeing a goblin in person—they don't like desert ruins. Forests, jungles, and abandoned radioactive cities like Chernobyl, on the other hand . . .

Rynn had a point, but he'd also developed a bad habit of discounting anything I had to say about security as a bad idea. I needed him to strike a balance with me here, which meant compromise—his compromise this time, not mine being lopped out a window.

"It's not only using a gun, Rynn. Depending on you to scare vampires and other supernaturals away is a bad idea."

He stopped and turned toward me, blocking the path, his face knit in confusion. "Why?"

Why. He genuinely didn't get why I didn't think letting him deal with supernatural logistics was just the logical thing to do. No question about my independence, my ability to solve my own problems . . .

I didn't say that though. Problem with working with a significant other is that they have feelings. Rynn didn't quite get the whole independence thing, not when in his mind that meant having to let supernaturals beat me to a pulp. And he meant well, it was just that despite the fact that he could sense my emotions, it was as if he couldn't tell the difference between me not wanting to *have* to depend on him to handle my supernatural problems and me not wanting him to try.

For someone who could read all my emotions, he occasionally had a remedial handle on what they actually meant.

Instead of reopening the "independent human" can of worms, I said, "Just because they're scared of you doesn't mean they can't afford to be reckless. They'll just send out more cockroaches." My term for vampire lackeys. "And what about the ones on the opposite side of your supernatural war?" I added, navigating a length of foliage that had overgrown the path. This was another sign that yaks hadn't been in the area for a while; all their footpaths were disappearing under the foliage.

"It's not a war. Yet. And there are no vampires on the other side. For all their bluster about eating people, they're terrified of being pushed out in the open. They're the first ones the humans go after." He glanced over his shoulder at me. "Besides, Alexander doesn't want you alone. He'll wait."

We both knew why. Because I didn't have Captain with me. Lady Siyu had my cat, a situation I was trying to rectify but the dragon lady was intent on blocking at every step. Which made no sense. She hated my cat, he hated her. It should be a no-brainer.

We continued in silence after that until we reached a section of the stream where the woods had encroached on its bank. The caves were still roughly five hundred meters away.

We both smelled the air. No trace of rotting flesh or urine-cured hides.

"I don't smell anything," Rynn whispered. "But it won't hurt to cover our tracks in the water."

"What if they're already watching us?"

He inclined his head as he crouched to roll up his pant legs to his knees. "If they're already watching us, then they've decided they don't want to eat us."

I shot him a skeptical look as I followed his lead and cuffed up my own pants before following him into the shallows of the stream. From everything I'd ever read about goblin species, that was highly unlikely.

He shrugged. "Or they're waiting until we get closer to their den to ambush us."

That sounded more like it. I shivered as the water came up a little ways past my knees, soaking the bottom of my pants.

I clenched my teeth against the cold as we headed toward the caves, some five hundred odd meters away now. We kept to the shallows, but they were icy from the snowmelt feeding in. I noted something else troubling besides the cold.

"No fish either," I said as we waded through the stream, my voice a whisper.

"You've read about goblins, Alix," Rynn said, keeping his voice just as quiet as he scanned the river and treetops. "They're not the smartest supernatural, but they are experts at exploiting their environment. They'll exploit it to starvation."

"Not a comforting thought."

He inclined his head to the side. "Like I said, not the smartest supernatural."

We continued our way along the stream in silence, my own adrenaline spiking as we drew closer to the caves. I could swear I smelled something rotting, like a dead animal left out in the sun.

"Do you smell that?" I asked.

Rynn inclined his head. "They're watching us now—I can feel them—more or less. No anger—curiosity more than anything. And hunger. They are definitely hungry."

I stole a look around us, trying not to fall over in the water. "Why don't we see any of them?"

"The yeti have trouble with these trees. For one there's two of them stacked under the yak hides they wear making climbing difficult, and second, this time of year the camouflage would be a giveaway against the green foilage. My guess is they're waiting to see what we do."

I reined in my own visceral panic as the scent of urine and rotting flesh grew stronger. I kept close to Rynn as we made our way down the stream. Three hundred meters now, tops.

Yeti were a unique subspecies of goblin. Unlike their warmer-climate brethren, who made their homes in old abandoned ruins and cities that had been reclaimed by the forests and jungles, the yeti had to deal with the mountains and cold. To combat the cold, they'd evolved two behaviors. The first was that they'd learned to use yak hides for clothing. Not well tailored, mind you; the hides were shredded by sharp teeth into loose-fitting tunics and cured with, well, the only thing the yeti had on hand that could do the job. Goblin urine. The second behavior, well . . .

"It's the mated pairs under the hides, right?" I asked Rynn.

He nodded. "Females stand on top of the males' shoulders, and the yak hide is draped over them. They hold the yak horn as well, probably to make them look bigger and scare other predators away."

I always figured the stink of goblin urine would do that.

"Unless they're fighting, that is," Rynn continued.

"What happens then?"

"Well, the female makes the male hold the yak horn out while she throws spears made out of bone usually—or shoots arrows—since she's the one with visibility." He gave a reluctant shrug. "The horns probably make for another kind of intimidation as well."

I gave a quick shudder, not from the cold. The phallic yak horns had definitely not made it into the IAA handbook.

We were approaching the rocky hillside the caves were situated under, where the forest and river ended and barefaced open rock and mountain cliffs began. No noise, no movement . . . no phallic horns . . . nothing that signaled a yeti ambush.

I spotted the path, worn into the rock and dirt. Rynn stepped onto the bank first and stood, watching, waiting, before motioning me to follow him out of the river.

I followed Rynn as he started up the hillside, both of us silent and me not willing to breathe.

"Son of a bitch!" I jumped as something buzzed loudly in the silent forest.

Rynn jumped too, one of his guns drawn, searching.

It took a second for his eyes to fall on me, my jacket to be precise, and another few seconds for me to feel anything beyond the adrenaline coursing through my blood.

My jacket pocket was buzzing.

I swore as I fished out my phone. Nadya's number flashed across the screen.

I shook my head and answered it. "Nadya—you have no idea the scare you just gave me," I said as softly as I could.

"Then you should get better about turning your phone off" was her curt reply. "Besides, you were the one who told me to call as soon as I could."

The email I'd managed to get off last night before crashing in the backseat of Talie's glittery jeep had said to call me when she could.

"How are things over there?" Nadya asked.

I heard a rock skitter down onto the path a moment before a pebble struck the ground beside me. "Ah, let me get back to you on that."

Rynn had decided to move a few feet ahead and check the cave entrance. I watched as he stuck his head inside, waving the beam of his flashlight before glancing back down at me.

"It doesn't look like anyone's used these caves for some time—including the yeti," he said, and waved me up.

"Well, the caves we need to look at aren't infested with yeti-goblins," I said to Nadya, balancing my phone between my ear and shoulder as I made my way up the path to join him.

"That's a good start," Nadya offered.

"Yes, though it does beg the question what the hell scared them off. Rocky crevices, multiple caves, good view of the valley—it's a prime yeti breeding den."

I reached the cave entrance and spared a last look around the valley. I couldn't shake the feeling someone—or thing—was watching us. For a second I thought I caught a glimpse of a tattered piece of white cloth fluttering in the trees, but when I looked again it wasn't there.

Figment of my imagination caused by adrenaline. Still, I lost no time following Rynn inside.

"No hint or mention about the yeti in the notebooks?" Nadya asked.

I'd sent Nadya a quick email with the short version of what I'd found—namely that there was a journal the World Quest duo had left at a site under suspect circumstances and that a number of mercenaries were crawling around. "Nothing, but they weren't exactly transparent on the notes either. Probably spent so much time worrying about someone stealing their research it never occurred to them someone besides them might actually need to read the journal."

"Send them to me and I'll see what I can do, but no promises. I'm on my own tight deadline myself."

"Nothing in Vegas I hope?"

"Nothing so bad. Look, Alix, I need to get back to Japan and soon. There's something going on with my club."

"I thought you left Murasaki in charge?" Murasaki was one of Nadya's senior girls. The name was a stage name of sorts, after her favorite author—but if the imagery of Japan's first novelist, a woman, denoted a classy, educated, and refined woman, then the stage name was appropriate. Also, she was the kind of girl the patrons wouldn't try to take advantage of. Not like some of the more . . . schoolgirl-like women, we'll say.

"I did. And it's not her. She knows how to run the club. It's my silent partner."

I frowned. "I didn't know you had a partner."

"*Silent*. And I needed one to open the club—someone Japanese. It makes things work better."

"Why am I only hearing about it now?"

"Because it wasn't a problem until now." I heard the sigh over the connection. It was slight; no one else would have noticed it, but I knew Nadya. Despite her assertions otherwise, she was stressed.

"Really, it's probably nothing. I just need to go and threaten some sense into a few people, but I need to go sooner rather than later. For my own peace of mind."

I won't lie—part of me did want to let it go. I had enough of my own problems at the moment. I mean, goddamn it, there wasn't a single bird *anywhere*.

"Why do I get the feeling this isn't as straightforward as you want me to think it is?" I asked.

Nadya sighed again, this time louder. "Because you have a modicum of sense inside your head? Look, don't worry—yet. Wait until I get there and see what's happening."

"Not comforting," I sang into the phone.

"If you want comforting out of life, work at a Starbucks. I'll update you when I arrive, and I'll see what I can make of the journal codes when

I get them. Just be careful and keep ahead of the mercenaries. These aren't archaeologists, they're dangerous. And don't fight with Rynn this time."

"Don't tell me you two have been talking about me behind my back again," I said. Rynn pretended not to hear me as he continued to check the cave.

"Only when he starts to worry. And mercenaries make the both of us worried."

I ran my hand through my hair. It caught on the tangles I hadn't had the time or inclination to brush out yet. Funny thing was, as much as it was in my nature to resist, she didn't have to warn me this time. Am I good at infiltrating dig sites and decrypting tombs and artifacts? Definitely. Dealing with mercenaries, real ones? Not so much.

"I'll . . . do my best," I said.

I noticed Rynn had disappeared around a corner. I didn't want him accidentally disturbing something before I got a look at it. "Got to go, Nadya," I said. She said a quick good-bye, and I slid my phone back inside my pocket before turning my attention on the cave.

The entrance led into a natural circular chamber roughly the size of a medium apartment with a high ceiling reaching a good twenty feet into the mountain. No stalagmites or stalactites, but there was the sound of water dripping somewhere. Probably pores in the rock above us allowed both water and air to flow through. Rynn had placed glow sticks at even intervals in the main chamber and was doing a second pass now, dropping a glow stick wherever he found an alcove or anything else that could be used for a den.

I found a series of rough paintings near the entrance; not the clean lines and pigments of the ancient-looking pictographs from Neil and Frank's notebook, but dark brown and crudely made symbols and letters.

I fished my UV flashlight out of my bag and turned it on the paintings, which confirmed my suspicions. "Rynn, I've got goblin paintings."

He came up beside me. "They're not camping in here. This is old. It's a warning of some sort for other goblins to keep away, along with mention of something new they ate that didn't agree with them, an electronic, maybe a phone or a radio."

Great. Goblins finding new and exciting things to eat. "What's it a warning for?"

"Hard to say. I think they're talking about a door. 'Beware doorway,' maybe, but beyond that? Most goblin writing deals with things they've eaten, want to eat, or lamenting that all the food's gone."

Doorway . . . doorway. I searched the cave with my flashlight, but there wasn't anything that looked like a doorway. "Could it be the cave entrance?"

"Doubtfully. Goblins don't really think like that. To them, doors and buildings are man-made things. They'll exploit them and they understand what they are, but they don't associate them with natural structures."

Where was it then? And where did it lead? And was whatever the goblins were afraid of a danger to us?

"Come on—I think I found something toward the back of the cave, though I'm not sure what to make of it," he said, touching my shoulder gently and steering me away from the yeti drawings.

Using the light from the glow sticks, I followed him to the back of the cave, the air getting more metallic and stale with each step. Rynn came to a stop by the very back of the cavern where a hidden alcove broke off into a slightly smaller cavern no more than five hundred square feet around with the same vaulted ceiling. Rynn waited until I was inside to shine his flashlight on the far cavern wall.

It was much more bare than was shown in the journal. The base images were there, those I recognized. Rings of gold, orange, white, blue, and red adorned the wall from the floor all the way to the ceiling, before branching onto the ceiling itself. There was a handful of colorful depictions of animals drawn in the centers of the double- and triple-lined rings—birds, wolves, small rodents, even some crates being dragged by yaks with stick people following behind. Your run-of-the-mill ancient pictographs. Pretty—and old, from the looks of it, but nothing occult beyond the storytelling symbolism.

And there were parts missing.

"Are you certain it's the same one?" Rynn asked. "There are a lot of caves."

"You know as well as I do looks can be deceiving." I rifled through my backpack until my fingers closed on a heavy plastic handle. "You ever wonder why so much magic was written in caves?"

Rynn shrugged. "Truth be told, Alix, I never felt that comfortable around magic. Seems to cause more trouble than it's worth."

I could drink in multiples to that statement. "They always stuck the inscriptions in caves so the sun couldn't get at them. Note, the pyramids were built as a substitute where there were no ready caves, since they couldn't really dig into the sand. So were some of the Greek and Roman catacombs for that matter." It was something that had boggled archaeologists for a real long time. Why were all the ancient magic inscriptions kept underground?

"So sunlight couldn't degrade them?"

"Good guess, but no, that's just an added benefit." I pulled out my heavier UV light floodlight, the one with multiple filters, and set it on the floor. "So we couldn't see them like you guys can." Supernaturals saw in different wavelengths than humans, particularly in the UV spectrum. A lot of their magic was only visible to humans when activated by light.

"Good hypothesis, Alix, but I can't see anything either. The wall is blank," he said.

Yeah. I had a theory about why the World Quest duo had been so set on this place. I fiddled with the filters and wavelength settings. If I was right about this, the settings would be critical. When I was satisfied, I turned it on.

Like invisible ink, the relief flared to life under the wave of my UV flashlight; symbols mixed in with pictographs that were so common in magic spells and inscriptions. Yaks, birds, people—all layered with the symbols to make a picture of sorts, then arranged in rings, swirling around each other not unlike a conga line done in oranges, reds, white, yellows, and blue.

"You couldn't see these inscriptions with your bare eyes because they weren't meant for you," I said to Rynn.

"Human magic," he said, staring at the images, now excited and visible under the infrared wavelength, not a spectrum supernaturals could see with their bare eyes but one that could be made visible with the right tools.

"Looks like ancient humans practicing magic here picked up on some of your guy's supernatural tricks."

Rynn let out a low whistle at the inscriptions both of us could now see under the infrared filters. They were beautiful. Breathtaking, when you considered this was one of the few existing examples on the planet of human magic—something that had been lost, not only to the history books but to the archaeological record as well, as if it had been wiped out.

I held up Neil and Frank's notebook, open to the diagrams. Now they matched. Human magic, hidden from supernaturals. "This is a find of the century, if not *the* find of the century," I said to Rynn. "They never would have been able to publish it, but if they had gone through the right channels, this could have made their careers."

"Or ended their careers spectacularly—like yours was," Rynn said.

I inclined my head. No wonder they'd been so secretive; if the IAA had had any idea what they'd been after, well, there was no shortage of tenured professors who would have been more than happy to steal their work.

"There's one problem, Alix," Rynn said as he gestured at the cavern. "There's nothing here. No refuse, no camping gear, no equipment, no blood, no remains. I've seen it all—supernatural renderings, murders, magic gone wrong. There should be some trace, something I can see, but there's nothing. Nothing at all."

I nodded and held up the notebook to check the pictures against the cavern wall again.

"Yeah, well, we've got an even bigger problem," I said, handing the open notebook to Rynn. "I've got absolutely no idea what any of these symbols or drawings mean." Which meant I had my work cut out for me.

3

THE ART OF FINGER PAINT

11:00 a.m. Still in the quiet valley of death, Nepal

"Goddamn it." I dropped the notebook and put my head in my hands. I was sitting cross-legged on the cold cave floor, still trying to figure out the damn notebook and pictures.

"Still nothing?" Rynn called from the entrance of the cave, where he was keeping an eye on the valley, a rifle resting on his lap. I could barely see him through the narrow alcove entrance, but he hadn't moved since I'd settled in to work. I think the fact that the yeti hadn't shown up yet was starting to unnerve him as well.

"It's not that they didn't take notes," I said, nudging the notebook none too gently with my feet. "They took copious notes. They even diagrammed the relief in detail. The problem is I can't make head or tales of *any* of their labels—not even with the research sitting right in front of me." I gave a loose rock a kick for good measure, sending it across the cave floor. It eventually struck the UV lamp propped against my backpack so I could study the reliefs. It would be one thing if I had weeks to go through them, but we had hours at most.

I let out my breath and tried to force my temper down. I was starting to think I'd have a better shot getting meaning out of the yeti-rendered paintings over this mural.

And the unintelligible chicken scratch that passed for notes.

I'd figured on Neil and Frank coding their research—I mean, it was a supernaturally derived cave with magic reliefs. It was standard practice to code stuff, but my God, how did these two pass their undergrad classes? Even the most paranoid and secretive archaeologists left a clue somewhere. What if you ran into a skin walker?

"I mean, some of it is obvious. Pictures of yaks, carts, people carrying bags of goods. Doesn't matter the culture or language, they're all symbols of trade."

"So that's more than you knew an hour ago?" Rynn called from the entrance.

"Not really. I keep seeing symbolism for a gate but nothing concrete—not where they were going, who was doing the trading. If there was a trading center here, there should be some remnants—outpost ruins, towns, agricultural centers. Nothing. It's as if it vanished."

"Maybe it did?" Rynn said. "It wouldn't be the first time something was lost to the ages."

Maybe. The difference between disappeared and hidden was finding the clues. I held up the book again. "And as for this? Up until Fikkal, it's just history of the region and the variations on the local Shangri-La legends. The rest of it? It's all in code. The pictographs make more sense than what those idiots wrote in their dig book." We'd searched the entire cave—not even a hidden jump drive. "And *those*," I said, tossing a handful of sand at the pictures, "I can't read."

I'd tried various filters on the wall mural and hadn't uncovered anything more. If I'd had a half-decent internet connection, I'd have been sorely tempted to give up cracking their notebook myself and load it on World Quest as a bonus code—something players did occasionally when they couldn't get past a particular puzzle; offer in-game loot for someone else doing it.

Seeing as nobody has seen them in four years and the World Quest duo ceased in-game communication with me and Carpe a month ago, right after they'd helped us get into the City of the Dead, I probably couldn't risk damaging my relationship with them any further.

Actually, loading some of this over on the message board at the Dead Orc Soup and a few other choice in-game bars wasn't a half bad idea. It'd certainly get their attention. I mean, why fish when you can trawl?

"Don't antagonize them any more than you already have," Rynn called from the cave entrance.

My temper didn't need much prompting. I hadn't even said anything that time. "Do you ever turn that off?"

"I *can't*," was Rynn's curt reply. Rynn might be a patient man, but we'd been here for two hours now. Even he had his limits—and they were a hell of a lot more substantial than mine with this damn notebook in front of me I couldn't for the life of me read.

I sighed. Maybe there was something in the sections on Shangri-La I missed.

"So that's what this bounty is all about?" Rynn asked. "Finding Shangri-La?" I saw him shake his head in disgust. "Foolish pursuits," he said.

For the most part I agreed. Shangri-La was what we in archaeology called a "white rabbit." You could chase it down as many holes as you wanted, but you'd never catch it—and probably lose what chance you had of a career. "*Many lives were ruined chasing after myths,*" an old professor of mine used to say. It was one of the few pieces of advice I'd taken to heart. If there isn't a good, concrete trail, I'm not interested.

But if Shangri-La had been found, an entire magic city based on human magic . . . "It does explain what the IAA wants with Neil and Frank." I knew the IAA. This bounty was pulling out their biggest guns and crossing a lot of jurisdictional red tape. It never made sense that they were throwing their arsenal at the World Quest duo for sticking a few restricted dig sites in a video game. Not even to set an example to potentially wayward graduate students chomping at the reins. They had me for that. "Still, I wonder why they didn't make the bounty for Shangri-La." If nothing else, the IAA always kept their end game in mind—and advertising they were after Shangri-La would have attracted more talent, the kind that chases after glory and fame.

"Too many treasure hunters would have been tripping over each other's toes. And maybe they sent them after Neil and Frank so they'd be certain to look in the right spot?" Rynn offered.

"Maybe." Despite the secrecy and false names they'd used, we'd still managed to trace them to the Himalayas through credit card purchases and email archives. The human magic, that had to be it; somehow the IAA found out.

And only Frank and Neil knew how to open Pandora's proverbial Shangri-La black box.

Which left me with more questions. Why hadn't the IAA been able to find this place on their own? Why launch a public bounty if they wanted things kept under wraps?

I picked up a loose stone and launched it at an undecorated wall. The echo was cathartic.

If Rynn had an opinion as to the IAA's motives, he didn't offer them. Instead, he said, "Alix, I don't need to pressure you, but we'll need to start hiking back soon. The longer we stay here—"

The greater the chance the mercenaries or yeti would make an appearance. Meaning unless I found something spectacular in the World Quest designers' notes or the cave itself in the next hour, I would still be running after the World Quest designers blind.

And I wasn't going to kid myself. Despite the fact that the IAA had either ignored or missed the place, it wouldn't stay safe from their attentions for long. I opened the notebook back up once again. *What the hell were you two after?*

Rynn abandoned his post and came over. "Let me see," he said, gesturing for me to pass him the book.

"Knock yourself out," I said, and handed it to him. Anything to stop myself launching it at the damn painted cave wall yaks.

He opened the journal, careful of the pages as he turned them. When he got to the images they'd painstakingly jotted down with the coded notes in the margin, he frowned.

I sat up. "Do you recognize them?" Maybe they'd pulled out some ancient dialect for their code.

But Rynn shook his head. "No, like you said, chicken scratch." He sniffed at the pages gingerly. "But it does smell faintly of blood."

Blood? There's only a couple reasons blood would be on the pages, and it didn't look like carnage splatter, so . . .

Rynn could see where my thoughts were going. "If there was supernaturally derived magic on the pages, I'd see it."

I went cold . . . unless it wasn't supernaturally derived.

Oh hell . . .

I picked the notebook back up and opened it back to the pages where they'd diagrammed the cave images. *All right, Texas and Michigan, gimme something to work with here.*

The chicken scratch notes diagrammed along the margins of the pages were grouped into circles and then attached to various symbols and pictographs on the wall with lines and arrows.

I palmed a UV flashlight out of my pocket and aimed it at the notes. Here went nothing. I flicked it on.

Nothing happened.

"It was a nice try, Alix," Rynn said.

"This has to be it. I'm missing something." I tried turning the page upside down and on its side under the UV light.

Wait a minute . . .

I stared at the page again. They wouldn't have put something from the game in here, would they? Then again, only someone who played the game would think of it.

"Rynn, do you have a mirror?"

He gave me a funny look but fished a mirror from his backpack and brought it over to me.

I took it and, sitting cross-legged, balanced the book open on my lap.

"I remember something like this from World Quest. A treasure map they released into the game a couple years back that was only half complete. There was a trick to getting the whole image." Okay . . . now, how had this worked exactly? I balanced the book again and lined the mirror up as best as I could. Next, I motioned for Rynn to pass me the UV flashlight again. I'd done this in game before. Nothing happened to the diagram on the first try either in the game. There'd been a trick to it.

"You know what you're doing?" Rynn said, glancing up at the painting, not bothering to hide his concern.

I thought about my answer. "Well, it's a little different than commanding an avatar. I mean, I have to balance the book myself, and you don't have to worry about angles in the game." A mirror could amplify any of the UV light from the flashlight. Activation from stray light was a risk, especially since I wasn't sure what the magic woven into the images *did*.

"The last time someone tried copying something from that videogame in the real world, I remember things going horribly wrong."

"That wasn't World Quest, that was a flight simulator game. And it was Carpe." All right, how to balance the mirror so it didn't slide off the page . . .

Rynn lowered his head and glared at me from under his eyebrows. "I really don't see the difference," he said.

I didn't dignify that with a response. I wasn't trying to fly a plane, I was looking for magic.

Figuring I had the book and mirror as balanced as they were ever going to be, I turned the flashlight on the page. Okay, World Quest, prove me wrong.

Nothing illuminated on the page itself; I hadn't expected it to. I was watching the mirror. It wasn't instantaneous, and it was a stretch to see it, but slowly and surely the reflected chicken scratch from the page began to elongate and change. Not on the page, mind you, just in the mirror.

"Son of a bitch," I said under my breath as I watched the reflected chicken scratch morph and change in the mirror, completing the sentences that had been drawn out on the pages. "The bastards figured it out."

I felt Rynn's breath on my hands as he came closer and crouched behind me, looking over my shoulder. "Can you see any of this on the mirror?" I asked him.

He squinted at the reflection, but after a moment he nodded. "Is that what I think it is?"

"Human magic." How many attempts of humans trying to do supernatural magic had I read about in history books? Every one had resulted in explosions and/ or missing limbs.

Yet here it was. Newly written magic code. Left by the World Quest duo. This had to be the first time in thousands of years that humans had figured out how to get human magic—once thought a myth or, at the very least, lost to the ages—to work. And yet here it was, right in my hands.

I looked up at Rynn. "The IAA doesn't just want Shangri-La. Neil and Frank are the first people—humans—in over a thousand years to get magic to work."

"Can you read it?" was all he said, nodding at the page, his face unreadable.

I turned my head at an odd angle. The writing wasn't coded; no point. If you got this far, why bother making you work harder? But it also wasn't neat.

"Ahh, it's not notes. A message," I said, and began to read it out.

" 'To whoever finds this book. If you've made it this far, things have gone bad. Before you is the door to Shangri-La. Beware—something is horribly wrong. Do not try to activate it. I repeat, do not turn it on.' "

A doorway. *This* magic-coated picture was the doorway to Shangri-La. I walked over and ran my hand gingerly over one of the yak-drawn carts. Son of a bitch. They'd opened the doorway. That's where they were, they had made it to Shangri-La.

"Alix," Rynn warned, keeping his distance from the doorway. "The last thing they said to *anyone* was not to follow."

"Or they didn't want the wrong person to follow them." It was as if the pictures called to my fingers, as if the door itself was reaching out, calling to me. But how to open it?

"That's an irresponsible jump of logic, even for you."

I turned on Rynn, not entirely sure why I was so irritated at his interruption. "If I don't find them, who will? The mercenaries? The IAA? Please explain how any of that is better than me chasing after them?" I was shouting now. I knew I shouldn't, but I couldn't help it. After how many false starts this month, I was so close. The doorway was right in front of me. Or that's what I reasoned.

I tried to go back to the painting, but Rynn grabbed me by the arm and spun me around until I was facing him. He waited until I met his eyes. I didn't need to be empathic like him to know he was barely covering his own anger. "I *agree* with you trying to help them."

"Then why do you keep arguing with me about treasure hunting!" There was more venom in my voice than there should have been.

"Because you and I both know that city is a golden treasure beacon, and treasure hunting is one of your faults, Alix. I care too much not to point it out."

I clenched my fists. This was verging on the first real fight we'd had in a long time. "I am *not* on a treasure hunt," I said, straining to keep my voice even.

"Who are you trying to convince? A lost mythical city that hasn't been seen for centuries?" Rynn shook his head. "There are other kinds of treasure, Alix, than the ones you can haul away taped to your chest or in your bag. And the fact that you seem to have an intentional blind spot for that right now should be a huge warning."

Rynn knew when I was lying—or strongly suspected was maybe more accurate. Incubus perk—or handicap, depending on the situation.

"I'm well aware that the part about Shangri-La being filled with treasure is a myth," I tried.

Rynn brought his face close to mine, until I could see just how much anger was hidden behind those eyes. "You don't believe that for one second. You think you were there, Alix."

I froze. I'd seen Shangri-La, or something very close to it, in World Quest while under the influence of an ancient curse. Granted, I'd been delusional at the time—and there with a talking Captain—but I hadn't told Rynn that, not in so many words.

He could have kept pushing, yelling at me. I could see it in his face. But he didn't. Instead, his features softened, and he let me go. "I don't want to see you get hurt, Alix. And I'm worried. Over the past month you've become . . ." He paused, searching for a word. ". . . *obsessed* with finding them. At first I thought it was having the IAA threatening you again, but now? I wonder if it's the shadow of that city, and I think those," he said, nodding at the murals, "just made things worse."

A snarky retort was on the tip of my tongue, but looking at Rynn, the worry written on his face, I wrangled hold of my temper and forced it back down.

Rynn's concern wasn't lost on me—not completely. "Look, if they're living in there and running World Quest, it stands to reason it's not cursed."

Rynn shook his head and gave me a sad look. "Not the same thing as safe."

No, it wasn't. I drew in a breath. "I'm not trying to find the city for a thieving free-for-all. For once I'm not on a treasure hunt," I said, though I wondered who I was trying to convince: Rynn or me?

"Then what are you trying to do?" he said, crossing his arms. "Because right now, standing here . . ."

I met Rynn's stare and said something that might not be the entire truth but was part of it. "Saving those idiots from their self-righteous, egotistical selves."

Rynn watched me with those gray eyes, but instead of nodding, he turned his head to the side in confusion, as if he'd seen something in my face that shouldn't be there. "There's something else," he said, his brow knitting as his eyes flickered blue. "I can't put my finger on it, but there's something not right."

He looked like he wanted to say something else, but we both heard the crash of a tree outside. In the silent forest, that couldn't be good.

Rynn swore and turned back to the entrance. "Stay here—and whatever you do, don't touch the doorway."

I watched him disappear into the cave's shadows. I tried to focus on sounds outside—anything that might tell me what was happening—but I found myself staring back at the images. A moment later my fingers were tracing what had to be the arches of the portal. . . .

I frowned. Hadn't I been on the other side of the cavern? There was something worrying about that, but the worry vanished, drifting away on a warm breeze.

I was standing in front of the doorway to Shangri-La.

And it wasn't like touching it would open the gate. Blood, maybe UV light, but not my bare fingers.

No, I'd only touch.

But what if Neil and Frank were waiting for me? What if they were trapped? In need of my help . . .

"Alix!"

I stepped back from the portal and shook my head as Rynn's voice broke through whatever fog I'd fallen into. I turned in time to see him slide through the alcove. "Mercenaries, the South Africans, to be precise."

Goddamn it. Any thoughts of the doorway vanished as I followed Rynn back into the main chamber. Sure enough, we could see the trees and brush moving, giving the mercenaries' movements away. "Have they seen us yet?" I said.

"No, but they will. I don't think they've seen the goblins either, but with this many humans in their valley . . ."

It wouldn't be long before the bloodlust at so much food kicked their caution to the wind. "What about Talie?"

Rynn shook his head. "Gone. She would have seen them coming."

"Great, couldn't she have warned us?"

"She's a luck demon, not a soothsayer."

Regardless of the why, the result was the same—we were on our own.

"We need to leave now if we want to have any chance of slipping by them undetected," he said, and began collecting the glow sticks. "If we hug the far side of the valley, they may not see us."

"Rynn! We can't leave them the portal," I said, surprised at the panic in my own voice.

Rynn frowned at me but shook his head. "We don't have a choice. I'm sorry, Alix. If we're lucky and they don't find the cave . . ."

We could always come back.

I nodded and headed back into the alcove to grab my things. I shoved the lab book into my backpack, than collected the glow sticks, careful not to look at the mural—no point in tempting myself.

Flashlight, floodlight. I frowned as I came across a squirt bottle—my squirt bottle, the one filled with chicken blood that I carried with me.

When the hell had I brought that out? I hadn't planned on activating the gate. Rynn was right about that one. I started to put it back in my bag . . . and stopped.

What if there was another way? Maybe we didn't need to sneak out the cave entrance and play peekaboo with mercenaries.

"Come on, Alix. Hurry it up!" I heard Rynn call, but it sounded more distant this time. I turned to face the mural, bottle of blood in hand.

I was the expert on this stuff, I reasoned. And it was my gut telling me not to leave the gate here, untouched, unopened.

I was Owl, infamous antiquities thief. Since when did I take the wise or easy way out of anything? And since when couldn't I handle a few activated inscriptions on a rock wall?

I had to know.

"There's another way out." It took me a moment to realize it had been my voice; there was something that should bother me about that. I frowned, trying to chase the thought down, but I already had the bottle of water and blood ready.

I started to spray the mural.

"Alix!" Rynn said, but it was too late.

There were still two UV flashlights on the floor. Under the light I could see the magic contained in the images begin to activate, glittering and flickering as they brightened, the swirled designs churning in on themselves, the animals taking on a life of their own as they danced toward the gate.

Someone gripped my shoulders and turned me around. Rynn, an incredulous look on his face as his attention went from the portal to me. "I cannot believe you just opened the portal, Alix, what the hell . . ." He trailed off as he stared at my face, his anger disappearing, replaced with worry. He swore under his breath and started to pull me toward the cave entrance.

I shook him off. "Which one of us is the expert on antiquities here? I made the call to open it, all right?" It still didn't sound quite like my own voice—and my thoughts were foggy, churning, slipping past me.

Rynn's mouth set in a hard line. "Something isn't right. There's magic at work in here, one I'm not familiar with."

I shook my head, trying to shake the fog clouding my thoughts, weighing them down.

There was a furious shock of anger that coursed through me—then, slowly, as if a wind had picked up, the clouds lifted off my thoughts.

The cave rumbled behind me.

Shit. I ran my hand through my hair. What the hell had I been thinking?

The cave rumbled again as the portal continued to turn in on itself.

Whatever had happened, I didn't have the luxury of kicking myself now. The two of us backed away slowly. "Let's just wait and see what it does before we panic," I said. "If it malfunctions, we run." And if it didn't? What then?

Rynn swore in supernatural—the few words of supernatural I understood—as we watched the magic unfurl. The air filled with the tangy scent of citrus and warm, heavy spices. The wall began to waver under the UV, showing glimpses of somewhere else, a place with green grass and snow-covered peaks.

"It's working," I said. I didn't know whether it was the gate itself or the air coming through, but my breath fogged the air in front of me.

Then it changed. The lights fumbled and the scent of orange and spice was replaced with something metallic and sharp. The image began to flicker with dark shadows. Letters started to scrawl along the gate, but quickly faltered and fell apart.

The cave groaned this time. We both jumped back as the far walls crumbled, spilling onto the floor.

"Please say you know how to turn it off," Rynn said, his voice quiet, as if it might upset the portal.

I shook my head, backing up toward the larger cavern a little faster.

More words attempted to scrawl out over the top of the mural, instead twisting violently into tangled and fragmented strings. "The mercenaries will have heard that for sure," he said.

"Is this the part where you try and tell me I told you so?"

"I don't do that until after we avert the disaster."

There was a respite in the shaking cave as a last series of iridescent words made their way across the portal itself. These were in English—and legible.

We tried to warn you. I'd run. Now.

Shit. "You were right, back up faster," I said. I turned and bolted through the narrow passage and out into the main chamber. Rocks had started to fall in here too as the caves had begun to collapse.

"Alix!" Rynn said, and knocked me out of the way as rocks from the ceiling crashed to the floor.

We grabbed what we could and made for the entrance, skidding to a halt just outside the cave entrance as the main chamber collapsed behind us.

When the adrenaline subsided I looked up at Rynn, who was watching me, his jawline still clenched.

"Do you think they heard us?" I said hopefully.

Rynn started to say something.

Instead, his attention was drawn to the ping of metal striking the cliff face above, followed by two more. Darts. Metallic and modern, the contents from the broken glass vials dripping onto me, smelling acrid and chemical.

"I'd say yes," Rynn said and knocked me downward, into the cover of brush.

I landed on my back, the air knocked out of me—which is why I saw the ripples of white tattered rags in the trees above us.

"Oh no."

"That mercenaries have seen us? Yes, I'd say that's an issue," Rynn said, still holding me to the ground.

I shook my head. "No, we have another problem." I pointed as best I could at the yeti balancing in the tree above us. This yeti was about seven feet tall, give or take, the combination of two goblins, one standing on the other's shoulders and draped with a ratty yak hide, which I smelled as the wind shifted.

At the top and the middle of the hide, holes had been randomly cut—what I imagined were eye and mouth holes. There were also holes in the sides for all four of its spindly brown arms, and though I couldn't see their feet I imagined they'd have the same dried-twig-like texture. The only thing out of place was the yak horn; instead of being held up top like a horn on an animal, the lower half was holding the horn out, curved end up, looking like an extremely disproportionately large phallus.

It made a low chirping noise, not unlike Captain when agitated.

Rynn said something in supernatural that I most definitely did not recognize, and yanked me under a bush as a spear hit the loose dirt where we'd been a moment before.

One of the goblins shouted down at us, a screeching, garbled sound this time.

Rynn said something back at it, his voice low and rough but nowhere close to matching the yeti-goblin.

"They speak supernatural?" I asked.

He shook his head. "A few words here and there. Badly translated.

They called you 'meat,' then said something about a yak horn. I think it was offering it in trade, but considering where it's got the horn placed..."

Not something I cared to be left open to interpretation...

More voices drifted toward us, shouting various orders and directions over each other. Mixed in were the screeches of the yeti.

"Run," Rynn said, and with a hard shove sent me down ahead of him toward the trail. When we hit the bottom, Rynn steered me to the left, into the brush and away from the river.

"This way. They'll expect us to head toward the river. Yeti-goblins don't like to get wet."

"So why the hell are we going into the forest?"

"Because we're desperate."

Damn it. "I thought your plans weren't supposed to involve running?" My cardio had gotten better over the past few months, but I was already feeling the run in my legs and lungs.

"My plans most definitely didn't involve you deciding to fuck with magic and setting off a cave-in!" Rynn said, and pushed ahead of me. "Keep up."

Keep up. I could hear men and women yelling out in the valley. It might have been my imagination, but I could have sworn they were closer this time.

"How many of these supernatural jobs have you followed me on now?" I said, my voice coming in short bursts. "How many of them end in some kind of supernatural cave-in or explosion?"

Rynn shot me a dirty look over his shoulder. He'd pulled ahead a few paces, partly because of the dense brush and miniature trees, but also because of my quads protesting loudly.

"Run faster" was all Rynn said as he somehow navigated the nonexistent path.

I swore as Rynn skidded to a sudden stop in front of me, his shoes sliding in the damp forest floor. I slammed into his back, but oddly enough he seemed to be ready for that.

"Booby trap," he said. I followed his line of sight to a series of wooden spikes hanging precariously from a tree. The scent of rotting hides and days-old cat urine hit me. Yeti-goblins, cackling and screeching like cats in the trees all around us, as if they were arguing. There was a scuffle in the nearest tree before one of the yeti fell, crashing to the ground.

That was the only warning we had before they let the trap loose.

Rynn pushed me out of the way as the spikes crashed to the ground. "Since when do goblins have booby traps?" I hissed.

"Since they've been breeding like rabbits and ate all the food. They've been selecting for the smart ones who figured out there was one food supply left."

The ramifications of that hit me. I guess it was already cold enough up here that they'd had to figure out furs. Put the right selective pressure on them—namely, make it warm enough for a couple breeding seasons and then have them eat all the food—and it was only a matter of time before a few of them figured out they could eat each other. The blueprint was set. "Cannibalistic phallus toting yeti-goblins?"

Rynn inclined his chin. "I was going to say hyper-aggressive, but your description is apt enough. It'll be the smart ones that survived and bred."

We both turned as more shouts came from our right this time—probably picking up on the screeching yeti. "They're herding us all. We need to go another direction."

As if his words were premonition, something slammed into the tree trunk behind us, narrowly missing my head. Darts. And not primitive ones made out of bone and feathers, but plastic-and-glass encased. For the second time I smelled the sweet metallic contents as they trickled to the ground. I had a feeling whatever was in those darts would put down a supernatural as easily as a human—and I doubted the mercenaries cared what it did to my liver and kidneys . . .

Rynn sprinted to the left as something else whizzed by our heads—whether from the yeti or the mercenaries, I couldn't be sure and wasn't about to look.

I pushed my legs to keep up—or not collapse underneath me. I figured they were about the same thing.

"The jeep should be up ahead."

"I thought she took off?"

Rynn gave a shake of his head. Even he was starting to look and sound winded. "She wouldn't leave us here. We'll have a window if we keep running while the yeti try to pick off the Zebras."

I caught sight of it up in the tree. I mean, it was a glimpse of white, and for a second I thought it was moss or pieces of some animal's nest that had been shredded and left hanging from the limbs.

"Ow!" I came to a halt as something sharp, like a bee or a fire poker, bit into my cheek before slamming into the tree behind us. I touched my face, my fingers coming back covered in blood. I looked at the tree behind me. A nasty jagged arrow, with a smaller, feather-decorated shaft, was lodged into the tree trunk. And my cheek was numb. Shit. They'd figured out poison.

I heard the gleeful cackle before the yeti began to step out of their hiding spots. The one nearest us had a *pair* of yak horns protruding from its middle. It was the kind of disturbing visual that you wanted to look away from but couldn't.

It took me a sec to figure out that the bundle of mish-mashed feathers in its spindly hands was an arrow. And the rough feather-and-hide-decorated item in its other hand? A bow. I ducked, this time pulling Rynn down with me as it readied and launched another feather arrow at us with unnerving speed. This one hit the tree trunk where we'd been standing a moment before.

Rynn took in the scene as the yeti-goblins readied more arrows.

I could hear other shouts, human ones, and the odd crash and yell coming from the other directions—back near the caves and toward the river.

Rynn looked from the yeti closing in on us to the direction of the mercenaries crashing through the bush behind us. I watched his mouth move as he spoke to himself silently.

"Rynn, definitely your area of expertise now. Plan of action?" I thought I could see red eyes under the yeti hides, but it was hard to tell.

The eye holes weren't exactly cut even—I could now see that each of the faces had been made from multiple attempts—and I figured it was the sheer volume of holes that gave them their vision, since clearly they could shoot.

The shouting was getting closer, and the yeti began to look at each other—or as well as they could under the hides. One of them made a high-pitched chattering screech, returned by another.

"Any idea what they're saying?"

"Haven't a clue," he said, taking a step back. He turned his blue-gray eyes on me. "Do you trust me, Alix?"

"Oh God, you're going to throw me over a cliff."

"In a manner of speaking." He pulled me up and shoved me hard to the right, arrows thudding into the trees behind us. He kept his hand on the small of my back as we ran, pushing me any time I slowed.

"Human here!" I managed to shout out in between painful, lung-searing gulps of air.

"Not much farther," Rynn said, though even he sounded winded. I realized we were heading back toward the caves.

"Here!" he shouted, as we spilled out of the bush and skidded to a halt before a rock face—steep, but with enough crags and outcrops that it was scalable. "Quick, climb, Alix. The brush should hide us."

Yeah, but for how long? My muscles protested while I inflicted a new and painful torture on them as I climbed, taking the easiest way, while Rynn took the fastest, spilling onto the top of a ledge a few paces before me, helping me up the last few feet.

"Take this." Rynn pressed a rock into my hand that was a little larger than a baseball, and much heavier and sharper.

"And do what?"

"Throw it at those trees over there when I say so." He reached over my shoulder and used his arm as a sight, making sure I saw exactly the trees he meant, a copse of evergreens like miniature Christmas trees.

I waited a count of five breaths, listening as the chattering and grunts and human yells and orders continued toward us, getting louder and more excited, figuring they had cornered their prey. They had. "This is not my kind of plan."

"Just wait, Alix, and trust me. I'm taking a page from your book."

"My book? What the hell in my playbook dealt with getting cornered by mercenaries and goblin kin?" My playbook was run—and if that failed, see if I could lose myself in the crowd . . . or a protest, or a riot. . . . Oh shit. Nooo, that was a bad idea.

I didn't get a chance to register my objection as Rynn picked that moment to shout, "Now!" as loud as he could. I tossed my rock at the copse of trees. I'm not much of a thrower, but I was impressed with how well I did, all things considering. The trees gave an impressive shake as if there might be some animal hiding amongst them. The yeti-goblins seemed to think so too. With a universal screech that echoed throughout the trees, almost every yeti seemed to launch some sort of weapon at the copse, momentarily distracted by the potential of dinner.

Rynn tossed something—but it wasn't a rock. He threw a grenade.

I dropped and covered my head as the first one detonated, sending up a cloud of debris and making my ears ring painfully. He threw three of them; one behind the goblins who had moved into firing range to explore the copse of Christmas trees, and one each behind the mercenaries' tight lines. The point hadn't been to kill any of them; it was to scare them. The mercenaries and yeti. Though, from the catlike shrieks I figured some of the yeti might have been incinerated— I wasn't feeling as bad about that considering they'd called me meat.

I watched from the ledge as if in another world as the debris and devastated vegetation settled, and both the goblins and mercenaries shrieked bloody murder.

Then, one by one, the goblins saw the mercenaries, who'd moved forward to escape the grenades, tightening their ranks. If they didn't look like a threat before, they did now.

The mercenaries, twelve of them, stood perfectly still, considering their options.

Rynn wasn't going to give them one. The mercenaries couldn't see us yet, as we were still hidden by the tree line and the ledge.

But some of the yeti could, the ones still in the trees. One of them, in a nearby tree, chittered and started to point at us.

Rynn threw another grenade at it. It caught it and tried to bite, sharp white teeth showing through the holes in its hide. I ducked and covered my head as it went off. Something wet hit me. Oh man, the smell. It was all I could do not to puke.

I looked at Rynn, who'd thrown himself down beside me. "Their population needed some thinning. Come on," Rynn said as he stood and started to climb over the top of the rocky hillside, in plain view of the mercenaries and yeti. I followed. The mercenaries and yeti didn't pay us one damn lick of attention this time—they were too busy attacking each other. The gunfire and yeti battle cries still punctuated the air as we climbed over the last set of rocks.

The opposite side of the hillside was sloped, and we dropped down onto a flat area covered in soft grass. A ways from where we started, but I thought if we ran due east we'd eventually find the road we came in on.

I heard a shot echo through the field and dropped down. Rynn pulled me back up, shaking his head. "Backfire, not gunfire."

Sure enough, Talie's jeep turned and barreled out of the brush, then rounded toward us, the brakes squeaking to a stop.

"The lines of fate broke quite wildly, but I was able to follow the tether that led me back to you, though we have a very narrow window," she said.

"She means get in," Rynn said.

"You said it, little demon." Not wanting to waste time, I tossed my backpack onto the seat and dove about as gracefully as a walrus after it.

As soon as we were in, Talie stepped on the gas, the engine grinding in mechanical revolt as she steered it down the grass-paved back road.

"They'll have the jeeps on us, Talie," Rynn said.

To that she shook her head. "The mountains tell me their two off-road jeeps are very happy to stay where they are in the"—her face squished up—"well, not so quiet forest, the forest with many screams of carnage and pain."

We both stared at her this time. She frowned, looking very childlike. "The engines are missing many parts." She tapped the dashboard of her jeep. "Kitty needed them more than they did."

I glared at Rynn. "I notice you're not on the Apsara's case for theft."

He shrugged. "Different perception of ownership. Besides, it was an emergency."

I sure as hell didn't have any problems with it. Now that we were more or less in the clear, I sat back and let everything sink in. My God, an entire lead—a doorway to Shangri-La—*gone*. "Goddamn it, Rynn, I had them." This was just like when I'd had Carpe try to trace their location two weeks ago. Every time I'd gotten close to Michigan and Texas, it was as if something had been rigged to explode . . . like my computer. . . .

"This isn't a dead end. They were here."

"That's just it—this *was* it! No more credit cards, no email, no face recognition, no phones. *This* is where they vanished." I let my head hit the back of the seat and closed my eyes. I'd been so close . . . if I hadn't pulled a Pandora and knocked the lid off the box.

Rynn turned to face me, letting some of his anger show through. "It wasn't entirely you. There was something else back in the cave—magic of some sort, either the doorway or maybe something behind it." He leveled a measure stare at me. "I'm starting to think Neil and Frank are doing everyone a favor not wanting to be found."

For a moment I pushed aside thoughts of the magic that had briefly taken me over. There was only so much I could worry about at once. "Well, they're being idiots. Do you realize the extremes the IAA will go to in order to uncover human magic?" What would that be worth to the IAA? And more importantly, what would they do with it?

I wasn't sure I wanted to know the answer to that one.

"I hate to say it, Alix, but maybe they don't want to be saved."

Yeah. I was getting that distinct impression. "Think we have enough to pacify Lady Siyu?" We'd been on the road for three weeks straight, chasing after Neil and Frank on Mr. Kurosawa's dime.

Rynn let out a long breath and seemed to consider it. "The Delhi bowl you picked up last week should be enough. There's another artefact they made noise about in Kathmandu. Provided the mercenaries aren't as thick as they were in Nepal, you could try for that."

I nodded. A set of suspected supernatural jewelry. "How much do you think your friend Talie the Royal Kumari is going to care if we hit her temple?"

"Talie?" Rynn called out. "Did you hear that? Alix wants to raid the Kumari Palace."

I smacked him on the arm. "Don't say it like that," I said. "It makes it sound like I'm going to destroy the place."

But Talie turned to face me. "Lady, you can raze the place as far as I'm concerned. Sticking children in the temple as my reincarnated self? Do you have any idea how stupid that sounds?" She added something in Nepalese I didn't catch, but I was pretty sure it included a derogatory word for priests.

"Wise spirit once said the trick to being a God with a long life? Make sure the world ignores you. That beacon of worship gives me more headaches than you can imagine."

Maybe Rynn was right—maybe the majority of the supernatural world didn't want a war or to come out in the open. Funny though how a few choice individuals always end up making the rules. What's that saying, he who speaks the loudest?

My phone started to buzz in my pocket. I checked the name and swore. Lady Siyu, aka Dragon Lady, my boss's second in command. Lady Siyu's intimate dreams included seeing me gutted by the next supernatural that stumbled along. The fact that she'd recently had to cure me from a curse had put her into a foul mood to no end.

"Stop thinking about Lady Siyu," Rynn said beside me, where he was strapping our gear in.

Rynn might not be able to read minds, but there were very few things

I got that angry about. "Next to impossible, Rynn; the damn snake is calling on the phone." I took a deep breath before answering it. "Lady Siyu," I said.

"You will return to the Japanese Circus Casino at once," she said without any greeting or attempt at niceties. "Your flights are arranged. You will be at the airport in two hours' time. Tell the incubus I've relayed details to him, since you can't be trusted to follow anything except the human lust for treasure and gold."

"Ah, in the middle of something, so, no."

There was a hiss of breath on the other end. "It is *not* a request. And you would be best not to make me angry. Your *cat* ruined yet another piece of Louis XIV furniture." I wondered if he was going for the set. If it smelled like her . . . "The stupid beast thought it was a scratching post," she hissed again.

Yeah, I doubted that very much. "You know, he wouldn't destroy your furniture if you just gave him back to me."

"And my orders remain. You and the incubus are to be on that plane in two hours."

"Give me my cat back and maybe I'll think about it. Goddamn it!" I held up the phone. "She hung up!" I shoved my phone back in my pocket. "You heard?"

"Alix, she can't give you the cat back, she made a deal."

"Yeah, I know." Supernaturals had a difficult time breaking their word. I wasn't certain on the details, but it had to do with magic and biology. "There's nothing stopping her from trading him back."

"It doesn't work like that."

"Clearly. She won't actually hurt Captain? Will she?"

Rynn inclined his head. "Well, that depends."

"On?" I asked when he didn't elaborate.

"If we miss the flight."

I let out a long breath. Well, there went the rest of my expedition. If I had to guess, I'd say Mr. Kurosawa, my boss and a dragon, was as interested as I was in finding out what the IAA wanted. However, he also had his own agenda, which I was paid and contracted for. Meaning anything to do with the IAA and their hunt for World Quest would have to take a backseat.

Dragons have a reputation for eating the odd thief.

"On to the Japanese Circus, Incubus," I said, doing my best to imitate Lady Siyu's imperious tone, if not her precise British accent as the jeep made its way back onto the more traditional-looking back roads. Yet another dead end on my search for the World Quest duo.

I leaned up front by the driver's seat. "All right, you heard the lady, Talie?"

She took her eyes off the road, a downtrodden look on her face. "I thought you were going to destroy my temple."

I frowned. "I said break in, not destroy."

She glanced back at Rynn. "Typically when the Owl enters a site for confrontation with historical elements, the result is a cataclysmic event," she said.

I shot Rynn a dirty look.

"You have a reputation for destroying things," Talie said, assuming I hadn't understood her the first time. "Like Kali. Rynn said as much." Talie took her eyes off the road again and looked at me like a puppy might. "I was hopeful your presence might result in its destruction."

"She was locked in that palace for a long time," Rynn offered. "Two hundred years."

"*Three* hundred," she said, her pretty face etched with a frown.

Rynn acknowledged her. "My mistake. Three hundred years she was locked in the Kumari Palace after the human priests trapped her the first time."

"They didn't just trap me, they lured me down from the mountains with a promise of a party—with lanterns and children," she said as she looked at me woefully. "I like playing with children. They rather look like me."

"It's rigged to imprison her if she steps foot on the grounds," Rynn added as way of explanation.

Oh God. That was so sad. I mean . . . "Why didn't you just use your powers?"

She shrugged. "My powers don't do as well in Kathmandu. I work better in these mountains."

"I remember you distinctly raining avalanches and snowstorms down on the surrounding areas," Rynn said.

Her eyes furrowed. "Only for the last hundred years of my imprisonment. What can I say? I got desperate."

"She escaped in the eighteen fifties."

"Thanks to you and that onryo."

Onryo—a Japanese vengeance demon. The corrupt version of a kami, a very powerful supernatural being that appears throughout Japanese mythology. Loyal to a fault and bound by a strict honor code, kami were one of the few species that tolerated humans, even advocating for them occasionally. And they were terrifying warriors. An onryo was what they became when they died, a monster not tied to any code beyond vengeance. I imagined there couldn't be too many onryos out there, and fewer that Rynn knew. It could only be Oricho.

"And a lot of good it does me," Talie continued. "I can barely enter the capital without those priests trying to track me down and put me back." She turned to me again, treating me to the full effect of her large, sad, painted eyes, which reminded me of a doll's. "Did you know fifty years ago they tried luring me back to Kathmandu with another party? 'Oh no, it won't be like last time,'" she pantomimed. "'You can leave whenever you want, we promise we won't trap you in the palace. We're different.'" She spit out the jeep window and uttered the kind of phrase that would have been more appropriate on a sailor, not a small, childlike supernatural. "Humans get to break their word. *We* don't, but them?"

Rynn interrupted her tirade. "She's been trying to come up with a way to destroy the palace bindings *without killing anyone.*" He stressed the last words, as if that was not exactly a forgone conclusion between them—or as if he needed to remind her.

Talie shrugged. "I was hopeful," she repeated to me with the doll eyes.

"Ah, sorry, but your temple will have to wait. I promise," I rushed to add as her face fell, "that I'll take a crack at it another time and see whether I can't trash the bindings." Actually, if she hadn't been in the palace since the 1850s, this generation of caretakers might not realize they were there. Often with supernatural bindings, all it took were a few misplaced rocks. For all I knew, it might have already happened. "Mr. Kurosawa's list isn't going anywhere."

That seemed to brighten her up. "You're certain?"

"Kid, if there's one thing I'm certain of, it's that the dragon has one hell of an appetite for treasure and I don't want to be eaten by vampires. Trust me, I'll be back."

"Kathmandu it is," she said, sounding more cheerful than she had a moment before as she kicked the dilapidated orange-and-fuchsia rhinestone-encrusted jeep into a higher gear.

World Quest, IAA, and whatever else had been lurking inside that cave would also have to take a backseat to whatever it was Mr. Kurosawa and Lady Siyu had for me now. I just hoped the mercenaries didn't catch up—for Michigan and Texas's sakes.

4

ROCKS AND HARD PLACES

4:00 p.m. The Japanese Circus Casino, Las Vegas

The great thing about working for an obscenely rich dragon? Private jets. Rynn and I pretty well had the plane to ourselves—including a shower—with minimal interference from Lady Siyu. Guess she figured that since we were already on the plane, she could wait to yell at me in person.

The downside? Rynn and I had been locked together inside a plane by ourselves. For twenty hours . . .

Don't get me wrong; we were nowhere near an off-again state, and it's not like we hadn't exactly enjoyed having the plane to ourselves for the first few hours. I just wish he hadn't started in on the cave again and hadn't been so damn smug about being right. It wasn't like opening the doorway had been entirely my fault. . . .

Rynn turned and frowned at me as we got out of the car. "Alix, you're still angry at me."

And why the hell couldn't he turn off the whole empathy thing? For once, was it really too much to ask for? Or at least he could pretend he didn't know what I was feeling. I mean, my *God*.

I stopped myself from saying any of that though as we walked through the sliding glass doors that led into the lobby of the Japanese Circus. "I'm not angry. I'm disappointed. In you," I said. There, that wasn't so bad? No name calling, no yelling, nothing inflammatory . . .

Rynn made a derisive noise.

Okay, well nothing too inflammatory . . . but he'd crossed a couple lines on the way back. I turned on him. "Seriously! Why do you have to think that every job, everything I do, is about treasure?"

Some people in the casino glanced over at us—well, me. All right, so maybe I'd raised my voice a little. Rynn pulled me into an alcove.

"I'm not a treasure whore!" I said.

Rynn's brow furrowed. "I did not call you that, Alix, though God knows you've called me worse. We agreed no more name calling." He sighed and ran his hand through his hair. "I believe you want to stop the IAA—and I agree with you, I don't want to see them with human magic any more than you do, which is the entire reason I'm helping you. I wouldn't be if I thought it was just over Shangri-La."

"But?" I could hear it in his voice, and he knew it.

I watched him hedging his answer. "Treasure colors your judgment, and what's worse, some of the time you don't seem to realize that's what you're after."

I breathed and tried to calm my nerves before I said something stupid. "I won't be finding anything at this rate, not after destroying our only lead. It's like something in that cave wanted me to self-destruct." I still couldn't believe I'd tried to activate the gate; I *knew* better, and it wasn't like something had been controlling me. I'd gone over it in my head a hundred times: I'd just been convinced it was the right choice.

It hadn't been like me.

"Or something was desperate for you to open the gate," Rynn offered. "I have no doubt you or the *elf* will find another lead." Every time Rynn said "elf," he made it sound like a dirty word.

We started back through the foyer toward the elevator, the casino patrons no longer paying us any mind. We had a meeting with an angry

Naga to attend. I jostled Rynn. "And Corona is not a bottom-tier beer," I said. The other thing we'd managed to fight about on the plane.

He didn't bother hiding the eye roll.

"It is a safe bet in foreign harbors. Do you know how many times I've had to drink really bad beer?"

"That's because you've spent your adult life hanging out in the dives universities call accommodation and backpacker hostels."

"And considering my career choices, that's not likely to change, so . . ." I held out my hands.

Rynn leaned against the elevator. He'd bothered to dress in casino-appropriate attire of jeans, T-shirt, and leather jacket. I was wearing jeans, but I hadn't given up my cargo jacket. We didn't exactly make a matching pair.

"It wouldn't kill you to consider branching out your horizons," he said as we waited for the elevator to arrive.

"Why do I get the sinking suspicion we're not talking about beer anymore?"

"Because we aren't." Rynn's phone buzzed, and a pained expression passed over his face as he checked it. "Wait here. I need a few minutes to check in with security before we face Lady Siyu."

I nodded. Facing Lady Siyu was not something I ever tried to do alone. The fact that she hadn't figured out a way to kill me without royally pissing off her boss was a huge point of contention for her.

I watched as Rynn headed down the hall toward the security room. The casino employed mostly supernatural creatures, and Rynn had been recruited into running security for the casino since Oricho had betrayed Mr. Kurosawa almost four months back now. Half the time I was amazed I was dating a supernatural—I did not have the best track record—and half the time I was amazed I'd started letting him come on jobs with me instead of Nadya. Not that I didn't like having him with me; it was just hard to get used to having people in my life on a regular basis.

My own phone rang, interrupting my train of thought.

Nadya. On the plane I had managed to scan the World Quest duo's lab book and fill her in on what had happened in Nepal, but we hadn't had a chance to talk. She should have arrived back in Tokyo by now.

I found a spot by one of the casino's pillars—a quiet one, away from the casino proper traffic and the bells and whistles of the slot machines but still in sight of the elevators.

"Everything okay?" I answered.

"Fine. I heard through the grapevine that you just got in." Meaning one of the many employees at the bar had told her. Where my natural state was to infuriate people, Nadya made friends easily. Not just because of her looks—those didn't hurt; she was a Russian bombshell with a thing for extreme red wigs—but because of her personality. She had a way of getting people to listen to her. A skill I was often deficient in.

"I just landed in Tokyo, about to head to my apartment, then the club," Nadya continued. "I've been looking at the notes, and I have a couple ideas I want to check into, some old accounts from Siberia and China, but it will have to wait until I get things in order here."

She sounded distracted. "Everything okay?" I asked again.

"Let us just say things took a complicated turn for the worse. Look, there's no sense me going into details yet, not until I have a better idea what they are, but you're on your own from the archaeology side until I get this cleaned up."

"Nadya, seriously, what's going on?" She'd never passed up a job like this. Sure the club was important and paid the bills, but both Nadya and I had been grad students together. Her passion was archaeology, just not the BS that went with it.

She let out a breath. "Someone's trying to squeeze more money out of me for licensing, which is a fancy term for protection money. And not just me—" There was a muffled sound, as if Nadya had covered the mic of her phone. "Look, give me an hour to clear customs and check my emails."

"Nadya, who is doing the squeezing?"

"That's just it. I don't know yet. Everyone is being very tight-lipped as to who is orchestrating the push. That on its own wouldn't bother me. I could negotiate if it was just more money they wanted."

"What, then?"

"They're trying to wrangle a piece of ownership of the club. And without knowing who . . ." She let the sentence trail off.

Golden rule of business. Always know who it is you're working with or for.

"No sense worrying about it right now, Alix, not until I get a better grasp of things." Too late for not worrying. "Look, the customs guard is trying to get me to hang up my phone. I'll call you back."

"All right. Let me know if there's anything I can do to help."

"You have enough on your plate. Let me handle this. I'm hoping it's just a new gang trying a newer business policy—a very intricate cash grab and way to force us to launder money."

"But?" I asked.

"But if it's not, I want to make certain I'm there when everything hits the fan."

"Be careful." I saw Rynn turn the corner. I gave a half wave so he'd know where I was, then turned my attention back to the phone.

"That's not my weakness, that's yours. Say hello to Rynn for me." And with that she hung up.

I rejoined Rynn by the elevator and related what Nadya had told me about the squeeze in Tokyo. "The thing is, she said it wasn't just her. You haven't heard anything, have you?"

"Unfortunately, yes. I've got someone looking into it, but, like Nadya said, they've kept their identity quite secret. Eventually they'll have to expose themselves, but there's not much anyone can do until then." The elevator door slid open and he nodded at it. "Come on, time to see Lady Siyu before she decides we're late." He corralled me through the ornate elevators with a squeeze to my shoulder. After the doors closed and the elevator began to ascend, Rynn shot me a sideways glance. "You still have it, don't you?"

I couldn't help but smirk. Rynn might prefer following me on my jobs, but he was not interested in keeping track of the details of what I was actually taking—or where I kept it.

I reached into my backpack and pulled out the carefully wrapped bowl I'd picked up in a New Delhi sewer—yet another supernaturally derived artifact on Mr. Kurosawa's ever-growing list. Granted, I was getting paid a percentage for each one I managed to find, with expenses.

"You know, it's not really stealing when you're taking the artifact from a long-forgotten tomb." Or in this case, a tomb that had been hijacked by a Kali cult in the mid-1800s. It took me a couple days to realize that the offering bowl for Ganesh I was searching for and the cult's sacrificial bowl had been one and the same. Funny how the context changes our perception so much. In our heads, harmless bowl used to burn incense and offer fruits does not look the same as the bowl you hold under someone's slit throat.

I held it out for Rynn's inspection, but he passed. I couldn't help but smile. Supernatural he might be, but never would he be comfortable with the thieving aspect of my job . . . or his, now that Mr. Kurosawa had his black claws into him as well.

Silence stretched between us until the doors finally slid open to the hall on a hidden top floor that led to Mr. Kurosawa's private casino. "You warned your friend," Rynn said in an offhand manner.

It took me a second to realize he was talking about Dev Rai. "I wouldn't call him a friend, he's just one of the very few people from my archaeology days who isn't a complete asshole."

We reached the massive black doors embossed with gold characters. Rynn stopped in front of them. He was waiting for something. He never started on these seeming tangents without a reason or a point he was trying to get to.

"I wanted to help him out," I persevered. "He doesn't deserve to be thrown under the bus." After a pause I added, "He never got screwed by the IAA, but his father was. Big time, from what I understand. Was kicked off a local dig site when some bigwig European decided he was interested in Tibet. Some trendy spiritual quest back in the nineties when it was trendy to find yourself in the mountains. Someone higher up wanted a vacation, so Dev's dad got the boot."

"Interesting," he said, but he didn't step away from the embossed doors or make any move to open them. "I've heard you talk of lots of people's families except your own."

That was what he wanted.

My family was definitely not something I liked to talk about. "Not much to tell. My mother died a long time ago. Car accident—tragic, quick, and dealt with by a litany of counselors at my high school during my teen years. My father is still alive. A retired academic. We talk. At holidays." Not for the past two years, since my career imploded, but I like to think we both enjoy a comfortable distance. Also I was not great at hiding things from my father. He knew enough about the world of archaeology that I was pretty certain the first thing out of his mouth, *without* me telling him anything, would be I *told you so.*

"Archaeology?"

"God no—anthropology. He was not happy about my choice to chase after artifacts over the pursuits of culture . . . but by that point the university tuition was already free, sooo . . . headstrong daughter one, overbearing, opinionated father, zero." There hadn't been anything he could hold over my head at that point as far as telling me not to do something. "What's with this line of questioning?"

Rynn only offered me a casual shrug. "Curiosity. You usually blame your old colleagues or pick a fight with them. Often provoked," he added as I started to argue, "but still. It was interesting. You didn't turn it into a fight. I was curious why."

Rynn placed both hands on the massive doors that reached up to the nine-foot-high ceilings and pushed. They swung open, a plume of white smoke billowing out and exposing the cold, black marble floor and rows upon rows of slot machines.

I took one last deep breath in the semi-clean air before stepping inside Mr. Kurosawa's lair. Enter the dragon—or more like let the circus begin. "You could have just asked," I said.

"Where would be the fun in that?"

As I followed Rynn through the haunted rows of slot machines, I fidgeted with the bowl. He knew where he was going. Me, on the other hand? Being human, if I lost track of him, I'd end up lost in the slot machine version of an evil enchanted forest.

"You know, your anxiety over the Naga wouldn't be such an issue if you didn't spend all your time baiting her."

"Yes. I agree. Which is why I'm not going to bait her. Seriously," I added when I caught Rynn giving me a sideways glance. "No yelling, no baiting, no name calling. Cross my heart," I said, and followed through with the motion.

As opposed to assuaging his fears, that only made Rynn glare harder at me. "Who are you and what did you do with Alix?"

"I want my goddamned cat back, okay?"

Rynn snorted. "And as you keep pointing out, yelling at the giant snake lady isn't getting me anywhere, so I'm going to try playing nice."

Either by the stirred air or the sound of our footsteps, a few of the machines came to life, their lights flickering. I startled as one of the slot machines chimed behind me, followed by the clinking of coins hitting the smoky marble floors. It was one of the antiques from the 1930s. I never knew the reason behind the displays, whether they were to get my attention, warn me, or lure me off the path. Regardless of their intent, I backed up against Rynn so none of Mr. Kurosawa's gold could touch my feet.

The thing you noticed quickly about Mr. Kurosawa's private casino was that the slot machines were an eclectic mix, from 1905 Reys all the way up to modern electrics. There was a reason for that. At first I'd thought it was just one of Mr. Kurosawa's many antiques collections, but no. They were souvenirs, or trophies of a sort—the kind you trap someone's soul in. And every time I came in here to deal with Kurosawa or Siyu, there always seemed to be a few more.

A reminder of what happened to thieves at the Japanese Circus Casino—like an eleborate dragon mousetrap . . .

"It's best to ignore them and keep moving," Rynn offered.

Easy for him to say. I stared at Rynn's back as another machine spat gold coins at me. Sensing my discomfort Rynn picked up the conversation.

"You haven't called me any names recently," Rynn noted.

"We agreed not to call each other names." There was a pause, filled by another gust of smoky, cold air. "Besides, I never meant it in the first place."

There was that noncommittal shrug again. "I'm just saying when you change your behavior too much, I start to worry. Besides, bottling things in doesn't help either."

"How the hell can I bottle anything in when you can feel everything I feel?"

"It's not for me, it's for you."

"Okay, can we stop with the pop psychology? At least while I'm trying to figure out how to deal with Lady Siyu?" I let out a breath and reminded myself that Rynn wasn't the one I was really angry with. "I'm sorry. I don't mean to snap. Just that every time I'm in this damn place I can't help but wonder if I would have been better off running from the vampires."

Rynn fell silent for a moment. "Perhaps," he said after a moment. "But you'd still be running."

Which was the crux of everything: was it better to run from, or face, your problems? I still wasn't sure I knew the answer.

Rynn looked like he was going to add something, but the click of expensive heels on the marble stopped him.

Lady Siyu rounded a row of slot machines a moment later, appearing out of the smoke like a fairy-tale monster.

The first time I met Lady Siyu she was dressed like a modern kabuki girl, in a slightly shorter, more tailored, patterned minidress with less emphasized makeup. Today she was wearing her usual tailored black suit with a matching pencil skirt and the kind of white shirt I'd have wrinkled and stained in a matter of minutes. The shirt set off her black hair and bloodred matching nails and lipstick. Even the clipboard she carried was colored the bloodred shade she preferred.

Lady Siyu looked every inch the powerful businesswoman—and trust me, Mr. Kurosawa's right-hand monster was snake enough to topple any boardroom.

And she hated me. The feeling was mutual.

I was also terrified of her, so much so that I didn't realize I was holding my breath until her red lips curled up, exposing a single thin fang.

She wasn't wearing her sunglasses either—the ones she used to conceal her yellow snake eyes when she was angry, both of which flicked between the two of us.

Lady Siyu did a good job keeping up her human guise, but she had a tendency to drop it around me. I have that effect on a lot of supernaturals.

"Alix," Rynn whispered. I realized I was clutching my hands, digging my nails into the palms. I stopped and stuffed my rising temper.

New leaf, Owl. Do not pick a fight.

Lady Siyu turned her attention on Rynn, not bothering to hide her apathy toward him but also not willing to drop her manners like she did with me.

"Incubus," she said.

He gave the slightest nod. "Lady Siyu." Not quite a slight, but close. And he was the one warning me about baiting her. . . .

"Here," I said, and held out the wrapped bowl. The best way I'd found to avoid a fight with Lady Siyu was to keep the meeting as short as possible. I'd found through trial and error that the best course of action was to keep talking to a minimum. Explanations—make that any speaking— she didn't specifically ask for were dissuaded. She glanced at me, then began unwrapping the bowl, gingerly, careful not to tear the paper or even let her red nails brush the bowl.

She examined the outlines. It wasn't particularly impressive—dull brown colors, shallow etching.

Finished with her examination, she glanced back up at me. "You were tasked with retrieving a Peruvian artifact, not this," she said, holding up the bowl between two fingers.

If she had any idea how much easier the Peruvian job was compared to lifting that from a sewer full of rats and the remaining undead priests . . .

"Don't look at me if you don't like the bowl, go glare at Mr. Kurosawa, he's the one who sent me to retrieve it."

Confusion flickered across her face for a moment until she realized I meant the clay bowl. "This? This is exquisite in ways your simple human eyes can't *begin* to comprehend. My disgust is at your inability to deal with the IAA." Her lip curled, exposing the tip of both her fangs this time.

I bristled at the insinuation and the open, yet still subtle, threat. Lady Siyu was a Naga, and a poisonous one at that. "I'm dealing with them as best I can," I said.

The lip curled higher, exposing more fang. I thought I saw the glint of yellow venom. "Clearly not efficiently enough," she said, and handed me a tablet."I suppose the disaster we had to supress in New Delhi was another of your careless accidents?"

I took the tablet from her and checked the news articles—mostly video clips covering the sewer fire that had raged through part of the New Delhi downtown. Damn it. I'd hoped my antics hadn't warranted making the 6:00 p.m. New Delhi news, with no mention of the upside blow I'd dealt to their sewer rat problem. "Yeah, about that—I ran into some undead cultists in the tunnel." I wasn't certain if they'd counted as zombified or mummified. I hadn't stuck around long enough to ask.

"A fire and a collapsed section of the road?" Lady Siyu continued.

I winced. "Better than undead walking the streets of New Delhi looking for new victims." And if I'd known the undead monks' hearing was that good; their ear canals should have decayed decades ago . . .

But Lady Siyu only nodded at the tablet.

I glanced back down at it and frowned. As opposed to giving the usual reason—gas line, electrical fire, spontaneous combustion of a rat—that the IAA typically employed to cover a supernatural mishap, the article instead cited a robbery gone wrong.

"'An internationally infamous antiquities thief, known only to insiders as The Owl, is credited by sources in law enforcement as having been responsible for the fire and all attributed damage,'" I read. Although the article didn't provide a picture, it went on to describe me accurately. It was when I got to the last part that my temper flared. "'Individuals are warned not to engage The Owl. She has a long-standing reputation for property damage and has little regard for people's safety.'"

"Oh come on!" I said as I handed back the tablet to Lady Siyu's outstretched hand. "This is a smear campaign," I protested.

"Clearly," Lady Siyu said, her lip curling into a sneer.

I closed my eyes and counted to three. "The IAA contacted me a month ago. They wanted me to track down two archaeology dropouts who run a video game." I thought about mentioning the Shangri-La connection and evidence of human magic, but decided against it. It would confuse the issue, and it wasn't relevant. "I told them no, and this is their attempt to not take no for an answer."

"It keeps speaking," Lady Siyu mused, "yet it offers no contradicting evidence to my original statement that it has *failed* to manage the IAA."

Oh for crying out loud. "And I would argue that you and Mr. Kurosawa are incapable of preventing other organizations from coercing me into working for them instead of you! And this is what? The second time? First the elves and their book, now the IAA. Why don't you stick a tattoo on my forehead, Pimp Our Ride?"

"It is your responsibility to manage disagreements with other organizations. Not ours. And for your information, we have dealt with the elf's transgression interfering *directly* with Mr. Kurosawa's workings." She was referring to Carpe's sidetracking my last job for the dragon, trying to stop a thief stealing cursed artifacts from the Syrian City of the Dead . . . something that had almost gotten me killed. "*This*," she said, holding up the tablet, "is not interference, it is an accurate report of your activities in New Delhi."

Of all the warped, twisted— What the hell was the point of having a contract thief if you let everyone else push them around?

Instead of saying that though I took in a long breath and forced myself to calm down and employ something resembling a filter. Anything I said in my defense would just be used against me.

On top of that, I was going to have to deal with the IAA anyway. And once they realized I wasn't just a reluctant thief but was actively trying to screw them over . . .

Time to switch to a much more productive topic—solving the other result of Lady Siyu's supernatural streak of stubbornness. "When can I get my cat back?" I asked.

Lady Siyu's lips quirked up, once more exposing the thin fangs.

"What do you want? Ancient artifacts? Something from my collection?"

"I am not able to discuss the return of the Mau with you."

I ground my teeth. That's what she'd said last time, and the time before that.

Yelling won't get you anywhere, Alix, not with her. "All right. When *will* you be ready to discuss the terms of return of my Mau?"

She inclined her head down at me like a predator. "When I *feel* like it," she said, pronouncing each word oh so carefully.

From what Housekeeping had told me, Captain had already destroyed two Louis XIV chairs, one antique coffee table, and a number of vases. The vases he'd crashed into chasing an errant pen, as he was wont to do. Oh yeah, and he'd taken offense to the red soles on Lady Siyu's Louboutin designer shoes and chewed through half of two pairs. I didn't think mismatching shoes were in Lady Siyu's fashion repertoire.

She wasn't happy, clearly Captain sure as hell wasn't happy, and it was only a matter of time before he really started to exact his vengeance.

My nails dug into my palms. "Look, just tell me what I need to do before my cat chews through one of your designer suits."

Her usually stony expression cracked, a tic escaping through her carefully controlled veneer. "He wouldn't," Lady Siyu said, the words tinged with the telltale hiss.

"Don't leave your closet open," I warned. "You think the shoes were bad? *Warning* shots."

Her face paled as her yellow snake eyes narrowed and glistened in anger. Rynn, who'd been silent up until this point, squeezed my shoulder. "Alix," he warned.

I didn't take my eyes off the Naga. "You're enjoying this, aren't you?"

She made a noise that might have been a snort if it hadn't been for the fact that I figured those kinds of sounds were beneath Lady Siyu's immaculate appearance—minus the venom dripping fangs. "How dare you. I enjoy so *very* few things in this human-dominated world, and believe me, being caretaker for your barbaric, untrained cat is *not* one of them."

Yeah, yeah. *Be nice, Owl. Baiting her into a fight isn't going to help at all.*

"Just tell me what you want so I can buy my cat back, or so help me—"

"Or you'll what?" Lady Siyu said, baring her fangs at me. "Come on little thief, what will you do?"

Whether in warning or anticipation, one of the nearby slot machines began to whistle. Its friends joined in, bathing the casino in a veritable cacophony of bells and lights. I heard the clink and sputter of tokens and coins as they were ejected onto the marble floor.

I'd tried, God help me, I'd tried . . . not even a saint could keep polite with the likes of Lady Siyu.

"You no good piece of . . . of . . ." I sputtered as I tried to come up with something that might serve as an insult to a Naga. ". . . of rattle snake." Not one of my shining moments, but there you have it; I can't always be a genius on the fly. "You have no intention of giving him back!"

It had the desired effect as she bared her fangs at me and hissed.

Rynn stepped between us, putting his back to Lady Siyu and holding me back. "Let it go, Alix. Lady Siyu is baiting you. And you?" he said, turning to Lady Siyu, his eyes flaring blue, though I wasn't sure if his powers of persuasion worked on other supernaturals.

She let out a long hiss. Her jaw had extended to accommodate the Naga teeth, and her red fingernails had elongated into sharp claws.

Rynn didn't take the bait. Instead he turned back to me and arched a single blond eyebrow. "See? Nagas do that, bait their prey. Like snakes with mice."

Lady Siyu let out a shriek. "I will not deal with your insubordination today, incubus," Lady Siyu said. "I did not invite you to this meeting."

Rynn tsked. "Yet as Mr. Kurosawa's security, I figured I should stop in and at least say hi. Before you accidently killed his archaeologist."

"*Thief*," she said, with more venom dripping off the word than I'd heard from her in a long while. "She's Mr. Kurosawa's hired *thief*."

Rynn's face turned serious. "You have a bad habit of forgetting the job at hand when it comes to dealing with the thief, so . . ." He let the thought and open threat trail off.

Considering the way Lady Siyu was glaring daggers at Rynn, I expected her to launch herself at him, claws and fangs first. She didn't though. Her fangs retracted and she closed her eyes, her nose flaring as she composed herself. When she opened her eyes back up, they were a human-looking brown.

Now that was a changed dynamic. Usually she was more than happy to push Rynn's buttons, though not today, for whatever reason.

I didn't have a chance to ponder it more as Rynn turned to me. "Lady Siyu can't bargain the cat with you, Alix, as much as she'd love to, because we've already set a price."

"*What?*" I grabbed him by the arm and steered him a few feet away from Lady Siyu, hoping she wouldn't hear. "When did you arrange a trade for Captain?" I said, keeping my voice low.

He frowned at me. "I told you at Artemis's that I would get your cat back. Please, can we discuss this later?"

I wanted to push things, but not in front of Lady Siyu. "This isn't over," I said before heading back to the Naga.

Lady Siyu glared daggers at me but continued. "I've brought you back to the casino for a purpose beyond collecting the bowl and discussing your atrocious cat. Mr. Kurosawa has a new task we wish for you to expedite."

"*We wish.*" Interesting choice of words. Supernaturals never used words lightly. "Let me guess, you want me to drop everything and head to Peru?"

"Hardly." Lady Siyu turned on her heels and clicked her way past the slot machines to the empty casino's bar—a long slab of black marble set into the back wall and stocked with a variety of liquors, all very top shelf. Off to the side was a set of black leather couches that had replaced the white ones after the fire that had gutted the room four months ago. The color scheme had changed drastically after the top of the casino had almost burned down. The marble on the floor and the bar itself had even been replaced with duskier versions. I suppose stone burns much less easily than wood counters and floorboards. . . . Again, long story that can be summed up as supernatural bullshit.

Lady Siyu retrieved a manila folder tucked away behind the marble bar. I'd noticed in my dealings with her that whereas everyone else used email, a tool designed for circumventing people you have to deal with but hate, Lady Siyu still preferred using the analog copy. Or maybe she was aware how easily Carpe, my World Quest partner and elf, could get in and look around. Now that was a thought.

She held the folder out.

Keeping an eye on her, I undid the heavy string. Inside were documents—copies of very old documents, to be precise. A cursory glance told me they were from a variety of periods and locations— ancient Japan, India, Rome, Greece, Eastern Europe, medieval Mongolia. It was like a who's who of ancient civilizations throughout history. And the only thing they had in common was that they all depicted a suit of armor, each different and unique.

But the documents were sparse to the point of omitting what it was exactly I was supposed to do with them.

I held them up. "What's this?"

"Your next job."

"Fantastic. Ready to get started. Only problem is there is no job in here. Only a handful of half-complete documents and pictures from around the world."

Lady Siyu made a face. "That is the package the elves requested I deliver to you."

"The elves? What the hell do the elves want with me?" I knew how these things went. Sparse envelope filled with pictures of a bunch of artifacts . . . "Whoa, okay, I don't know what the elves have said I've taken from them, but I *haven't*—"

Lady Siyu hissed. "Unlike the vampires and every other supernatural you seem to cross, the elves do not want your head, nor are they accusing you of anything except your proffered profession, which you readily admit. They have requested your professional services."

"*No.*"

We both looked over at Rynn, who'd said it with more force and determination than I expected in one of these meetings. He was staring at Lady Siyu with bright blue eyes and an expression I had difficulty reading, but if I had to guess, I'd say it was verging on hostile.

Lady Siyu didn't quite seem to know what to do either. She opened her mouth, but Rynn beat her to it.

"Out of the question. She's not working for the elves."

It did not surprise me one bit that Rynn had a problem. He was not a fan of the elves. For that matter, neither was I. I believe his more colorful description of the elves was that "their version of planning a fight is sending everyone else off as cannon fodder" and "they couldn't plan their way out of a locked dungeon without a committee meeting and census."

"Why wasn't I apprised of this first?" he continued, advancing on Lady Siyu. I took a step back. Good rule to follow? Try not to get in between a couple supernaturals facing off.

I also now knew why Lady Siyu had requested that Rynn not be here for the meeting. His dislike of the elves was legendary at the casino. I certainly had my own issues with them after Carpe had almost gotten me dead over some stupid book.

Oh hell no . . .

"This wouldn't have anything to do with that spell book?" I said. Carpe had at one point threatened to go through Mr. Kurosawa on his quest for the spell book. It hadn't come to that; Carpe had stolen our cargo plane and crashed it near the dig site he'd wanted me to infiltrate, but the threat meant the channels were there and open.

I could see Lady Siyu hedging her answer. "It might have come up."

Great. Get coerced into doing one favor for a friend, and the rest of his little buddies figure they can strong-arm me too. Carpe was going to get one hell of an earful for not giving me a heads-up on this. I waved the folder. "What is it they want, exactly?"

"I couldn't say what the elves want at the best of times," she sneered, "even when they manage to deliver memos that are half legible through their clauses and conditions. But in this case they want you to find an ancient suit of armor. That one, to be precise."

I held up the collection of copied documents. "There isn't one suit here, there are ten, and next to no descriptions. There isn't enough in here to even start looking." Don't get me wrong. Things went wrong all the time on jobs, but that didn't mean I invited blind spots. I went into every job as prepared as possible, especially when there was the chance of the supernatural. "How the hell do they expect me to start finding it?"

She arched one of her perfectly painted black eyebrows. "I haven't the faintest idea. All I know is they wish you to retrieve."

"What about that little clause in *our* contract? The one that says I work for Mr. Kurosawa exclusively?"

Another hedged answer was coming; I could tell by the way her eyes flicked left. "While not accepting responsibility," she said carefully, "they have offered to recompense Mr. Kurosawa for one of their ilk circumventing his permission. They are offering him a great deal for your services."

I couldn't believe this. "So what? Coerce the thief into stealing something and they get rewarded with another job? How the hell does that make any sense?"

Lady Siyu's jaw clenched. "They claim it is a routine artifact."

The last run-of-the-mill retrieval I'd done for an elf had involved taking a spell book from a mummy who'd still been using it. And that had just been Carpe's wild-goose chase. Looking for something the lot of them wanted? I was really thinking Rynn had the right idea on this one.

Rynn had remained silent while I'd discussed the details of the job— or complete lack thereof—with Lady Siyu, but even I could see he was seething now. "Owl is not working for the elves," Rynn said. "It's suicide."

"The decision is not yours to make," Lady Siyu started, her eyes bleeding back to yellow.

"It *is* in fact my decision to make, if you remember the terms of *my* contract." One of the things Rynn had done before agreeing to work for Mr. Kurosawa was to have overview of all my jobs. "They're dangerous," he continued, raising his voice. "And not just because they can't accurately count bodies on a field. Those bureaucrats have no inkling what an actual job of *any* kind entails beyond passing a description around each other's desks adding protocols that make no sense to anyone with half a mind to self-preservation."

I don't think I'd ever seen Rynn this worked up about anything, including my own screwups, which he'd been spectacularly pissed about on multiple occasions.

"That is an *exaggeration*," Lady Siyu tried, getting visibly flustered now.

Rynn ignored Lady Siyu and turned to me. "Did I tell you that the last time I worked in the supernatural community as an enforcer some elf put in a clause that I had to ask the supernatural in question three times if they were sure they didn't want to surrender?"

"That is not an unreasonable request—" Lady Siyu started.

Rynn turned on her. "While they were *shooting* at me?"

Lady Siyu shifted uncomfortably under Rynn's gaze. "Still," she tried.

"*And* eating a village of humans." Rynn glanced at me. "It was a troll—certainly not innocent—who was boiling five-year-old children, who, we are positive, are innocent beyond killing a few bugs, snakes and frogs. Not *my* standards—theirs, the elves. Try explaining to the elves not shooting the troll immediately means the children get eaten alive. It breaks their inflated brains."

Rynn had worked *for* the elves? How the hell had that never come up in conversation?

"The point is that if the elves told you whatever they want Alix to get is 'routine,' you can be certain it is anything but and should have charged substantially more." His voice started to rise again. "Which you'd have known if you'd bothered to ask me, the only one here who has a *modicum* of experience dealing with the internal workings of elves!"

Lady Siyu was looking less confident as the moments ticked on.

"Did you even bother checking to see what they were asking for, or did you let the elven bureaucrats snow you over with platitudes like they do everyone else?"

Okay, the roles here had changed in an uncomfortable way.

I stopped Rynn before he could continue his round of verbal sparring with Lady Siyu, something that I was usually on the receiving end of. "Just what is it they want me to find, exactly? What does this suit of armor do? Where is it from? That sort of thing." If I knew where to start looking for information, I'd have a better chance of finding it.

"They . . . were not clear on all the details," Lady Siyu said carefully.

"Jesus, you didn't bother to ask, did you?" I said. Rynn snorted beside me.

"*But* they provided information about the armor, including a description of the location where it should be."

Okay, a location. That wasn't sounding nearly as disastrous. "That's not a horrible start." A location I could work with. A location meant history, civilizations that had risen and fallen. "Where?"

Lady Siyu stared at me, and I saw her white throat move as if she was swallowing. "Ah, not the location, but a description of the type of temple it should be buried in."

"A *description*?" I couldn't believe what I was hearing.

"They assured me it is quite distinct. As you are the archaeologist—"

I was starting to get the impression the elves had snowed everyone over. Carpe—for all his asshole-ness and hijacking antics—had at least known the exact site.

"Where the hell is Mr. Kurosawa in all this?"

"Indisposed," Lady Siyu said, her tone indicating there was to be no more question.

I opened the folder back up. A few hastily copied inscriptions, a handful of temple drawings I didn't recognize. The descriptions of the armor collected in the pages came from Mongolia, Southeast Asia, the Middle East, and Japan. The exact details of the armor changed with each place, but the name . . . now, that was interesting. Everyone gave the suit a different name, but they all roughly translated to mean the same thing: 'the Lightning Suit,' or 'Storm Armor.'

The oldest and most detailed account was from ancient Japan . . . 150 AD, give or take, where the armor and resulting legends seemed to originate. A suit of magic armor imbued with lightning from the storms, given to a farmer by a river spirit to protect his peaceful farming village from a particularly violent and sadistic neighboring warlord. I skimmed the details, but from what I could gather, the farmer won but paid a hefty price—his life. It was a common enough thread among fables and stories: be careful what you wish for and such.

But other than an old fable and a collection of pictures? No maps, no specific locations, not even a city name for me to start with. One detail caught my eye—a footnote near the end. The armor changed its appearance with each new wearer.

Shit.

I turned to Lady Siyu, who was pursing her red lacquered lips as she held up the printout of the fable. "Tell me, when you had your meeting with the elves, did you put on the fancy heels and a nice dress because you wanted them to fuck you?"

Rynn covered his mouth—I think to hide a laugh—but I couldn't be certain, since Lady Siyu lunged at me, hissing, with her fangs out, a glint of yellow venom on each tip. Rynn intervened and held her back.

I wasn't about to let up though. One would think that if you kept an archaeological treasure hunter on retainer you might maybe, just *maybe*, confer with her before arranging a job. "Like he said, the elves snowed you," I told her as she fought against Rynn. "It changes appearance. I'd have no idea I was looking at it even if I was standing in front of it."

"Wait. A suit that changes with the wearer?" Rynn asked, his brow furrowed now, even as he did his best to restrain Lady Siyu. "Translates to 'the lightening warrior'?"

I nodded.

Rynn didn't look nearly as hopeful as I did about the fact that he recognized the reference. "And the elves want to retrieve it—are you certain?" he said, this time directed at Lady Siyu.

"Yes," she hissed. "They say they require it to complete our *other* negotiations."

I was pretty sure Rynn swore in supernatural; it sounded like a curse word, even if I didn't recognize it.

I looked between him and Lady Siyu. "What am I missing?"

"This isn't retrieval for profit like she's tried to make it out to be. It's *politics*, thinly veiled politics." He turned again to Lady Siyu. "Did they give you a reason?" Rynn was barely keeping civil now as he bared his own human-looking teeth at her.

Lady Siyu shot me a glance but for whatever reason decided it wouldn't be worth her time to argue with Rynn. "They said that they are not comfortable with our odds of success if the suit is left out in the open and in play. They feel it is one of the artifacts that *they* will go after."

They. Oh shit. "This is part of your supernatural war, isn't it?"

Rynn inclined his head, but he kept his eyes on Lady Siyu. To her he said, "You swore you wouldn't involve Alix in any political negotiations."

"Mr. Kurosawa agreed to try, and unfortunately we no longer have that luxury. In any case, the decision was taken out of our hands, as they specifically requested *her*."

All because of that damn spell book. Oh, Carpe was going to hear a hell of a lot about this, like why there hadn't been any goddamned warning.

Rynn took the folder from my hands and began perusing the contents. "They've cobbled these together from their archives," he said after a cursory glance. "Where did they get the idea?" he asked Lady Siyu. "They weren't looking for this ten years ago, even a hundred years ago." Rynn turned his attention back to me. I couldn't shake the feeling I was a ball in a tennis court. . . .

"The elves don't like weapons," he said to me. "They chase spell books, documents, and artifacts so that they can rot in their archives, but rarely do they chase after weapons. They don't like the message it sends to other supernaturals."

"So what? They leave all the dangerous stuff like the scroll and the City of the Dead for us humans to stumble across?"

Rynn gave me a wry smile, but before he could add anything Lady Siyu snatched the folder back. "What the incubus forgets is that the elves are the only body of supernaturals capable, let alone *interested*, in enforcing our laws and *keeping* an archive. This is the simplest way to end the war and prevent a goblin or troll from ending up on the six o'clock news. Do you know the media storms I've already had to put out? Between her fiasco in New Delhi," she said, pointing at me, "and the minor supernaturals, I'm running night and day trying to keep up with these infractions. Everywhere. Why, yesterday I just had to cover a goblin army raiding a supermarket in broad daylight! Do you have *any* idea how much manpower that costs? And those are only the opening volleys. This isn't the Middle Ages where an incident can be contained and written out of history after all the humans are dead. It's global, even with Mr. Kurosawa's multimedia company. And now that the IAA has ceased to cooperate—"

"Whoa, wait a minute. I thought the IAA was supposed to keep the supernatural under wraps?"

She turned her smile back on me. It wasn't nice. "I was wondering when your slow brain would finally stumble onto that question. They've gone silent in any negotiations we had and will continue to do so until *you* deliver the video gaming thieves."

Oh shit. That was why Lady Siyu didn't give a shit that the IAA was stepping on Mr. Kurosawa's toes; they had something she needed. "They're designers, not thieves."

"They did not use that word."

I shook my head. "But they really weren't thieves."

"It does not matter!" Lady Siyu screamed and stamped her foot. I backed up.

"Look, if getting the IAA back in whatever negotiations you have is the problem, I'm close to finding them." Hell would freeze over before I handed them over to the IAA, but that was another bridge to cross when I reached those deathly rapids.

But Lady Siyu shook her head. "The elves are a higher priority. Mr. Kurosawa has deemed it so."

Yeah, and if the mercenaries found them while I was off chasing artifacts for the elves . . . Something occurred to me. "Wait, isn't the other side, the supernaturals who want to come out of the closet, already breaking the rules?" They both turned to look at me. "If the elves are neutral and capable of enforcing laws, shouldn't they be dealing with them?"

"They like their neutrality more than their precious rules," Rynn said. "All the elves do is make a declaration that they find something unappealing—empty threats. Unless, that is, you're a low-powered supernatural and make a minor infraction. Then they throw the rulebook at you because it's easy and makes them look like they're doing something. Anything important or dangerous? That might actually piss someone off who might decide to eat a few elves."

My God, the more I learned about supernatural politics, the more they mirrored our international ones.

"So they hand out parking tickets and leave all the real weapons and battles for everyone else to deal with?"

"Now you see the problem with *fucking elves*," he said, directing the last bit at Lady Siyu.

Lady Siyu stamped her heel loud enough I was surprised it didn't crack. "They've agreed to throw in the full support of all their governed people and political influence *if* we retrieve the suit for them," Lady Siyu said, sounding more and more desperate.

That made Rynn pause. A tense silence settled onto the casino floor.

"What does that mean?" I said, acutely aware how loud my voice sounded.

Rynn broke his stalemate with Lady Siyu. "It means they are bound to the gesture, the intention of the deal, not what's on paper. The only other times elves have actually had to get their hands dirty and fight was under a similar accord, which I imagine Lady Siyu and Mr. Kurosawa know."

"Regardless of their neutrality, if the elves throw in their support," Lady Siyu continued, "it will mean an end to the war. Immediately. No more fighting, no more disobedience."

But Rynn didn't look convinced. "The elves specialize in circumventing their deals. They will promise you the world, provided they figure they can squirm their way out of getting their hands dirty later. Trust me. I know."

"But you are in agreement?" Lady Siyu said, letting enough hope into her voice that I knew she had to be under stress.

Rynn inclined his head. "No, but I don't see that we have much choice, since you've already signed the paperwork. But this?" he said, pointing to the folder holding the sparse information on the suit. "This just means they're already hiding something. They have new information; they must have, to go after something dangerous like this."

Wait a minute. New information in the hands of the elves? Shit. "Could it have anything to do with the spell book?" Carpe had said it was a matter of life and death—he just hadn't elaborated on whose. . . .

Rynn hedged his answer. "It is a distinct possibility. It's a spell book. Elves deal mostly with magic so them wanting it isn't out of the ordinary, but there might be something inside that's made the suit more appealing—like how to dismantle it so no one would bother trying to take it, or something that could alter what the suit does."

Or use it for their own gain. I don't care how antiviolent the elves claimed to be; they weren't getting me to chase after an ancient suit because they wanted to give power away. I'd dealt with enough bureaucrats over the years to know they lusted after power as easily as the next tyrant or dictator—more so, considering attacking people from behind a wall of paper is easier.

"Regardless of the elves' motivations, it's too late now. The deal has already been struck."

Rynn shook his head. "That may be, but I'm vetoing Alix's involvement in the entire thing," he said.

"You wouldn't dare."

Rynn closed in on Lady Siyu until he was staring down at her. "Try me," he said.

I watched as Lady Siyu licked her lips with a forked tongue. "*Fine,* I'll agree to your terms," Lady Siyu said.

Rynn gave her a wary once-over. "Everything?"

"*Everything,*" she said between clenched teeth.

Rynn held out his hand. Lady Siyu, looking none too happy, removed a pen from her bag. She stabbed Rynn's hand and red blood flowed out. The tip of the pen sucked it up before it could spill on the tiled floor. She strode over to the bar and removed a clipboard. She brought it back and handed it to Rynn, and before my eyes, black ink appeared on the page, though I couldn't read it. "The terms are as you stated earlier."

Without looking at Lady Siyu or me, Rynn signed.

Lady Siyu snapped her fingers. A door clicked open somewhere in the back and a man with tattoos of a dragon covering half his face stepped out. He was dressed in an expensive suit; one of Mr. Kurosawa's kami servants. He was carrying something that looked suspiciously like a cat carrier. It—or whatever was in the carrier—let out a baleful howl. Mr. Kurosawa's goon didn't slow his stride, but I did note he held the carrier farther away from his suit.

"Captain?" I said, my voice breaking.

On hearing my voice the howls amplified, coming in faster bursts.

"Congratulations," Lady Siyu said, her voice dripping with dry condescension. "Your demon spawn cat."

The goon handed me the carrier. Captain, scenting me in the air, let out an inquisitive chirp and began digging at the mesh. I couldn't believe it—after an entire month of pestering and insulting Lady Siyu, I had my cat back.

I clutched the carrier tight. "What's the catch?"

"There is no catch. The incubus bartered your cat back. More's the pity. If he's half as right about the elves and this suit of armor, none of you will live to enjoy it." Without another word, Lady Siyu spun on her heels and headed back into the darkened casino, the goon close on her heels.

"Come on, Alix, we're leaving," Rynn said.

Hand on the small of my back, he started to steer me through the maze.

"Incubus?" Lady Siyu's voice rang out through the hall, echoing off the slot machines. A few of them began to chime at the sound of her voice, and those nearest me began shooting out gold coins. I backed up, not wanting them to touch my feet.

Lady Siyu stood at the very back of the casino, backlit by red Exit lights and what looked like smoke trailing around her. Intentional, I imagined.

"Just remember, she needs to deliver." And with one last flash of her fangs, the smoke engulfed her.

I shook my head and held the carrier tight, despite Captain's struggling to get out now that he sensed freedom. "She likes to torment me."

"She likes to torment everyone, she's a Naga. They hold grudges."

I kept close on Rynn's heels out of the maze. It wasn't until we reached the elevator that I mustered the willpower to break the silence. "Rynn?"

He didn't say anything, didn't look at me—just pushed the button to the elevator. I grabbed him by the shoulder and made him turn around.

"What did you do?"

I watched as he chose his answer. "Nothing I hadn't already been willing to agree to. This just gave me an opportunity to negotiate the terms." We rode the elevator upstairs in silence—except for Captain, who still wanted out of his carrier.

The elevator door opened on our floor and Rynn stepped out, setting a fast pace down the hall to our suite. "What agreement? What terms? For my cat? Rynn, I was perfectly capable of handling it."

"Alix, can we please deal with your frustration with me later?" he snapped, then stopped and breathed. "I'm sorry, this has nothing to do with you. It's hard to stomach being treated like the empathic grunt." He hit the side of the wall. There was a dent, but since no one ever came up to this floor, I didn't think he was particularly concerned.

I realized what the bargain was over. "Lady Siyu traded Captain to do things her way."

"I said I would help you get him back."

A pit formed in my stomach. I hadn't wanted that, I hadn't asked for it.

"You couldn't have offered her anything she would have wanted," he explained. "She made up her mind weeks ago when we hit a stalemate over the elves. This was her first opportunity to get her own way." After a moment he added, "And, as much as I hate to admit it, Lady Siyu isn't wrong about getting the elves on our side or covering up supernatural mishaps. So far it's only trolls and goblins, but every time they misbehave . . ."

Eventually someone was going to get a video up on YouTube.

I pushed past Rynn and opened the door. The suite was exactly how I'd left it, clean and sterile, not really my home.

Captain, smelling his old territory, took that moment to let out a baleful howl from inside the red carrier. "Just wait," I told him.

"That's not all of it," Rynn said. "The cat has a sense for supernatural things. Even a half-trained Mau is an invaluable tool."

My pride at Captain's progress reared its head. "He's not half trained."

Rynn nodded to the carrier, where Captain had gone quiet.

I looked down. Captain had decided it was time to eat his way out.

This carrier was new and had stronger mesh; I was guessing Lady Siyu had had some incidents over the past month. But still, I gave him an A for effort . . . or would that be for eviscerating? Or ability to generate pet damage? How do you assign RPG stats to a cat?

I maneuvered inside our suite and closed the door before putting the carrier on the ground and opening it. "There you go, Captain." He darted out and made a pass of the living room and kitchen, checking that everything was still marked by rubbing everything with his chin and the top of his head.

I glanced up at Rynn, who was watching me. I recognized the look as one he got when there was something important he wanted to talk about.

There was a conversation or two we needed to have about just how intertwined our personal and professional lives had gotten lately. I wasn't sure where things ended and began anymore, and now with the mess that was this suit for the elves and the IAA's bounty on World Quest . . .

I held up the folder. "Whatever it is, Rynn, it'll have to wait. I need to start looking now, because between the IAA breathing down my neck and the elves, this suit is going to be a real bitch to find."

5

THE ELECTRIC SAMURAI

7:00 p.m. The Japanese Circus Casino

It wasn't the alarm I'd set on my phone that woke me, nor the chime on my computer, which I'd set to wake me up. It was the crash of shattering glass.

I swore as I sat up in my chair, almost knocking my half-finished Corona over. I readied a slipper to throw at Captain, but he was already out of sight.

The glass wasn't though. The one Rynn had left on the coffee table for me was now on the floor in a million odd pieces where I couldn't help but see it.

Whereas I'd spent the last two hours working, Captain had spent the time re-scenting everything in the apartment and making sure all the nooks and crannies were where he'd left them. Every now and again, when he remembered he was supposed to be punishing me, he found something to knock off a table.

I swore and checked the time on my computer screen before grabbing the dustpan and broom. It was the second glass since Captain had been reintroduced to his territory.

"Seriously, the first one was fine, the second one was overkill," I called out. Captain let out a muffled baleful meow in response from whatever hidey-hole he'd crawled into.

I deposited the broken glass in the garbage with its predecessor. Well, at least Captain was destroying things in pairs.

Two hours I'd been poring over the file Lady Siyu had given me. No wonder my eyes were so damn tired. I closed them again. Rynn was checking security and updating himself on the situation in Tokyo, which worked well for me, since it gave me time to work without him hovering over my shoulder. Considering the mood he was in . . .

I'd memorized what the elves had given me to the point where the notes were burned into the back of my eyeballs. I couldn't not see them, even with my eyes closed.

I took another pull of my now-warm beer and went over what I knew. Despite the incomplete notes, I now had a grasp of the time line and the armor's path across the ancient world. And the picture it was painting was one of uncomfortable death and destruction.

Around 300–150 BC, the suit of armor made its first appearance in ancient Japan, well before the time of samurai, geishas, and emperors. I'd managed to find a few more versions of the legend online. They varied in details, characters, and periods of history, but they all had the same kernel: a beautiful water spirit, possibly a demon or elemental of some kind, felt sorry for a group of farmers who were at the mercy of a neighboring warlord. One brave soul, a man from the village, petitioned her for help. Depending on which story you read, her motivations change. This was not uncommon; legends and myths had a funny way of changing to suit the time they were being told in, to communicate some sort of culturally acceptable message. In this case, some of the stories said she felt sorry for the villagers, others said she was in love with the man, and yet others claimed she was in a vindictive mood that day for having been slighted.

Regardless of intentions, she offered to help. Some say it was a magic sword, others claim she cast a spell on the villagers, but the earliest refer to a suit of armor gifted with the power of the storms, that could down a field of enemies with a sheet of lightning.

Of course, any old fable with a grain of truth in it tends not to have a fairy-tale ending. This was no different. Powerful gifts from supernaturals always come at a high price. The stories all ended more or less the same. Sacrifice for the greater good, be careful what you wish for, everything has a price—take your pick of the lessons, but the result was the same: the man saved his village but at excruciating costs.

Whatever the true version, it had been lost to the ages. The armor itself though . . . Lining up the periods represented in the folder, the suit had somehow made its way to the mainland, appearing briefly in Korea, then India, then disappearing for a hundred odd years until it surfaced in Roman times, around the reign of Caligula. From there it vanished again until it reared its head in Genghis Khan's army during the early Middle Ages.

And that was it. According to what the elves had given me, the suit hadn't been seen since.

I polished off my warm beer and sat back to give my eyes another rest.

One thing was certain and corroborated by every sighting of the armor recorded in the elves' notes: like the four horsemen, the armor brought death and destruction with it, though whether it was the cause or the catalyst remained to be seen.

I let out a deep breath. Maybe I was missing an angle. Maybe if I started looking at Genghis Khan's rule . . . I could always probe the university archives a little deeper.

I was about to open a browser when I heard yet another crash, from the kitchen this time.

Son of a bitch, that was the third time. I turned to see what the hell Captain was up to now.

He was standing in the middle of the suite's kitchenette. Waiting for me, braced to run. When I looked at him he meowed, a long, baleful, accusatory moan.

"Look, I'm sorry. I didn't mean to give you to that harpy, and certainly not for an entire month."

He meowed again. I narrowed my eyes as I peered at him. It sounded muffled, as if he had something in his mouth.

Shit.

I bolted for Captain, and he leaped onto the kitchen table. "Get back here!" I yelled. I don't know how, I wasn't sure why, but Captain had my cell phone in his mouth.

I cornered him on the counter, blocking off the easy exits. "Drop it," I said.

There was a crunch as Captain bit down into the glass. "Son of a—" I lunged, but he was faster and skidded around me.

"Don't you dare chew! Stop it!" With my luck he'd manage to break the screen and swallow the glass before I got to him, then it'd be a trip to the vet and a whole new wheel of spawned vengeance over the indignity of a cone. . . .

"You no-good, rotten cat. Get back here!" Finally he dropped the phone in order to man an escape up the cupboards. Served him right for breaking his diet. He hunkered down above the kitchen cabinets, swishing his tail and glaring at me.

I checked my phone. Shit, he'd cracked the screen.

I held the phone up so Captain could see it. "A hundred fifty bucks down the drain. Are you happy?"

He meowed, and swished his tail again.

The front door clicked open and Rynn stepped in. He took in the scene.

"I'm fairly certain the cat has no idea what you said. Maus are smart, but not that smart," Rynn said.

"No, but he can understand intonation. He lulled me into a false sense of security so he could go after my phone. It smells like me and he knows I need it."

As if in answer, Captain settled in to clean himself, satisfied with whatever cat point he'd been trying to make.

At least he hadn't peed on something. Yet. Served me right for thinking all I was going to get were a few indignant mews, a couple broken glasses, and demands for a filled food dish.

I turned my attention to Rynn, but before I could say anything he stopped me with a shake of his head. "Give me a minute, Alix." And with that he headed into the bedroom. I heard the door close, and a moment later the shower turned on.

Something was definitely still bothering him, well beyond our meeting with Lady Siyu. Part of me wondered whether I should push, but I scrapped that idea. Part of a relationship—any kind of relationship—is trusting the other person to tell you something's wrong when they're ready, not when you'd like them to. Though I was tempted to join him in the shower . . .

I grabbed a fresh beer from the fridge and returned to my desk and laptop.

Cohabitation. Regardless of the whole supernatural angle, I was still getting used to it. Not that things weren't going well, or that we didn't have our disagreements.

I was used to freedom—sort of. Truth be told, I didn't think there was any such thing, between university, being on the run from the IAA, and Alexander and his cronies chasing me . . . But this was a wholly new kind of containment. Before, it had just been me and Captain. Now I wasn't the one in control anymore.

Or maybe it was just the illusion had been removed. I'd be lying if I said I wouldn't have jumped on a plane for Nadya at the drop of a hat. And Rynn? I'd spent three months avoiding him specifically because I hadn't wanted to care. Even Carpe had known who I was online; he'd only kept it secret so I wouldn't delete my profile and run.

I'd been buying into my own fantasy of independence—not living free. There's a difference, subtle, but it was there.

Captain let out a piercing howl as my browser window opened back up. I glanced over my shoulder to where he was sitting, shifting from paw to paw in front of his half-full food dish. "Goddamn it, I just filled your dish and you repaid me by eating my phone?"

He meowed back.

My view of independence had been not unlike my cat's: I'd made a lot of noise about not needing anyone, but at the end of the day I'd still needed friends—or, in Captain's case, someone to open the kibble bag.

I reached for the fresh Corona as I turned my attention back on the search engine. The one problem before me I did have control over.

Since Genghis was the most recent sighting of the armor according to the elves, I decided to start there. I headed for the IAA university archives and used an old set of passwords I kept handy, rotating them so one never set off alarm bells. I found the red folders, the ones containing supernatural references, and typed *Genghis Khan* into the search bar overhead. "Let's see what kind of supernatural monsters hung around your court, shall we, Genghis?"

A couple vampires, at least one skin walker, succubi . . .

I looked for anything concrete; diaries, journals, inventories. But even the online stuff was sparse . . . now hold on, that was interesting. At the bottom of the search results page was a footnote reference to someone's thesis. I clicked through to the summary.

It was a detailed analysis of the fall of the Khwarezmian Empire during the early middle ages, whose border had covered parts of modern Iran, Afghanistan, Uzbekistan, among others. The Mongol horde had ransacked the empire and burned most of it to the ground—to the point where there really wasn't much left of an archaeological record. I suppose it made sense at the time. Genghis didn't want to allow anyone who might hold a grudge to have a roof over their head. Grudges tend to fester the dryer and well fed they are.

The supernatural link had to do with one of the palace treasure rooms that had been ransacked. A large portion of the king's treasure went to one of Genghis's generals. Jebe. Including a suit supposed to have magical powers.

I frowned at the screen. Could that be it? Regardless, I now had a name.

I checked the source material and swore. It was on a secure server.

The IAA had a bad habit of doing that lately in an attempt to keep the information they really didn't want out of the wrong people's hands. Like mine. They'd taken to using secure servers that traveled with the collections and never met a high-speed connection. They had the ports removed before anything was even installed. This was one such collection.

I opened the thesis, hoping the contents contained more about General Jebe and the fate of the armor, but when the thesis loaded all I saw were swaths of black mixed in with the print. It had been redacted like crazy.

I was starting to think a scrub job might not be so much paranoia....

I heard the door to the bedroom click open as Rynn came out.

I did a double take—I couldn't help it. He'd thrown on track pants but had otherwise forgone clothes. Though he pretended that there wasn't anything unusual about that . . .

I watched him as he headed into the kitchen and grabbed a beer out of the fridge. Something was still bothering him. I was at a loss for what to do. I mean, my go-to was not exactly touchy-feely talks with people about their feelings. I've never been particularly in touch with my feminine side.

"How goes the research?" he asked, nodding at the dossier open on my desk as he took the seat beside me. I felt my own temperature and heart rate rise. Touchy-feely I was not, but I wasn't immune to Rynn's physical charms, not by a long shot.

I shoved down a couple ideas that popped into my mind and set my brain to answering him, not undressing him. "Besides a general time line? Not much. The records the elves gave us are next to useless. Though it looks like the last stop was in Genghis Khan's horde."

Rynn closed his eyes as he drank his beer. "Tell me about the Mongolian connection," he said.

"It's not concrete. Genghis Khan's army stumbled across a suit that vaguely matches the description of the armor, buried in a Khwarezmian king's treasure room. After that, the reference shifts to one of his generals, Jebe, who led part of the army north to invade what's now Russia and

Poland. And that's as far as I was able to read through the redacted the-sis." I shook my head. "It's like someone's actively trying to scrub it from history." I hesitated, not entirely certain what kind of mood Rynn was in.

"Ask," he said, not opening his eyes.

"When we were dealing with Lady Siyu, you mentioned you'd heard of the armor."

My phone started to ring, and Nadya's name and photograph flashed across the screen. It took me a second with the cracked screen to answer.

"Nadya?"

"Are you alone?"

Hi to you too. "No, Rynn is here."

"Put me on speakerphone. Rynn should hear this too—it concerns him."

I did as she asked. "You're on, Nadya," I said, and sat back.

"I just finished a meeting." There was a brief pause while Nadya chose her words, something she always did carefully. "I don't have time to be subtle about this. Rynn, has anyone contacted you about changing your fees at Gaijin Cloud?" Gaijin Cloud was the bar Rynn ran remotely.

Rynn frowned. "Yes. I've got someone looking into it. Why?"

"Because they've started asking for more."

"More payments?"

"No. They're demanding—or should I say suggesting strongly—that I change my financial manager."

Rynn frowned. "You don't have a financial manager. Neither does Gaijin Cloud."

"My thoughts exactly. They want to put one of their people in the club to run my money." She made a derisive noise. "I made a few calls, not everyone was forthcoming or even willing to answer, but I'm not the only one who is being squeezed."

Rynn's brow knit. "I'll make some calls and see what I can find out from some of my more-connected contacts. Nadya, whatever you do, don't let them anywhere near your books."

Nadya snorted. "Like I'd leave the money somewhere it could be found." Her voice took on a more serious tone. "Look, I don't know if this is serious. It could just be a simple cash grab, some new lowlife in power who wants to see how far he can push the local clubs, but my nose tells me something else is going on. And Alix?"

"Yeah, still here."

"No stupid risks—or no more stupid than usual."

"Just keep me up to date on what the hell is going on in Tokyo."

And with that she hung up.

I turned to Rynn. "Protection money?"

He nodded. "Yakuzu most likely, but the timing is odd. And so is the other request, unless they're looking for another way to launder money. It happens every now and then. One gangster moves in on another's territory and decides he—or she—needs to make sure everyone knows who's boss."

I frowned. "Odd? As in supernatural dangerous?"

"Let's hope not," Rynn said.

I shook my head and took another sip of my beer. "I hate it when you supernaturals use qualifying verbs."

"We'll see what rodents scurry out of the trash. And they will scurry."

Great, as long as they didn't bring guns. I hoped Nadya knew what the hell she was doing.

"You were about to tell me what you know about the Electric Samurai," I said, changing the subject to stop me from worrying about what might or might not be going on in Tokyo.

"The Electric Samurai?" Rynn said, frowning.

I shrugged. It seemed as good a name as any. "It's what I've started calling the suit. It has a better ring than Lightning Suit or Storm Armor."

He gave me a strange look as he took another sip of his own beer. "You realize it's incredibly inaccurate? There were no samurai until the medieval times."

I shrugged. "The sentiment was there even if the name wasn't. Besides, I think I know a little something about archaeologically accurate terms."

Rynn ignored my attempt to troll him, and instead nodded to himself, his brow furrowed as he stared at a spot on the ground. "Was he successful, this Jebe?" he asked after another long moment had passed. "On his campaign into Russia?"

I shrugged. "In a sense. Technically Jebe's army won, but only after burying themselves and the Russians under a river of blood and steel."

Rynn nodded. "And what happened to Jebe?"

"No one says, at least not in these records."

A silence that was palpable stretched between us until he said, "I've seen the suit before. I didn't know what it was at the time, but it fits the description. I lost track of it; when you live long enough you start to skip through parts of history—except for my cousin. He'd rather get a good seat and watch things burn."

Yeah, that sounded an awful lot like Artemis.

"The point is I remember the armor during the reign of Caligula. I was working as an enforcer for the elves. Artemis at the time was playing minor warlord in Rome. His antics were inconsequential, so for the most part I left him alone. Until one of his men stumbled onto something, an incubus named Atticus, who found it after a battle. It was magic, that much they knew, so of course they squabbled over it—except for Boadicea."

"Wait, Boadicea, the real one?"

Rynn nodded. "A succubus. She was recently from the north and claimed she recognized the suit. Not as it was, it had changed its appearance, but she recognized the magic. She said a Viking warlord had stumbled into town wearing it, on his last legs and burning up from fever. He died and one of her Celtic warriors took it. As you so aptly put, it allowed the wearer to strike at his foes with electricity. At first they thought it was a holy object—or the humans did and she didn't argue—but then it started to change him, turning him into a monster. She described it as watching someone's soul being devoured slowly from the inside out." Rynn paused to take another sip of his beer.

"And?"

"And one day he left. Without any warning. Unsettling stories reached them of a sole warrior devastating villages with no mercy. No, the suit didn't look the same, but the magic?" Rynn stopped to finish off his beer. "Most of Artemis's men listened to her warnings. Except for Atticus. Convinced she was scheming to keep it for herself, he took it. The others said it was as if the armor called to him. Artemis never had a backbone for telling people no, so Atticus took the suit."

"And it burned him up? Like the Viking?"

Rynn shook his head. "No. Much worse. Boadicea described what had happened when humans donned the armor, but Atticus was an incubus." He turned his eyes on me again. "It turned him into a monster the likes of which I've never seen. It took seven of us to defeat him— seven trained supernatural warriors to subdue one incubus. He was very powerful—and unstable. Every time he lost his temper, the armor would take on a life of its own, lightning dancing across the metal."

I didn't want to ask, but I knew I had to. "What happened to him?"

"He'd gone half mad by the time we caught up to him. Once the seven of us had him pinned down we tried to remove the armor, but it wouldn't come off. Three of us ran him through the heart. Artemis has never forgiven me for it," he added after a moment.

Despite my disastrous run-in with Artemis, I could understand his anger at Rynn now. I didn't sympathize with it, but I understood it. "What did you do with it?"

Rynn shrugged. "It disappeared a few days later before we could entomb it. Calling to a new victim I imagine, as if it had a mind of its own. Alix, the suit chose him. That's why it's so dangerous. It might not think, but it searches people out."

I sat back in my chair. "And if the elves want it, who's to say it isn't calling to one of them?"

"They claim it is too dangerous a piece to leave on the playing field."

Magic was bad on its own, but magic that gave things a life of their own? It would also explain why the Electric Samurai wasn't exactly at the forefront of the monster hordes; they preferred to control the chaos, not be controlled by it.

"It's like a larger more violent version of a monkey paw," I said.

Rynn nodded. "A similar effect. After that falling out? I went north and didn't see my cousin again for many hundreds of years. I didn't return to Rome until it had fallen and the Dark Ages had set in."

I sat back and emptied my own beer while I thought. If anything, this made me more determined to find the suit. Something that dangerous shouldn't be in anyone's hands, especially supernatural ones. And with this many supernaturals involved, something was bound to go sideways soon.

Rynn retrieved our empty bottles and headed into the kitchen. "And in the meantime, what do you plan to do about the IAA and World Quest?" he asked, the sink running in the background.

Not much until I got a handle on the armor. "Part of me is inclined to head back to the Himalayas and start there, but now that the mercenaries are involved—"

"They'll entrench themselves and branch out," Rynn said. He paused before adding, "The Zebras are dangerous. Their leader, Captain Hans Williams, is smart. He'll know from that explosion you found something."

I turned around in my seat so I was facing him. He was kind enough to return, holding two new beers. "My gut tells me the answers are in here, not in the Himalayas," I said, sliding the World Quest notebook across the table. "I know they left more clues. I just need to figure out what they are." Preferably by having my brain mull things over with alcohol; I lifted my new beer and took another sip. "Besides, like you said, we need to deal with the elves first."

Rynn stood and headed for the bedroom we shared. I was inclined to follow. I almost did, but my brain was still chasing the files and this new mystery to solve. I refreshed the screen and opened my browser to search for where the current archaeological collection of artifacts pertaining to the Mongolian horde was currently housed.

"Hello, Canada," I said. It was doing a tour of the Canadian universities, the University of British Columbia in Vancouver being its most recent stop.

I pulled up flights from Vegas heading out tomorrow. If the elves weren't going to cooperate with me, let's see what Charity Greenwoods could glean from under the noses of the IAA's Canadian branch. . . .

I was still mulling over my search results and travel plans when Rynn stuck his head out of the bedroom. "Alix, come to bed."

I gave a noncommittal response, not able to tear myself away from the screen.

He came up behind me and rested his chin on the top of my head before removing the beer from my hand. "Come to bed, Alix. I don't need sleep. You do."

The computer screen called to me, but Rynn was right—and warm. I took a deep breath and turned away from the screen and the paltry excuse for intel the elves had deigned to give me.

I had a lot of blanks to fill—needed to fill—so the Electric Samurai didn't fall into the wrong hands. But it wouldn't happen tonight.

Rynn pulled me up out of the chair and into his arms. I let out the breath I was holding and pushed away thoughts of the Electric Samurai as he kissed me.

I didn't spare even one glance back at the computer as he led me into the bedroom.

6

THE TRIUMPHANT RETURN OF
CHARITY GREENWOODS

11:00 a.m., Sunday
The University of British Columbia, Vancouver, Canada

You'd be amazed at how hard it is to keep an eye on your surroundings when there are trees and artistically placed totem poles in your path. And I don't just mean one or two trees, I mean they stuck the campus in the middle of a forest with brush and wildlife besides rats.

I glanced around the path again. I could not shake the feeling someone was watching us, even though Captain was settled into his carrier and hadn't even lifted his head in the last hour. Rynn didn't seem concerned either. It was possible it was just the onslaught of nature—something I expected from a dig site, not a university. Canadians were definitely not concerned about visibility.

I chalked my pinging spider sense up to too much travel over the past few days. I just needed to get my fingers into the exhibit.

"You didn't have to come with me," I said, needing to break the silence. "Up to the university, that is. We could have arranged a meet-up."

I didn't add, *Somewhere that you would fit in a little better*—like an upscale bar in the trendy Kits area just outside the campus, where he wouldn't have garnered looks from the female student population that was up here on a Sunday. Me? I could hide in plain sight. Nadya could too when pressed. But Rynn? Every coed we'd passed had given us a second look. Well, no, they'd given Rynn a second look. . . .

"Nadya isn't here," he said.

"Yes, but I don't *need* Nadya or you to watch my back. It's not like I haven't done this before." Since long before I met Rynn.

"Consider me insurance the vampires don't show up."

"I have Captain for that."

Captain, at the sound of his name, issued a noise that was a cross between a growl and a meow from inside his carrier-turned-backpack, perpetually hopeful for a treat. "See? Vampire detection at its finest."

"Fine, then consider me backup if something besides vampires shows up."

I fell silent, and not just because the totem poles that decorated the front of the anthropology museum had come into view through the campus trail. Rynn had a point. And to be completely honest, I'd rather have Rynn around even if it was only vampires that showed up. Especially since they tended to travel in numbers, cockroaches of the supernatural world that they were.

Even though it was a weekend, there were only a few couples milling outside the anthropology museum entrance. I kept my head down as we passed by and headed around the side of the building, where the researchers' entrance would be.

It was a Sunday morning and, as I'd suspected, there wasn't a single grad student on a smoke break. I took my collection of white access cards out of my bag. "Canadian . . . Canadian . . ." I said to myself as I searched through the thick ring holding them together. I'd made a habit of collecting university access cards over the years. Trust me, when it comes to research facilities, outside military and medical research of the narcotic pharmaceutical variety, security measures barely kept the riffraff out. And no, that doesn't include me. Changing security systems is expensive. The cards get reworked every five years or so—at most. And even then I figure they just cycled through the old codes.

"There it is." I pulled out a white security card labeled UBC in smeared blue marker and swiped it along the back research entrance door panel. As I'd suspected, the green light went on and I heard the door to the museum click open, just for yours truly.

"God, if half the world's museums were this easy to waltz into—" I was halfway tempted to bet Rynn that the card would work on most of the buildings . . . "Think there's anything interesting in the chemistry building?" I asked.

He made a face. "I'm amazed they bothered with the cards at all if they weren't going to keep track of them." Rynn was frowning at me. I shrugged. "They turn away the odd klepto and burgeoning drug dealers looking for free equipment, but beyond that? I don't think they figured on antiquities thieves waltzing through. I kept it after an excursion up here for some Inuit artifacts last year." I'd had a collector who'd gotten in a beef with the university—or one of the curators up here. It'd been a shockingly easy job, and totally legit—I mean, they'd practically been planning on selling it to him until an argument . . .

Still, Rynn's frown didn't go anywhere. "You've been here before? Using *that* card?"

It took me a second to figure out that Rynn wasn't concerned about the general principle. I shook my head. "Seriously, this is one of the least guarded IAA facilities on the planet. It's Canada—might as well be a research station in Greenland. I'd be surprised if they even realized I took anything last time." Skeleton crew campus security, rooms full of boxes that hadn't been opened since 1970, an ever-revolving roster of three-month grant employees and student interns hired to curate the boxes they did manage to open. It was a wonder anything ever got unpacked, and even more unlikely that anyone actually bothered to check the boxes, drawers, and shelves to see if everything was still there.

If I wanted to do them a real favor, I'd label and sort a couple things for them while I searched.

"Last time I found a handful of early Viking settler artifacts from back east mixed in with the First Nations display stuff. On *display*. Do you realize how much of a screwup that is?"

Rynn stared at me.

"Seriously, if it had been one of my undergrads who couldn't tell them apart, they wouldn't have heard the end of it."

"Like I'm not hearing the end of it?"

I made a face. Rynn might know guns, the supernatural, and mixing bar drinks, but understand the finer points of archaeology he did not. "I did that Inuit totem a favor. At least it's appreciated and properly labeled now. You know I have a point."

Rynn inclined his head as I pushed open the door. "A point? Yes. I'm holding judgment on whether it's a good one. How many of those do you have exactly?" he asked, taking the ring of white cards from my hand, holding them out as if they were some morbid collection of animal feet . . . or a graveyard where lost academic security access cards went to die a slow and slightly zombified death.

I grabbed them back before he could do anything to them. "You'd be surprised," I said.

Sensing motion, the hall lights flickered on, illuminating the 1970s off-yellow beige paint in cheap fluorescence. Now, which way was the research room?

I turned around and tried to remember which way I'd gone last time . . . there! I remembered the cracked ceiling.

I eased my way around Rynn and headed left.

I kept my ears open for any sounds, but to be honest, running into someone wasn't at the top of my list of worries. I'd picked the time and date for a reason. At 11:00 a.m. on a Sunday, there were people milling around the museum proper, which meant that was where the sole security guard's attention would be. As far as grad students in the research facility were concerned? Even the keeners wouldn't be in until at least

2:00 p.m. There's only so far dedication takes you past free overtime on a Sunday morning.

Well, that and having to put up with weekend museumgoers; they had an uncanny knack for finding your research lab on the way to the snack machine, and they just had a couple of questions . . . not that they've noticed your hangover and the lousy cup of coffee you're clutching between your hands like a shield or blessed relic, the only silver lining you've seen this morning, but more importantly the only thing on the planet standing between you and them. . . .

"Are you sure we shouldn't come back at night?" Rynn asked.

I shook my head. "On a Sunday, they might actually set an alarm for after hours to prevent real thieves from getting in." Though I doubted that would apply to the graduate student section, I preferred to be careful.

"The *real* thieves? Please, tell me more. I'm quite curious how their patterns of behavior differ."

I ignored him as I counted and examined the beigey-yellow doors. Behind which one was the loaner stuff? Hmmm, should be near the middle, about where the loading dock would be . . . bingo. I placed my ear against the door labeled Research and Loading Bay to see if anyone was inside. Unlikely, but it always pays to check. Never know when someone hits a Saturday-night dorm party or campus pub crawl and ends up passing out in their office watching sci-fi flicks.

Before I could swipe my card, Rynn shouldered me out of the way and listened himself. Finally, once he was convinced the room really was empty, he let me swipe the key card. I pushed open the heavy, hermetically sealed door to a large rectangular room about half the size of a tennis court. Arranged in rows down the long side were three research bays—basically tables that stretched the narrow width of the room, fitted down their length with chairs, lights, and Bunsen burners.

The most used equipment in the room, the tanks at various stages of soaking items, were balanced on the benches, bowing them in the process.

On the left wall were the fume hoods, the fans and vents above buzzing on autopilot. Interspersed amongst those were the sample tables fitted with special lights and microscopes to get a better look at, well, whatever it was you were looking at.

Now, where would I stick the Genghis exhibit? I spotted five crates, barely unpacked, on the far side of the rectangular lab, still stacked by the loading bay door. The computer tower and large monitor, however, were parked on a bench beside them.

Well, the computer and self-contained servers were up and running. At least they'd gotten that far. Saved me twenty minutes trying to get them up and running on my own.

I motioned Rynn to follow me as I headed over to see whether the rule of Genghis Khan had left any pertinent information on the Electric Samurai.

I jostled the screen and was met with a login window.

"Now what?" Rynn asked.

I checked around and under the monitor before looking behind the computer itself. Taped to the back of the tower was the operating manual and inventory manifest. I flipped open the manual. Login codes were on a yellow note that had long lost its stickiness and had been taped to the inside. I was hitting the jackpot today as far as time savers went.

I retrieved my jump drive from my jacket. I didn't trust it with Captain, not after the phone incident. Speaking of which . . . I sat down and let Captain out of his carrier. He darted out to investigate what was around. Not that I figured on vampires showing up, but it paid to be careful. Besides, he needed the exercise.

Rynn pulled up a chair as I logged in and waited for the computer to grind on.

"Doesn't sending the passwords with the boxes defeat the purpose of having passwords?"

I shrugged. "Well, only if you've actually got the computer. It can't connect to the internet. The only way anyone is accessing these files is through this computer, and since the boxes and archives are almost constantly moving with the exhibits . . ."

"It's a colossal problem if someone like you or Nadya wants access. Or what if some student or janitor decides to sit down and take a look? What if they pick up something dangerous?"

"First, Nadya just logs onto the Russian Archaeological Associations servers or gets a contact to deliver the information. She doesn't burn her bridges. I do, hence the need to break in. As with regards to the janitor? Anything that dangerous is stored in some IAA vault, not passed around like a joint between research departments. And second, you'd need to know what you were looking for. To the uninitiated observer, this just looks like any old file system. Here, see for yourself."

I let Rynn look at the screen over my shoulder. After a moment he said, "These are generic colored labels. It's coded?"

"Give the incubus a prize." I used the cursor to highlight the green series of folders with lettered names. "Green folders contain information that your most clever undergrad couldn't find a supernatural element or reference under. They're green because they're considered clean—safe enough you could leave your volunteer students with the folders and accompanying items for a month and they still wouldn't suspect there was a supernatural connection. Blue folders are iffy. If someone knows what to look for, or say you gave them to an astute third year, they might get suspicious by some of the text references that don't quite match up. But the red ones"—I ran the cursor over one of the red folders labeled simply Alpha—"now, those folders will absolutely mention an artifact or text that's related to the supernatural. Those the undergrads aren't allowed to touch."

"What if they open them anyway? Curiosity killing the cat and everything."

"If you were them, would you believe there was such a thing as the supernatural?"

Rynn shook his head as he abandoned me to the computer in favor of opening one of the crate lids. "They're as bad as the elves."

"Think of it this way—no one knows the supernatural exists, so why would they look for it? Besides, if you added Fort Knox or CDC level security, someone *would* start looking. They'd figure we were hiding gold, jewels, a grow-op. Who knows what they'd convince themselves had to be inside."

He furrowed his brow at me over the box he'd busied himself with. "That's not comforting."

"It's not supposed to be. Remember? Bureaucrats. Look, Rynn— stop fidgeting and take a seat—I'm copying all of this, but we're talking terabytes off a system that's been upgraded in patches. It'll take awhile."

"I'd rather take a look around if it's all the same to you."

Rynn's usual problem with being up close and personal to the thievery. I turned my attention back onto the file progress bars, watching as they ground along, copying onto my drive. All the images and papers that would never actually be published. *Don't break anything. And keep your eye on Captain.*

The files were copying, slowly but surely, but that didn't mean I couldn't run a search. When starting from scratch, best to kick off with the bloody fucking obvious.

I typed *magic armor* into the search engine and waited as the computer spun its chips to churn out a list.

There was a lot—as in pages of mentions as far as the translations were concerned.

"Shit." I mean, I'd expected Genghis and his ilk to have found some magic weapons and armor over the years. I'd assumed it had come down to a few pieces, but apparently that was not the case.

The Mongolian horde had created a massive empire. You didn't do that back then without a little supernatural help. And Genghis, much like Alexander the Great, had assimilated everything in his path. The Mongols had found everything from an eleventh-century Russian cloak that allowed the wearer to turn into an animal to Korean demon hide armor.

It could take me months to sort through all of this, especially since the armor changed its appearance with each wearer.

Okay, let's try this again. I typed in *Storm Armor*. No luck.

"Try Lightning Armor," Rynn offered. I typed *Lightning Armor* in the search program. This time three references came up.

Now these odds I liked an awful lot better . . .

The first two I traced back to a blue folder. I opened the individual files, but they seemed to mention markings on the armor itself and the speed with which the user had been able to move. Magic, most likely, but I didn't think that fit the description of the armor the elves wanted. I made a mental note of their location in the files anyway; I'd have a longer look later.

The third reference, though, now that was the doozy. I whistled. "Jackpot," I said, and opened up the file, then waited for Rynn to join me.

Subatai Jebe, or General Jebe. "Now this one, this is interesting. Do you know much about Genghis Khan's army?"

Rynn shook his head. "Northern Europe. By the time stories of the horde reached us they'd been muddled with the retellings."

What people must have done in the days without cell phones and internet . . .hearing your news in stories and having no idea if it was real or if some asshole was trolling the unknown world.

"Well, Jebe was unique. He was one of Genghis's four generals, or 'dogs' as they were nicknamed. He also was known as 'the Arrow.' Jebe wasn't like the other generals. He started out on the other side and was recruited by Genghis after almost killing him with an arrow to the neck."

"He made him his general?" Rynn sounded skeptical of the decision. "Keep your friends close and your enemies closer?"

I inclined my head. "Not quite. Jebe was good. Really good. Let's face it, he was on the opposite side and almost managed to orchestrate an end to Genghis's reign."

"Most warlords would kill such an opponent to maintain order in an army like that."

"Ah, but you're thinking of a figurehead, like a king or a noble who is put in a place of power or inherits it from their forefathers. Genghis was the director of his own orchestra of mayhem and destruction. His horde terrorized the Asian continent and eastern Europe. He didn't have anything to prove to anyone—and Jebe had the balls to admit he was the one who shot Genghis in the neck." I shrugged. "Honesty and loyalty are hard to come by. Probably worth more to Genghis by that point than the fact that he'd been born on the other side." Rynn didn't look convinced, so I added, "Think of it like a corporate takeover. Jebe was the best up-and-comer on your rival company's roster. You could take over the company and scuttle him, or do the smart thing and hire him. Genghis went the hiring route. This time," I added. There were plenty of cases when he'd gone the marauding evil army route as well. Maybe he had a karma thing going—50 percent of the time kill everyone, 50 percent of the time let everyone live.

"Humans never cease to surprise me."

"Why? Because we can occasionally put our own hate and indignation aside when we can see a use for something?"

"No. Because no supernatural I know of, except maybe a dragon, would be able to put its own passions aside to consider the alternative."

I turned my attention back to the file contents. "What about incubi? You're pretty even-tempered."

"Not so much with other supernaturals. It can be hard to put aside . . ." He paused, as if searching for a word. ". . . past transgression. It's complicated. It's why we tend not to surround ourselves with other supernaturals for prolonged periods of time. It's not often you see succubi and incubi traveling or working together for more than a few decades at most. In your words, we tend to piss each other off. If you're smart, you part ways before that happens."

"And if you don't? Didn't you say your cousin had a troupe of them or something?"

He inclined his head. "Then you end up like Artemis—with problems and well over a hundred years' worth of hate and grudges built up."

The more I gleaned about Rynn . . . half of me wanted to keep him talking, but the other half?

The file was a translation, along with the original documents that had been scanned in. "This is an account detailing General Jebe and two of the other dogs' parts in the downfall of the Khwarezmian Empire." Rynn shook his head, and I continued. "Ah, second Persian empires, Muslim dynasties? During the Middle Ages they held parts of Persia—Iran, Afghanistan. Basically they controlled the lower half of the Caspian Sea and a swath of the Persian Gulf. They were a silk road choke point between the Mediterranean and Europe and Genghis's empire." A trade route Genghis had wanted very badly.

"Brilliant general perhaps, but not a ruler. Why didn't he barter for trade instead of razing an empire? It would have set trade back a century."

"Because the shah sent back the head of Genghis's ambassador in a bag. Apparently he took offense to Genghis sending a Muslim." I scrolled through the document's translation. "Takes two to be civilized, Rynn. This is one of the original accounts of the entire invasion into Persia written by one of the horde's scribes—everything from the number of people killed to accounts of all the loot taken."

I frowned. This was the kind of document that was usually on display in the museum's public exhibit, meaning it had to list the supernatural items. I scrolled through until I found them—jewelry, sacrificial bowls, swords . . .

And there was my magic suit of armor.

"The scribe makes a footnote about the suit. Claims Jebe found it while they were sacking the capital, Samarkand, near the end of the campaign. It was mixed in with the shah's treasures."

I ran the time line through my head. The first Persian empire sacked Babylonia and parts of western Europe while the Roman Empire was still going strong . . .

Times like this I wish I had a photographic memory. "Okay, correct me if I'm wrong, but weren't Persia and Rome locked in battle for a few hundred years?—after and during Caligula?"

Rynn inclined his head. "I wasn't around for the majority of it, though Artemis might have been—not that he's in any state to answer questions about much of anything these days."

"But the suit disappeared, and considering it has a mind of its own and a penchant for violence, what better place to run to? It's got a pattern. The Storm Warrior legend first appears around 150 BC in Japan. My guess is it reached the continent through Korea, found itself a couple nice wars, got some traveling and sightseeing done across northern Asia until it fell into the hands of the early Vikings, again for who knows how long. It reaches Ireland, where you have your next eyewitness account from Boadicea. It falls into the hands of the Romans, where Artemis and you encountered it. From there, a few more battles lost to history and time, and it's right on Persia's doorstep. Persia enters a time of relative peace, so the suit has nothing better to do than sit around in a vault—that is, until Genghis and Jebe come along."

"And the violence begins all over again."

The scribes' account of the suit as the invasion progressed read like a journal of sorts. It wasn't a diary; you had to find the entries between accounts of sacking towns and cities for slaves, food, and gold and how it was all divvied up, but there were glimpses and comments about Jebe's state of mind and the suit throughout.

Things started off fine. The horde continued their incursion and, with Jebe's newfound armor, defeated one town after the other, collecting the spoils. His men began calling him the "Lightning Arrow" on account of the electricity that danced across the plates before battle.

I skimmed—I didn't care about things going right, I cared about things going horribly wrong.

It didn't take me long to find it.

As the war with the Poles and Russians progressed, the scribes began noting changes in Jebe, who was by all accounts an even, patient general, but who had become impatient and volatile. Little things at first—lapses of temper, punishing his men for small infractions, jumping into battle before all of his intelligence was delivered, not something Genghis and his men were known to do. At first it earned little more than a footnote, but as the army progressed north, that changed.

"The cracks start to show outside Kiev," I said to Rynn. Rynn peered over my shoulder. "A battle with losses, more than Jebe was used to."

I nodded. They'd come upon a walled city. The Mongols didn't do well in close city quarters; their strength was being on horseback with ranged bows. Usually they put the town to siege, starved everyone out. But this time the general didn't have the patience. They won—with heavy losses. "After that, Jebe's temper only got worse, more volatile and reckless. He started to take pleasure in humiliating and torturing his foes." The scribe noted he also stopped taking the armor off after that.

Bad tactical decisions, poor battle plans. He'd become so caught up in the killing that he'd stopped being a general. "The suit is its own worst enemy."

Wait—that was it.

"It still doesn't tell us where the armor ended up," Rynn said.

I shook my head. "My point isn't that this tells us where it is. My point is a question we haven't asked. Why doesn't it ever stay in one place? There was plenty of fighting in the Roman Empire for the next few centuries, not to mention northern Europe and the Celtic clans, yet the armor appears sporadically—sometimes hundreds of years apart. Why?"

Rynn arched an eyebrow at me. "You clearly have an opinion."

"I think it's doing more than looking for the next, nearest, biggest fight. If that were the case, it never would have left Japan and Korea. I think it needs the right wearer—so much so it had to propel itself across the entire ancient world."

Another thought occurred to me. "We assumed it was evil from the start because it burns up its host. If the host is that specific, that rare . . . Back in the ancient world, wars would have been the easiest way to find a large pool of people."

"And eventually the need for a host and violence entwined, warping whatever it started out as."

"And unless there's a war nearby, when it eventually kills the wearer . . ."

". . . it has nowhere to go but a treasure room," Rynn finished.

That was the problem with magic artifacts and supernatural weapons—they might be powerful, but there was always a price and always a weakness.

Rynn swore in supernatural and ran his hands through his hair. "I'm about ready to tell the elves and Lady Siyu where they can shove the armor."

"There's another option I'm thinking we have," I said. If there's one thing I've learned over the years, it's always keep your eye out for the back door.

He gave me a skeptical look. I poked at the screen and the item inventory that went with the translated documents. "Jebe—*he* wore it, the suit picked him. And someone was nice enough to document the entire campaign until it either killed him or someone figured out a way past its defenses. Our other choice is to figure out what the hell it is the elves want with it." Once you know what someone's end game is, negotiations get so much more interesting. Regardless, the first concrete clues would be in here.

Rynn still wasn't appeased. "And if we can't figure out what it is they want? You don't know them like I do, Alix. You know one of them, who by elven standards is semi-tolerable and apparently clueless to internal politics."

"I thought they were neutral?"

"Exactly—neutral. They haven't made waves during the past five hundred years that Mr. Kurosawa and his predecessors have been in charge, but mark my words, that doesn't mean there isn't a large faction of elves that enjoyed playing gods throughout Europe during the Roman Empire and Middle Ages as much as the other side did. If things hadn't shifted, they'd still have human slaves underfoot, just like they used to, and they'd still be chasing after minor infractions and protocol violations. Just because on the surface they have a handful of traits your kind consider admirable doesn't mean there aren't plenty of rotten ones running the show underneath."

"Then if we can't find out what it is they plan to do with it, we do the next best thing. They said they wanted the suit but didn't specify what condition it had to be in, correct?"

He gave me a wary nod.

"We figure out a way to make the suit unusable."

He wasn't convinced. "*If* we find the suit, *if* we find a way to disarm it—that's a lot of ifs, Alix." His eyes drifted to something behind me, on the screen. "What's that?"

"What's what?" I searched the lists, but I didn't see anything beyond the war trail accounts.

"Not there. The thumbnail, on the side." He reached over my shoulder and tapped one of the comments made by a previous grad student. Sure enough, attached to the notes was an embedded icon—a link to a longer set of notes contained in the folder . . . and it was directly related to a passage about the suit.

I clicked on it and waited for the second window to open. It was a brief two-page analysis on a section of the records I hadn't gotten to yet—the records of a later campaign into what's now Poland. But as opposed to discussing the locations or items looted, the grad student entry talked about something else entirely. It was only two lines, but it was about a possessed suit of armor that drove Jebe to madness . . . and it cross-referenced Jebe's journal.

Son of a bitch, Jebe kept a journal while he had the suit. Jackpot. I needed that journal. I searched the computer for the journal file and found it. . . .

There was nothing inside. "Oh, you've got to be fucking kidding me." Someone had erased the fucking soft copies. I opened up another window to see when the files had been removed; maybe if I was lucky they were still in the trash.

"What?"

"Jebe's journal. The entire entry is gone—photos, the documentation . . . everything!" I frowned at the screen. "That can't be right." I turned to look at Rynn. "This says the files were erased from the hard drive twenty minutes ago." Right before we got here.

Rynn and I both clued in at the same time. "Someone knew we were coming—someone who doesn't want us finding that suit. They must have been watching us, or had an informant from the casino."

Goddamn son of a . . . "They must have found out about Mr. Kurosawa signing a deal with the elves." If the other side of the supernatural war figured the tide was about to turn in Mr. Kurosawa's favor . . .

"Whoever it is, they do not wish us to find it."

Or worse, they wanted it for themselves. I went back to the hard copy and started to search the inventory list. Twenty minutes—that meant they might not have had time to track down the journal itself. It might still be here. "Rynn, I need you to check box 3A." *Please, please say they didn't make off with the original . . .*

"Alix, if I were them I'd make sure you didn't have enough time to find it . . ." He trailed off as an alarm began to sound elsewhere in the building—not the fire alarm, which was designed to get people to leave as fast as possible, but the other kind, the one that says a door's been left open, or broken . . .

"Time's up," Rynn said.

I swore and turned back to the computer screen. The files were almost finished copying. There was something in Jebe's journal; there had to be, and I *very* much planned on finding out what it was. "Find that journal."

"Is this it?" Rynn held up a leather-bound book that had been wrapped in a set of packing cloths. I took a quick look through it and shook my head. "No—this is the account keeping, not the journal. Keep looking." Maybe they hid it in the room. That wouldn't be stealing, just misplacing, and if the journal got left behind when the crates moved . . .

The files finished copying, so I pulled out my thumb drive and shoved it back into my pocket.

"Well what is it I'm supposed to be looking for then?" Rynn said.

"How am I supposed to know? They deleted all the pictures and descriptions!"

I grabbed the inventory list and rifled through to the packing sheets.

Box 3A . . . 3A . . . there it was . . . I found Jebe's journal halfway down the page. "Ah, should be packed in the bottom drawer, a metal box labeled 'journal' and decorated with yellow tape. Look underneath the tray of arrows. No, not that one," I said as Rynn pulled out a metal box labeled with yellow and white tape. "The other one, should be . . . ah . . ." I consulted the packing slip again. "Underneath where you found that one."

Rynn pulled the right one out and tried to replace it with the other. "No! Don't put them back in the wrong order!"

Rynn glared at me as he put the right metal box on the table.

"It's important—you have no idea how easily that stuff gets lost." The incredulous look didn't dissipate. "Look, you've never opened a box only to find the thing you needed went missing. Oh, for . . . I don't need to explain proper artifact curation to you, just open the damn box so I can steal the book." I realized there was a large dose of hypocrisy in that statement, but we were getting short on time.

Rynn popped open the metal latches and I heard the air seal break. He frowned and held it up. "Empty," he said, and showed it to me.

No, no, no . . . I ran over to check the box. It should have been in a wrapped plastic bag; maybe someone's idiot grad student hadn't bothered to put it back in the case.

There was nothing loose in the crate. Everything, including the dusting kits, was immaculately tucked in their places.

"Son of a bitch!" I slammed the top of the crate down. "They took it. They beat us here and took the journal."

I couldn't believe it. So close again. A dark black pit settled inside me, and for the first time in a while I wanted to throw something, break something. I deserved to find that journal. I saw red as my eyes fell on the computer. I bet they made a great shattering sound—and who knows? Maybe I'd find the missing files inside . . .

I thought I heard Rynn call my name over the alarm, but I was so furious, so angry . . .

I might have gone through with breaking the computer if Captain hadn't started to bleat . . .

Even through my anger I saw he had his nose pressed in the space between a bench and the wall. Normally I wouldn't make anything of it—there were plenty of bugs and rodents to keep Captain's interest—but the way he was twitching his nose and his tail, and sniffing at the air as if he was trying to figure out what it was . . .

There was no way I was that lucky.

"Rynn, get me something thin," I said as I ran over to the bench. Captain let out a bleat, the same noise he made around any supernatural who wasn't a vampire.

"Why would they hide it?"

"Who cares? We can worry about that later, after we have Jebe's journal."

Rynn passed me a broom handle and I lost no time shoving it between the benches. Something was definitely back there—it moved as soon as I touched it with the handle.

I swore as I heard multiple footsteps coming down the hall. They should have spent way more time clearing the exhibits. Whoever had sounded the alarms must have also included a helpful call to security.

"Alix, we're out of time—and a hallway. We'll need to find another way out."

"Gimme a second." The book moved a few more inches. I pushed Captain away as he tried to wiggle in and help.

Come on, come on . . . don't tear, not now . . .

I heard the electronic lock click open as someone swiped their card, followed by the rattle as they tried the handle, which I'd manually locked.

The wonders of light-sensitive experiments: they'd had to design the manual locks to override the electronic in all the labs.

"You don't have a second," Rynn whispered.

I reached my hand in up to my shoulder. The tips of my fingers brushed it. "Then make me one!"

Rynn swore, ran to the door as they tried swiping the card again, and relocked the door. The card was swiped again, and yet again Rynn reset the lock. I heard the chime as the key card was swiped a third time, this time followed by "Is anyone in there? Campus security."

Maybe I got lucky and they'd left their manual keys in their office?

I heard the muffled jingle of keys.

Nope. Why wouldn't the goddamned book come out—there!

"Got it!" I whispered as the book slid into my fingers. I dragged it out of its hiding spot and started flipping through the old pages carefully, ever so carefully. . . .

Medieval Mongolian dialects weren't my forte, but I could make out enough of the characters to read, " 'I am Zurgadai of the Besud Clan, also known as Jebe, the Arrow of Ghengis Khan.' " I closed it shut and fit it into my backpack. I then held it open for Captain. He mewed at me. "Inside. You'll get a treat after," I whispered.

He sat on his haunches and curled his tail around his legs, sniffing at me. Yeah, I got it; he'd had bad luck getting into carriers of late. "Listen, unless you want to end up back with Lady Siyu—I promise, treats. After!"

He sniffed at me again, but whether he decided my tone meant business or he was just bored with the lack of a food dish and litter box, he caved and crawled in.

Finally. I zipped up the bag and tossed him on my back as carefully as speed allowed. Normally I wouldn't put something like the journal in there with him; Captain had spent most of his life as a wild cat out by the Egyptian pyramids, so he tended to stake out territory—places, people, *things*. I just hoped he didn't decide to take any residual anger out on the book.

I turned to Rynn as the banging on the door intensified.

"You're the thief," he whispered. "Do something."

I took a quick perusal of the room for alternative exits. Windows were too suspicious to any bystanders. Now, the loading bay door, that was another matter entirely.

I ran to the cargo bay door and found the latch. Wonder of wonders, it was only locked shut by a set of bolts.

I undid both of them and used my back to get the door open enough to crawl under while Rynn played lock footsies with the security guards.

I checked under the metal loading bay door to make sure the coast was clear. Our luck held out. No one was waiting for us—or even looking our way.

I waved to Rynn. He waited until the guards had unlocked the door, locked it for a last time, then ran. He baseball-slid under the garage door lip, and both of us dropped the four feet to the cracked concrete below. Rynn crouched down and turned his head to the side, listening for something. Satisfied it was safe, he nodded that the coast was clear. "Wait," I hissed as Rynn started away from the building.

"They'll be in the lab any minute, Alix. They were rebooting the system."

Which meant the locks would reset and open. "Just trust me." I slid my hands under the door, and carefully, as quietly as was humanly possible, I eased the loading door back down.

The bolts would give it away, but if luck held they wouldn't notice for a while.

I started backing away, Rynn beside me. Running would attract attention on a university campus, but we needed to walk away quickly before the guards figured to check around back or get a buddy in the office to do it.

I turned to Rynn. He was the one with mercenary tendencies, after all, and navigating security and getting away were his specialties. "What now?"

He inclined his head. "Head to the jeep. With any luck no one will spot us."

"With any luck?"

He frowned at me. "This is a university—a little out of my experience. It's not like they follow any real best practices when it comes to security—it's a bit like dealing with a two-year-old. With that much inexperience and incompetence comes unpredictability."

I shook my head and grabbed his arm. "Come on. This way," I said, and started out of the loading bay. We kept an even pace until we turned the corner. Free and clear . . . so far so good. I crossed my fingers inside my pocket that that was in fact the case.

As we headed down the empty promenade, I checked a couple times to see if anyone was following behind. No one was.

We were halfway to the car lot where we'd left the jeep. We were passing by a copse of maple trees left to grow in a ring in the center of the road when there was a piercing howl in my ear, followed by hissing and scuffing at the inside of my backpack.

Shit. Both Rynn and I scanned the area as Captain tried to claw his way out of my bag. When that didn't work, he let out another ear-piercing howl. Damn it, his claws were going to destroy the journal.

"No, Captain. You're not getting out of there to eat vamp—Ow!" I yelped, and madly tried to get my bag off my back as Captain dug his claws into my spine.

While I tried to pry Captain off, Rynn found the source of his fury—a pink-hoodie-clad woman in beige cargo pants, wearing a pair of heavy sunglasses. A shock of blond hair peeked out from under the hood, which was pulled up high and covered most of her face.

And she was not happy at having been found. "Hey!" came a high Valley Girl voice as she struggled against Rynn. "Let go of me!"

If I hadn't recognized the voice, the scent of rotting lily of the valley that wafted my way and the surfer girl getup would have given it away.

Rynn pulled the hood down, exposing her face, and dragged her to the edge of the shade from the trees, just short of the sunlight. I did my best to wrangle Captain.

Bindi. Alexander's most recent lackey acquisition.

"What are you doing here and why shouldn't I kill you?" Rynn asked, leaning in and using his more menacing voice.

"That's two questions," Bindi whined. "Which one do you want me to answer first?"

"I guess you'll have to guess which answer is least likely to convince me to kill you."

Bindi made a sound halfway between an exasperated sigh and a whine. "Look, I'm not here to do anything. Okay, okay!" she said as Rynn's hand clamped down on her shoulder. "Fine. I was *thinking* about it, but come on— Vampire? What do you expect?"

I closed my eyes. I'd managed to finally get my backpack off my back, but Captain was still trying to get out, though now that he could see Bindi his howls had quieted to a continuous growl.

"I'm here for a reason other than trying to kill Owl. Promise!"

"What are you here for then?"

"Alexander sent me!" she whined.

"And that's supposed to make me feel better? Alexander has tried to kill Alix not once, not twice, but *three* times now."

"But not this time. I *promise.*"

And closing my eyes wasn't going to make Bindi go away. Goddamn it, why did vampires have to squeeze themselves in everywhere? I opened them back up to find Rynn looking at me, eyebrows raised. "Well?" he said, and I realized he'd asked me something while I'd been lost in my musings on the problems with vampires. "Do you want to hear what she has to say or not?"

One thing was certain as I gave Bindi a once-over. She looked scared more than murderous, though that might have been Rynn. From the way Captain had focused himself on her, pressing his face as far as it would go against the mesh, he didn't think there were any other vampires around.

"Alix?" Rynn asked again.

And we sure as hell couldn't stand around here forever.

I nodded. Rynn let her go. "Finally!" Bindi said, and stumbled back away from the sunlight further under the protection of the shade of the trees. She pulled her hood back up, tucking her surfer blond hair underneath. "*Seriously—*" she started, but I cut her off.

"Your message. And whatever it is Alexander wants better be good, otherwise I'm going to rethink this whole chat real fast."

"Okay, okay." She took a breath and tried to compose herself. Not easy to do with my cat making his feelings well and vocally known. Bindi shot the carrier a concerned look before saying, "Alexander says that you have a common interest and he wants to help you. He wants to call a truce. A real one this time."

Fat chance Alexander was going to help anyone, especially me. Not after the fiasco in Ephesus, or Bali, and especially not after L.A.

I sighed and turned to Rynn. "It might just be easier to give her to Captain. I mean, it'll shut him up—"

"No not the cat!" Bindi shrieked. "Honest, I'm telling the truth. Alexander really does want to help you. Look, if you let me reach into my pocket, I'll get his message out!"

I nodded at Rynn. He was the one who approached to take the message from her, while I took a step back further out of range of the lily-of-the-valley-scented pheromones that acted like a narcotic. It weakened humans and made vampires look pretty. It was also more addictive than heroin. I had a gas mask, but it would draw too much attention if anyone walked by.

Rynn took the note and, after sniffing it for the pheromones, brought it to me.

It was an off-white card, addressed to me with flowery gold script. Definitely Alexander's style.

I opened it.

Dear Owl,

Though I'm certain this proposed truce will come as a shock to you as much as it has to my superiors, it is—suffice it to say—necessary. Though you may find this hard to believe, we vampires rather enjoy not being hunted, nor do we appreciate the idiots after a source of immortality. Much as I enjoy her work, the famous vampire writer did not do us any favors.

I have information that you need, but I am not trusting it to Bindi. Suffice it to say it is information that you will most certainly want concerning a number of supernaturals we've both had dealings with recently and the humans who are currently under their sway. Call me at the number below and I will explain more.

PS: Oh yes, and please have your incubus let the girl go. I've grown rather attached to my assistant. Selfish and obtuse in that way you Americans seem so fond of—very much like one of those characters on your horrid reality TV shows. But, she has her uses.

It was signed *Alexander* in flourishing script and, as promised, a number was included below.

I shook my head and gave the note to Rynn.

The worst part was it made sense. Rynn had said as much about the vampires. They might be cockroaches of the supernatural world, but they were also one of the most vulnerable to humans—*if* they found out. It was logical that Alexander and the rest of the vampires really didn't want anyone knowing they existed, as much as they enjoyed eating and enslaving people.

Minor thug versus career criminal. Goddamn it, I was actually buying it.

Meanwhile, we still had Bindi to deal with. Rynn was waiting for me to throw in my two cents.

"Well, we sure as hell can't trust her," I said. Despite the fact that she was a vampire, she was bat shit crazy and a serial killer. But on her own? Cowering in front of Rynn? As much as I'd like to see her suffer for killing innocent people, it didn't seem very sporting to let Rynn hurt her.

Besides, it would just give Alexander another excuse for his vendetta against me.

Against my better judgment, I was certain, I nodded.

Rynn jerked his head at Bindi. "Get lost. And if I see you again—" He left the threat open.

Bindi glared at both of us in turn as she gave her neck one last rub. I wasn't going to have Rynn kill her, but like hell was I going to feel bad about a few bruises. *Serial killer.*

She pulled her pink hood down and readjusted her sunglasses before taking off at a jog for the shaded forest trails. "Later losers," she called out over her shoulder at us just before disappearing under the trees.

Rynn shook his head. "Later losers? Why is it the gutter trash are always the ones who do well as vampires?"

That I couldn't agree with more. "Probably has something to do with the bottom feeder supernatural part of the ecosystem they inhabit." I nodded toward the parking lot. Time to get out of here before whoever had tried to set us up figured out we had Jebe's journal.

"You're considering it, aren't you?" Rynn said, waving Alexander's note. "Don't answer that. I can tell."

"At this point, I'm willing to take just about any help we can get."

Rynn didn't disagree. "I think I know just the place. Somewhere not even the elves' best spies could listen in. "

7

THE PARIS BOYS

1:00 p.m. The Cambie, Vancouver East Side

We ditched the jeep in a downtown parking garage. Rynn hadn't found any bugs or tracking devices, but we couldn't be certain one hadn't been placed since someone had tracked us to UBC. I'd skimmed through Jebe's journal in the jeep, but I wouldn't have a chance to take a much more thorough look and crack at a better translation until later.

From the garage it was a short hike down the street, our heads down and sweatshirt hoods pulled up, until we reached a bar that doubled as a backpackers' hostel. Right in the downtown core of Vancouver.

"A little odd location for a dive bar," I said as I pushed open the beaten metal and wood door. Vancouver has a certain expensive veneer to it . . . and a strange dichotomy. A forested, picturesque city built for outdoorsy hikers who couldn't actually afford to live here. The hiking pathways and park trails that wound through most of the city had an abandoned feel to them, even on a Sunday afternoon. Don't get me wrong—it's very pretty, a lot like Seattle. If you like the abandoned zombie apocalypse feel.

Except for this part of town. As we'd entered the waterfront district, the people packed the sidewalks—younger and less polished-looking than everyone else in the city. And as for this place? The Cambie was the ugly duck hanging out with the swans, but rather than trying to fit in, it had accepted its status in the world as a dive bar and embraced it.

It wasn't like there was sawdust strewn over the floor or drunks from the night before passed out under the lip of the bar, but the old wood floorboards, picnic tables, and booths hadn't been refinished in decades, and the scent of almost a century worth of spilled beer had permeated them. As I followed Rynn inside, the scent of stale beer hit me—but, pleasantly and surprisingly, not the scent of urine.

Lucky for us, 1:00 p.m. on a Sunday was slow. Besides a few back-packers who'd managed to crawl out of bed to nurse their Saturday night hangovers, there was no one here.

Even so, I pulled my hood down further over my face and slouched over as we headed for the bar. I glanced over at the open garage-style windows, open to the street outside because of the warm weather. "Are you sure no one will find us here?" I said to Rynn. We still had no idea who had tried to sabotage us at the university.

He shook his head. "Not even the elven spy networks. They hate this kind of place. Even if they know we're here they won't do much."

"Why do they hate bars?"

"Not bars, this kind of bar. Old, historied, *human*. Besides, it was built at the turn of the century from the old-growth forests. It takes centuries for the feeling it gives elves to fade. Even if they wanted to, they won't come in. We're safe for now."

I shook my head—not just at him but at the beer selection. Corona was not on the menu, so I settled for a lager on tap. We took our drinks and slid into one of the many empty booths in the back, as far away from the windows as we could get.

"All right, so spill. Who do you think tried to sabotage us?"

Rynn had refused to tell me on the way over. "The elves," he said now.

"What? Why?" My paranoia was rubbing off on Rynn. "That makes no sense. They're the ones who hired me to get the armor."

"Why do the elves do anything? Different factions, a disagreement amongst themselves on policy. Back at the university when we were leaving the museum I picked up on their scent, and it's faint but layered on the journal. Green, not unlike the forests and trees. It fits with their methods; elves like nothing more than to control the flow of information." He nodded at the book. "It also explains why they didn't outright steal Jebe's journal. Elves can't steal, not outright—or lie. They use other forms of deception. There is something inside there they don't want us to find."

Considering the sparse dossier they'd given me, it wasn't so far-fetched. "Okay, I get that they want to keep information hidden, but then how do they expect me . . . us," I corrected, "to find their damn suit?"

"Because human bureaucrats make so much more sense?"

He had a point. I felt Rynn nudge me with something under the table. It was a gray-blue windbreaker he must have brought with him from the jeep. Not a bad idea. Blond girl in black hoodie and cargo jacket walks in; generic gray-blue windbreaker walks out. "My methods are starting to rub off on you."

"I've never had a problem admitting the things you have a talent for. Hiding in plain sight and getting lost in a crowd are two of them. It's your lack of planning."

I took off the pink hoodie and slid the windbreaker on. "Like I said, your lack of planning is my thinking on my feet."

Normally Rynn would have continued to argue against my more laissez-faire methods, but this time he sat back and took a pull of his beer. I could count the times on my hand we'd been out at a bar and Rynn hadn't been the bartender.

"In this case your thinking on your feet might have been the better set of methods. I can't believe I didn't pick up on them from the start." He took another drink and hazarded a glance outside the large windows. "They know me and my methods too well."

I frowned. I could also count the times on my hand Rynn hadn't been a step ahead—of me or the competition.

He glanced back at me. "I rarely dealt with them one at a time. The elves like to pretend they are a unified mind. They aren't. There are layers and layers to their dealings with outsiders."

"No offense, but the elves don't strike me as the most competent bunch when it comes to dealing with the real world," I said. That was certainly the impression I'd gotten from Rynn, and the one elf I knew, Carpe, hadn't exactly challenged that perception. Carpe might be a world-class computer hacker and programmer, but when it came to the real world, well . . .

"Incompetent isn't the right way to think about it. The elves are individuals, just like you or me. The trick with them is that they always pretend they are one unit, even when they're trying to stab each other in the back."

I frowned. What was it Rynn had said about the elves? That they ended up tying up any and all of their regulatory responsibilities in what amounted to parking fines? "So they spend just as much time fighting amongst themselves as the rest of the supernaturals?"

Rynn nodded. "They never break the rules, but they are masters at figuring out how to bend them to their whims. It doesn't always work out in their favor, but that doesn't stop them from trying."

"So what? One of them wants us to find the suit, another one doesn't?"

Rynn inclined his head. "It's hard to say. Think of it as a chessboard. It could be someone doesn't want us to find the suit at all, or that someone else doesn't want us to know anything about it—and that's only considering two differing opinions. It could be a third group or individual hopes we stumble into something completely different. Hiding and censoring information using minor rule infractions is the easiest way for them to disrupt the chess pieces while still playing by the rules."

The more I learned . . . "How did you end up working for them in the first place? I mean, no offense, but you—" I'd been about to say that he hated backdoor espionage almost as much as thieves. "Your code of ethics doesn't seem to fit." I didn't know if that was an incubus thing— not if Artemis was any indication—but it was a Rynn thing.

"Because you don't figure it out until you've been working for them for a few decades. They're as good at hiding their intentions and lying to your face as they are at disrupting the chess table, all while you're sitting across from them, watching them do it."

"Why play chess when you can win by moving the chessboard and distracting the players," I said. Rynn nodded.

The more I learned about the elves, the more I was starting to wish I'd avoided this job. "Is there any way to know what they're after?"

Rynn shook his head. "No. They lie about everything with half-truths and wording. The ones in power can't be trusted. It's layers and layers of games and manipulations with them; not even the best spies in the supernatural world ever truly figure out what the elves are really up to. Most of the community never sees the duplicity, only a subtly incompetent group of politicians enforcing parking tickets—and even that I think is an intentional device. They know me. They'll be more careful than usual."

Wait a minute . . . that was assuming we didn't have someone on the inside who owed me one hell of a favor. "What if we knew an elf we could ask to snoop around for us?"

"Carpe?" Rynn snorted. "Alix, I think you'll be surprised how little you'll get out of him."

Yeah, we'd see about that. I took out a cell—a burner for this exact purpose—and entered Carpe's number. "Watch me." The elf owed me, especially considering he'd almost gotten me killed—twice.

The phone rang twice before Carpe answered. "If you have this number there's a good chance I don't want you calling me," he said.

"Fuck off, Carpe. I'm calling in favors. *Multiple* favors."

There was a pause. "What favors?" he said, in a decidedly unfriendly voice.

What *favors*? That's what I got for socializing with good-for-nothing

World Quest sorcerers. "That favor for coercing me into getting that spell book for you. The one you never paid me for. Doesn't that go against your elven creed or code of ethics?"

Silence. And another pause. "That was a matter of life and death," he said, his voice still carrying that formal and distant tone.

Oh for crying out loud. "So is this, you Lord of the Rings reject. *Mine* if I don't deliver."

There was a drawn-out sigh on Carpe's end. "The dragon isn't going to kill you if you can't retrieve—whatever it is you're after this time."

"Maybe, maybe not. But he will kill me if I don't put in the effort. So start spilling on what you think you know about my job. And while you're at it, you can tell me what the hell is going on with all of your bureaucratic elven Grand Poobahs."

"Look," Carpe said, raising his voice to cut me off. "I sympathize with you, Alix, really, but I had to get you to steal that book because the world was at stake. Don't you care about saving the world?"

The condescending tone in his voice made me just about throw the phone. Who the hell did Carpe think he was?

"*Told you so,*" Rynn mouthed at me before taking another sip of his beer.

I settled for glaring at him instead of throwing the phone. I put the receiver back to my ear. "No. Frankly I don't care about saving the world, I care about my own skin."

Carpe snorted. "Okay, I know you're selfish, but even you and your friends need somewhere to live."

Who the hell was the person I was talking to, and what had he done with Carpe? "Maybe I think the world could deal with a little reshuffling."

There was another pause. For a second I thought Carpe might have hung up, then he responded. "Good thing I made you get me that book then." His voice was cold, as if we barely knew each other. I think that pissed me off more than the refusal to even entertain my favor.

"Why, you—" I stopped myself. Whatever was going on with Carpe, yelling at him wasn't going to get me anywhere.

I lowered my own voice. "You know what, Carpe? We didn't have to stick around and help you. We could have stolen a jeep, a boat, had Rynn call in a few favors. I helped you because you were supposed to be my friend. I figured if you had gone to all those lengths, it had to be important—so important that as your *friend* I didn't even consider leaving you on your own, because as my *friend*, I assumed you'd do the same thing."

"You punched me in the face and threatened to shoot me!"

"Yeah, because you fucking deserved it!" People were looking again.

"See you in World Quest, Owl," Carpe said, no trace of my gaming buddy of the last two years in there at all. I heard the line disconnect as he hung up on me.

"I don't want to say I told you so," Rynn started as I sat there staring at the burner.

I downed a large portion of my beer. "No kidding." I am a fucking lousy judge of character. . . .

Rynn sighed. "I hate to say it, but it might not be entirely him. I don't like him better than the others, but he didn't strike me as a political climber. Chances are good whichever elf or elves are involved know of your connection. Since you have the journal now, it might be that they've upped the stakes, or maybe they thought of it and cornered him earlier."

So much for loyal friends. I swear to God, if you can't get to know a person's soul raiding dungeons in World Quest, where the *hell* can you?

"I just expected more from Carpe," I said, glancing back up at Rynn. "Does that make me an idiot?"

Rynn had known me long enough not to toss me empty platitudes. "No," he said, considering his words carefully. "It means you don't know elves."

Maybe Rynn was right. Maybe the elves were putting the squeeze on Carpe, or had something on him. Maybe I'd do the same thing in his case.

I didn't think I would, though. Not even if push came to shove. There are just some things that aren't worth it. Or maybe I just don't have a hell of a lot left to lose. . . . Funny thing about having the carpet yanked out from under you. You start to reevaluate your priorities in life.

Maybe I'd start my own smear campaign at the Dead Orc . . . tell everyone Carpe had a couple resurrection scrolls lying around for the taking . . . he was a powerful sorcerer, it might take an army of newbies to defeat him, but where there was the empty promise of treasure and a litany of new players, there was a way.

"Well, now what?" Rynn asked, breaking my musings over ways to mete out righteous vengeance on Carpe.

I sighed and took out the card Bindi had delivered to me. Despite not having any trace of pheromones on it that Rynn could detect, I still gave an involuntary shiver as I opened it and placed it between us on the table. "Well, since I'm getting desperate . . ." I waited for a nod from Rynn before I typed Alexander's number into my burner and hit the Call button.

The phone barely made the second ring before someone answered.

"Why, hello, my little bird. Fancy hearing from you, to what do I owe this pleasure?" Alexander said in his thick French accent.

Rynn rolled his eyes.

"Cut the crap, Alexander. I'm not in the mood—but you probably knew that, otherwise you wouldn't have sent Bindi to come find us."

"My, my," Alexander tsked. "Someone certainly has you in a fury. I'm going to wager a guess your problems are of the . . . long-eared variety?"

I snorted but exchanged a glance with Rynn. Like I was giving him anything that good information-wise in an opening shot. "How the hell did you know we were in town, Alexander?"

He feigned a sigh. "Can't I keep tabs on my favorite birds?"

"No. You can't. You're a vampire. 'Bird' is just a euphemism for fried chicken. You've wanted to kill me for almost two years, Alexander. I fail to see what's changed."

"Perhaps I'm willing to bury our differences. Maybe I have simply bored of our game."

"Game? Trying to assassinate me is not a fucking game, you tooth-less French dandy!"

"Just a minute, Alexander," Rynn said, interrupting me before I could do any more damage. He then reached across the table and muted the phone. I *knew* Alexander would bait me, and I knew I should have kept my cool. It's always harder to follow advice than give it. A *game* trying to kill me and Captain.

Rynn arched an eyebrow, asking if I was ready.

I took a deep breath and counted to five—long counts—before nodding. Rynn took it off mute.

"All right, Alexander," Rynn said. "You've had your fun. You have five seconds to tell us what it is you want before I hang up the phone."

Alexander sighed. "For a species who feeds off lust, you incubi are as boring—"

Didn't get to hear what Alexander was going to compare incubi to. Rynn hung up.

A moment later the phone rang. This time I picked it up.

Alexander didn't bother with the niceties or insults this time. "I want a truce."

Yeah, not falling for that bait again. "We have a truce, one you interpret as provided you or one of your minions doesn't get caught—"

"*And* I acknowledge that I am fully the party at fault for said transgressions and offer my sincere apologies."

I pressed Mute and glanced up at Rynn, whose expression I couldn't quite read. To actually get Alexander and the Paris boys off my case, not just pretending to not be trying to kill me in public, but actually not trying to kill me . . . Or torture my cat . . . But there's a saying about three times and a fool.

It was Rynn who unmuted the phone. "Vampires don't need to keep their word, Alexander," he said. "Nothing that starts off human does," he said in an even, neutral voice—no confrontation, simply stating a fact.

"Ahhh" came Alexander's smooth voice. "But there are other ways."

Rynn muted the phone again and glanced up at me. "He's not lying," he said grudgingly. "There are types of magic that can force all parties to keep to the deal. They're expensive though."

Expensive. "In other words, Alexander is going to want something awful good out of this."

Rynn gave me a single nod.

I thought about it. What the hell, I had nothing to lose from listening. I unmuted the phone. "All right, supreme cockroach, you've piqued my curiosity. *Hypothetically*, suppose I'm entertaining the idea of believing you. What do you want?"

To his credit, Alexander ignored my jibe. "It is really not so complicated an arrangement. I wish you to make sure certain parties do not succeed in upsetting our current . . . status quo."

Alexander had said as much in his letter. "Would have pegged you as the kind of vampire who'd like being out in the open. Munch on whoever you want, lacing entire cities with that god-awful pheromone, star on a reality TV show."

"Those of us who have survived a few hundred years have no interest in becoming the outlet for righteous human vengeance. It is a simple equation: we're high enough up on the supernatural food chain to prove a challenge, with enough weaknesses to exploit. We like the supernatural community, but . . . Do not let your incubus take offense, but . . . how do you say? We don't like them that much."

I couldn't help it—I snorted at that. Selfish preservation and looking out for number one. Sounded like Alexander and every other vampire I'd met. Still . . .

"I don't know, Alexander. I have the utmost faith in your ability to crawl back into the woodwork when the need arises."

"Ahh, you wound me," Alexander said, adding his brand of false drama in. "Though I suppose some vampires might adapt, what with the current cultural predisposition to violence and technology. Some may do quite well and run over the cities. The food supply would become a concern, 'dry up,' so to speak. Then we'd turn on each other; as I'm certain you've ascertained, we are not the most altruistic bunch. I suppose it would be no time until a vampire got hungry enough to feed on another, then well— Oh, my goodness, I forgot!" he said with feigned surprise. "My apologies, Owl. You know exactly what happens when we begin to feed off each other. You do remember how well that went last time, with the vampire Sabine."

Yeah . . . a new vampire that had become incredibly powerful a lot faster than she should have been able to. And gone crazy. Not a good combination.

"Trust me, Owl, despite our many differences and mutual dislike, we have a mutual goal. Being killed by a self-made vampire hunter while I sleep or having to fend off my own crazed starving kind does not appeal to me. I like the world the way it is," he said, dropping the thin veneer of civility he usually used with me.

"Alexander," Rynn warned. "You've told us why you want to help us, but not the how."

"No fun," Alexander tsked. "Suppose, Owl, you are starting to walk in your namesakes' footsteps and philosophize—or whatever your foul-mouthed brain calls it—apologies," Alexander said. "Old habits die hard, even for vampires."

"No shit."

"The question you need to ask yourself, little Owl and decidedly dour companion, is what the elves who do not wish this current status quo want. And, to show how sincere I am in this venture, I will offer you a clue. They were the same ones behind those artifacts emerging from the City of the Dead."

I frowned at Rynn and muted the call—again. "For a group of su-pernaturals who feign neutrality, these guys suck. Or don't care whether they're caught anymore."

His eyes narrowed. "I hate to say it, but in some ways it makes sense; they are the ones with the archives. If there was any mention of that place and what it held, it would have been kept there."

And Alexander had been screwed over by whoever had been behind the attempt to raise a zombie army in L.A.—and kill me with an ancient curse. If it had been the elves . . .

Rynn took the phone and unmuted it. "An accusation like that, Alexander, would need proof."

"And I am willing to bargain it—and so much more—*if* you accept my truce."

Rynn gave a reluctant shrug. Not the most ideal scenario, working with Alexander, but it wasn't like we had a lot of options—or supernaturals—offering help. There was one more thing I needed to ask though. "Why? Why me, Alexander? You hate me."

"Because begrudgingly I have to admit that you have a bad habit of following a code of ethics the opposition has no intention or interest in observing. Sometimes it's better to side with an honest enemy than entertain a camaraderie with parties who may or may not stab you in the back."

While I was still processing that answer, I heard a click on the other end.

"Goddamn it." He'd hung up on me. Fantastic. I didn't know if I was more concerned that Alexander got the last word in or that I was seriously considering striking a deal with the homicidal cockroach. I finished off my beer while I mulled it over a little more. "What do you think?" I asked Rynn once I'd put the empty glass down.

Rynn opened his mouth to offer his insight, but he didn't get the chance to say anything before my own phone began to ring. I pulled it out of my pocket; probably Lady Siyu to yell at me again, damn it.

I frowned as I got a look at the screen. Instead of the hissing cobra icon I expected, there was a number I didn't recognize. I turned the phone around and showed it to Rynn. He raised his eyebrows and shook his head.

Shit, what now? "Hello?" I said.

"Alix Hiboux" came the clipped female voice.

I recognized the voice, and it definitely wasn't a pleasant memory. It was a female IAA agent, the same one who'd been waiting for me at my apartment in Seattle a month ago. The one who'd pulled a gun on me and tried to recruit me to go after World Quest with the promise of a blood money pardon.

"I take it your trip to India and Nepal was productive?"

She'd also never given me a name.

"Why hello, Black Suit Number 31, and how might you be hoping to ruin my day today?" I mouthed, "*IAA*" at Rynn. He took another swig of his beer and swore. I agreed wholeheartedly with the sentiment, and if I'd still had a beer, I might have joined him.

We were having enough trouble with elves and vampires; the last thing I needed was to toss the IAA into the mix right now.

If the IAA suit was at all rattled by my less than respectful tone, she didn't let on.

"You can call me Agent Dennings, Ms. Hiboux."

Rynn gestured for me to hurry it up. Probably worried about them tracing my phone. I'd be ditching it after this. "Your name doesn't answer my question, like, at all."

"It's quite simple. This is a progress update call, you'll remember those from your PhD?"

Oh, that was a whole new level of reminiscing anxiety. "I think I'd rather deal with the vampires."

"My superiors have decided you're not moving quickly enough on the World Quest project."

I snorted. Rynn once again made the gesture for me to wrap it up. I held up my hand, placed the phone on the table, and set it on speaker-phone. "Ummm, apparently there's been a huge fucking misunderstanding," I said.

"I assure you, there isn't."

"Yet you just spoke to me as if I was your employee. Let me clear that up for you real fast. On no planet, in no universe, on no deserted island where the IAA is the only source of clean water and I'd be sentenced to a slow dehydrating death, could you convince me to work for the IAA." Rynn was checking the rest of the bar now.

Dennings was stalling.

Even so, I needed to know what it was she thought she had on me. She was many unpalatable things, but stupid wasn't one of them. If she was acting like I was back in the IAA fold, she—or the IAA—figured they had leverage. "Correct me if I'm wrong, but I'm pretty sure I didn't take your job—because, you know, your organization has an abysmal track record of paying the fuck up."

"We prefer the term *contractor* in this case, not *employee*."

"No benefits and crap pay? Yeah, that sounds like the IAA." Rynn was scanning the windows now. He'd seen something. "Ah, let me think about that. No. Besides, I already have an employer. A Japanese red dragon who won't be very happy with your assumptions. Neither will the Naga dressed in a suit. You might think you have teeth, but let me assure you, she does. And they're actually poisonous."

"Be that as it may." She cleared her throat, and I detected a nervous hitch in her breath. "We wish to see more results."

"Well, sometimes I wish I had a pink unicorn and free rein of the British museum, but as neither of those are likely to happen—"

"The terms and our conditions are nonnegotiable," she said.

Rynn got my attention and shook his head at me, brow furrowed. Time was up, we needed to move.

I cleared my throat. "Apparently, Agent Dennings, you are under the impression that I am your bitch. Let me assure you, I am not."

Dennings let out a dramatic, exasperated breath. "Yes, well, I told my supervisors you would say something along those lines. Good thing we have backups."

I snorted. "I saw your mercenaries. A little rough round the edges, definitely not into preserving archaeological sites, but then again, they actually think you might pay." For all I knew the IAA did pay them, what with their being small and heavily armed private armies.

"Funny you should say that. And you're right. I don't think they can find the World Quest designers either." And with that, Dennings hung up.

I stared at the phone, then at Rynn. "Am I missing something?"

Then it occurred to me. The IAA made no bones about their displeasure with my motivation, and they'd admitted they weren't thrilled with the skill set of the motivated folks . . .

If you were a soulless, evil organization that wanted things to move faster, what would you do? Shit.

I grabbed Captain's carrier and strapped it on fast. "We need to go—now," I said. I could feel my hands shaking. Captain, either hearing something in my voice or sensing something was wrong, let out a soft, inquisitive mew.

"Alix, what do you know that I don't? You're terrified," Rynn asked, but he also threw his jacket on and once again scanned our surroundings.

I checked the door and the open garage windows. There was no sign of the zebras, but then again, this is what they did. "Rynn, I think the IAA sent the mercenaries to find—"

I didn't get a chance to finish my sentence, on account of the pinging clink of something metal striking the floor. Both of us turned in time to see a round metal ball roll through the doorway. The bar was quiet enough that everyone heard, and for a moment deadening silence filled the floor as everyone fixated on the tennis-ball-sized silver canister. The vortex of the storm, where nothing moves or happens.

It didn't last long.

The first shouts sounded as the metal canister hissed. Smoke billowed out the sides, filling the bar. The violent scrape of chairs and tables followed as people clamored for the two exits, managing to block both of them. A few bright people squeezed out the open windows.

I started that way, but Rynn grabbed me and pulled me back, pushing me under a table as two more smoke grenades landed in the bar, further obscuring the scene of panic unraveling. I pulled the blue windbreaker hood down over my face and rifled through my bag. Good thing I came prepared for this sort of thing. I pulled out my goggles and gas mask, usually for dealing with vampires, and fixed them to my face.

The chaos intensified as folks from upstairs got wind of the smoke. Convinced there was a fire, they began flooding the stairs, putting more pressure on the exits, limbs and shouts mixing with the thick smoke coiling through the room.

A few people tripped over tables and chairs. It wasn't an attack. It was exactly what it seemed like—a smoke screen. Which begged the question; where were the mercenaries?

Problem with a smoke screen was the prey could use it too.

I turned to Rynn under our still-standing table. "Well, if there was ever a good time to see how well my hide-in-plain-sight plan works—"

Rynn stopped me. "It's a trap, Alix. They'll be waiting outside."

"And they can take their chances spotting me amongst all the other backpackers."

But Rynn gave another shake of his head and nodded toward the windows, where people were scrambling out now. I still saw no sign of the mercenaries, or whoever had lobbed the smoke grenades.

I spotted a group of students moving in a herd and holding hands so as not to get lost in the smoke as they moved toward the back door. I was sure they wouldn't mind another fellow backpacker joining in. Again I started for them but Rynn stopped me, more forcefully than he had the first time.

"Come on, I see our opening," I told him and nodded toward the students. In a few moments they'd be out.

But Rynn only shook his head. "They won't be looking for you. They'll be looking for me. They probably already have an idea where I am depending on the range of the equipment they're carrying."

I swore. "What about splitting up and meeting at a rendezvous?"

Another more insistent shake of his head. "If the IAA gave them halfway decent intelligence on you—" He gave me a hard look. "These are professionals, Alix, they won't give you a chance to escape. If you think the IAA is bad, these people really won't take no for an answer."

Well, regardless of chances, we were fast losing our window of opportunity. Against all odds the bar and hostel had emptied, and soon the smoke would clear enough for anyone waiting to come inside.

I caught sight of a group of men across the road exiting a fire truck. But there were no sirens, and though the men milling around were dressed in fireman gear . . .

"Shit. Rynn, it's them—the firemen across the road, the Zebras. I recognize the big one from Nepal," I whispered. The one who'd passed me on the stairs.

Rynn swore. "I figured as much. I think I have a better way," he said, and pulled me behind him as he started for the stairs that led up into the old hostel.

When there's smoke, typically people don't run up into a burning building, they run down; we could use it for cover. Not a bad idea, all things considered. I checked to make sure Captain was still okay. He was not happy with the smoke, but otherwise . . . well . . . himself.

When we reached the first landing I hazarded a glance back. Whether they'd seen us run or it was a matter of timing, the fireman-dressed mercenaries entered the bar. It looked like five, but with the smoke still filling the room, I couldn't be sure.

Regardless, the smoke had no effect on my ears. I heard orders—not in English but in Afrikaans—being barked out as we disappeared around the corner. Rynn tried the first door we came across on the windowed side of the hostel. "Locked," he said, and moved on to the next. I followed his lead. The first three I tried were locked as well. Locking your door in the middle of a fire—shows how trusting the hostelling world is. . . .

I heard the lock break as Rynn lost his patience and forced one of the doors open.

The room had been abandoned quickly, clothes left in piles and bags upended as people scrambled to grab their valuables and electronics before leaving. The window to the dorm room was bolted down to prevent exactly what we planned to do, but Rynn made short work of the latches before I could reach for my lock picks. Benefits to being an incubus with inhuman strength.

The window opened up to an alley—not droppable, but then again, that's what rope is for, which Rynn had had the forethought to pack for just such an emergency.

"I think it's clear," Rynn said after taking a quick survey out the window. "Regardless, even if they are watching, they won't be able to maneuver in the alley."

Rynn was testing the rope attachment when my phone buzzed. I swore and pulled it out to silence it; I did not need the mercenaries hearing it.

Carpe. Son of a— I should have known. Lousy timing; I was thinking it was a species trait.

I declined the call, only to have a text appear next.

Not that way. They're covering the windows.

Oh for Christ's sake. I hit Redial.

He answered before the first ring had a chance to go through. "Now you want to help us, you miscreant elf?"

"Can the insults and just listen. I've been watching the South Africans online for a couple days now. I don't think they're on to me, but these guys are packing some serious tech and muscle, and they're totally on to your boyfriend."

I heard noise on the stairs. "We figured that out, thank you very much," I whispered into the phone. Rynn nodded to me to close the door and I did, as carefully and silently as I could, then reinforced it with one of the cheap metal chairs that furnished the dorm. "And why the hell couldn't you have mentioned the South Africans were watching earlier?"

"Because unlike you, they aren't fuckups. They've been using code words and keep radio silence. And I couldn't tell you before because I'm being watched."

I paused. That was what Rynn had suggested.

I heard footsteps in the hall, followed by the sound of metal jarring against wood. The South Africans were trying the doors now. "Carpe, if you are trying to fuck me over, I swear to God—"

"If you don't do exactly what I say right now, you'll be in no position to exact revenge from whatever cage the mercenaries put you in."

I covered the mic and turned to Rynn, who'd been listening. He was watching the commotion on the street below. "As much as I hate to admit it, the elf is right, Alix. The mercenaries have the streets and external building covered. We need another way out."

Rocks and hard places . . . I uncovered the mic. "All right, Carpe, shoot."

"Okay, I've got your location. There's a side passage in the room, inside the closet."

I checked. Besides some towels, bags, and bed linens . . . "I don't see it," I said.

"It's behind the wall. An old laundry chute that was covered over—accident hazard—but the pulley lift was never removed. Too expensive. The side passage below is covered over too; it's behind the walls and was taken off the official blueprints decades ago to avoid building code questions."

Rynn pushed me aside and checked the wall. Then he took a knife out and started to cut through the drywall.

I listened for the mercenaries. The sound of doors being tried was getting closer. I fixed my eyes on the door and hoped that the door handle wouldn't start turning.

There was still something bothering me about what Carpe had said. "Carpe," I said while waiting for Rynn to cut through the drywall, "why would the elves care about you warning me about the IAA?"

"Because who do you think told them you were there?"

I went cold. Rynn was almost through now, but I could have sworn I heard the door across from ours being tried. We were next. "That makes no sense—the elves hired us to get the suit."

"And some of the higher-ups really don't want you to find it. I don't know why. I just know they're watching me close and passed on your whereabouts to the IAA."

Son of a bitch. Why the hell would they hire us to get the suit, then try to stop us?

I heard the door to the dorm turn then jiggle as it met with resistance from the lock, then the metal chair. The attempts abruptly stopped, but instead of shouting, silence filled the hall. I think that made it worse; the shouting would have been easier. I was really starting to hate competent bad guys.

"Just a sec, Carpe," I said, and put the call on hold before shoving my phone back in my pocket. "Found us," I whispered at Rynn.

He abandoned the knife and, holding onto the closet doorway, kicked the drywall in. "They can bill the South Africans," he said.

Sure enough there was a passage inside, along with an old rope-and-pulley-system metal laundry bucket. Rynn slid through first, testing the rope and rusted metal crate. It held. He waved for me to join him. Not exactly the most stable getaway, but it had to be better than facing off with the South African mercenaries. I grabbed Rynn around his middle before stepping onto the bucket. It rocked and squeaked on the rusted hinges, but it held both our weight and Captain's.

"How far a drop?" I asked.

"I wouldn't look."

I swore and made sure I had a good handle on Rynn's jacket.

"Since when do you have a fear of heights?"

"Since I started letting you come on my jobs. Shit!" The sound of wood cracking and the pop of metal hinges came from inside the dorm room.

Before I could register anything resembling an opinion on the matter, Rynn cut the pulley's anchoring rope, and the bucket started its rapid descent down.

"Son of a—" Rynn clamped a hand over my mouth to stop me from yelling anything more. I think I heard a commotion above us, but I was too busy hitting the ground. The bucket struck the basement floor, and a cloud of dust rose up around us. For the most part, Rynn absorbed the shock from the impact—wonders of not being human. Captain, not impressed with either the landing or the cloud of dust, let out an indignant mew.

"Sorry, buddy, trust me, neither of us wanted that to happen. Blame him." Captain snorted—whether in agreement with me or dust in his nose I didn't know and didn't care.

I took a look around. From what I could see in the very low light coming down the hole in the shaft, we were down in the closed-up guts of the building, amongst stuff that probably hadn't been seen for a good few decades. The rodents, bugs, and dust had had a field day. I found a spot under the rafters that was out of the way and hopefully out of sight of any flashlights from above. If the mercenaries weren't in the room yet, it would be moments.

Now where to go? I pulled my phone back out. "Carpe, are you still there?"

"To your left—there's a shortcut, it'll circumvent the mercenaries."

I felt around in the low light. "It's a wall, Carpe, a stupid wall. I'm not magic."

"Feel around the corners—there should be a latch at the top. It's an old rum runners' route from Prohibition. It'll take you out to the water. They won't know it's there, I promise."

They might not know now, but they would soon. I made Rynn check, since I'm all of five four. He found said latch, and, with a push from both of us, the hinges creaked and the door swung open, sending a metallic, moldy taste of stale air our way. I covered my mouth and nose with my sleeve and pulled my gas mask back out. I ducked out of the way as flashlight beams were aimed down. The last thing I needed was to be hit with a chemical dart of unknown origin.

Rynn stepped into the passage and shone his flashlight, illuminating a brick tunnel that was damp and slick with groundwater from above and a shallow run of water pooling in the bottom. We could see cracks where the bricks had buckled from decades of settling, but otherwise it was empty. More importantly, it continued as far as the light path stretched.

"It'll take you to the freight docks," Carpe said.

"And from there?"

"I got you out. If you two can't handle it from there, then you deserve the mercenaries. See you on World Quest, Byzantine. Carpe out." And with that lovely sentiment, my World Quest buddy extraordinaire hung up.

With friends like Carpe . . .

More banging sounded upstairs, and a pair of light beams shone above before being aimed down. No time for considering our options. I followed Rynn into the tunnel and shut the door.

I started to search for something, anything, to block the door. Rynn found it—a pile of broken and discarded crates. Good enough. I grabbed one of the pieces and wedged it in as tight as I could on the hinge side of the door, then followed it with two more. I stepped back and regarded my work. It'd keep them out for a while, but not forever.

I refixed my gas mask and goggles before turning my flashlight on so there were two sources of light.

Definitely time to run.

We set off at a jog. Carpe hadn't said how long this tunnel was, but I hoped it wasn't more than a few kilometers. If it was, well, my cardio had improved over the past few months, but it was far from good enough to handle a serious run.

I also really didn't want to see what the mercenaries wanted with me—or Rynn. I forced myself to keep pace as we ran for the end and the water, hopefully without the South Africans trailing behind us.

Carpe hadn't sold me out. Part of me was happy about that. The other? Maybe I was just being paranoid, but Carpe had played his part on the phone just a little too well. I wondered how far our friendship stretched when it came to the elves..

For once I'd survived an encounter with the bad guys without being beaten up. That had to be a win for me, but then again, I now had both the elves and the IAA to contend with. Two birds that were going to require two very different stones.

I sure hoped Nadya was having better luck in Tokyo.

8

BREAD AND THE JAPANESE CIRCUS

Midnightish back in Vegas

We stumbled into the Japanese Circus around midnight. I'd spent the flight poring over Jebe's journal and what I'd been able to copy off the university servers. After our run through the rain sewers of Vancouver, followed by an uncomfortable helicopter ride to the airport with a pilot who wouldn't stop staring at our mud-covered clothes, we made it home. At this point though, I really didn't care.

"Of all the times you could have used your incubus powers," I said.

"There was no point. He was going to take us to the airport regardless, and he probably won't want to admit we were even in there."

"He certainly didn't make an effort to hide that fact."

"He didn't have to."

I noticed a free spot by the bar out by the pool—the Garden Café. It was still hot despite the evening hour, so people were avoiding the outdoors in favor of the air-conditioned venues inside. There was one nymph behind the bar I recognized. Fantastic. The one thing I appreciated about nymphs? No need for small talk. They didn't really have the muscle and nerve development for speaking. Might be pretty, but they were still ghouls.

"I need to debrief with security," Rynn said beside me. "I'm not happy with how quickly the IAA tried to push you around—I expected it at some point, just not so soon. I want to make sure whatever mercenaries they send next can't get in."

That sounded just fine to me. I started for the bar.

"And don't get drunk," Rynn called after me.

I waved over my shoulder. I doubted very much I'd be paying attention to that piece of advice. "I do not start a bar fight in every bar I visit," I called without turning around or looking back.

"No, but you have a bad habit of ending your fights there," Rynn called after me. "And don't let Siyu find you in those clothes."

"I'll clean up after that drink." I didn't need to see Rynn's wry expression to know it was there. I was going to need that drink before attempting to clean up Captain. He'd been getting restless ever since I'd made him crawl his muddied self into the carrier.

I exited into the pool area and grabbed a seat at the garden bar before letting Captain out in all his muddied glory. I figured the layers of grime Captain was sporting couldn't do too much damage to the patio furniture. Captain lost no time finding a spot to dig in the garden, and I lost no time ordering a beer from the nymph. Out of all the supernaturals that worked at the Japanese Circus, I'd decided I preferred the nymphs—outside Rynn, that is. They never seemed to judge me; they always handed me my beer with a smile, not the once-overs I got from various other species, especially the radish and frog demons. Then again, that might just be their lack of facial nerves.

For all I knew there could be an onslaught of prejudice and judgment behind those pretty green eyes and genial smile. I doubted it though. Killian, as his nametag read, brought my beer way too fast to be nursing any well-hidden contempt.

I settled into my seat and tried to enjoy the quiet. I was on my second Corona, staring out at the empty garden where Captain was rolling in the grass, trying desperately to scrape the mud off, when I became vaguely aware of my phone buzzing.

It was Rynn. He'd been gone what? A half hour now?

I answered the phone. "Tell me there's good news," I said.

"There's been a security breach," Rynn said, his voice strained. "Some of the cameras in the lobby and main casino floor were accessed and are being monitored from off-site. We're trying to trace it now."

I almost let it go, but there was something in his voice besides just the strain of the last few days. "What are you not telling me?"

There was an uncharacteristic pause. "There might have been some fallout from Delhi," he said carefully.

I frowned. "More fallout?" We'd both already seen the news footage. I took a sip of my beer and glanced up at the TV screen. I spit my beer out over the bar.

Oh no.

I reached over and grabbed the TV remote before Killian could stop me, despite his best efforts.

It was blurry on account of the low-quality traffic camera, and you couldn't quite see my face, but it was me. Crawling out of a New Delhi sewer and tossing a Molotov cocktail back inside . . . then diving out of the way to avoid the flames from the oil embalming that had gone up like candle wicks.

That hadn't been in the newspapers. I winced. "Rynn, I think I found the New Delhi fallout," I said as I watched the sewers go up in flames. "How about I call you back," I said before hanging up.

I flipped through the channels, which all showed the same thing. One Charity Greenwoods. What the hell were they getting at? Flushing me out? Not with images that blurry. The scroll across the bottom included a few more details about me; weight, hair color, age, but nothing definitive. One thing was for sure, the various channels were very fond of the Molotov cocktail shots . . . and me diving away as the flames boiled out of the grates. If nothing else, the embalming on those priests had certainly been flammable.

I didn't regret it; letting the undead priests crawl out of the sewers would have been multitudes worse. But the resulting fire that had spread for an entire block had most definitely not been part of the plan. Luckily the fire had been mostly contained and there weren't any casualties being reported, but still. . . .

My phone began to buzz again on the bar. Not Rynn, but a number I did recognize this time around. I needed to ditch it—and soon. Too many people had this number now. "Dennings," I said, answering.

"Hiboux. I take it you've seen the evening news?"

"Bad shots, awfully blurry, didn't catch my winning smile. You guys are losing your touch in the surveillance department."

"Just a reminder that we expect you to start delivering."

"Really?" I took a sip of my beer to give myself a pause. "Because I think it's a sign of something else."

"Oh?" Dennings said in her condescending tone.

"All this tells me is that you're running out of leads," I said, and hung up before she could add anything else.

I continued to watch myself, over and over, tossing the cocktail into the sewer and running before I could see the flames burn through the grates, all the way down the street. I flipped through the channels and watched as various reporters tried to analyze one Charity Greenwoods. Well, there was one passport and set of credit cards that was about to be shredded . . . and burned . . . then dumped down the garbage disposal. After a few reruns, even I had to admit my antics really lost their touch. I flipped to the Discovery Channel instead. Killian, if he'd been watching, didn't say anything.

I waited until I finished my beer and watched some cute, large African lions maim their prey before calling Rynn back. "They're getting desperate," I said as soon as I heard him pick up. Mercenaries, not too subtle threats, and now a smear campaign. The IAA was digging far into their card deck. I didn't think it was bottomless; then again, it was the IAA.

"Yes," Rynn agreed. "The problem is, when people get desperate they do stupid things."

"And try to screw me all over again." If their offer had already deteri-orated this far . . . "There is no way they'll hold up their end of the deal."

"They will—they'll just make sure they have a loophole. That spec-tacle on the international news I'm guessing is their loophole."

I think I preferred it when I was trying to burn the institution to the ground—from well outside their walls, like across the continent.

"They still haven't given out your real name or location. It's a smoke screen, meant to scrare but not incapacitate you. It means that you have time to think how you are going to play this."

I shook my head. This is why Nadya had gotten out. All the IAA did was screw over grad students. No one ever does anything about it because there's the chance you'll get one of the few cushy post doc or teaching positions and then the circle of abuse continues. . . .

Rynn kept his voice even. "They need you, and someone's figured out you aren't playing ball. This—the news cheap shot—is almost cer-tainly a knee-jerk response to the fact that you're not behaving the way they need you to. It is poor strategy, and it is going to cost them."

"How? How is it going to cost them?"

"Because it tells us just how desperate they are. By the time we're ready to deal with them, we're going to make sure that they're going to have to meet our terms, not us theirs."

I leaned over the bar. Killian lifted a fresh beer with something re-sembling a questioning gaze. I nodded. This was turning into a three-beer night. "You don't know them like I do, Rynn. They don't make stupid mistakes."

"There's a lesson I learned years ago from a general who used to abuse his commanders: take credit for their wins, blame them for their losses. This applied especially when he lost his battalions using them as cannon fodder."

"Don't those people usually win?"

"For a time," he admitted. "This one became a minor emperor."

"Not convincing me of the bad strategy here."

"The point is, eventually every monster like that needs his army one day. This minor emperor used and abused them so much that he didn't have a commander left who could—or was willing to—command what was left of his troops. The smart ones had seen the writing on the wall and deserted—while the going was still good, as you like to say."

"What happened to him—the emperor?"

"The invading army won and stuck his head on a pike—or maybe it was an anthill. The point was that well before his head was severed from his neck, the minor emperor realized that he was the sole source of his own crumbling empire."

"The IAA isn't an empire."

"No, but the analogy still stands. They've sown so much discord in their own ranks that now, when they need people, they realize they've burned all their bridges."

I shook my head. "That doesn't make them any less dangerous."

"No," Rynn agreed. "If anything it makes them more dangerous and less predictable. But when the other side doesn't have a plan, it makes it easier for us to stay a step ahead."

There was some truth to that, I had to give Rynn that.

"Rynn, I can't let the IAA get to them. This, all of this," I said, meaning the TV news coverage, "just proves it. If they get hold of human magic—*real* magic that they could use . . ." I let the thought trail off. I didn't want to add that every time someone in the world of archaeology tried to explore magic with a more hands-on approach, regardless of whether they were a student or academic, the results were always disastrous. Humans using supernatural magic? They were lucky if all it did was blow up a building. But *human* magic . . . The IAA was dangerous and abusive enough as it was, but with magic they could access . . . ?

I heard the phone muffle as he spoke to someone else. "I'm going to double-check security, make sure all the surveillance is secure one last time before it's time to meet Lady Siyu," he said.

Right. I checked the time. It was fast approaching the hour mark before our audience with the dragon lady. So pervasive was my dislike of any time I had to waste in the monster's presence that I was imagining the click of her heels everywhere I went. Only that wasn't my imagination. . . .

Shit. I swiveled in my chair only to make out Lady Siyu, immaculate black suit and all, weaving her way along the cement garden tiles, her heels clicking with a less-expensive-sounding clack than they did against the more expensive marble floors.

"Speak of the devil, looks like she brought the meeting to me," I said as I watched Lady Siyu make her way down the cement path. Her suit and heels just seemed wrong in the more natural setting.

I eyed beer number three. Normally I kept the drinking to a minimum before having to deal with Lady Siyu or Mr. Kurosawa. I took a generous swallow.

Rynn swore. "Try not to pick a fight before I get there."

"No promises," I said, before I heard the click of Rynn hanging up.

Lady Siyu stopped a few paces away from me, hands on her hips and sunglasses firmly in place, even though there was no one else in the Garden Café. "Do you have the elve's artifact yet?" Lady Siyu said. I noticed Killian had vamoosed. Smart nymph.

I watched as Captain stopped his rooting in the garden and shot his nose in the air, sniffing madly. His eyes fixated on Lady Siyu and he began to creep forward, letting out a tentative growl.

Damn it . . . I scrambled off my chair and around Lady Siyu to grab him before he could launch himself. He wasn't impressed; he squirmed against my grip, but I held on—at arm's length so he couldn't eviscerate me.

"No," I whispered as Captain twisted and tried to push his way out, keeping his eyes on Siyu the whole time.

Lady Siyu's sunglasses turned down, and I got the distinct impression she was examining my cat.

Captain, sensing the same thing, bellowed at her in all his muddy glory.

Lady Siyu took a step back—but not from Captain's bellow. Lady Siyu didn't scare nearly as easily as the vampires. It was the mess. Lady Siyu's crisp white shirt, expensive skirt, and shoes did not look like they would take well to an angry Mau's mess.

Captain wasn't stupid. He'd hit her where it hurt.

Lady Siyu offered a fanged sneer to Captain before turning her yellow gaze on me. "If you do not retrieve that artifact soon, the deal with the incubus will be null and void. Then I will wish *my* cat returned."

"Whoever gets Captain gets to clean him," I said. "Here, be my guest." It was a bluff; being passed back and forth as a bargaining chip would give Captain more of a complex than he already had, but Lady Siyu didn't need to know that.

Captain bared his teeth, set his ears back, and let out a hiss from behind my arms.

Lady Siyu hissed right back, her jaw protruding to fit the elongated fangs. Captain huddled closer to my chest. He was still growling, but the hissing stopped.

"Seriously? Hissing at a cat?"

Her lip curled, exposing a single upper fang. "I prefer the animals of *any* species around me to know their place. Come, you and the incubus are being summoned."

"Now?" I'd hoped to at least clean up.

"And I thought if you didn't bring me back an artifact, I'd get to kill you. It appears Mr. Kurosawa's whim is to watch as we live out our disappointments, over and over. Though," she said, her head tilting in a pensive gesture, "if you do ignore this summons, perhaps Mr. Kurosawa will allow me to kill you." She glanced around the garden. "On second thought, stay and drown what's left of your pitiful life in vice." And with that, she spun on her heels and headed back into the Japanese Circus.

Captain didn't come out from behind my legs until the doors had slid shut. Fantastic. I downed the remainder of my beer and placed the carrier in front of Captain. Of all the people on the planet for him to pick a fight with . . . "As if the vampires weren't bad enough. You realize I can't actually protect you from her?" I told him.

He mewed at me before settling inside, if for no reason other than to get the last arguing noise in. I shook my head and pulled my phone out to text Rynn the change in plans, then hefted Captain over my shoulder and headed back inside the Japanese Circus's immaculate lobby. We were garnering stares this time—not that there were many people lingering, but still, it was enough to make even me self-conscious.

"Paintball," I said to one couple who looked a little too long for my liking as we stood outside the elevator doors. "They added mud in the arena for realism."

They nodded as if in understanding but picked up the pace.

A woman dressed in a light pastel blue suit who had also been waiting for the elevator ahead of me gave me a long once-over and quickly took a few steps back.

"Must be my winning smile," I whispered to Captain under my breath.

Then again, I doubted any of these people would know a winning smile unless it was packaged in a wrapper they could digest and understand.

Three months ago that would have bothered me. Now? Their loss. I had people who went out of their way to see past my shell. People who couldn't be bothered to actually see the world around them? Like Rynn and Nadya said, they should be pitied.

As I watched the couple and woman retreat, it occurred to me again that even if the supernaturals did manage to crawl their way out of the proverbial closet, it might be that the people at large would decide as a collective that they didn't want to see any of it.

The elevator door opened. "Time to face the dragon, cat," I said before stepping inside the mirrored and decorated car.

—m—

Rynn was waiting for me outside the massive black-and-gold doors. So was Lady Siyu. In contrast to me and Captain, somehow, somewhere between checking security and arriving here, Rynn had managed to clean up.

I hadn't, and decided I wasn't going to bother apologizing for the bits of crumbling, stagnant mud my shoes left with each step.

Lady Siyu glared at me, then turned her attention to Rynn. "I expected an incubi to at least attempt to keep your pets cleaner than the humans do theirs."

Rynn gave me a once-over and shrugged. I just stood there, Captain slung over my shoulder, rumbling in his carrier—whether at the fact that he could smell Lady Siyu or that he wasn't out on his leash, I couldn't be sure and frankly didn't care.

Lady Siyu flared her nostrils. Apparently neither of us was rising to the bait on that one today.

She turned her back on us to push the massive doors open, the plumes of gray smoke billowing out into the hall, curling around my feet. I shivered. Despite the heat, this room always gave me the chills.

Rynn followed her in first. "I assume there is a point to this appearance besides threatening Alix and her house cat?" he asked.

"There is business to be discussed with Mr. Kurosawa. You and the thief," she added, nodding toward me.

"What about?" I asked.

"He didn't say and I didn't ask." After a moment of only the slot machines chiming around us and the click of Lady Siyu's heels against the marble floor, she added, "Mr. Kurosawa is in a mood."

Fantastic. Assuming that Mr. Kurosawa had been in good moods whenever I'd dealt with him before, I was pretty damn sure I didn't want to see his bad mood.

"If they want the artifact so badly, they'd let me get back to the damn job," I said to Rynn.

"I know," he replied. He sounded tired—something that almost never happened. And distracted.

"Are you—okay?" I hesitated over the "okay" part. I was not usually the one on the asking end of that.

He shook his head, and it occurred to me we were keeping a very respectable distance behind Lady Siyu.

"Just worn out from the political infighting. Between the elves and the IAA." He trailed off and let Lady Siyu turn a corner ahead of us before giving me a pointed stare. "I'm starting to think the two are connected. There's too much coincidence," he said, lowering his voice to the point where I didn't think even Lady Siyu would be able to detect it.

"Now you're starting to sound like me with the paranoia and conspiracy theories." Elves involved in the IAA's current witch hunt for World Quest—to what end?

Rynn took my arm gently and steered me down a corridor I hadn't realized was there, hidden from my human eyes. "To hinder us or coincide with our search? It's questionable whether they know behind their own machinations. I left this work for a reason, Alix," he added. "I wanted to avoid being dragged into supernatural plots and games."

"Do you think they'd have left you alone if you had stayed in Tokyo?" I don't know why I asked it exactly, but I did.

He inclined his head, considering, then sighed. "No. As tempting as it is to blame leaving Tokyo, it wouldn't be true. They'd have found another way to involve me—the elves, Mr. Kurosawa, or whoever else might have a stake in this game. No, I prefer this. This way at least they haven't blindsided me completely. You aren't the only one trouble has a habit of finding."

A slot machine went off beside us, and I had to do some fancy footwork to avoid touching the stream of gold coins that shot out. I swear the ghosts in a few of those things had a twisted sense of humor. Probably from being locked up in a slot machine for so long.

I caught Rynn watching me as I avoided the coins. "And there's you," he said. "If I had stayed in Tokyo, I might have avoided being dragged into the confrontation a few more months, but I wouldn't have you."

I felt the same way, though I didn't always express it eloquently. I might have said something to that effect, but we'd cleared the last corner of the maze.

Mr. Kurosawa was waiting for us on the black leather couches facing away from us. I probably would have missed him if it hadn't been for the billowing smoke—and the red, emberlike glow emanating from his skin.

I held Captain's carrier a little tighter and drew in a deep breath to calm my nerves. *All right, Alix, gird your loins and let's see what's got Mr. Kurosawa in a mood.*

"I hear you have yet to find the artifact," Mr. Kurosawa said, still facing away from us.

If there was one thing I'd learned about working with supernaturals like Mr. Kurosawa over the past few months, it was to make sure expectations were managed.

I cleared my throat. "It's not that simple," I said. "First, the IAA decided to involve themselves—"

"In other words, *no,*" Lady Siyu offered.

I stuffed my temper and started again. "Look, finding the suit the elves want so desperately while the IAA breathes down my throat is a *significant* mitigating factor." It would have helped if he'd turned around so I could see his face. You could tell a lot about a dragon's temper by how well they were holding their human form. I didn't think it was my imagination that the room's temperature went up a fraction.

Lady Siyu arched one of her perfect black eyebrows. "And taking out jobs for third parties is in direct violation of your contract with Mr. Kurosawa."

I stopped myself swearing. Outright denying Lady Siyu's well-worded accusations rarely went my way. I was always better off with the facts.

"*Actually,*" I said, "they seem to be under the impression I work for them. I tried to explain I work for a dragon and wasn't interested in their job, but they don't seem to give a flying fu—"

Lady Siyu didn't give me a chance to finish. "And you expect us to believe that you, a thief, refused their prize?" She gave a derisive sniff.

Oh, hell, screw diplomacy. Never had a talent for it anyway.

"You think I'm a greedy thief? Then why the hell would I accept a job from an organization that I *know* won't pay the fuck up. And speaking of getting screwed over, the situation with this artifact the elves oh so want me to find isn't nearly as straightforward as you seem to think."

Lady Siyu frowned at that, and I caught the movement of Mr. Kurosawa's head as he turned to watch me with his black, white-less eyes. Whether with feigned or genuine indifference, I couldn't be sure.

"Look, I realize I'm not as familiar with elven politics as you—"

"Then maybe you should hold your tongue. Unless you'd like me to take it," Lady Siyu started, but she was silenced by a hiss of breath from Mr. Kurosawa. I took that as my signal to continue.

"But *something* is very wrong."

"Are you suggesting the elves are being dishonest?" Mr. Kurosawa said, deliberate with his words, no trace of his Japanese accent over his cultivated American.

It always paid to be very careful with how I worded answers to Mr. Kurosawa. "Depends what you mean by dishonest. Have they lied? Probably not, but they most definitely didn't give me all the information they have on the Lightning Armor, and—"

"Which you have no proof of," Lady Siyu snapped.

Deep breath . . . "Like I said, it depends what you consider dishonest." I shrugged and took a gamble. "Despite what the elves claim, I don't think they necessarily all agree on whether they really want it. I think the elves are fighting about it, and it's spilling onto this job.

"The last record of the armor was in the early 1200s, when Jebe had it. It disappeared after that. Jebe is the last known link, yet the elves went out of their way to try and keep any information he or the Mongols recorded out of my grasp. Why? Why go to all the trouble of negotiating a deal, then crippling my efforts to actually find it? That's the question you should be asking."

"And while you're at it," Rynn added, "ask yourself why the IAA has taken such a sudden interest in Alix with an army of mercenaries. It reeks of the elves—"

Lady Siyu turned on him. "And I am sick and tired of listening to your heavily prejudiced objections to the elves' business practices—"

"Because I'm the only one in this room who has ever worked with them!"

"*Enough*," Mr. Kurosawa's voice echoed through the casino with a preternatural amplification. Both Rynn and Lady Siyu fell silent.

Silence settled in the air, only interrupted by the buzz of the electric slot machines and the odd chimes of a winning hand.

"An interesting hypothesis," Mr. Kurosawa finally said.

I took that as permission to continue. "First they don't give us nearly enough information to really track the suit down—a few descriptions, piecemeal bits. From what I gather, the elves have the best supernatural archives around. They have more on the suit; I mean, some of the diagrams are so off kilter that the only way they could suspect the suits were the same is that if they had other text to go with it."

"And the IAA?" Lady Siyu asked, her voice poisonous.

"Like Rynn said. I think it's an awfully big coincidence that the IAA only pulled out their big threats right after we managed to find the book the elves tried to hide."

Silence fell across the room again as plumes of smoke flowed out across the casino floor from where Mr. Kurosawa sat perfectly still. This time not even the slot machines ventured a sound.

Mr. Kurosawa finally stood and faced us. He was dressed in one of his expensive suits, but his skin was bright red and his teeth were black and serrated. Smoke trailed freely out of his nostrils as he strode to where Lady Siyu was holding a folder.

"This changes a number of things," Mr. Kurosawa said to her. I got the distinct impression something else silent was said.

Then Mr. Kurosawa turned to me. "It is imperative that you deal with the armor while I . . . discuss some issues with the elves."

I opened my mouth to argue, but I stopped short at the smile Mr. Kurosawa gave me and the glimpse of his black, pointed teeth. I don't think I'd ever seen his skin quite this red—was that steam rising off of it? I stifled a shudder. Dragons had a harder time than most hiding their form, though Mr. Kurosawa was good at it, probably because of his penchant for ten-thousand-dollar suits. There was very little a dragon liked more than his treasure.

"You will also need to deal with this IAA issue," he added.

Wait . . . *what*? "Since when do I work for them? Or take care of two contracts at once—with mercenaries?" I said.

"The IAA is a mess of your own making," Lady Siyu snarled, slinking in a slow predatory circle around me.

"Like hell it is. Oh shit!" I stumbled back as she dropped her clipboard and lunged for me, red lacquered claws out.

I ducked behind a nearby slot, narrowly avoiding a grazing claw. Served me right for baiting a Naga.

"Okay, before you try to kill me, hear me out. Hey!" I ducked as she made a swipe around the slot machine, aiming for my left side.

"If they are not after you for your transgressions, then what?" Lady Siyu wasn't hissing or lunging at me anymore, but she also wasn't backing down.

"Because I'm the best and they don't stand a chance of tracking the World Quest designers down without me."

"Then why have you been pursuing them? You think I didn't know about your side excursions searching for them? If not for the reward of treasure, then what interest could it possibly hold for your thieving hands?"

Shit. This was the part I'd been hoping to avoid. I was not about to tell Lady Siyu and Mr. Kurosawa, of all people, that I figured the World Quest duo had stumbled across a lost city made of human magic. I didn't like whatever idea it might churn up if left for too long; on the other hand, lying to them was suicidal. "Because I am sick and tired of the IAA crushing everyone under their heels. Me, World Quest, any graduate student that doesn't kowtow the right way—"

Lady Siyu snorted and looked at me with disgust. "If you expect us to believe for one minute—"

"Believe whatever you want. Look, you want a selfish reason? Fine.

If the IAA finds them first, they'll shut down World Quest. Forever. I've sunk three years of my life into that game. Do you have any idea how long it'll take to reach the same level in a new one?"

"That is the most idiotic reason I've ever heard."

"Make up your mind, then! Do you want honest or selfish?"

Mr. Kurosawa stopped us midargument with a derisive noise.

My heart pounded as he turned those black, calculating eyes on Lady Siyu, then me.

"It appears the IAA was not truthful with you, Lady Siyu," he said.

And just like that he turned his back to us and headed back to his black couch, where he returned to a magazine that had been left upside down on the coffee table.

"Mr. Kurosawa—I *implore* you." Her heels clicked furiously against the tiles as she chased him.

He held up a hand that silenced her voice and brought her to a standstill. "And it will cost them. Explain to them that they were most clearly and sorely mistaken upon any assumption that my antiquities thief agreed to any contract. Furthermore, she has emphatically expressed her intent to refuse any future contracts offered due to egregious outstanding payments. Any further attempts on their part to contact or interfere with Alix Hiboux's employment with me shall be severely frowned upon."

When Lady Siyu didn't immediately turn on her heels, Mr. Kurosawa added, "You are dismissed."

With one last hate-filled glare in my direction, she turned on her heels and headed back into the maze. I almost pitied the IAA agent who was on the receiving end of that call.

I held my breath and waited for the other proverbial shoe to drop. It was when Mr. Kurosawa worded things that way—that legal way—that I knew there was a catch.

"Not that I don't appreciate it, Mr. Kurosawa, but I'm pretty sure all that will do is piss them off more," I said as Lady Siyu's clicking heels faded.

"Oh, I am almost certain that will be the effect. In fact I fully expect them to retaliate," he said, smiling at me with those black teeth. "The IAA bureaucrats and the elves share a common habit of getting so caught up in their own internal games they forget the external consequences."

"No offense, but me being dead or tossed in an IAA jail—"

Smoke billowed out of Mr. Kurosawa's nose. "Who do you think in the supernatural community helps their . . . problems disappear? Eventually my lack of cooperation will reach someone in charge and the carefully arranged dominoes in this scheme will begin to fall and expose their hand. In the meantime? I suggest you do what you do best."

Steal things. And run. Not necessarily in that order.

Smoke was filling the room now. It was up to my knees, curling around my calves in a manner that could only be described as predatory. And the temperature was decidedly getting warmer. I felt the squeeze from Rynn on my shoulder. It was time for us to leave.

"I will offer you one more hint, Owl," Mr. Kurosawa called when we were already deep in the maze, his voice carrying through the slot machines as if he was standing there beside us. "The politics being played by the IAA and elves reek of someone arrogant enough to ignore my favorite force of nature."

"Which is?" I called out.

"Chaos" came the dark hiss of Mr. Kurosawa's voice from the closest slot machine. I jumped back out of reflex.

I waited for him to add anything else, but the maze was silent. Even the slot machines seemed to be wary.

As Rynn led us out of the maze, I made sure to keep him in my sights despite the wheels churning in my head, trying to tease things apart.

We rode the elevator up to our floor in silence. When it opened, I stepped out into the empty top-floor hall where my suite was and opened Captain's carrier. He shook his front and back paws a few times and grumbled his discontent about the dirt, but he headed toward the door with his tail up.

Rynn stayed in the elevator. "Security?" I asked.

He nodded. "I want to be somewhere I can watch things when Lady

Siyu delivers her message to the IAA. The mercenaries won't stop, Alix. Not when there's a pay day at hand, and not now that the IAA has made you a target, despite whatever sway Lady Siyu can scare out of them."

I nodded. I'd figured that. I waited for Rynn to reach out and touch me, kiss me, like he usually did when we parted ways to work, but he didn't. He only stared at a spot on the mirrored wall as the doors slid shut.

Preoccupied. I knew it wasn't me, but still . . .

Captain meowed beside me.

I cleared my thoughts and followed him down the hall to our suite. "Come on, I can fix the mud, but you're not going to like it," I told him as I opened the door and let him waltz inside.

He headed straight for the food and water in the kitchen. Me? I finally had the chance to strip off my muddy clothes. I changed into sweats and dropped my computer on the desk before heading into the bathroom to start the bath water running.

While the tap ran, I grabbed a beer out of the fridge—one of the Belgians Rynn had me trying—and turned on the TV over the bathtub to see if the coverage in New Delhi had changed. It hadn't, which, all things considered, wasn't a bad thing.

I settled in and watched the news, the door slightly ajar so Captain could get in when he was done stuffing his face with kibble. Lady Siyu had succeeded where I'd failed; enforcing his diet.

Beyond my exploits in India, the news was filled with basic stuff. Normal world problems: terrorists, politics, people getting fleeced out of millions, some innocent man who had been locked behind bars for fifteen years because of a corrupt local legal system, etc. I really was starting to wonder whether helping Mr. Kurosawa was making things better. Would things really change if the supernaturals came out of the closet? Or maybe it would just add a new flavor to the same old problems.

I'd had my eyes closed and was only half listening to the TV while I rested my head and let the warm water penetrate my bones. It felt as if

I'd been on my feet for days; come to think of it, I had. The last time I'd had a good sleep had been in the hostel in Nepal.

I almost drifted off, and if I had, I probably would have missed it entirely. Just in time, I opened my eyes and frowned at the screen. It couldn't be . . . there was no way.

I upped the volume and sat up.

"Vampires in Las Vegas? Really?"

"Yes, there has been a reporting of vampires in downtown Las Vegas."

Shit. I hadn't heard wrong. They had said the magic *V* word. Rynn was going to love this. So was Mr. Kurosawa. Lady Siyu? She'd be pissed someone had dared break Mr. Kurosawa's rules, but as far as what she'd actually think of a vampire jumping the girls? Probably, deep down, she thought it was an improvement.

But before I could catapult myself out of the bathtub and probably break my neck, the hosts continued.

"An elaborate prank orchestrated as a publicity stunt for the upcoming 'Noir by Night,' the newest show coming to Vegas this October."

Relieved, I settled back down into the water. Now, don't get me wrong, it was a horrible prank to play on tourists, but man was I ever happy to see it wasn't real vampires. Still, I left the channel on.

They drifted off into more benign news on the upcoming weather— no rain and hot, real fucking surprise for Vegas . . .

It had all been an elaborate prank. Still, I suppose it was a window into what things might be like if vampires and other supernaturals started to slip through the cracks out of the closet. I remembered what Alexander had said would happen—self-made Van Helsings and towns overrun with crazy cannibalistic vampires.

I took a swig of my beer. I think I was happier not being in the supernatural know.

Captain chose that moment to stride in. He chirped and sniffed around the room before jumping up on the bathtub sill to sniff the water. Cats: they might hate water, but they can't stop themselves from investigating. A love-hate thing I suppose.

He mewed at me again. "You so aren't going to be impressed with this," I told him. But, since Captain was a cat, and only had a rudimentary understanding of English, he ignored me and went back to sniffing at me and the water.

"But you also need to get that mud off, soooo . . ." I continued.

There were two ways to give a cat a bath. The first was to let them know what was happening. I really don't recommend that with their hating water thing.

The second was to make sure they didn't see it coming.

I waited until Captain was looking away—that was the other critical part. You can't ever let them blame you.

I batted the water at him. As the drops hit his fur, Captain swung his head around to see where the offensive water had come from annndd slipped.

For a moment he just sat there in the water. Soaked, eyes wide in shock at the humiliating offense that had just befallen him, he made a clumsy grab for the edge to pull himself out but slipped right back in.

"Not so fast." I grabbed the pet shampoo and had him soaped up before he knew what hit him. I think he was a little shell-shocked.

He let out a baleful mew as I massaged his head. "Tragedy of your own devices, buddy," I said.

After I had Captain rinsed and cleaned, I did my best to dry him off. Still damp, he slinked away, probably to find a pile of my clothes to finish drying off in. I pulled my clean sweats back on and headed into the living room.

Rynn still wasn't back, so I decided to delve once again into the mystery of the samurai. I pulled Jebe's journal out of my bag and opened my laptop.

There was a note from Nadya sitting for me in my inbox.

Got your message on the journal and the IAA. It's disconcerting but there has been no sign of them over here.

That was a relief. What I read next though wasn't.

Things are . . . more involved in Tokyo than I'd hoped. I'm still figuring out a way to fix things. Don't worry, it isn't unfixable, just . . . complicated. I'm working with Rynn's people at Gaijin Cloud and I think we've come up with a plan.

I thought about texting or calling, but if things were as complicated businesswise as Nadya hinted, then me throwing in a beeping or buzzing cell phone was going to hinder, not help.

I opened up my email to fire off a response. *That had the opposite effect of making me not worry*, I wrote, and sent it off before setting attention back on research.

I don't like working in a void. I do better with details. And right now I was going on too many assumptions where the IAA and the elves were concerned.

And, with Nadya out of commission in Tokyo, that meant I was the one who was going to have to ping my contacts. I went to the fridge and poured myself a shot of tequila and grabbed another beer, which I needed in order to swallow the ass-kissing I was going to have to do.

Oh God, I was going to get an earful from Benji . . .

I noticed a flickering message in the bottom left-hand corner of my screen.

Hey, Byzantine—you up for a World Quest session?

I closed Carpe's message without responding. I wasn't up for dealing with the elf just yet.

After I sent off a few emails, I settled back in to read Jebe's journal and his accounts of the horde's invasion of the west.

9

TEMPLES, TOMBS, AND OTHER ASSORTED CRAWL SPACES

10:00 a.m. My suite at the Japanese Circus

I stared at the set of files on my screen from the cache I'd taken from the university. A possible treasure room in Mongolia . . . If I was right about the referencing, there was a good chance a chunk of Jebe's treasure had ended up there.

It was worth a shot, since everything else had been a dead end. I stifled a yawn as I opened a search window for one of the many IAA databases Nadya and I still had access to. I needed more coffee. After a phone call full of my threats and Benji's snide replies, he had managed to chase up a few more mentions of the armor on his end, but even combined with the details Rynn remembered and what I'd dug out of Jebe's journal . . .

Well, let's just say there weren't a lot of options.

"Come on, Jebe, don't fail me now," I said as I scanned through the recorded digs and excavations that had been done in that region of Mongolia. I'd finally given up last night around 2:00 a.m. after I'd hit my third dead end in search of Jebe's treasure horde and headed to bed. Still, I was working on a sleep deficit and was having trouble focusing on the screen between yawns. Captain's pleas for food weren't helping either.

"Shit." Found in 1920 while excavating a horde. I skimmed through; they'd found treasure, records, and a large number of skin walkers who'd taken up residence. I hit the keyboard with more force than I needed to in order to close the window. Fantastic. Yet another temple the horde had used to store treasure that I could cross off my list. And that had been the last one recorded in the files. I'd known it was a possibility that the horde's scribes might have left out what happened to Jebe's armor, but I'd been hopeful. . . .

I hate finding things people went out of their way to lose.

There was the clinking of dishes from the kitchen as I went back to Jebe's journal. "What this time?" Rynn called. He'd returned a few hours ago, after I'd given up and decided to sleep. Incubi didn't need much sleep, provided there was a surplus of energy to sop up. Still, it irked me that after only two or three hours he had none of the exhaustion I felt.

"Another dead end," I said. I rubbed my face, but this time it wasn't just the sleep in my eyes; it was the fact that as Jebe's condition had progressed, his handwriting had gotten much worse. As if he was battling the armor itself to put anything to paper. Considering what he had to say, I wasn't surprised.

I was vaguely aware of Rynn coming up behind me as I turned the pages. The references got sporadic after Kiev—after they'd killed the ruling princes in a very gruesome way. As if that was when Jebe had realized the armor was more than it seemed. I tore my eyes away from the pages to the cup of coffee Rynn placed beside my computer before pulling up a seat.

"Well?" he said, settling in with his own mug. Incubi might not need sleep, but they were not immune to the many wonders of caffeine.

I held up the journal. "The entries after Kiev get sporadic, but he knew something was up. The armor, however, figured it out too and dug its claws into his head, so to speak."

Rynn nodded thoughtfully. "Any mentions of its location?"

I shook my head and paused to sip the warm black coffee, willing it to filter into my veins before answering. "Despite the fact we know Jebe wore the suit, there is no mention of it anywhere after this journal. Not even the scribes bothered to mention what happened after Jebe died." Not one inkling of it beyond what Jebe and the scribe had recorded. As if the armor had just vanished from history.

"What about other treasure troves? There must be more of them. Ones that were left off the records."

At this I inclined my head. It was possible, but I wasn't about to bet on it. "I'm thinking they took it a step further and buried the suit with Jebe himself." It wasn't a bad idea. After Jebe died, his body had been buried in an unmarked grave—a Mongolian tradition so no one could spoil the remains or loot the grave for treasure. I had to hand it to the Mongolians: where others had spent fortunes building impenetrable tombs, the khans had taken it a step further. Instead of creating a beacon for grave robbers, they hadn't advertised at all. Considering all the tombs I'd managed to get into, and the countless tomb robbers through the histories before me, they'd had a point.

Not having an exact location for the grave was a significant problem, but there was another, bigger concern consuming my thoughts now that I'd had a chance to rummage through Jebe's thoughts as the suit had consumed him. "There's no report on how he died," I said, once again holding up the last page of the journal and indicating the files I'd stolen from the IAA research cache.

Rynn sipped his own coffee and frowned at the screen. "Arrow to the heart, axe to the head, festering wound," he offered. "There were a lot of ways to die on a battlefield in the 1200s."

"That's just it." I gestured with my coffee at the screen. "I mean, battles, spoils, even the numbers of civilians killed and enslaved—hell, they balanced the ones they used as human shields in the margins." The Mongolians had been awfully well managed for a horde of murderous barbarians; they'd even calculated how many of the conquered civilians they needed to kill versus enslave depending on how much grain they had for horses and supplies.

"So they were conscientious of their murderous activities and kept good records," Rynn said.

"Exactly. Injuries sustained by a general—and not just any general, but one in charge of a quarter of an empire's forces—is like a king dying. Someone somewhere should have recorded what happened. If not in here," I said, holding up the journal, "then somewhere."

"If there is a battle missing—" Rynn tried.

I held up my hands. "That's just it! A lost batch of documents I could understand, but this reads as if it was intentionally left out. Not something removed by the elves after the fact, but never recorded."

Rynn stared at the screen, a thoughtful expression on his face.

I rested my forehead in my hands then rubbed my eyes. I was cranky and frustrated. "No offense, but unless you happened to be awake during the Middle Ages and remember hearing something about a general dying after destroying most of eastern Europe?"

Rynn made a face at me. "I think I would have remembered a marauding Mongolian horde passing through. And I already told you, unlike Artemis, I did not enjoy sitting back and watching civilizations burn. After Rome fell and the Christians took power, I spent a few hundred years up north with the Celts until their civilization started to fall under the heel of the Christians. I slept for a few hundred years and woke to find the Christians were well entrenched and out to hunt supernaturals as much as before." As Rynn had pointed out, it had been only five hundred years or so since supernaturals had changed their rules.

"After that?"

Rynn shrugged. "I moved farther north into the lands the Vikings, Danes, and their ilk still held. They didn't care so much about supernaturals as long as they proved useful in winning raids and new kingdoms from the Christians, which I did so no one ever bothered confirming any suspicions."

"You helped the Vikings raid cities?" Somehow I had trouble imagining Rynn as a raider; it didn't quite fit with his persona.

He swayed his head, considering his answer. "I suppose, though, I was more concerned with finding the people who were hunting down and burning supernaturals during their medieval witch hunts."

"I always thought they just used those as an excuse to kill women who tried to think for themselves."

"Eventually they did, but in the early years, especially in the smaller villages and towns, they were terrified of supernaturals. Not without reason, the ones running the cities were dangerous, but like most movements, they didn't go after the dangerous ones that were eating humans and their children, which, for the record, I would have been fine with. They went after the harmless ones, the odd wood nymph or brownie they stumbled across. Even had to pull a young succubus out of a cloister of monks. They found her hibernating in the old ruins of the church and were convinced they held the key to power." He snorted with distaste. "Sorcery. The monks were the ones guilty of sorcery, yet they called *her* evil."

"What happened to them?"

Rynn actually looked at me this time and held my gaze. "Nothing nice," he said. "She was fine; she recovered. They didn't." His lips curled up, exposing his teeth, not unlike Lady Siyu did, though his were perfectly human.

I turned my attention back to my coffee, lost in my own thoughts. On the one hand, the idea of Rynn beating up and very likely killing humans sometime during the Middle Ages wasn't exactly comforting despite the fact that at the time killing and raiding was kind of like going to the mall for a movie. And I couldn't say I blamed him. It'd be like my finding a bunch of vampires with old classmates tied up and drugged out beneath one of their hidey-hole clubs as snacks. Probably wouldn't want anything nice to happen to them either. I know I wouldn't think twice or have any regrets about doing something awful.

And yet half a year ago—four months ago, even—if you'd asked me,

I would have sided with the humans. No questions asked, the monsters must have done something to deserve it.

And though many of the supernaturals I'd met were complete fucking assholes who tried to kill me, the majority, like the turnip demons and nymphs, were harmless. God help me, I was starting to agree with Rynn in that they were the ones who needed protecting from the humans.

Seriously universe, do you just sit there waiting to completely fuck with my belief systems?

"Alix?"

I glanced up from where I'd been staring thoughtfully into the depths of my coffee.

"Just thinking to myself."

Rynn looked back at the screen. "I heard about the Mongolians at the time, even heard about the destruction in Kiev, but it was years after the fact. The tales were always too far removed to be accurate by the time they reached me. And the Vikings were only interested in writing down financial transactions and trade." He shook his head. "I've got nothing useful. What is in there?" he said, nodding at the journal.

I flipped back through to the very last few entries. My grasp of the Mongolian script used was suspect, but it was close enough to some of the ancient Chinese scripts that I could follow. I was glad for the translation that had accompanied it. "Details, mostly his suspicions about the suit after Kiev, and a few entries after that where he sounds like he's fighting to get a word on the page. Ah, there are a couple of lines, dialect I don't follow, but here he talks about the suit corrupting his heart and mind until all he could see was death and darkness. It goes like that until near the very end." I flipped the page to the very last passage. " 'I'm trying to control thoughts that I know are not my own, and I fear this is one battle I cannot win and come out alive.' "

"And after that?"

"That's it. That was the last one. No pages missing. The only other useful thing I've found is a mention of what happened when someone else tried the armor on. Here it is. Jebe talks about finding the armor—ah, don't understand that word, or that one. He mentions a soldier who decided to test the armor before he got to the room—burned skin, screams, charred remains. Not a pretty way to go."

"It does confirm the suit wanted Jebe," Rynn said. "Either by choice or some necessity."

"Yeah, and after that things got really interesting, in the magical sense," I said, the details of which had me worried.

Rynn frowned. "We knew the suit was magic. For that matter, so did they."

"Yeah but I don't think anyone realized to what extent until it was much too late." I flipped through the pages until I found the entry I had read three times last night before finally letting myself drift into a restless sleep. "Jebe puts the suit on, it decides not to fry him, and pretty fast they figure out it is more than happy to fry enemies with electricity—hence the Lightning, or Storm, Armor. We know from the scribe that Jebe got progressively more violent as they moved into Russia." I count off on my fingers. "Quickness to anger, impatience, arguing with his officers, recklessly going into battle without intelligence. All of that alone could be written off as bad days—which he did, considering what the armor offered."

"The armor was manipulating him," Rynn mused.

I inclined my head in agreement. "Listen to this," I said, and started to read a passage from their invasion of the walled city outside Kiev. " 'It was a stupid military move, and one that has cost me valuable men even though we won. But I fear it is a sign of worse things to come. I suspected it before, but now I am certain—the suit, though powerful, is affecting my judgment. The more I use it, the more powerful it grows. I am reluctant to continue the campaign and unleash its power so freely, but I see no other choice. The armies here are not as weak as we'd hoped, and not so easy to die on our blades and arrows. I fear we are in too deep to turn back, and I must persevere. In hindsight there were subtle signs the armor did more than grant me powers. I was foolish not to question the cost.'"

"So why not take the armor off?"

"Because he couldn't: 'I know now that the armor is possessed by a malevolent demon that feeds off death and despair. The more my army wins, the deeper and more desperate that thirst goes, so much so that I fear the suit now lusts so much for death that it no longer cares whether I live or die, pushing me into battle and caring little whether I survive with an army, so long as there is blood. I fear its reckless influence will be the death of us all. It would be a simple thing to remove the armor and rid myself of it; in my more lucid moments I have tried, but it will no longer relinquish me, bonded to my flesh like a second skin. Or maybe it is my new skin, wearing my body like the prize I thought it was. There is an irony in that.'" I glanced up at Rynn from the pages.

"When was that entry?" Rynn asked.

"About a month before this one." I skipped to one of the last entries of the journal I'd bookmarked. "Listen to this: 'I write this in a moment of lucidity, as they are so few and far between now, and I am certain I will forget myself once again in the coming days. I both wake and dream its blood lust—there is no escape and even in my bloodiest moments I am no longer able to satiate it. I am now the source of its frustration, and I think it has ceased to care whether I am the source of its victims, or the next.'" I glanced up at Rynn again. "It's like the armor is an addiction—or has an addiction. The more it feeds, the worse it becomes."

"'The priests and sorcerers have been unable to dampen the armor's hold over me. Nevertheless, once these lands are conquered and we are on the road home, the suit will be retired one way or the other, until greater, wise men may learn to tame it.' And that was the last one," I added, and closed the journal. "No mention of his death, not even a footnote from a scribe marking the occasion."

"You think the suit killed him? Forced him into battle?"

I shook my head. That was the part that had kept me up in bed, worrying until I'd finally fallen asleep. "No, I think it wanted to. I think it tried, but ultimately Jebe dug in the last knife. Remember, he was a genius of a general, maybe one of the best the world has ever seen." I held up the journal again. "However much control the suit had, Jebe knew he was at war with it and that he couldn't win by conventional means. What do you do when you know you're going to die fighting a battle you can't win?"

"You make certain your opponent's victory is a hollow one."

I nodded. Which, considering the Mongolians were known to scuttle entire civilizations to prove a point . . . "*I* think the suit had used up Jebe and was ready to move on to another host. *I* think Jebe figured out a way to make that impossible, which is why no one has seen the armor in eight hundred years."

Rynn's face grew pensive. "Not suicide, not unless he was certain he could control the resting place. And somehow I doubt a suit of armor that survived that many centuries would let him. He couldn't have been the first host to try. Maybe poison, but again, he would need to keep it hidden from the armor." He glanced up at me.

"Perhaps," he said, his voice not argumentative but distant. "The elves don't go after items like this. Not in the entire time I worked for them. Why this, why now?"

"Maybe they've changed. I mean, you worked for them, what—over a few hundred years ago?"

Rynn made a face. "They don't change, Alix. Not like that." He gathered both our mugs and headed into the kitchen.

There was another possibility. "Rynn, bear with me. What *if* they want to use it?" I said.

Rynn shook his head from the sink. "They don't get involved."

"I know, I know. They love their neutrality more than life itself. But what if? What if they decided the benefits outweighed the costs? A powerful weapon that drives its user mad in a relatively quick time frame, more so if they're supernatural. Wouldn't you want to keep that information under wraps from the potential next wearer?" Or the suckers you want to have steal it for you?

Rynn paused, but only for a moment. "Anyone else I'd consider it, but not them."

I clenched my teeth and thought about my next words carefully. On the one hand, I got it—Rynn hated the elves. But on the other hand, I was getting the distinct feeling it was blinding him from looking at any of the other angles. "Rynn, you know more about the supernatural world than I do—"

He shook his head to stop me, the dark look still on his face. "Leave this one alone, Alix," he said, his voice cold, disinviting any argument.

I stopped. I don't think Rynn had ever used that tone with me before. It wasn't cruel or mean, just . . . icy. And unlike him.

His expression softened and he added, "I know you're trying, and normally I wouldn't dismiss it, but you don't know them. I do." He disappeared back into the kitchen, shaking his head as if a dark cloud had descended on him.

I turned back to the computer and the files. Captain decided now was as good a time as any to hop on my lap. As much as I balked at Rynn's insistence on what the elves would and wouldn't do, I had to admit he was right about one thing. Even if we knew what the suit did, we had no idea why they wanted it now. Unless . . .

"Shit." Captain jumped off my lap with an indignant mew as I pulled up my message screen. Oh man, if that spell book was behind all this . . . but what were the odds?

You already know the answer to that, Owl. Highly probable, considering your track record.

The World Quest message box flickered open. Surprise, surprise—there was already a message from Carpe waiting.

Call me. We should talk. And you owe me game time.

Yeah, sure. Right after he told me what the hell the book had to do with anything. "Rynn, I think I know what changed the elves' mind. Remember the spell book Carpe had me find?"

It didn't take Rynn long to return, looking colder and more contained than he had a moment ago. "Explain," he said.

"What if they found a spell that they thought would control the armor? Even you have to admit the time line works."

Rynn didn't say anything as he stared at the screen where my empty message window with Carpe was now open.

"Well?"

His eyes didn't move from the open screen; his expression only turned darker and more inward. He nodded at it. "What is that about?"

"Getting Carpe on the line. With any luck, I can get him to answer some questions without getting myself roped into a World Quest game."

Rynn turned his dark expression on me. "So let me get this straight—the elves go out of their way to deceive us, you think they are planning to resurrect a possessed suit of armor, and your first instinct is to run to that *elf*?" His voice was civil, but the contempt was there. Bad moods were one thing, those I could understand, but this went beyond that.

"I know Carpe. I'll get the information out of him. I'll have to think about how to word it . . ."

Rynn said something under his breath in supernatural.

"*What?*" I said.

"Lady Siyu and Mr. Kurosawa I can understand striking a deal with the elves. They're arrogant. But you? After all I've told you?"

I couldn't believe he was pissed at me. Over *Carpe* of all people.

"What I think is that he can get me information we need," I said, letting some of my own frustration into my voice.

Rynn made a derisive sound. "I like that even less. Why bother listening to me? I'm just the incubus, what do I know about complex politics and elves?" He headed back into the kitchen.

"That's not what I said."

I heard the dishes in the sink rattle. "Even you, Alix. You barely listen to any of my warnings, especially when it comes to that elf. Look where it got you last time! Now you want to ask him questions? All you'll do is let him know what we've found out."

"I'm not an idiot. I'll be careful. If you're worried about Carpe and what information he might feed me . . . I don't know, you can sit behind the computer and watch."

He returned from the kitchen, the storm still apparent on his face. "Close the screen."

"What?"

"*Now.*"

I drew in a breath and held it before I said something I might regret. This was not the first fight Rynn and I had ever had about my methods and work. I had a track record for shooting my mouth off in ways I regretted later, but this was the first fight Rynn had ever started.

What alternate universe had I stepped into?

"No," I said just as forcefully, refusing to break eye contact. I didn't let any supernatural push me around—not even Rynn.

For a hairsbreadth of a second, I could have sworn he was going to double down. Then he sighed, and closed his eyes. "I'm sorry, Alix," he said after a moment and opened his eyes. The anger was gone, if not the dark mood that had settled on him as of late. "I'm letting my temper get to me and cloud my own judgment." He nodded at the screen. "Forget what I said. Contact the elf if you think that's the best route."

Funny thing; if Rynn was the empathic one, why couldn't I shake the feeling that I was the one left gauging the emotions?

Rynn ran his hand through his hair. "I need to get some fresh air and clear my head. And it won't hurt to check in with security again and see if they've got a fix on the mercenaries."

"Whoa, what?"

He made a tsking noise, chiding himself. "I'm sorry, I was preoccupied and didn't mention it. A few of the mercenaries have been spotted in Las Vegas. Apparently the IAA has decided to ignore Lady Siyu's decree."

He didn't sound surprised. Considering the current climate, neither was I. "How many?"

"At the moment? Just the ones stupid enough to use commercial flights and their own passports. The Zebras I'm still tracking, but they'll have someone here if the others have surfaced. I'm not too worried about them—yet. They'll wait and see what happens, let the other outfits do their dirty work."

I wasn't so concerned about them getting in. I was more worried about what happened when we tried to leave.

"I'll be back in a couple hours," Rynn said. "I need to clear my head." He reached over and gave me a quick kiss on the forehead, but still, there was that preoccupation and distance.

There was something else though that was bothering him. God knows how I figured that out, but I was sure of it. I reached out and grabbed his arm. For once, I seemed to have surprised him. A lot of firsts . . .

"It doesn't just have to do with the IAA and the elves, does it?"

"It's everything. The elves, the possibility of a change in power." He shook his head and gave me a weary look. "The powerful in these games never run any risks, but the nymphs and radish demons downstairs?" He narrowed his eyes. "Working in a casino for a dragon is a far cry from what any of them dreamed of doing with their lives, but it's a sight better than being hunted down by humans. And they would be the first. The elves, dragons, the real monsters? It's like your human struggles. The poor man always ends up paying for the rich man's war," he said.

As hard as I might, I couldn't offer up any disagreement, which is why I didn't stop Rynn again as he left. Sometimes, apparently even incubi need to be left to settle their own emotions.

Me? I had an elf to deal with. I refilled my coffee and settled my strategy before maneuvering around Captain and back to the desk where my laptop was open. Let's hope I could get Carpe to talk.

Captain hopped back into my lap as I settled in. "Let's see if we can't deal with the asshole elf, shall we?"

He turned his big green eyes on me and let out a long, drawn-out mew.

"Yeah, yeah," I told him. "I'll try not to let it degrade into insults, okay?"

Captain huffed.

"Fine. I'll keep it civil for the first ten minutes."

That seemed to appease him, and he finally settled in. Apparently, Captain had a thing for setting realistic expectations. Who knew? If only negotiating with Carpe were as easy.

I set my fingers to the keyboard. First rule of negotiations: if you can, pick the location. *I've got a job for us, Carpe,* I wrote in the message window.

What you thinking, Byzantine? scrawled below my own message a few moments later.

I didn't bother answering through my mic. Like I said, I was trying to keep things civil. *No raiding low-level goblin hordes this time, promise.* I got a noncommittal huff over my headset.

"I'll take that as a yes," I said to myself and shot Carpe off the map I'd settled on. One I'd wanted to explore but wouldn't put any cards on the table.

"A Norse treasure trove?" Carpe said over the headset after a brief moment.

That's what the map says. A wise player once said to never trust what's on a map—right before something ate him, I imagined.

"Hardly seems worth it to share. You could handle this on your own."

Second rule of engagement? Never open with what you want to bargain for, but also don't waste your time.

"Consider it a peace offering. I'm bored. Then we split the treasure fifty-fifty." I waited to the count of two before adding, "Of course, if you have better things to do . . ." Or need more time to plan how to double-cross me . . .

"Wouldn't think of it."

And that was the crux of the problem. No one ever warned the person they were about to double-cross.

Holding the warm mug of coffee in my hand, I ported Byzantine into Dead Orc Soup. Let's see if I couldn't pump Carpe with some carefully worded questions on the evil elves trying to screw me over . . .

And figure out just whose side Carpe was on.

10

WORLD QUEST

11:00 a.m. Somewhere in the middle of nowhere, World Quest

"I don't know. Looks awfully good to be true, Byzantine," Carpe said over my headset. It was in reference to the town we'd reached, a small, picturesque walled city set in a fjord, modeled after the fortified Viking cities that used to dot the coast. From what I gathered from the buildings and NPCs, it was supposed to represent the early to mid-medieval ages. It was the right city; my in-game map said as much. All we had to do was find the treasure.

I took a sip of my coffee. An Americano this time. I'd finally managed to summon up the energy to run the espresso machine . . . and suffer through Captain's pleas for food every time I'd set foot in the kitchen. Currently he'd settled for batting the food toy around. I was impressed. It had been out in the apartment for almost twenty-four hours and it wasn't in pieces. Yet. "Those who never take chances never find resurrection scrolls," I told him.

"No, but they also don't get eaten by dragons and fried by fireballs."

"Gird your elf balls and stop whining, Carpe. It's *barely* a Level eighteen dungeon, and as far as the map says there's only one major monster guarding the treasure."

"And every map in World Quest should be trusted implicitly?"

"No, but what kind of treasure hunters are we if we don't give it a chance and hear it out first? I don't think I want to live in a World Quest where a treasure map has to cough up proof of its good intentions before a couple dungeon crawlers like us will take it out on the town."

I could hear the sigh along our comm channel. "There is something seriously wrong with you. What level is the monster?"

"Thirteen."

Carpe swore. Level thirteen meant it'd be packing some serious fire-power, and we'd have to do some reconnaissance to figure out what kind of Level thirteen monster it was.

"Giant or a Medusa," Carpe said.

"A Medusa this far north? More likely an ice troll, or a baby wyvern." I'd been reading up on Nordic monsters. Most, like the sea monsters and dragons, were in the low twenties, meaning a team of three or more, but the under-fifteens were still more populous than one might imagine.

Carpe went silent.

"Look, are you in or not?" I asked, wondering for a minute whether Carpe would play along.

"Yeah, yeah, I'm in. Just changing up my inventory. Here, hold these in your magic thief bag, will you?" A set of scrolls and three knives appeared in my inventory, which I transferred into my bag of holding. How did the thieves of World Quest end up the RPG game's equivalent of a packhorse?

"To be honest, I kind of expected you to throw me something besides a treasure map," Carpe said.

"Hunh," I said, as I began to scope out the area for any magic wards we might want to avoid. "As I'm not a mind reader, what were you expecting exactly?"

"Oh, I don't know, Byzantine. You're the one who uses World Quest to plan out your personal treasure hunts. How about you tell me what it is you're looking for?"

"Wow, personal insults and dragging up my past transgressions. You really must be off your game today, Carpe. You ever think I'm not all about the treasure hunts? Maybe I just want to spend a couple hours playing a video game with my friend, the elf—who occasionally stabs me in the back." No magic anywhere. Not on the gates, not set in a trap to catch thieves past the threshold; I ran into one of those once. They aren't pretty.

"What is it I heard someone say to you once? Something about a guy in a whorehouse visiting his sister . . . ?"

"First, that's a low blow to the working whores of the world."

"I suppose your boyfriend would know."

"Wow. Carpe. Wow. Jealousy and misogyny. Diving through the Looking Glass real fucking darkly today, aren't we?"

"Just like to make sure I've lowered myself to my teammate's level. Wouldn't want to give anyone an inferiority complex. Now just where the hell does the map want us to go?"

"Town square."

I set my avatar on a course for the center of town, a wooden structure set in a courtyard of rough-hewn wood surrounded by hay and sawdust. I did another check for magic, traps, anything as we approached. To be honest, I'd been expecting at least a magic trap . . . maybe a party of NPC protectors of the faith.

Everyone was just going about their business. Like a normal village.

"Is it me, or are the townsfolk a little, well, normal?" Carpe said into my headset.

I won't lie, it was surreal. And a little uncomfortable. Aping real life a little too much as far as oblivious townsfolk. "Map says we're supposed to stand in the center," I said.

"Then what?"

"I don't know. It'll either tell us what we need to do next, or teleport in a monster. Or a combination of the two."

The two of us headed for the center. As soon as we reached it, a circle flared into existence, denoting in-game magic. "A teleport point," I said to Carpe. Not uncommon in World Quest. It made the treasure hunts more interesting; you couldn't completely map out the area. Took a home game advantage away—you can't dominate an area if you don't know where the final map point is.

Still no sign from the crowds milling around that anything was amiss . . . or even that we were there.

"Okay, don't tell me you aren't creeped out now," Carpe said.

"Just look at the map and see what it wants us to do next," I said as I kept my avatar on a very high lookout. Carpe was right. This was way too easy for World Quest.

Carpe's avatar huddled on the ground beside mine in the center of the magic circle, a signal that he was preoccupied with a spell. "The map's showing me a teleport spell, a specific one. Shall we?" Carpe asked.

I gave the NPCs around us one last good look. Still nothing, as if the blaring pentagram in the center of their square wasn't there. I shook my head. World Quest NPCs weren't exactly known for riveting conversation, but this was a little meta, even for them. "Just get the teleport spell working, and get a couple defensive spells ready. I'm betting the monster is waiting on the other side."

"Roger Wilco, Byzantine. And I'm holding you responsible if we end up in a bottomless pit of death."

I watched and waited. The screen air around Carpe lit up as he activated the spell contained on the map, and I braced myself for the worst as the screen flashed opaque white and our avatars began to reappear in a matching teleport circle in another region of the game—a field, set amongst arid low hills and mountains that reminded me vaguely of the Mediterranean.

I circled my avatar, waiting for an attack.

It didn't come.

"Where the hell are we?" Carpe asked. "And when?"

Good question. I took stock of the area and the structures that were now starting to fill in on my own game map. I recognized that we were on the outskirts of a late Roman town—the amphitheater was still a prominent structure—but eyeballing it I'd guess that the newer structures had been built over an older Greek city. I spotted the lake down the hillside. Wait a minute . . .

I turned my avatar around and checked the hillside to be sure. "We're in Macedonia. Lychnidos—or Ohrid, to be exact. Home of Alexander the Great. As to the when . . . ah, after the Greeks, but still in the later Roman period, I think."

Hunh. Supposedly a burial mask made of gold for Alexander the Great went missing in this town, right around this period or a little before. No one had been able to find it, not with the medieval town that had been built over the original structures . . . might be worth taking a look around. Just because I was here to probe Carpe didn't mean I wasn't above a little reconnaissance while I was at it. Yes, I had sworn off using World Quest for my treasure hunts, but come on, there had to be points for good behavior.

It also distracted me from the nagging thought in the back of my mind that kept insisting this was way easier than a World Quest treasure hunt had any right being. I did another check on the screen map, casting my Detect Magic spell for good measure.

Still nothing. The in-game time was early morning, and as far as I could see the only things moving around were vaguely Roman NPCs, going about their daily business.

Weird. I realized Carpe had said something. "What?"

"I said, I figured you'd have me crawling around some ruin in Tibet for sure, not a generic treasure map."

I ignored the probe. Carpe had thrown a few vague ones at me over the past hour. I wasn't biting. Instead, I was keeping him off balance with a quest that had absolutely nothing to do with either of my real-world problems. "It's not a generic treasure hunt . . . it's crossed into the realm of metageneric. And maybe you don't know me nearly as well as you think you do."

"Brothers visiting their sister in the whorehouse. And why the hell aren't you trying to get me to spill on the elves?"

"Because I'm maturing and working on developing a deep respect and understanding for all things supernatural. Starting with you. Now how about we start with a conversation on why you really had me risk my life for that spell book?" I searched the game screen. There really was nothing here—or nothing that raised any alarms or posed an immediate threat.

"Touché. And the town is up the hill."

Round one to Owl. The lack of any monsters or guards trying to protect the treasure might be unnerving, but far be it from me to turn my nose up at easy treasure. I set my avatar headed toward the old gated city on the hillside above us on autopilot, then pulled up the notes I'd been making on Jebe and my list of most likely burial sites—the ones I'd been compiling while playing with Carpe.

Despite our differences over the past few months, there were two things I knew without a doubt about Carpe. One, he took World Quest seriously. Determined, focused seriously. Two, he wanted to know what I was up to and liked to spy on me digitally.

Oh no, wait. There was a third thing I knew. He couldn't do both at once.

I'd had my search window open on and off for the past hour and not a peep from Carpe on my recent history.

To be sure, all my notes were handwritten. I courted disaster, but I didn't jump in bed with it.

I went over my list as our avatars approached the town. There were six or so sites that looked promising as final resting sites for Jebe. The problem was that regardless of which one I went with, it boiled down to two bad choices.

Tibet or Nepal.

Mercenaries or the Chinese. At the moment, neither of those were particularly appealing options. The mercenaries were obvious, but the Chinese? Let's just say we'd had a disagreement about a handful of terra-cotta warriors last month, which Rynn didn't know about. Oh the joys of breaking that one to him. . . .

I turned my attention back on the screen as our avatars reached the city gates.

"You weren't wrong, Byz. The World Quest version of ancient Lychnidos has a Roman feel to it."

Good thing the dates were never exact—and neither were the people. Otherwise they probably would have reacted a hell of a lot more aggressively to our dress and appearance as we approached. Hazards of an RPG: people tended to err on the side of obscenely flamboyant when dressing their avatars, so the NPC—non-player characters—that inhabited the game had to interact as if everyone thought pink Hello Kitty armor was perfectly normal. Otherwise, every time a player tried to sell their goods or start a quest, there'd be chaos.

As it was, the Roman NPCs offered us about as much of a look as we entered the gates as they would give any other travelers or traders.

The city guards only nodded at our weapons as we strode in. Early in the history of World Quest, players had been forced to hand over their pointy bits, but that got tedious. Easier to make all the towns noncombat zones. Not the entire town, mind you: cellars, dungeons, and ruined tunnels were still try-to-kill-you fair game, but you couldn't attack other players when they were, say, pulling out their coin purse to pay someone. The game designers were above taking cheap shots . . . unless it was me, in which case cheap shots were fair game.

Now that we were in Lychnidos, the map had changed once again to show a dotted line leading to a dwelling of some sort—or that's what the map made it look like. I checked the area on the screen. Though the layout was familiar, the buildings didn't quite match.

"I think the map and town are supposed to be separated by a couple hundred years," Carpe offered.

Fantastic. "Just keep your eyes on the line and make sure we don't stray too far off it." Carpe's in-game sorcerer had access to more of those kinds of spells than my thief did. Counterintuitive if you thought too long about it . . .

"Done," Carpe said into my headset as our avatars turned down a small alleyway.

Sure enough, Carpe set the lead, taking us toward an alley that looked vaguely like the one on the map, though much narrower. Then again, there weren't a lot of places for a mountain fortress town in the hills of Macedonia to expand.

"You know, despite your complete lack of social skills, I figured even you would have at least *tried* to scrounge up a thank-you for me by now," Carpe said.

"A thank-you? What the hell for?" *Thank you for almost getting me killed?*

"For getting you out of that hostel in Vancouver, for starters. And you're welcome."

I was not going to fall victim to Carpe's bad attempt to draw me into a verbal sparring match well off my script. There was power in keeping to my notes. "You owed me for that book. In fact, as far as I'm concerned, you still owe me," I said, and hovered the cursor over the spot in the alley that the map seemed to think was the entrance to the next checkpoint on the treasure map. "It says we need to take a right here."

"That's a brick wall."

"Well, no one ever said following a treasure map was supposed to be easy, now did they? Sometimes you need to be creative—or break through walls, or help a friend out with clandestine organizations."

Carpe swore. "Cheap shot. And I repeat, I did not have to put my neck out to help you out of that hostel."

"Sure you did. After I twisted your arm all the way down to the joint."

"No offense, but I think the incubus's temperament is brushing off on you. That's a little overboard on the violent imagery."

"Better him than you." And it was an accurate reflection of my feelings.

"What's that supposed to mean?"

I ignored Carpe and concentrated on the treasure map.

"No, seriously. How am I a bad influence?"

The current path stopped right here, which usually meant stairs—probably down, since the dwellings above didn't look like they could be housing much of a dungeon. I wondered if that's where the Level thirteen monsters were hiding. "It means the incubus, as you so like to refer to him, actually thinks I'm a good person. You? You just relegate me to the gutter with the rest of the thieves. No reevaluation, no second chances."

"But you are a thief."

I shook my head at Captain. *Clueless.* "And I repeat. If you're trawling for a thank-you, you can start with why you skipped over the corrupt and clandestine nature of elves."

A large window popped up on my screen, shunting my World Quest game screen to a corner. Carpe's familiar, frowning face was nestled inside. A mirrored video window of me popped up in the lower left corner of my screen, despite the fact that I had disabled the camera—manually.

Today Carpe was sporting a man bun and a flannel shirt on his slight frame. The funny thing was I didn't think Carpe had the wherewithal to realize he was emulating the hipster movement. Or maybe he did. Maybe his whole not caring was just an act. Regardless, the furrow to his brow and frown told me he was pissed.

I minimized the window.

"They aren't corrupt," he said, "exactly. And I did tell you about their bureaucratic tendencies."

"You told me about the ones who saved innocent chicken livestock over people!" Crazy? Yes, but not clandestine.

Carpe frowned. "And you seriously didn't think that was a huge warning sign?"

I killed the camera with my finger as I sat back and shook my head at Captain, who was perched behind my computer, roused from his nap and interested in who I was yelling at now.

That didn't stop Carpe though. "And explain to me how the incubus telling you you're a better person than you actually are is a good thing? I mean, let's face it, you are a thief—an unapologetic one."

"The IAA owes me years of back pay and grievance money."

"See? Unapologetic!"

I muted my mic with my other hand. "I swear to God, Captain, if he was sitting here . . ."

To Carpe, I said, "Believing that I'm a bad person and can't become a better person isn't helping me either! It just reaffirms that I should be a thief."

"Has it ever occurred to you that me accepting that's your nature makes me a better friend?"

Completely clueless . . . I didn't dignify that with an answer. "Just get off your ass and cast Crumble, will you?" Crumble was a low-level spell Carpe had stumbled across a while back. That was another bonus about World Quest; you often found new and interesting spells or skills as the designers invented them. It made things like sightseeing from town to town interesting.

Carpe grumbled something I didn't quite catch under his breath, but he parked his avatar in front of the brick wall. I stood guard at the street entrance. Remember what I said about the NPCs ignoring our flamboyant nature? Yeah . . . that went out the window if they see you trashing a brick wall. Once you've done it and crawled inside, however, it's like it never happened. It's while the damage is being incurred you need to worry.

A section of the brick wall and cobble road crumbled into pebbles, exposing a tunnel underneath.

"See? Told you." I shoved Carpe's avatar inside before he could give me a snarky comeback, as NPCs were starting to look down the alley in the direction of the noise. I hopped in afterward and watched the screen shudder as I landed. Well, it had worked. As my avatar adjusted to the dimmer light, I saw that we were in a generic, circular tunnel lined with bricks.

"This way," I said, and started my avatar down the end of the tunnel pointed north.

The headset was silent. Not surprising, since we didn't have anything in game to talk about until a goblin decided to attack us. My screen pinged though, and I glanced down from scanning the tunnel for traps and writing—anything that would either give us a hint of what was up ahead or . . .

Let's hope there was treasure left. And no more comments from Carpe about the doomed nature of Rynn's attempts to encourage me to be a better person.

I vaguely clued into the fact that my phone was buzzing on the table. I scrambled to grab it from underneath Captain's impressive bulk before it went to voice mail.

"Speak of the devil incubus," Carpe said.

I muted my game mic before answering. "How goes security?" I asked Rynn.

He exhaled a sigh. "Well, no more sign of the mercenaries. How about on your end? Any ideas where Jebe's resting place might be?"

"Yeah. About that. There's good news and bad news."

"Good news."

Yeah, he usually went for the good news. "Well, I've narrowed the burial site down to my top two." I'd gone on the idea that, sentient or not, the last thing the suit would want was to be tied to a corpse. It was attracted to death and destruction. So, in order for Jebe to foil it, he had to eschew the traditional unmarked burial place: it was too easy for the suit to call out to passersby to dig it up. Which meant it had to be in a location that deflected magic or kept people out, meaning temple. "One is a temple in the Tibetan side of the Himalayas, and the other one is back in Nepal in the Mustang region." Thankfully far away from where the mercenaries were still looking for me. "Both were used by the khans to hide their treasure."

"That sounds promising," Rynn offered. "I'd recommend we start with Tibet. Less chance of running into the mercenaries, and if it's the right location—"

"Yeah, about that," I said, cutting Rynn off. I glanced up at the screen. Still no monsters, and Carpe hadn't said anything. "There's a minor complication with Tibet."

Rynn waited.

"I might have had a less-than-friendly altercation with the Chinese antiquities authorities last month."

I counted to three while I waited for Rynn. "Over?" he finally said.

"A handful of terra-cotta warriors I was relocating."

Rynn swore. "Why am I only hearing about this now?" He kept his voice civil, but I could hear the strain.

"Because I knew you'd be upset, and I figured it was on a need-to-know basis."

"How is an altercation with the Chinese authorities on a need-to-know basis?"

"Because now we need to go into China so now you need to know?" I offered.

I knew he had to be frustrated and tired, because he let it go. "Fine, I'll look into it. Anything from the elf about the spell book?" There was tension in his voice as he asked.

"Not yet. Working on it."

"Let me know when you have something," he said before hanging up. Less personal than usual, but considering I'd thrown the China problem at him, he was taking it in stride.

I glanced back at the screen. There was a single word written in our pop-up messaging window that hadn't been there before.

Thief.

Asshole. I closed the message screen and got rid of Carpe's video.

A moment later it was back up. "Look, I'm not saying you are a bad person. What I'm saying is that things can't change their nature. It's like asking a tiger to be a pigeon. It's just not going to fucking happen." He inclined his head as if he was thinking about it. "Unless you used a lot of magic."

I unmuted my mic. "No magic!"

"And even then I have a feeling the tiger-pigeon would try and cannibalize his new pigeon buddies in a nascent reign of terror."

And that was where Carpe and I fundamentally disagreed on life. A tiger might not be able to turn itself into a pigeon, but a person could change who they were. And at the very least they could try.

Carpe was right about one thing; Rynn's views had been rubbing off on me.

"No, you're right, Carpe, I am a thief, but as opposed to settling for whatever dark and gloomy reflection you keep shoving at me at every turn, I'd much rather sign up for the one Rynn tries to show me." I muted the mic once again. I realized that the way Carpe saw me—an unchangeable thief—didn't sit well with me. Not one bit.

I caught the red light on my screen map indicating monsters. Finally. "Goblin up ahead," I said. I saw a series of magic missiles shoot past my avatar's head and registered the audio as they all found their mark. If there was one sorcerer's spell to level the heck out of the playing field, that was it.

There was a pause in the action as we waited for the smoke to clear and any remaining goblins to take their turn.

"So what you're saying is that you, Owl, international antiquities thief extraordinaire, believes what she's doing is wrong and is attempting to turn over a new leaf?" Carpe prompted.

I clenched my teeth. "I'm saying I can see Rynn's point and I'm not ruling it out—one day. After I finish exacting my revenge from the IAA in sweet, sweet, expensive antiquities."

The smoke cleared off the game screen at the same time that one last bad guy light appeared on my map in faint yellow. One goblin left, and he was running. Though he might not be dead, the yellow meant he'd be an easy kill. "I'll do it," I said. Easier for me to sneak up and put the goblin out of its misery than to have Carpe cast Magic Missile again. I set my avatar down the tunnel.

"And it's not like I haven't ever changed my mind before," I added. "Look at the supernatural thing. I used to hate supernaturals."

"And now there are a handful of supernaturals that you've decided are an exception to the rule. Again, tiger dressed up as a homicidal pigeon."

Okay, Carpe's pigeon analogy was starting to unnerve me. "You have an unhealthy obsession with homicidal pigeons," I told him.

"Look, let's just get back to the game," Carpe sighed. "And whatever it is you really brought me here to ask."

"Why does there have to be an ulterior motive? How do you know I want to ask about something other than World Quest? Maybe I just want to play a game?"

"Because you don't! Look, will you just cut the crap?"

I turned the corner and found the dazed goblin shaman panting in a corner. Blood spurted up as I did the coup de grace. "Hunh. Since when did World Quest go for the blood splatter?"

"Player feedback. Said it wasn't realistic enough."

I got a good look at the goblin blood that stained my avatar's face and clothes. "No offense to our upstanding community of players, but—"

"Ah, you know the rules. Question not their sanity or anything else that comes out of their mouths. Just give the horde whatever the hell it is they think they want, and maybe they'll go away."

"Elf proverb?"

"No. Best practices for dealing with the internet. Now fucking spill."

I started checking the goblins' inventory. Unlike other RPGs, when you loot a fresh corpse in World Quest, you actually see your avatar manhandle the body, looking for things. You start off gently and respectfully looking through their items, but the longer you hold down the button, the rougher and less respectful it gets. You also uncover more loot, sooo . . .

"Well?" Carpe probed.

"A couple spell scrolls, a couple decent knives, gold. Want a half-eaten goblin chicken wing?"

"I meant will you hurry up and ask me. . . . Wait, goblins don't keep chickens."

"I said goblin chicken. What lives in dark, dank tunnels underneath a city and are goblin-sized to eat?"

"No, I don't want a half-eaten rat! Gross. What the hell are the game designers thinking?"

"That if they have to do the blood spatter to appease the horde, they might as well trick them into eating rats?" I said as I finished looting the goblin corpses.

Regardless of the ease of the goblins, I wasn't detecting any more threats on the immediate game map, so I turned my attention back to Carpe. "All right, fine. Let's start with what it is the elves want with the Electric Samurai?"

I swear to God he had the audacity to lift his nose at me. "They don't want anything with the Electric Samurai."

"Jesus Christ, Carpe. If you were planning on lying in the first place, why the hell bother getting me to ask you?"

"Because otherwise you'll hold it over my head."

I started to say something and stopped. It was useless for me to argue with him. "All right, then. Why are the elves interfering with my investigation and attempts to *find* the Electric Samurai?"

"Now that I don't know. But technically they can't interfere."

"You used a qualifier in there, Carpe."

"They can't interfere because the elven council asked Mr. Kurosawa to get the suit for them. Scuttling their own deal would be against the rules."

I shook my head again. "You just told me they didn't want it."

"Since when has not wanting something stopped people from asking for it?"

Goddamn it. It was like talking to the Mad Hatter in *Alice in Wonderland.* I was starting to suspect Lewis Carroll had had numerous run-ins with elves. . . . "Okay, despite the fact that that makes absolutely no sense whatsoever—"

"Interfering would nullify whatever agreement the elves made. If you found the Electric Samurai suit despite our interference, then you wouldn't be bound to pay the fuck up, as you like to so eloquently put it. And if you *couldn't* find the suit, we'd still have to hold up our end of the bargain."

Okay. In a warped, roundabout way, that actually made more sense. The tunnel turned onto a dead end. The map showed a red *X* just ahead. We'd reached the treasure vault.

"Hold that thought," I said, and started another scan. "So, just so we're on the same page here, it has nothing to do with a sense of altruism or doing the right thing, and everything to do with making sure you don't fuck up your own deals?"

"Well, when you put it that way—"

"No, no. Leave it. I actually have an easier time swallowing that, all things considered. Still doesn't explain why someone would risk it."

"Again, you have no proof."

"Except we know it was an elf. Or something that smelled like an elf."

Carpe made a face. "Shit. I forgot about the incubus."

"Rynn."

"Whatever."

"Just answer the question. Why . . . or even better, *who* is trying to screw with my getting the Electric Samurai suit?"

"Okay, I probably shouldn't tell you this, but I doubt they're trying to prevent you from finding the armor. Why ask for it in the first place?"

"What about factions?"

"And they'd still be bound to the same deal. My guess is they're trying to hide something about it."

"Why?"

"There you have me. Probably don't want the dragon knowing what it can do. Or maybe they just don't like the idea of you knowing? Or maybe they think it'll piss off Rynn. He has a reputation amongst some of the higher-ups—and not a good one."

I watched Carpe's face. It was guileless, but somehow . . . "What are you not telling me?"

"Lots—because you're not asking me the right fucking questions."

I swore. "What do you want from me, Carpe? What does the suit do, who wants it, why can't you elves agree, why are elves a fucking pain in my ass?"

He held up his hands. "And none of that I can answer."

I shook my head and switched topics as I set about opening the vault door lock. It still didn't sit right with me though. The lock wasn't particularly hard, no traps . . . "Carpe, does it strike you that this tunnel is not what it might appear to be?"

"How so?"

"I mean, it's supposed to be Level seventeen with a Level thirteen monster, but even with that shaman those goblins were barely a Level ten, let alone thirteen."

"Maybe they were sent as a nuisance. To drain our spells? Or maybe the World Quest duo are going senile in their reclusive state."

Maybe. The treasure door swung open as the last locking mechanism clicked into place. I made my avatar hang back while Carpe cast light in the room.

Gold, ceramics, jewels . . . a decent treasure horde from the piles stacked against the wall. I even picked up a couple magic items mixed in.

No trap either. There ought to be some kind of challenge. "Okay, now I'm just plain weirded out."

"Maybe the World Quest designers really are losing their touch. Or maybe they just called this dungeon in?"

That struck me as the least-likely scenario. Still, we'd come this far, and it was only Level 18. We could handle it, even if I set off some hidden magic trap that brought a monster in.

Which reminded me. "Speaking about spells and traps, you still haven't answered my question about the spell book."

Carpe opened his mouth to say something, but he didn't get the chance.

The door slammed shut behind us. It *had* been a magical trap. Shit.

"Took you two assholes long enough" came a voice I recognized, heavy with a Texas drawl.

Both of us spun our avatars around until they were facing the back wall.

None other than Michigan and Texas—or their avatars—were leaning against the stone wall.

"You!" I said. Out of the two of them, I preferred dealing with Michigan. He was less abrasive than Texas—or Frank, as I'd recently found out. Of the two of them though, Frank usually spoke first.

"You just can't take no for an answer, can you, Hiboux?" His avatar's face might have been neutral, but his voice sure wasn't. "You want to tell us why the hell the IAA has every band of mercenaries on the planet looking for us?"

"Funny, I was kind of hoping you boys might be able to shed some light on that one for me."

"Well, sometimes you ask and someone decides to help you out. The rest of the time they tell you to fuck off and mind your own business. Kind of like I'm about to tell you to do—" Texas said.

"They know you're in Shangri-La," I interrupted.

Texas fell silent, and Michigan spoke up. "What else?" he asked.

I fished Neil's research journal, the one I'd found in Nepal, from under my other notes and held it open to the page coded with human magic. "Enough that I figure finding the city is just a bonus for them. I think they want whoever figured out how to do this."

I could see Carpe frowning at the screen. "What is that?" he asked.

Michigan answered for him. "You've got five minutes before I nuke both your characters from the game. Forever."

Great. Five minutes was all I needed.

11

THIEVES LIKE US

An hour later
Still trapped with Texas and Michigan in the
World Quest pit of despair

Okay, maybe five minutes was not all I needed. Especially when one of the people I was talking to was as stubborn as Texas.

"You know what I think?" Texas said, his voice screaming loud and clear across my headset. "I think you *want* them to find us. That this is all just some giant treasure hunt to you—one big excuse to hunt down Shangri-La."

"What I'm trying to do is stop them—" I heard an electrical snap across my headset. "Hey, asshole, what the hell happened to my audio?" I said, but the only place my voice sounded was around my room.

"How? By leading the fucking pack?" Texas continued.

Son of a bitch, he'd cut my mic output. No way was I letting them have an argument with me when I couldn't argue back.

Carpe, get my mic back on, I messaged.

"We've got your messages too, you know. We run the game, remember?"

I heard my mic click back on; apparently I was allowed to speak again. "I've been trying to find you because I *don't* want the IAA to win. Call me sentimental, but I'd rather not see anyone else subjected to their personal brand of screwing people over."

"And I'm guessing that the IAA offering you a pardon makes no never mind to you?" Texas said, his voice dripping with sarcasm.

Why did everyone always assume the worst of me? "Been there, done that. They fuck you over. The end."

"Look at it from our perspective, Owl," Michigan piped up again. "Even if your intentions were good, all you've done is lead them closer."

"And you keep underestimating them. If I'd left them to their own devices, one of them would have stumbled onto your hiding spot and you'd have been none the wiser. And if you haven't noticed, the mercenaries they've brought in are serious—as in guns and explosives serious."

Michigan and Texas went silent. The fact that the World Quest avatars had the best graphics in the game made it look as if Texas was glaring at me. Considering how well we got along, he probably was.

I closed my eyes. I didn't have time to convince them . . .

Texas sighed. "All right, say we believe you—big fucking *if*; what do you plan on doing about it? Let me guess, we just let you stroll into our hideout."

I made a face. "No, asshole, you can keep your fucking hiding place."

"Everyone calm down," Michigan said before Texas could add insult to injury. "Hypothetically, what is it you're proposing?"

"Okay, the first step in dealing with the IAA in my opinion is to screw them where it hurts—"

Texas snickered. I ignored him.

"In this case, figure out whatever the hell it is they're after and why now. I have the first part of that equation. I was really hoping you two could shed light on the why now—beyond the fact that they want magic they can use."

"How about you shining a giant floodlight on the game?" Texas said.

The more I'd run it over in my head, the more I wasn't buying it. Me turning up artifacts couldn't be the whole story. I was a pain in their ass, but even I didn't have those kinds of delusions of grandeur.

There was a pause on the line. Carpe was keeping oddly silent.

"What?" When there wasn't an immediate answer, I was certain. "What are you two not telling me?"

I heard Michigan sigh. "We were hoping you knew something on the IAA's motives." His avatar even took on a reticent expression. "To be honest, we were worried. Well, we kind of assumed—"

Texas answered. "What he's trying to say is that we figured *you* wanted to get your grubby hands into Shangri-La and were orchestrating this whole fiasco."

"Oh, come on. Seriously? I am not that much of an asshole." Petty thievery, maybe, but break into Shangri-La? I'd thought about it, fantasized in my dreams a couple times, but even I have lines. "Besides, I wouldn't know where to look. And you can be damn sure I sure wouldn't get the IAA involved. Do I look that stupid? Don't answer that, Texas," I added as one of them cleared their throat. "They came to *me*—"

"And offered you a deal."

"Breaking into my apartment to threaten me, then opening a bounty on World Quest is not a deal. Worse, now they know I'm not playing ball, so they've offered me up to the mercenaries. And no," I said, pointing at the camera, "you can't offer me to the mercenaries to get your own necks out of trouble," I added.

I waited, a prickly feeling like static crawling over my skin as their CGI avatars appeared to converse. It was like a flashback from when I'd had a fever and had been convinced I was in the game. I pushed the sensation aside. I was just watching a game with very good graphics and having an LSD-like flashback from the curse . . . probably happened all the time.

"They're not above making a show of things to set an example," Texas said, but without his usual bluster. "I've seen it before; remember the Aztec dig back in 2005?"

"They let them go free after a couple weeks in jail, said it was all one big mistake," I said as my memory jogged. A couple of grad students on a Mexico dig had been caught telling supernatural tales to impress coeds on spring break. A couple kilos of cocaine had ended up in their luggage.

Texas snorted. "Yeah, funny how they never told that to the drug lords the IAA lifted the cocaine from in the first place. They still don't get a good night's sleep."

"I think we should tell her," Michigan said.

"Why? So she can tell the mercenaries?"

I banged my head on the desk. "I already told you I'm not working with the mercenaries. Tell them, Carpe."

"I can't."

"What do you mean you can't?"

"I mean I don't think she's working with the mercenaries. They're chasing her too—but it's not like I know for certain."

"Carpe, you're a lousy World Quest partner," I said, then turned my attention back to the World Quest dynamic duo. "Okay, ignore the part about not being certain. You heard him, and you like him, and he doesn't think I'm dirty. That's got to count for something?"

Texas's avatar narrowed his eyes and glared at me. "What is that thing I keep hearing about you? Something about a brother standing in a Mexican whorehouse?"

I swore. I was blaming Benji for that one. "Look, will you stop it with the insults? I'm trying to help, not lead you to the mercenary slaughter."

Michigan piped up. "No offense, Owl, but intentions aside, you kind of have a reputation."

"He's got a point," Carpe said.

"Carpe—stop helping. And what happened to me saving the world twice? From an army of the living dead and getting you that stupid book."

"Okay, I had a pretty big hand in guiding you toward the book—but yeah, if you consider that three months ago an army of corpses flooded L.A., she kind of stopped it."

I gritted my teeth. "Thanks for that resounding endorsement. Really gets me right here," I said, slapping my chest over my heart.

"Hey, I'm trying to help. I'm not like you; I won't corrupt my own morals to do the right thing."

The audio feed snapped. "How the hell are you two one of the best teams in World Quest?" Texas said. "Jesus, it's like listening to a couple of three-years-olds. Fucking unbelievable. I'm starting to think we should say to hell with the game and take the whole thing down." There was a sigh. "All right, I've heard enough. You two are both in my asshole books."

"Me?" Carpe piped up. "What did I do?"

"You threw your teammate under the fucking bus. Who does that?" Texas said.

"Have you met her?"

Oh, for the love of— "Go to hell, Carpe."

Texas snorted. "I'm putting an end to this twisted three-ring circus now. Owl, you and your fucking elf can take your IAA shit storm and—"

"*Wait.*"

We all went silent as Michigan spoke up. "It's because they found out we're in Shangri-La. They weren't certain before, but somehow they got confirmation. That's what started this new hunt."

That wasn't what I'd been expecting. I'd assumed the IAA had known they were in Shangri-La. I mean, that was where the clues had led. "How . . . who told them?" I asked.

"You're my first choice."

"Frank—enough." Michigan let out a breath. "We know you didn't tell them. For the most part the last four years we got lucky. We weren't exactly high up on the food chain."

Texas jumped in. "They knew it was a possibility we'd found it, but I don't think any of them really believed we could find it—or any trace of it."

"In the last few weeks that changed. At first we thought it was one of you two figuring out that if we had it on the World Quest map, it had to be real. But then the time line doesn't work out," Michigan said.

"You're not the first treasure hunter they've gone after in the last few months. I don't think you even made their list of first choices."

"Let me guess, I trash just as many sites as I don't?" I said. Captain picked that moment to jump up from his nap, scattering my papers and letting out a startled chirp. I caught most of them before they cascaded off the desk, then shoved Captain off them before he could do any more damage.

"No, more than everyone knows the IAA fucked you over pretty spectacularly and even they're not stupid enough to go chasing rattle-snakes," Texas said.

"Fascinating character assassination aside, that still doesn't answer the why *NOW*—" The last part I had to shout because Captain decided to let out another long meow.

"What is that?" Michigan asked.

"My cat," I said, and scrambled to grab a glass he knocked over before it rolled off the desk. Captain hopped to the floor and slinked for the door.

"My God; not only are you loud and obnoxious but your animal is too?" Texas said.

As if in answer, Captain let out another wail. I frowned. He was crouching by the door, alert, his tail twitching rapidly and his ears back.

A cold chill hit me. My cat didn't do that unless there was something wrong. Like vampire or Naga wrong . . .

"Alix?" Carpe said, sounding hesitant. He'd met my cat.

I opened my mouth to say something but was cut off by a muffled bang in the hall, followed not by yells but by a deafening silence.

"Hold on," I said, and headed for the door, where Captain was hud-dled, growling. I peeked through the fisheye. A heavy white smoke filled the bottom third of the hall.

"Shit." I pulled out my cell and texted Rynn. *Rynn?* I texted into my phone. *Any idea what's going on in the hall outside our suite?* I really hoped that was some kind of security exercise, because the alternative . . .

An alarm sounded. Loud and piercing, not unlike a fire alarm. The dreams I had of an impromptu security exercise faded like most of my half-baked, hopeful wishes.

"What's going on?" Carpe said, a hesitant tone in his voice.

The heavy smoke was filtering under the door now. I tried to pull Captain away while I scrambled through my bag for my gas mask, but it was no use—he was back growling at the smoke coming under the door. Damn cat. "Hey, Carpe—you still have access to the Japanese Circus security systems?" I said.

"On it already."

If anyone could hack into the Japanese Circus security systems. . . . I turned my attention back to Michigan and Texas. "Look, guys, I hate to cut our conversation short—"

"Alix, I've got mercenaries in the Japanese Circus. They're on your floor," Carpe interrupted, his voice not panicked exactly but more animated than it had been a moment before.

"We'll be in touch," Michigan said.

"In the meantime, try not to burn the world down," Texas added before their audio feed snapped off. I slid my gas mask on.

There was a banging at the door.

"Alix?" came Carpe's voice across my headset. "Just getting into the cameras now. You've got a group of mercenaries outside your door."

Fantastic. "How many?" I said, lowering my voice as another muffled bang sounded right outside my door. I checked my phone, but still nothing from Rynn.

"Best guess, four, but it could be more. They've flooded the entire floor with smoke, and it's running havoc with the cameras and sensors."

Damn it. I glanced over to where Captain had wedged himself under a table by the door, as if waiting to pounce on whoever might be entering his territory.

Great. Now he was taking affront to non-supernaturals. So much for socialization. My cat was going to get himself killed.

And me with no weapons that would work on humans besides a metal chair. I grabbed Captain and pushed my desk over, forming a barricade before settling in behind it. He let out a growl of disapproval but didn't launch an outright attack on my hands. I took that as a win.

"Quiet," I whispered at him and did my best to tune into the mercenaries behind the door.

It was faint, but they were talking in Spanish, if the "*para*" and "*silencio*" were any indication. Hunh. Not the Zebras. I didn't think the South Africans would be stupid enough to break radio silence; they hadn't during any of our previous encounters.

If they weren't bright enough to keep their conversation down, maybe we'd get lucky with radio. "Carpe, are you picking up any of their conversation?" I whispered.

"My Spanish is rusty, but something about a door?"

I heard the unwrapping of something, and then what I thought was "*get back*" mumbled in Spanish.

Shit. I scrambled for the couch and grabbed a couple of pillows to press against our ears before diving back behind the overturned desk. I noticed the journals—Jebe's and Neil's. I grabbed them, shoving them inside my belt.

No sooner had I managed to get Captain under a pillow than an explosion rocked the room.

Even though I'd been prepared for it, I was dazed. It took my ears and head a few seconds to stop ringing. When I did take the pillow off, I wasn't alone. There was a barrel of a military-grade rifle pointed in my face over the desk—no, make that two of them—held by two men dressed in black paramilitary gear and wearing gas masks that rivaled mine.

I swallowed and managed to restrain Captain before he could launch himself at anyone holding a gun. Two more men moved into the room after hand signals from the one on my left, and I thought I caught a fifth taking up point in the hall by the door. It was hard to tell with the smoke.

"Hey? Alix?" came Carpe's voice in my headset.

I ignored him, keeping my eyes on the mercenaries.

They were all wearing masks. The one on my left, pointing the gun at me—the same one who had signaled the others and who, I reasoned, had to be in charge—motioned me to stand up with the barrel of his gun. I started to rise, slowly, buying myself time to think. He jabbed the barrel into my chest. "All right, all right, I get the idea," I said as I stood, still gripping Captain under my arm, much to his chagrin. Tough. If I got the chance to make a run for it, the last thing I needed was a loose cat behind enemy lines.

I waited for them to say anything, but all they did was secure my suite; the two who weren't holding me at gunpoint went from room to room. I let them. Always good to cooperate when the people holding guns weren't hitting me.

They found a couple of the weapons Rynn kept lying around, though I highly doubted that was all of them.

They should have said something by now. "Look, guys, isn't this the part where you talk and start making demands?"

They ignored me as one of the ones who'd searched my suite spoke into his radio, in English this time. "Secured the objective. Stand by to transport."

Objective? Wait a minute, the only thing they'd secured was me. Damn it, the IAA really was serious about handing me over to the mercenaries—apparently first come, first served.

"You're making a huge mistake—" I tried.

The one who spoke English—a large man over six feet tall—glanced at me this time. "There is no mistake," he said in a gruff voice, showing me his phone screen—a picture of my face with a lot of Spanish below it. "You are the rogue archaeologist we are being paid to retrieve."

"Rogue archaeologist? Is that what they told you?" From the way the others deferred to him, I was betting he was the one in charge. "Look, dude, I hope they told you more than that—"

I was cut off by one of the subordinates still holding a gun on me. I didn't catch all of it; it was a Paraguay accent, one I wasn't as familiar with, but I understood "*incommunicado.*" Their partners, or whoever they were supposed to meet up with, had gone silent.

But they seemed more surprised than they should have been. I mean, this was a casino full of supernaturals. It dawned on me . . .

"Dude, I hope the IAA told you more about this place than there was a rogue archaeologist inside."

"You're a thief," the one I figured was in charge said, as the others tried again to bring up their mercenary friends. "Antiquities, specialized."

They didn't realize who this casino belonged to . . . or, more importantly, *what* this casino belonged to.

Oh man, it was going to be a bad day for these guys.

I tensed as he began rifling through the folders that had spilled onto the floor. I was acutely aware of the two journals under my shirt.

More attempts to raise their friends led to a heated exchange.

"Look, I really think you guys are firing a few puzzle pieces short—"

"Quiet, and turn around. Slowly put your hands on your head or they shoot your cat," the one in charge spat at me before nodding at his two companions, still training their guns on me.

I did as they asked and placed Captain on the carpet, grateful that he didn't bolt. Then slowly, like the man said, I put my hands on my head. Maybe I could still talk some sense into them. "Look, there's still time to leave now and chalk this up to a big misunderstanding . . ." I started.

One of the guards behind me hissed. Still, I kept going. These guys might be assholes, but much like me, they were on someone's payroll. The longer this went on, the worse it was going to be for them. "I'm offering you guys a freebie here—"

"We can handle an incubus," the one behind me said, pushing the barrel into my lower back.

So they did know there were supernaturals in here. Still . . . "That's really not the one you need to be worried about. Didn't you guys wonder why the Zebras are sitting things out in a hotel at the end of the strip, drinking beer?"

"Cowards," one of the two behind me spat in heavily accented English—the one on my right, who hadn't spoken until now. "Lazy, waiting to see what you'll do next. We'd rather take the money now from under them."

Oh man. Greed and arrogance were the true downfall of people everywhere.

The rattle of a snake's tail sounded from somewhere down the hall. Another nervous look exchanged between the mercenaries.

I craned my neck until I was facing the one holding me. "Tell me, did you gas a Japanese woman on your way in? Expensive heels, designer suit, red lipstick and nails—hard to miss?"

One of them snickered.

"Because if you guys did, I so can't help you."

The sound of a rattle grew louder. The three other mercenaries in the room stopped in their tracks and looked at each other. Sometimes there really wasn't anything I could do to save other people from their own stupidity.

The gun jabbed between my shoulder blades, making me stumble forward. "What trick is this?" Captain started sniffing the air and let out a quiet growl from where he was crouched by my feet.

"No trick." Another shove.

I heard the hiss of green-gold leather scales sliding against the expensive carpet, and I licked the nervous sweat from my lip. Not that I was huge on the idea of handing a couple humans over to Lady Siyu to chew on, but at some point I had to pick my moral battles. The question was would she take these guys out before or after they got nervous enough to fire the guns.

Hands still on my head, I turned around and looked the mercenaries in the eyes—the only part of their faces that showed through the masks. "The IAA, your boss—whoever told you I was here? They must have it in for you, because they didn't tell you the most important thing."

They exchanged another glance as a louder hiss sounded through the hall, as if emanating from the walls themselves. The mercenary in the hall shouted a warning.

Once they had me outside the casino . . . I needed to stall. "Don't get me wrong," I said, "the incubus is scary and is probably going to hurt you really badly."

"*Quiet*," the mercenary said. He motioned for the two men to grab me, and the four of them, towing me, exited into the hall to join the fifth, who'd been on lookout. Taking point down the hall, each on edge, they picked up their gait, heading for the elevator.

I searched the smoke for Lady Siyu, but where there'd been the sound of her scales a moment before, now there was nothing.

I flinched as something wet dripped on my face. For a second I thought it was sweat, but sweat didn't burn. I glanced up as cautiously as I could.

Suspended on the ceiling of the hall, blended in with the gold-and-green baroque wallpaper, was Lady Siyu. She was Naga'd out, fangs extended and not a trace of her human guise remaining.

Whatever you do, Owl, under no circumstances are you to lick your lips. "So I'm curious; what does the mercenary handbook say about strolling into a dragon's lair?" I asked.

That got their attention. "Dragon?" one of them said.

"She's lying, there's no dragon."

I watched the numbered light move. The elevator would be here in a few more floors. Lady Siyu better hurry up . . .

I saw the glint of gold-green scales as she moved above me, closer to the mercenaries. I figured that was all the warning I was going to get. I made ready to jump. "Good news! You're about to become the cautionary tale."

The elevator chimed its arrival, and I dove out of the way as Lady Siyu dropped from the ceiling, taking out three of the mercenaries before they could retrain their guns, and knocking out at least one for the long haul. She moved like lightning after that, immobilizing the other two with her teeth while they were still on the ground.

Two left standing. Unfortunately, they were positioned in a way that made it impossible for her to take them out in one shot, even with her speed and the added length of her tail.

She went for the sure thing—the last lackey standing closest to her.

Time for Owl to exit stage left. I started to crawl toward the now-open elevator. Something grabbed my foot. They didn't let go. It was the remaining mercenary. "If you know what's good for you, you'll run," I shouted, aiming a kick at his face.

Whether it was pride or panic, he wasn't listening. Before I could deliver another kick to his face, he had me around the waist and positioned as a shield.

"That was about the stupidest—" I began. He jostled me to shut up.

Lady Siyu had finished with the other mercenary, and she hissed, turning on the remaining member of the group. "Stay back," he shouted.

I caught a glint in Lady Siyu's eyes.

Yeah . . . nuts to seeing just how far "accidents" got tolerated in the Japanese Circus.

I threw my weight into my hip and tried one of the throws Rynn had shown me. In theory, when I pushed my hip back and threw, my opponent was supposed to sail over my shoulder and fall flat on his back, splayed out. It hurt. I should know; Rynn had shown me enough times before I'd figured out the break fall part.

In practice, my hips went back and hit something akin to a brick house. I'd like to think I knocked the wind out of him, but that was being generous.

Well, on to tried-and-true methods.

I kicked back and up between his legs—hard. He didn't yell or scream, but there was an audible exhale of breath. I don't care how well trained you are as a mercenary; a well-trained kick to the groin loosens any man's grip.

It wasn't much of a gap, but it was enough. I stamped on his foot and got myself a little more space—enough to slide out.

He was blocking the elevator, so I turned and ran for the exit door, slamming into it before taking the stairs up, two at a time.

There was an inhuman shriek behind me, Lady Siyu I presumed, followed by another bang at the exit door. I sped up even as my legs and lungs protested, taking three steps at a time instead of two. *Ankles don't fail me now.*

I could hear the heavy boots behind me. He wasn't taking the stairs quite as recklessly as I was, but I had no doubts my cardio would give out before his did.

I rounded the corner and saw the twenty-third-floor door ahead of me—Mr. Kurosawa's floor.

I hesitated, but only for a second. I ducked as a bullet struck the cement above me. Didn't have time for smart plans—I threw myself into the door as hard as I could, then spilled onto the bloodred carpets and bolted for the massive black-and-gold doors. *Please be open, please be open.*

I threw myself into the doors. I don't know what I'd been expecting, but it hadn't been for them to swing open to the maze. Either Mr. Kurosawa knew what I was about to do, or the ghosts figured another pansy was about to join their ranks; as if in anticipation, the slot machines were silent for once, not even their lights flickering in the dark.

I heard the bang of a door behind me. Let's hope the ghosts and dragon were feeling altruistic today. I ran for the nearest set of machines, but something Rynn had told me over and over again made me skid to a stop short of the dark marble tiles that denoted the start of the maze itself: "*Never go in on your own.*"

Something told me that was not the rule to push today, so I searched for somewhere short of the maze to hide. One of the machines off to the side, a 1970s-era slot machine, started to chime and spew coins on the floor. I hoped that was a ghost's way of offering me an alternative. . . .

I slid behind the machine as the black doors swung open once again.

I didn't dare peek, but I did listen as the heavy boots slowed.

I quieted my breath.

"I'll give you the snake lady was a surprise," he called out as he made his way around the front of the casino, "though I still don't believe in your dragon nonsense." He spit on the black floors, as if punctuating the statement.

I listened to his footsteps and wondered if he'd stopped short of the dark, smoky tiles. Some instinct telling him not to continue forward.

Another step . . .

It would be so easy, so easy to just let him disappear into the maze. He'd been shooting at me—with bullets—and they'd been about to kidnap me. I jumped as a slot machine behind me spit out a single gold coin, of a denomination I didn't recognize. Nothing loud enough to attract the mercenary's attention, but enough to get its warning across.

I swore under my breath. "I really hate my morals sometimes," I whispered to it. I hoped the echo in this place would hide my location . . .

"Don't step on the dark tiles," I shouted. "Just put your weapon down and surrender." I swore, covering my head as gunfire sounded around me. A number of slot machines began to chime and spew coins. When the gunfire stopped and I wasn't dead, I continued. "If you thought the Naga and the incubus were bad, you haven't seen anything yet." This time though my voice didn't come from where I was. It twisted, as if coming from the depths of the maze itself.

"You're in there? Aren't you? Hiding." The mercenary made a derisive noise and spit on the floor again. "You can't fool me with your ghost stories."

As if that was a cue, one of the machines in the maze began to chime. Others followed, until there was a veritable path of lights and sound leading into the slot machine maze's heart.

"You can't cover your tracks with sounds, thief. I know exactly where you are!" he called out. Over the noise I heard the fall of his footsteps as he stepped over the line of smoky marble.

The maze went silent, and a few heartbeats later I heard the shout, then the bloodcurdling scream. I plugged my ears and closed my eyes. Damn it, this wasn't what I wanted. But there were only so many things you could do to save someone.

Still, it never sits well with me. Stupidity gets you dead, but it's awful final. Call me sentimental, but I'd rather see people learn from their mistakes. Not die from them.

The slot machines were silent once more, and through my plugged ears I heard the familiar click of heels against the tiles. I frowned. I hadn't heard the doors open again. I peeked around the slot machine.

Back to human form, Lady Siyu strode out of the maze at a leisurely pace, her eyes bright snake yellow and fixating on me as the click of her heels beat out a sinister tempo.

She might be human again, but she hadn't bothered to hide the blood that now covered her face and her suit. And she was dragging the mercenary behind her as if he'd been a feather doll, not a six-foot grown man.

"I never thought I'd live to say this, but am I ever glad to see you—" I started.

Lady Siyu hissed. "The feeling is fortunately not mutual," she said. She stepped onto the white tiled foyer and deposited the mercenary none too gently, before beginning to prod him with her foot and sniff at the air above him. She then turned her yellow snake gaze on me. "Wonders do not cease."

"What? That I didn't end up dead?" I said, scrambling out of my hiding site. "It happens, you know—"

"That you managed to execute a halfway decent strategy. Luring him into the maze and then pleading with him not to enter." She gave me a reappraising look. "Wonders never cease, thief. I am impressed."

A pit formed in my stomach. Lady Siyu thinking I'd planned to lure him into the maze was worse than the fact that I hadn't managed to convince him not to. Much worse.

Lady Siyu picked the mercenary up by the collar and continued to drag him toward the exit.

"Come," she shouted over her shoulder when I didn't immediately move.

"For what?"

She glared.

"I mean, not me . . . I know why you don't want me in here—" *Owl, stop babbling.* "Where are you taking him?" I asked instead.

Her red lacquered lips parted in a smile—the first one I had ever seen, I think. As vicious and cold as she was. "Why, so he can be questioned, of course," she said, and pushed open the massive doors.

And of course I'd been stupid enough to ask. Without asking I could have fooled myself into thinking they just tossed them out on the curb.

Okay, probably not that, but you'd be surprised what my imagination can come up with under stress.

I followed. I could lie and say I didn't have any option, and it was mostly true if you took out "death by angry Naga" as an option. But in all honesty? Like I said—some days you had to pick which moral battles to fight. Some of my brain wanted to fight out of principle, but mostly it decided that this wasn't the one to pick.

Did that make me a bad person? Days like this, I wasn't so sure.

12

MERCENARIES

8:00 p.m. The poolside bar at the Japanese Circus Casino

I stared at my open laptop screen as I sipped my beer, though I'd be lying if I said I was concentrating on the files I had open on Jebe.

A message box popped up in the corner of my screen. Carpe.

Hey—I've been trying to get you on your phone.

I'm taking a break. Ask me in another 30 minutes, I wrote back. Not that I planned on answering in thirty minutes; if things went as planned, I'd be too drunk to consider answering my phone . . . or at least turn it back on. See? Forethought.

I minimized the screen, only to have it pop back up a moment later.

So . . . you seriously led the guy into the dragon's maze? That's harsh, even for you, Byzantine.

I swore and minimized the screen again, hitting the keys with more force than was specifically necessary. Sometimes I wondered why it was I bothered to be a better person—not when everyone, including Carpe, assumed that every outcome was due to me trying to be an asshole.

I was getting a deeper and up close understanding of just how hard it was to shake a reputation. The world really sucked sometimes . . . and so did Carpe.

Ah, screw it. I polished off what was left of my beer and leaned over the bar. I'd seen that bottle of tequila hanging around here somewhere.

I heard Captain chirp from where he'd managed to make a bed for himself in one of Lady Siyu's many flower beds.

"So this is where you got off to. I might have known," Rynn said before sliding into the seat beside me.

"Watch it. Captain is now showing an interest in incubi," I said. *Come on, tequila bottle, where'd you go?*

"More likely he smells a trace of Lady Siyu on me."

Ah! There it was. One of the nymphs had hidden it behind a tray of glasses. Must be new. They usually did a better job.

"Tequila?" Rynn asked, taking the bottle unceremoniously from my hands.

I shrugged. "I ran out of beer, and this seemed like as good a substitution as any." Rynn didn't say anything; smart man—or incubus—that he was, he simply handed me back my tequila.

"You left," Rynn said as I poured myself a shot.

"Yup," I said. I stared at it, then at my empty beer bottle. I held up the bottle to Rynn and arched my eyebrows.

He sighed but stepped behind the bar to retrieve a new one for me.

The beer the nymphs always managed to hide.

I waited until Rynn placed the new bottle in front of me. I took a generous sip before adding a shot of tequila and taking another large swig.

Only then did I look up at Rynn.

The interrogation hadn't gone well—or maybe it had and I just didn't have the right perspective or stomach for it. I'd left as soon as Lady Siyu had broken out the fangs in front of the five mercenaries she'd tied to chairs while the three more Rynn had found in the lobby had waited, trussed up, in the corner.

Based out of Paraguay, they were a newer company of mercenaries who'd decided to branch out into the supernatural. They were still trying to establish themselves, which is why they'd decided to jump in on the lack of action at the casino. Or that was as much as I'd gotten before one of them had started to pray to Jesus . . . or maybe it had been to Lady Siyu. The gag had made it hard to tell.

"I am not cut out for mercenary work," I said, and took another swig of my tequila-laced beer.

When Rynn didn't answer, I added, "What happened to them?"

Rynn poured himself his own shot and passed me a second one. He even managed to retrieve a couple limes and salt. "We wiped their memories and deposited them outside the hotel. Or I wiped their memories. Lady Siyu wanted to castrate them and do something creative with their—"

"Don't want to know."

Rynn paused to shoot his tequila, and I joined him. "The Zebras are playing dirty. They were the ones who gave them the bright idea to try the casino—through indirect means, but it was them. They wanted to see how good our defenses were."

"Do you think they got what they wanted?"

Rynn seemed to consider that. "More than I'd like, but considering we didn't have to use any of our real defenses—"

"They made it to my floor." That was pretty damned effective if you asked me.

"Only because I let them."

I glared at Rynn, but he wasn't looking at me. I felt my own anger rise. "Seriously? You let them in and you didn't think to warn me?"

He did make eye contact, but his expression was anything less than apologetic. "You weren't in any real danger," he said, "but a far sight better the Zebras think our defenses are weak than to have any real idea of what we can do. Consider this one of those judgment calls that you make."

I didn't say anything. I was fuming too much.

"It wasn't a decision I enjoyed," he added.

I took another sip from my tequila-laced beer. "I think I preferred it when people were just pissed about me taking artifacts. Somehow, this just feels . . ." *More serious* I was going to say, but that didn't quite cover it. ". . . not the direction I would have gone," I said, and left it at that.

"In all honesty, neither would I, though the fact that there is one less mercenary group on our trail will make the other ones more cautious."

This was the second time now the South African mercenaries had almost caused disaster, directly or not. "At least Nadya got out before things hit the fan. That's a bonus."

Rynn snorted. "I just spoke to Nadya—said your phone was off." He hesitated before adding, "She said things are heating up, not cooling down as we'd hoped. There were break-ins at both our clubs. Minor damage, but the fact they managed to gain entry is the more troubling part, especially where Gaijin Cloud is concerned."

Rynn's club, and one I suspected had its fair share of supernaturals on staff. "Not what I needed to hear," I said.

"No, but if I didn't tell you now, you'd be more pissed off later."

I begrudgingly lifted my glass. He had a point.

"Whoever is behind the Tokyo mess, they're like a ghost," he said, and shook his head. "Things are strange, and let's leave it at that."

Not dangerous yet, but I held no illusions that that wasn't the direction things were going . . .

Rynn let out a sigh and brushed a loose strand of hair out of my face. "What about you? How are things on the treasure raiding end?"

"I'm not going to lie, I'm a little out of my league here, Rynn. I mean, mercenaries? That's you, not me. If I was a worse person I'd be tempted to leave the suit to the elves and World Quest to the IAA." I related my partial discussion with Michigan and Texas before the mercenaries had interrupted us.

"So Shangri-La is more than it seems," Rynn mused. "Leave the IAA problem to me for now. I can keep the mercenaries at bay a while longer. Meanwhile, you worry about finding Jebe's suit."

And that was part of the problem. "They're linked, Rynn. I'm not certain of the why but there is no way the IAA's search for Neil and Frank isn't connected to the elves bid for the Electric Samurai. And I think I might know the how." Rynn arched an eyebrow, and I pulled up the file on Jebe I'd been reading before I'd decided to drown my conscience in tequila and beer.

I showed him my laptop. "This is the original manifest we found in Vancouver—the household and campaign accounts for Jebe. This comment, written in the margins at the end?"

"You dismissed this before. Household goods, textiles, foods— hardly seems worth mentioning."

"Originally that's what I thought too, and so did the researchers who added their own translations over the years, but look here—" I showed him a section from a later academic paper that examined the Mongolian dialect used at the time. It had brought into question the use of some of the terms associated with households, and suggested they'd been much more inclusive than previously supposed. "According to this, 'household goods' refers not just to textiles and dry food goods but anything associated with Jebe—his army, textiles, slaves, horses, *weapons*."

Rynn peered over my shoulder and scrolled down the screen. "It says a large portion of household goods were donated to a monastery in the Guge Empire. That's in modern Tibet," he said.

I nodded and pulled the message that Neil and Frank had sent to both Carpe and me, along with directions to a location where they wanted to meet us. "Look what else is in Tibet," I said, and showed him the location the World Quest duo had forwarded me and Carpe only half an hour before.

He read the message before looking back up, a disquieted look on his face. "I don't like coincidences like this."

I inclined my head. "Coincidence or not, looks like we'll be hitting two birds with one stone."

Rynn started to pour himself another shot of tequila but then seemed to think better of it.

"Technically Tibet's in China." I winced as Rynn said something unpleasant-sounding in supernatural.

"You don't make things easy," he said.

"Maybe Carpe can wipe my photo off their recognition software."

Rynn started to say something, but Captain chose that moment to lift his head out of the garden he was destroying and chirp at the doors.

I spun, half expecting to see Lady Siyu stride out of the double glass doors. It wasn't Lady Siyu though, but someone shorter and lankier in build who stepped out into the Garden Café area.

I narrowed my eyes . . . slim build, dressed in jeans and a World Quest hoodie pulled down over his face. Even though he was standing, he was hunched at the shoulders the way I often see computer programmers and gamers stand. There was a bright green backpack thrown over his shoulders.

Showing more interest than he usually did with people, Captain chirped again and wandered over, sniffing at his shoes. The man tried to shoo him away, but to no avail.

It couldn't be him. . . .

". . . we'll figure out a way around the Chinese without the elf's help."

I was listening to Rynn, really I was, as I watched the slight figure try to repel my curious cat. The hood fell back as Captain went for a shoelace, revealing the long brown hair and pointed ears.

Oh, hell no . . .

". . . we're on the edge of a supernatural civil war, and all anyone can think about is moving their chess pieces," Rynn said, oblivious to the person at the door. "Politics is what they're all worried about. I wonder why I even bother—"

I grabbed Rynn's arm and nodded at the door. "Don't look now, but I think your bad mood is about to get much worse."

Rynn turned, his face twisting into a snarl at the sight of Carpe. "*You,*" he said, not bothering to hide his distaste. "I thought I told you never to come back."

"Um, yeah. Hi there, Alix, incubus—" Carpe started. Captain had hold of his shoelaces now and had decided they were his. Possession was 90 percent ownership . . . at least as far as cats were concerned.

"In those *exact* words," Rynn said, his voice rising to levels I rarely heard . . . if ever.

Carpe held up his hands. "I'm not here for your help this time, I'm here to help."

Rynn snorted. "That doesn't make me feel at all comforted. And the answer is still *no*."

I don't know what Carpe had expected his reception would be—especially from Rynn—but the way it flustered him, he hadn't expected this. "You need me," Carpe started.

Rynn stalked toward Carpe. Elf or not, Carpe had the good sense to step back. "The last time you accompanied us anywhere, you stole the plane, crashed it in the middle of nowhere, and almost got Alix killed crawling into a tomb."

"Now, that's not entirely true. I almost got Alix and her friend Nadya killed. You and me would have survived—but that's not the point." Carpe's voice shot up with the last part as Rynn gripped him by the front of his jacket and lifted him onto his toes.

I should probably have intervened. Then again, I was still pissed at Carpe for throwing me under the bus with the World Quest developers, among other things. And Rynn wouldn't kill him—at least I didn't think he would.

"I helped," Carpe said, straining to get the words out. Apparently incubus beat elf in strength.

"*After* I threatened to shoot you," Rynn said.

"Unfair." Carpe tried to say something else, but it was a losing battle against Rynn's grip.

"And I suppose the mercenaries let you stroll right in from the airport?"

"I think . . . they're all frightened of Lady Siyu . . . now," Carpe managed, and turned his brown eyes on me. "Look, Alix, let me help. At the very least I can monitor their communications. That has to be worth something."

Rynn looked to me. I had my misgivings about Carpe, but even I had to concede we could use the help—if only to monitor their communications.

"And last time I checked, you were down a delinquent archaeologist."

"You aren't a delinquent archaeologist, Carpe. And the last time I asked you for help, you told me to screw off."

"That's not—"

Rynn didn't let him finish. "What's to say you aren't here as their spy? That would be in their repertoire—send a friendly spy."

"I'm not!"

"And I don't believe you!" Rynn said, giving Carpe another shake as he struggled to wrench Rynn's hands off his jacket.

Okay, maybe I shouldn't have been so sure about Rynn's intentions toward Carpe. I realized both of them were looking at me. A pit formed in my stomach as I turned my options over in my head. I didn't trust Carpe—not completely—but he was my friend. He wasn't malicious, just selfish and single-minded when he thought he was right.

And prone to throwing me under the bus . . .

And he'd also found us a way out of the hostel . . .

"Why help?" I asked Carpe.

He gave me a confused stare—though that could have been the oxygen being cut off to his brain from the way Rynn had cinched his jacket.

I sighed. "Why offer to help? Clearly the elves don't want you involved, and the last time I checked, you were on their payroll. What's the incentive, Carpe?"

"Because I don't like the idea of World Quest being ruined by you or the IAA."

Rynn snorted, and Carpe turned his attention back on him. "And despite what you seem to think, I don't want to see a supernatural war spill out either."

The question was, how much did I believe that?

Enough.

I motioned for Rynn to put him down. He did, dropping Carpe in a heap before taking me off to the side of the bar.

"It's too much coincidence him appearing here now, Alix. I can't read elves like I can humans, but he's got an ulterior motive."

I glanced over to where Carpe was still slumped by the casino doors, rubbing his neck. Captain stood curious guard, sniffing and pawing at intervals. "He's never been malicious," I said carefully.

"Because being kind or helpful hasn't gone against whatever his orders have been. Yet. Mark my words, if he thinks for one moment that screwing you over will help the greater good or whatever agenda his higher-ups have given him, he'll be as malicious as he needs to be."

I chewed my lip and watched Carpe. I didn't want to think what he might be capable of—not after our fiasco in Egypt. I knew the kinds of lengths he was willing to go to when he thought he was in the right. That was part of the problem.

"He's right. We need him to keep tabs on the IAA and mercenaries," I said to Rynn.

He stared at me, incredulous. "You can't be serious."

"If he's going to screw us over— Call me a sucker for punishment, but I'd rather have him in our sights . . . or yours." What was that saying? Keep your friends close but your enemies closer?

Rynn looked far from convinced though. He shot Carpe a sideways glance. "This isn't play time in a computer game, Alix."

I felt my own irritation creep up the back of my neck. "Well, let's hear your idea for keeping tabs on the mercenaries, because I'm all out."

For a moment I thought Rynn was going to argue. But instead, he sighed and said, "All right, Alix. I'll go along, but at the first sign, and I mean the first, that he is working for the elves . . ."

"At the first sign that Carpe is here to screw us over, then you can deal with him," I said.

"By whatever means I deem necessary?"

I hesitated. That covered an awful lot of ground, considering the beef Rynn had with the elves in general.

"I'm sorry, Alix, but that's my hard line. Either you trust me to deal with him if it becomes necessary, or he's out."

I glanced over one last time at Carpe. Captain had gone back to battling over the shoelaces and the two were in a tug of war, but Captain didn't seem to think Carpe was a danger. I just hoped Captain's faith in Carpe was founded. And mine in Rynn. I nodded. "We'll do it your way."

"Thank you," Rynn said, squeezing my shoulder. He meant it.

I looked him in the eyes. "And I'm trusting you're not going to kill or maim Carpe outright."

Rynn nodded as he started back for the casino doors and Carpe, who was watching us, wary. "Now you just have to hope that he shares the same sentiment."

Thinking how close Carpe had cut it when warning us about the mercenaries and how easily he'd lied to me before . . . coincidences, close calls, and Carpe. Right now those were three Cs I could do without.

Rynn stopped just short of Carpe, who flinched. "We leave tomorrow morning," Rynn told him.

Carpe looked up from his tug of war with Captain with a mix of surprise and, I daresay, gratefulness. Maybe he really did just want to help. "Great. Where do I stay?" Carpe asked, pushing himself up and grabbing his green backpack.

"Pay for a room and make certain it isn't on our floor. Otherwise I don't care," Rynn said as he made his way through the sliding glass doors, a little less friendly than was maybe productive, but under the circumstances . . .

"Alix?" Carpe said, pulling my attention off Rynn's retreat into the casino.

I shook my head. I wasn't interested in pushing Rynn any more tonight. "Talk to the front desk, Carpe." I whistled for Captain, who hesitated over relinquishing Carpe's laces. Deciding there was a greater chance of food with me, he gave a last chirp and followed me into the casino.

So did Carpe. "Look, I was hoping we could talk without the incubus around—friend-like?"

"His name is Rynn."

"I'm pretty sure he prefers it if I don't use his name."

I glanced over my shoulder, ready to snap at Carpe, and stopped myself. He looked dejected. Rynn was at the elevators, watching as well, decidedly more hostile.

I shook my head at Carpe. "Not right now, Carpe. Tomorrow, okay? Go check in and get some sleep."

He opened his mouth to argue. Then, thinking better of pushing his luck any further than he already had, he drew in a breath. "Right," he said, nodding.

I started for the elevator, where Rynn was still waiting for me, watching Carpe.

"Alix?"

I turned to see what Carpe wanted. He was standing there, looking awkward and uncomfortable. "It's not the same, is it? Like when we're online."

That caught me off guard. Still, I shook my head. "No, it isn't."

"Why is that? Why aren't things the same between us?"

I thought about it. "Because things just aren't the same in real life as they are on the internet. In World Quest you get to be who you want to be, but out here?" I shrugged. "We're stuck with who we are. Just— I'll see you tomorrow, Carpe."

Without another word I turned back toward the casino. Rynn was still waiting for me outside the elevator.

I'd hoped he'd had a moment to cool off about my letting Carpe stay.

"I'm disappointed, Alix," he said as we stepped in the elevator.

Well, he wasn't yelling . . .

"I fear you've made a grave error with that elf," Rynn finally said to me, after the mirrored doors had closed shut.

I did not want to fight about Carpe. "He wouldn't do that."

"No, *you* wouldn't do that."

I stopped and really looked at him.

"*You* would never do that to someone you consider a friend, so you project that on those you call friends. I admire that about you, more than you could know, but it doesn't mean that he feels the same." He reached out for me, brushing my neck with his hands, then my cheek. "Or that he won't break your heart like so many people you've trusted have done before."

I felt Rynn's breath, warm on my face, as he leaned in and rested his cheek against mine.

I closed my eyes. "He's my friend," I said. And it was true. Despite his faults, despite the fact he pissed me the hell off, I considered Carpe my friend, at a time when I could count them on one hand missing a few fingers.

It might be stupid, but it earned him some leeway.

Rynn cupped my chin in his hand. "I know. And I'll be here to help you pick up the pieces when he betrays you, despite how much it hurts us both."

He kissed me before I could say anything else, his mouth warm and insistent on mine, more passionate than it had been since the search had begun for the Electric Samurai. He didn't let go or stop until the elevator announced with the chime that it had reached our floor.

I had to catch my breath as he took a step back. "I have to give him a chance. Otherwise, I'm no better than everyone who expected the worst from me."

"I'd be surprised if you did anything else."

We both exited the elevator and headed for our suite, Captain on my heels, though he had the good sense to keep quiet.

Neither of us said anything until we were inside. The suite looked as good as new, even after the mercenaries had rearranged the place. The wonders of supernaturally inclined house staff.

Deciding his attention and complaining weren't required, Captain went straight to scarfing down kibble in the kitchen, leaving Rynn and me alone. "You know, there's a way to handle someone who screws you over in Tibet," Rynn said. "Begins with a *Y* and ends in an *I*."

I snorted, happy for the break in seriousness. "With our luck they'll likely make the elf their fairy princess."

We'd deal with that hurdle when it arrived, though I hoped this trip wouldn't end up with having to throw Carpe to the yeti-goblins. I dropped my books back on the desk and glanced longingly at the bedroom. Sleep. That was what I needed—wanted—but there were still a few loose ends I needed to check on.

Rather than berate me, Rynn only came to stand behind me as I took my seat back at the desk. He leaned over to kiss my cheek. "Don't stay up too late," he whispered in my ear before disappearing into the bedroom.

For a moment I rethought joining him. Non-work-related time with Rynn had been in short supply recently.

In the end, that's what got me to turn back to my computer. The sooner we had this wrapped up, the sooner things could go to a relative version of normal and Rynn could stop worrying about a supernatural war. I started my computer. Sleep could wait for that.

There were new emails in my inbox, one a cryptic message from Nadya. *Things are getting worse and I still have no idea who is behind the thugs demanding a cut of the clubs.*

As if anticipating the questions that would raise, she'd added, *There are at least eight of us being targeted now, probably more who decided to cut their losses and pass the expense on to their patrons. Annoyances—nothing permanent yet, but things have a habit of getting worse before they get better.*

At the very end though was where I stalled. Nadya had added her own brand of personal advice relating to a paragraph I'd sent her regarding Carpe's eventual help in Vancouver. *Make sure you aren't helping someone throw you under a moving bus. This time I do not think that is what you need.*

She and I both. I sent a quick reply back, then opened up the information I'd collected on the lost Guge Empire in Tibet.

Let's hope I'm right about where you left the suit, Jebe. Otherwise you still might end up losing your last battle.

13

VIOLENT BUDDHISTS

12:00 p.m. Tsaparang, The Lost Empire of Guge, Tibet

I held on as the jeep rounded its way along the rocky mountain path. More desert than arid, there was no vegetation to speak of to soften the dirt roads or keep the dust down. It was hot like a desert as well, though I still wore my heavier cargo jacket and jeans. As soon as we hit the top of the city ruins the temperature would drop despite the sun, and then again once dark settled. The city fortress blended into the pale rocks of the mountain, all except the red monastery, like an imposing block, a beacon, signaling civilization in an otherwise hostile environment. It also completely negated any camouflage. Whether they hadn't needed it or hadn't cared . . .

During Jebe's lifetime, when the Mongol forces had been ravaging the eastern and western worlds, Tsaparang had been the capital of a small Tibetan kingdom called Guge, a trade point on the silk road linking India and ancient Tibet. For years now the IAA had written Tsaparang off as having no supernatural elements, meaning it was a favorite spot to train undergraduates, despite the remote area. Though lucky for us, the IAA student groups were still a few months away from their research visits.

Despite its reputation as a "safe" site, Tsaparang and the Guge had long been suspected of inspiring the Shangri-La legend, but no proof had been uncovered in the decades' worth of research that had followed. That didn't stop the rumors from persisting. Having an entire population disappear off the face of the planet will do that to a place. Shortly after they were discovered by Portuguese explorers in the 1620s, the entire civilization of Guge vanished. As in no trace. No descendants, no Be Back Soon notes, no *bodies*.

Theories abounded. Some historians claimed they were wiped out by disease introduced by the Europeans, while others claimed it was through centuries' worth of battles over the silk road trade route. Then there were those who thought the Guge had run afoul of the supernatural; cursed with infertility by a minor local deity, fallen prey to vampires or another local monster that decided they were a delicacy.

Seriously, it happened; look at the legends out of Transylvania.

None of them were perfect, but they earned you a respectable B to A- on a paper, unlike the remaining theory, which, although plausible, was still the stuff that automatically garnered you a D, C- grade on a paper.

That when invading forces came, the Guge simply up and left . . .

. . . through an entrance to Shangri-La. Hidden underneath the massive tunneled depths of the ancient Tsaparang fortress.

Not a bad theory as far as the hypothetical went, except for one problem; not one archaeologist in two hundred years had found a single mention of Shangri-La *anywhere* in the mountains or temples of Guge. Not a single magic inscription.

They also hadn't found any trace of Jebe's treasure horde—or at least not that I could find mentioned in the stacks of research.

What can I say? I liked a good wild-goose chase.

And one thing was certain, there was no way Guge was on the IAA's or the mercenaries' lists.

I sat back and watched as the dark clouds continued to ebb over the horizon, about as dark as my mood was going. If there was a secret entrance under Tsaparang for Shangri-La, then I had a much, much bigger problem than trying to outsmart elves and mercenaries.

If the IAA, with all their influence and power, hadn't found anything in the entire two hundred years they'd been looking, what hope in hell did I have?

At least we'd managed to outsmart the Chinese at the airport. Never underestimate an elf with a satellite connection and a penchant for hacking, or an incubus who hates paperwork as much as I do.

"Pretty, isn't it?"

I glanced away from the dark, roiling clouds to find Rynn watching me. "I'm not so much thinking they're pretty as I am worrying about where and when they'll start their downpour," I said. Not that I was against rain—considering the arid mountain range, they could probably use every drop they got. But hiking?

Though the city might have been abandoned and free of archaeologists at the moment, that didn't mean we could waltz right in. The IAA frowned on that sort of thing—and so did the Chinese, who happily provided the guns and guards.

Meaning we'd have to get creative.

Rynn pulled the jeep up into what passed for a parking lot at the bottom of the white city ruins—a faded red marker in the dirt and a collection of cars arranged in a haphazard ring.

"Just where are we supposed to meet this tour guide?" Rynn asked.

"It's called Adventure Tibet hiking tours," I said, and fished the confirmation email out of my phone to read it aloud. " 'Meet at the bottom of the Tsaparang city steps near the parking lot.' " I supposed "parking lot" was a euphemism for any collection of cars numbering more than three. " 'Your guide for the Tsaparang city and monastery will be waiting for you in the certified official Adventure Tibet red jacket.' "

"Certified official? What does that even mean?" Carpe asked, peering over my shoulder.

Carpe was getting as bad as my cat when it came to personal space. I shoved him back. "It means the only way to roam around this city without getting arrested by the Chinese is with an approved guide," I said, hopping out of the jeep and carefully easing Captain's backpack over my shoulders. He was taking a nap, and I hoped to keep it that way. The less I had to explain my "medical anxiety pet" on hiking trips, the better—especially considering how much Cat-pain had been chirping at Carpe.

Carpe struggled getting his own pack out of the jeep. To be sure, Rynn hadn't packed it light for the slight elf, but I got the impression the only hiking Carpe did outside World Quest was to the local coffee shop for his daily caffeine fix.

I headed toward the ancient white steps to the city, the red temple even more ominous-looking from this vantage point. Maybe that was why the Guge had forgone their natural camouflage: to instill ominous fear with a single temple painted red.

Rynn and Carpe fell in behind me. All three of us were dressed in hiking gear; boots, cargo jackets and windbreakers, baseball caps, and loose, Dri-Fit pants. Like I've always said, why stand out as thieves breaking in when you can stroll right through the front door?

I spotted a collection of brightly colored windbreakers gathered on a hill of dried grass. They were standing around what I assumed, due to his height, was a man. He was wearing a bright orange-red windbreaker. "I think I found them," I said.

"And how do you expect us to find the armor exactly if we're supposed to be on a tour?" Carpe whispered.

"Easy. Once we have our bearings, we get lost. Literally," I told him. I left out the part where I admitted I had no fucking clue where to start.

"And that doesn't strike you at all as reckless?"

Rynn snorted. I shot him a glare, but he otherwise remained silent. "You got a better idea?" I asked Carpe.

That caught him off guard. "Well . . . no," he said.

If I ever did amass a treasure room, someone, please remind me to at least mention where it's supposed to be hidden. "Then I'm going to recommend you stop complaining about my methods and start worrying about something much more important. Like how the hell to get us out of jail once the Chinese catch us." Unlike Rynn, who seemed to think we'd be able to bluff our way out of any misunderstandings, I had no such faith. The Chinese antiquities guards weren't stupid. Getting lost on a real hiking trail in the wilderness? Okay, sure, they might bite on a good day. Getting lost in an ancient city? They'd do the smart thing and figure we were thieves first and ask questions once we were behind bars.

"This is going to be a disaster, isn't it?" Carpe said under his breath.

"Usually is," Rynn said.

I tuned Rynn's and Carpe's squabbling out and turned my attention back on the hikers. Still no sign of the Zebra outfit or any other mercenaries. I hoped Carpe's intel was right and they were all still sitting in Vegas.

I spared another side glance at Carpe, struggling under his pack.

Friends close, enemies closer.

We reached the small group of hikers huddled together, and I took silent stock. Eight in total, nine if you included the guide. Fit-looking, all dressed like we were, in hiking gear.

One of them waved, and the guide turned for the first time to face us. I frowned as I caught sight of bright red hair under a yellow baseball cap. There was something familiar about him; the stance, the bright red hair. . . . I narrowed my eyes. "Oh for the love of— You've got to be kidding me."

I picked up my pace, Rynn jogging to keep up. "Alix, did you see something?" Rynn asked, on edge again, searching for mercenaries in the sparse landscape.

"In a manner of speaking." Yup, I was certain now. Not only the stance and red hair, but also the glint of too-white teeth as his grin spread ear to ear.

Hermes. Courier extraordinaire for thieves everywhere. I had used

Hermes for years to get antiquities to my buyers, but it was only recently I'd met Hermes in person and discovered he was yet another supernatural, a powerful one, who fashioned himself after the patron god of messengers and thieves everywhere. Or, for all I knew, he was the source of the legends. Regardless of reasons, he'd taken a recent interest in me and my involvement in supernatural politics.

I heard Rynn curse beside me as he caught on. He'd never met Hermes before, but I'd described him well enough, and it wasn't like Hermes was a recluse. A bit of a wild card if Rynn's sources were to be believed.

Not two, but three supernaturals now . . .

Hermes flashed me a wide grin, but with no outward sign of recognition.

"And here we have the final three of our group for today's hike. Did you find the place okay, ah . . . " Hermes didn't drop his smile or character as he glanced down at his phone. ". . . ah, Harmony, Greg, and . . ." He made a show of peering at Carpe. "You must be Bob. You can call me Hemey."

It took willpower to smile and wave at the group. Hemey. Hilarious. I just hoped he hadn't done anything drastic to the tour guide who was actually supposed to meet us.

Best not to think about those kinds of things when it came to supernaturals.

Rynn and Carpe followed my lead in waving and saying hi to the small group. Well, Rynn did. Carpe just stood there looking mildly uncomfortable—but considering it worked for him, I let it go.

Hermes turned his attention back on the group proper. "Today we'll be inside Tsaparang, the ancient fortress city of the lost Kingdom of Guge, one of the many Buddhist kingdoms that dotted this region between the eighth and sixteenth centuries. But don't let modern-day Buddhists fool you; these Buddhist kingdoms warred with each other and their neighbors like any other empire. The bloody and tumultuous reign of the violent Buddhists."

Hermes paused for the good-natured chuckles from the crowd

before starting up the steps to the fortress and continuing his intro-duction. "It's still debated how Tsaparang, the fortress city, became the capital of the Kingdom of Guge. According to some accounts, it was designated the capital by Namde Wosung around 838–841 CE, right after his father was assassinated. Others claim it wasn't until around 900 CE..."

I tuned out as Carpe jabbed me in the chest. I glared at him. "*What?*"

"Couldn't you have come up with something a little more original than Harmony? And Bob? Come on, I do not look like a Bob."

"He has a point," Rynn said, joining in. "Considering you just retired Charity."

"It's thematic. It helps me keep in character." Early lesson learned; it's real hard to remember whether you're supposed to be a Claire or Rebecca when you've gone through a couple rotations. Thematic names like Harmony, Charity—and my all-time favorite, Temperance—jog the memory on the sly. "And it's not like Bob is your new name. I was going with bland and generic."

"Accurate if nothing else," Rynn added. I gave him a jab for that one, before tuning back in to Hermes's lecture as we headed up the roughly cut steps toward the red temple.

"Regardless of how it came into existence," Hermes continued, "by the tenth century Guge was a regional power in control of an important trade route between India and Tibet. As you may have noticed, Tsapa-rang is a fortress city, perched on a pyramid-shaped rock rising about five to six hundred feet out of the sparse landscape. Whereas the commoners lived at its base, the royalty and nobility lived at the top, the only means to reach them this twisting stone staircase." A roll of thunder cut him off. "Which, weather and time permitting, we will see today. First though, we'll be stopping at the two public temples—the Lhakhang Marpo, also known as the red temple, and the Lhakhang Karpo, you guessed it; the white temple, which both lead to an extensive underground warren of tunnels."

Tunnels, finally, something I needed. I raised my hand. "Oh! Hemey, quick question," I said, in an excited voice like I figured a hiker named Harmony visiting Tibet for the first time might actually use, "you didn't mention what the tunnels were used for."

The smile didn't falter. "That's because no one really knows. A couple of historians suppose they were built for escaping from invading forces, but no exits have ever been found. It also might have been a labyrinth to disappear prisoners, or somewhere to hide goods, though I have a hard time seeing how they could have used them for storage. Over a hundred years archaeologists have been mapping Tsaparang and found mostly a collection of dead ends," he said and gave the crowd a sinister look. "At least that's what they figured when the various explorers didn't make their way back out."

"People get lost?" a German woman in a white windbreaker asked, a concerned look on her face.

"Hemey" turned his watt-level smile on her. "Not to worry, Camille, I guarantee you we'll only be exploring the mapped sections."

"You thinking what I'm thinking, Alix?" Rynn whispered as we approached the red temple.

"That if I was a treasure, a set of lost tunnels is very well where I might be? Oh, you've got no idea." The three of us had fallen to the back of the line.

"And what are we supposed to do when the guards come looking for us? Have you thought of that?" Carpe whispered.

"Run like hell and hope they're a lousy shot?"

"That's not a plan at *all*." Carpe shook his head. "Is she always this comforting on missions?" he asked Rynn.

"Not a mission, Carpe," I told him. "It's a clusterfuck of a job we've been roped into—and for your information, I've gotten much better when it comes to plans. You should have seen me before I met Rynn."

He stared at me, mouth open.

Captain rustled inside my backpack and made an inquisitive mew; I guessed it was because Hermes's scent was joining in the mix. "Yeah,

I'm wondering what the hell he's up here for too, Captain," I said. "Let's go ask, shall we?"

I figured Carpe couldn't get into too much trouble with Rynn watching him, so I left them to complain at each other as I trudged past the other hikers to where Hermes—sorry, tour guide *Hemey*—was talking with the keeners of the hiking group. I fixed a smile on my face and waited patiently.

Finally, he turned his bright green eyes on me. "Hey there, Harmony. Any questions you'd like to ask me about the ancient city of Tsaparang?"

"You can tell me what the hell it is you're doing here, Hermes. I've already got two too many supernatural entities on this derailing train ride. The last thing I need is one more." And definitely not the king of fucking thieves . . . though I didn't say that. It was implied.

The smile didn't falter one bit, though it did drop from his eyes. "Let's just say I doubled down on this new endeavor of yours."

Supernaturals betting on whether humans lived or died . . . "Rule of bets, Hermes: get out while you're ahead."

Hermes glanced over his shoulder to make sure the main group had gotten ahead.

"You know," he said, "sometimes I think you get it, and the rest of the time . . ." He sighed. "Piece of advice? Stop thinking about this being a one-off."

I went cold, a black pit twisting in my stomach.

"Just accept it, kid. You're caught up in something bigger than you, bigger than your two supernatural buddies over there. And since you just so happen to be one of mine—" He gave me a once-over. "I'll tell you, no one, like seriously no one, ever expected *that* to happen. I mean, you thieves are twitchy at the best of times."

"I'm not one of *yours*, whatever the hell that's supposed to mean."

Hermes shrugged. "Well, the details are sketchy on that part, and really I have like no say in the matter, so we'll just have to accept the lot we've both received, as lousy as it might seem. For both of us."

I opened my mouth to tell him exactly what I felt about supernaturals divvying up humans into boxes as they saw fit, but Hermes didn't give me the chance.

"You realize Cooper didn't stumble across the cursed artifacts on his own?" he said. "I mean, I just assumed you figured that part out on your own—your grades before you got kicked out suggested some form of intelligence."

I bit my tongue at the derogatory and unconstructive names that popped into my head at the thought of Cooper. Cooper had been the postdoctoral student in charge of the dig that had led to me being expelled by the IAA, not in small part due to him lying through his teeth. He'd been behind the theft of the cursed artifacts that had led to an undead army being raised in Los Angeles—and framing me. "Yes, I realize Cooper didn't figure out how to resurrect an army of living dead on his own," I said.

"And if you think that waste-of-space incubus Artemis just stumbled across some old incubi rituals, I've got a fantastic magic bridge to sell you as well."

"It's a bridge or magic beans, not both."

"Thief, remember? Don't like rules cramping my creative nature." Hermes, Hemey, or whatever the hell else he wanted to call himself, continued. "The problem is that no one's wanted to talk about it because no one really had any clue about who was behind it. Supernaturals get sketchy that way. They'd rather avoid problems than hit them head on. Consider it a collective fault." He gave me another appraising look. "Until, that is, the elves threw their hats in the game. A suit of dangerous magic armor, what would those librarians want with that?" Hermes said, making a tsking noise.

If I wanted anything out of Hermes, I was going to have to play his game. "Maybe they're being manipulated by the same person—or thing—that arranged Cooper and Artemis. It doesn't tell me anything except someone is serious about screwing with everyone." And I was stuck smack in the middle of it, not running for a safe hiding spot while the whole thing blew over like everyone else with a brain.

Hermes chuckled to himself. "I can see the wheels churning back there, slowly, but at least they still work. You should see this other thief I'm working with."

"Do you know who it is?"

Hermes shrugged his shoulders. "I've got some inside intel and leads, but that's not either the question or the game, which is what you seriously need to start worrying about."

"That one group wants to come out in the open and the other doesn't? Already got the memo, but thanks for playing."

"Your attitude? I just can't even—" Hermes sighed. "Not wrong, but that's the bigger picture. Think smaller. What is it the elves—or someone manipulating them—want the armor for?"

Yeah, not like I already hadn't been trying to figure that exact thing out, but there were still too many options. "It could be anything, from a supernatural wanting to take the world over by violent force or beat his fellow supernaturals into submission. Or any countless idiotic reason. It could just be another collector like Mr. Kurosawa wanting a fancy new paperweight."

"If you think anyone wants this suit for a paperweight."

"I know, I know. Catastrophe, then."

Hermes was silent for a moment. "Let's try this from a different angle. What do you know about the suit?"

I shrugged. "It's dangerous, drives the wearer mad forcing them to pick fights, eventually takes over their mind and body—"

"Too deep, kiddo. Surface superficial stuff."

I thought about it. "It's picky about its hosts; it doesn't want just anyone."

"Annnd?" he prompted, glancing over his shoulder back at the tour. "Seriously, I don't have all day here. The hikers are going to start thinking I'm hitting on you. So is the boyfriend. Incubi are more territorial than the bastards let on."

I remembered what Rynn had said about Atticus, the sole supernatural the armor had encountered. "Things get really violent when it takes over supernaturals."

"Ahhh," Hermes said. "Now that is interesting."

"Great! Fantastic! How about you help me along here and tell me what the hell that means."

Hermes made a face. "Ah, yeah, no can do. Against the rules. As you might have deduced by now, I'm more of a neutral party."

"Then why do you even care who wins?"

"Because one side is much worse than the other."

Whatever insult I'd been ready to throw next caught in my throat at the look on Hermes's face. He wasn't playing games this time.

"Let me put it this way. You need another big win, kiddo, otherwise there's going to be big trouble on the very near horizon, the kind neither you nor your friends can handle or hide from."

"Great. Is that all the advice you have for me?"

He shrugged. "Well, sometimes the decisions you get to make are not the ones you'd like. Other than that? I got nothing."

More riddles than help . . . that's what I got for asking a supernatural. "Has anyone ever told you that as an ad hoc impromptu mentor you kind of suck?"

"Has anyone ever told you you're a bit of a train wreck to be a hero? Got news for you, kid—I didn't sign up for this either, but every now and again even us thieves have to get our hands dirty." He narrowed his eyes at me. "And no more get-out-of-jail-free cards. You'd be amazed the disaster that caused my side. Well, maybe not disaster. More ker-fuffle."

Oh for Christ—"Fine. If you can't help, what are you even doing here?"

"Simple. To make sure the other team at least makes a show of playing fair. FYI—I don't expect them to."

Hermes turned and started back for the tour. He only made it a few feet away from me before he added, "I'm impressed you kept the guy around; good on you for not screwing that up. I'd watch the elf though. The incubus is a bit pedantic about them as a whole, but he's right; they're a tricky bunch on a good day. Then again, sometimes they surprise you.

Guess you can't brush an entire race with the same stereotype, kind of like you can't brush all thieves with the same criminal coat of bad paint. Tends to peel off."

"Do you ever give out useful advice?" I asked him. "Or only the half-ass California Zen spiel?"

Hermes made a show of checking his fingernails, which were way too clean and polished for a hiker. "I'm a thief. Another piece of wisdom for you? Sell the snake oil you have."

He continued toward the waiting tourists. "All right, folks, who wants to hear about the assassinations that led to the creation of Guge and the invading armies that lost themselves in the underground tunnels?" he called out. And just like that, Hermes went back to being tour guide "Hemey."

I stood where I was, watching Hermes until Rynn and Carpe caught up to me.

I don't know if it was an ingrained knack for distraction or something to do with his supernatural nature, but not one of them spared a glance back at us, not once.

"Negative on the supernatural bullshit," Carpe whispered. "Your terms, not mine."

Distraction it was. "Well, the good news is Hermes doesn't want to screw us over. I think. He's also not going to help us. Says he's here to make sure the other side plays by the rules," I said.

"Whose side?" Rynn mused.

I remembered what he said about having one of "his" in the game. "Considering his track record so far, I'm optimistic he's on ours," I said. The tour had turned the corner toward the white temple. As good a time as any to get lost. . . . I headed for the red. "Is it me, or does the addition of another supernatural to the mix, however seemingly friendly, signal imminent disaster?" I asked Rynn.

"If you think having more supernaturals around is in any way, shape, or form a good thing, I have a bridge to sell you."

The entrance to the abandoned monastery was before us, open, nothing blocking the way except the demarcation of red against the white. Deserted and bare on the inside, it sent a chill down my spine. The white stone didn't repel me though. Rather it drew me in, a welcoming cold rather than repulsive. It was a strange sensation—and unnerving. I shivered as I stepped over the threshold.

Standing in the sparse temple room, no trace left of the religious trappings that would have adorned it, I could have sworn something whispered at me on the cold breeze that came through the windows. Like a voice trying to start a conversation. I strained to hear it. . . .

Captain mewed as his claws dug into my back through the carrier.

I snapped out of it to find Rynn watching me with a wary look. "Everything all right, Alix?"

I shook the cold off and took another good look around the bare room. Nothing. A figment of my imagination from being surrounded by supernaturals. It had to be.

"Fine." Even though I said it, I wasn't so sure. "Just odd seeing a meditation room so sparse. They're usually decorated. This one's had all the trappings removed, as if someone tried to erase it."

"Let's get to finding those tunnels," Rynn said. "Because chances are good the mercenaries will get here soon. Then things will get really interesting."

Carpe, who had busied himself opening up his computer, looked up. "You two really know how to brighten up my day, don't you?"

We both ignored him and started scanning the meditation room the violent Buddhists would have used.

Violent Buddhists. If that wasn't ominous, I didn't know what was.

"All right, look for anything out of the ordinary, you two. Secret passages, hollow walls, anything remotely supernatural. Use your imaginations," I said, and ducked into a second, smaller meditation room.

There were three meditation rooms in all—one large and two smaller side chambers, cut out of the rock itself. Much to my frustration, the two smaller ones proved as barren as the first. No closets, no alcoves. There weren't even benches or shelves to rifle through. In fact, the only decorations in the rooms were a couple of spots of chipped paint and a single replication of a prayer altar holding a pot of incense that had long since burned out. Considering the temple's bright red exterior, the insides were downright plain.

Carpe and Rynn joined me in the smaller chamber. "Nothing?" I asked them as I crouched down to check a corner where the plaster had chipped substantially. I was hoping to find some sign of a panel or secreted space underneath.

"Not even a statue, just some bad plaster and rushed whitewash," Rynn said.

"Same," Carpe said.

Nothing. It was just chipped plaster. "Not exactly surprising. With the exception of a couple hidden idols and frescoes, the Chinese cultural revolution did a spectacular job stamping out religious artwork across China."

Tsaparang, along with a large swath of Tibet, had been no different, it would seem—anything left out in the open was wiped out. Never underestimate the power of a large group of people determined at all costs to reshape their culture overnight.

I wondered . . . I'd read somewhere about a different temple, farther east in Tibet, that had managed to hide artwork from the Red Guards.

I found a piece of plaster higher up on the wall that had cracked through. I stood on my toes and peered at it. Was there something black underneath?

"Rynn, help me out with this, will you?" He was taller than me and could reach, versus me, who had to jump. "I read once about a group of helpful archaeologists showing a group of Tibetan monks how to cover their artwork with plaster to hide it from the Red Guards."

A piece crumbled off as Rynn pried at the plaster, revealing an image underneath.

"They hid them," Carpe said.

"Yup." *Hiding in plain sight.* I shone my flashlight up on the patch that Rynn had uncovered. They were faint and more worn than I would have liked, but there were definitely frescoes hidden underneath. I was searching for anything that might indicate there was something more hidden underneath.

I found a corner that had the trace of a border, with lotus flowers drawn in the traditional style peeking out.

The only question was, was it magic or another false start?

Only one way to find out. Heart beating, I pulled my chicken blood water out of my backpack and sprayed the corner—carefully. I remembered what had happened the last time I sprayed chicken blood on a mural.

Nothing happened. Not a flicker, not even a pulse. I let out my breath. I'd been so sure. I turned to Rynn and Carpe. "Any bright ideas?" Both Rynn and Carpe shook their heads.

Great. Even the two supernaturals were stumped.

I turned back to the mural and removed more of the plaster. More lotus flowers and pretty designs, but a far cry from anything I'd seen in the Nepalese caves.

Come on, Jebe, you even said it yourself—the armor was wrong. Corrupted. I've got to think you had something to do with the fact no one has seen it in almost a thousand years. . . .

There was a scratch at the back of my backpack, followed by a tentative mew. "Picked a great time to wake up from your nap," I said.

Captain replied with a more insistent mew followed by more scratching. Either he needed to pee really bad, or he smelled something.

I let him out. Instead of running for the nearest corner or looking for somewhere promising to dig, Captain sat back on his haunches and sniffed the air—and not in Rynn's or Carpe's direction.

Without any warning he darted out into the main meditation room. I swore and scrambled to grab my things before he got out of sight. So much for training.

Rynn beat me to it. "Alix, over here," he called out. Captain was digging at a corner of chipped and crumbling plaster. No, wait, scratch that . . . he had the plaster between his teeth and was pulling it out while growling.

Somehow I didn't think he was after mice in a stone city. I grabbed him before he ingested any and took a look. Captain did his best to wrest himself out of my arms to get back at the plaster. He chirped to get across the point. First supernaturals, now magic . . . "I've seriously broken you, haven't I?" I said.

I examined the spot Captain had found. It looked identical to the other, right down to the faded lotus petals. I took out my bottle of watered-down blood and started to spray. Nothing happened.

Maybe Captain *had* been chasing mice. There was something about this mural though—again I heard the whispered voice on the breeze that came through the temple, pushing me to keep looking.

"We're running out of time," Carpe said. I glanced up from the mural. Sure enough, Hermes's voice was carrying down the stairs. The steps and height amplified his voice, but Carpe was right. We didn't have much time until the tour group returned.

I turned back to the mural. Looks could be deceiving. "Maybe the portal part is central on the wall," I said to Rynn. That would have made more sense; the center would be less likely to crack with age.

I winced as Rynn kicked the wall with his boot. Plaster crumbled away, revealing more of the fresco and the start of a colorful tree of life. I tried with the chicken blood again. Still nothing.

Yet Captain wriggled around my feet and started scratching at the wall once again.

Wait a minute.

Plastering. Shit—Jebe would have come through here in the twelfth century. There was no way the inhabitants of a Tibetan stone fortress had any reason to plaster anything—not when they had the smooth stone surfaces to work with.

"Guys, I think whatever magic they hid here is on the rock itself, underneath the plaster." And there was no way we had time to excavate it properly. I grabbed a small hammer out of my bag, along with a medium pin. I lined it up against the wall. Seeing what I planned to do, Rynn followed suit with a knife.

I closed my eyes and lined up the hammer over the pin. Oh God, this wasn't how I wanted to start my day, ruining a four-hundred-year-old fresco . . . I struck the pin and watched it crack the surface plaster and the heavier one with the fresco underneath. Rynn had better luck, sending a large swath crumbling. I took another swing and hoped the meditation room had been built with some sound dampening in mind.

On the third strike the remaining plaster slid down the wall, taking the four-hundred-year-old relief crumbling all the way with it, revealing the artwork underneath.

Unlike the paints that had been used on the plaster, this was a scene of carved and colored bones set into the stone. It wasn't a gate at all but a battle. "I think that's Jebe," I said, brushing the remaining plaster off one of the images, a white-gray figure in a sea of black and red, shrouded in what looked like lightning.

There was something written underneath.

I set to work brushing away the remaining plaster to uncover the script with my hands, and when that failed, with a brush from my back-pack.

"Careful, Alix," Rynn said.

"I am being careful. It's a warning—in Sanskrit, Chinese, and Cyrillic. They all say the same thing. 'Beware he who searches the Lightning Suit'—or something to that effect."

As I said the words, a chill fell over me—and anger, deep red anger at the scene before me. I shook it off. What the hell was coming over me? The suit was here; I didn't have time for my brain to take a vacation. All I had to do was figure out where the next stop along the treasure trail was.

"Remember what happened the last time, Alix," Rynn said, the warning heavy in his voice. I looked down at my hands, where the spray bottle was. I hadn't realized I'd picked it back up until Rynn said anything.

Carpe rounded the corner from where he'd taken up a lookout just outside. "Hermes is stalling them in the other temple, but you need to hurry."

"Yeah, ah, let's start taking photos—fast—then we'll run some tests with UV before I get the blood out." Less likely to make the whole thing explode.

I placed the blood bottle by my feet and tossed a camera to Rynn before turning my UV light on the image. It was ominous—and strange for a Tibetan temple, with the blacks and reds whirling together . . . angry at Jebe, for coming here, for staying, for locking everything up.

I shook my head again, clearing it. "What?" I asked, realizing Rynn had said something.

"Nothing active, not in any of the different spectrums." It looked like Rynn was going to say something else—he was frowning at me—but there was a noise back in the hallway that even I heard.

Carpe was no longer hanging by the doorway.

Rynn swore. "Stay here, I'll see what the elf has gotten up to. I'll be back in a second."

He added a few choice words, but my attention was already back on the mural of Jebe.

I picked up more bits of color mixed in with the dark blacks, grays, and reds. Pinks, oranges, even yellows—the details on the various armies' dress. The colors were well preserved; not all that surprising, considering the arid nature of the place and the fact it was hidden away from bleaching sunlight.

I blinked as I picked up a line of pink—no, make that red. Thin red lines peeking out from pieces of bone inlay. Something made me lean in and smell the stone. The metallic singe of magically preserved blood flooded my senses. Now that, I most definitely recognized. . . .

I held my flashlight up to get a better look. There were a few etches made into the wall where the red had been laid. I could see the lines of blood now woven into the mural, brilliant red, surrounding the combatants with their strange phosphorescent-like glow . . . if the phosphorescence was on an acid trip. . . .

I blinked. Then again . . . Wait a minute, those were active. How the hell had they been activated? I took a step back and swore as it continued to spread.

The ground shook. Rynn and Carpe both ran back in to find me backing away from the mural. Son of a bitch, I'd only touched it.

Rynn took one look at the activated magic inscriptions and then back at me. His face was white. "What the hell did you do?" he said.

I stood there shaking my head. "Me? Nothing. I swear to God, all I did was touch it . . ." I trailed off as my eyes fell to where both Rynn and Carpe were staring. At the spray bottle of chicken blood still in my hands. What the . . . ?

"We left you here for less than a minute, Alix—" Rynn started, not bothering to hide his anger.

"I swear, Rynn, I don't know how this got here. I didn't—" But before I could finish my defense, the floor began to shake.

"*No. One. Move,*" I mouthed to Carpe and Rynn, not willing to risk whispering. No one made a sound. Not even Captain, who gripped the floor as if his life might depend on it.

The room stopped shaking. Carefully, oh so very carefully, I edged my foot along the stone floor—the solid stone floor that should be stable.

Shit! With a crack that echoed through the red temple and likely through the entire city, the stone floor crumbled out from under us. We dropped, not down but along a wide stone chute leading down. Rynn was the only one who didn't scream, Captain included, as all of us madly tried to find a handhold on the smooth sides.

After sliding down for longer than I cared, we hit the ground, sending up a cloud of dirt that probably hadn't been disturbed in almost six hundred years.

I rubbed my tailbone. Oh, that was going to leave a mark. "Is everyone alive?" I called out.

"Yes" came Rynn's strained reply.

"Define 'alive'?" Carpe said.

Captain decided to join in and mewed as well.

Okay. Everyone alive and un-maimed. Score one for lucky streaks. I winced as my head revolted. I hoped the cave-in was restricted to the one room and Hermes got the tourists out. I did not need that on my conscience. I extracted myself from Carpe's and Rynn's limbs while I coughed and scrambled to find my flashlight. I swear I'd heard it clatter somewhere around here.

My fingers brushed against the handle, and I turned it on. We were in a cavern—or cavern-like space. Originally a natural structure but definitely altered and excavated by human hands.

The ceiling was only seven odd feet—high, considering how far down we were. And it looked like it expanded. "How far down do you think we fell?" I asked, stifling a cough as dust filled my lungs and throat.

"Five hundred feet or so, give or take," Rynn said, sounding like he wasn't doing so hot with the dirt and dust either, despite his supernatural constitution. Carpe? I just hoped he wouldn't die from sneezing or coughing.

I checked the slide. Even if we could boost ourselves up, we'd never be able to climb the polished surface. I moved my flashlight over the rest of the cavern and found a circular opening with a graduated ramp headed down.

"Guys, where do you think this goes?" I said, highlighting the ramp for them.

"Considering how far down we are? I'd say it's a tunnel out of the base of the mountain—for escape, or trade, or a combination of the two."

Well, it was certainly wide and tall enough to fit carts—a caravan, by the looks of things—and it beat carrying goods up the stairs one by one.

Something reflected my flashlight off the ground near my feet, and I made out what looked like a pattern worked into the floor. From what I could see through the grime, it was the same kind of colored bits of bone inlay that had been fixed into the wall above, only instead of a dark and gloomy battle accentuated with swaths of red, these looked to be depictions of brightly colored animals . . . and they were traveling in various directions. I don't know why, but my eyes fixated on a particular procession—pink elephants decorated with bright orange . . . tiny, but still intricately done.

A rarity if not completely unknown this side of the Himalayas, especially at the time these images would have been laid. But on the other side of the mountains, in India and Nepal, when Guge would have been a flourishing trade center . . .

I wondered . . .

The parade of various animals all disappeared into the darkness past where my flashlight could reach. I got up and followed the winding procession of elephants along the cavern floor.

"Remember what Hermes said about the labyrinth nature of this place," Rynn called out as he examined the chute. "That part I don't think he was lying about."

"Don't worry, if I get lost I'll look for the pink elephants," I said as I followed the pink parade until they ended fifteen feet away, at the base of a mural that stretched along the wall. It was painted in the outline of a gate not quite like the one I'd seen in Nepal; different styles and colors had been used. But the fact that it was here . . .

"Guys," I called out. "I think I found something." Maybe it was the drop in altitude or the fall itself, but a thrumming in my head had started. I blinked, trying to clear my vision.

Both Rynn and Carpe turned in my direction, looking none too relaxed.

I shone the light on the bone mural carved and set into the cavern wall. "Looks like the people of Guge really did escape through a gateway to Shangri-La," I said.

Unlike in Nepal, where there had been yaks, oxen, and horses dragging wagons and ware through the gate, this time there were elephants and tigers.

Was it functional, or did it just signify a different region? Before I could stop myself, I found my hand stretched out to the wall.

I squeezed my eyes shut. Something was clouding my thoughts; it wanted me to touch the mural. It was so intense I couldn't think.

Rynn came up beside me, evaluating me, as if trying to solve a puzzle, before turning his attention on the mural.

"It looks like another doorway, like the one we found in Nepal. Only difference is, this one is still active." He crinkled his nose. "I can smell the magic leaching off of the paints."

Well, Neil and Frank had told us they'd meet us here—they'd said as much in the directions. They just hadn't said anything about a slide of death and a large pit. And the mural above had been of Jebe and the armor; it hadn't even hinted at Shangri-La. We should have been stumbling into a treasure room.

There was something about the gate that was mesmerizing. I leaned closer to brush away the centuries of dust caked over the small bone elephants. The cold chill descended over me again.

Captain, who'd been sniffing the nooks and crannies, had made his way to my feet. He sniffed at the mural. Jumping back, he arched his back and let out a long, drawn-out hiss.

"What's his problem?" Carpe asked.

I frowned as Captain continued to back away. He hissed again until he reached the back of the cave, the farthest point from the mural possible. "I don't know, could be the magic."

"Or he remembers what happened upstairs," Rynn warned.

"Don't worry—I'm not turning this one on." Well, not yet, anyways. There was time for that. And why wouldn't I? How many people could say they'd been to Shangri-La?

"That's what you've said twice now—back in Nepal and right before the floor collapsed upstairs."

I didn't answer. There were more bone animals; yaks, oxen, cows, pigs, even horses pulling carts.

"How does it open?" Carpe asked this time.

I tore my eyes off the mural. "If Nepal was any indication, there's a substantial trick to it. One Texas and Michigan didn't see fit to share."

Carpe frowned at me. I sighed and added, "No, I have no idea how to open it, not without causing a massive explosion of magic."

But that's not true. You know how to open it. All it takes is a little blood.

I frowned at Carpe. Where the hell had that thought come from? "Maybe the Guge left clues—or an instruction manual."

I stepped away from the mural, a pang of loss coursing through me. Something was wrong . . . very wrong. For the life of me I couldn't put my finger on it.

I shone my flashlight on the rest of the massive cavern, and Rynn and Carpe followed suit. "Look for pictures, diagrams—anything that might be a reference for the gate." With any luck there'd be a set of instructions, or, at the very least, a hint as to how the door opened properly—as in, without the explosion parts.

"We're supposed to be looking for Jebe's treasure, not the gate to Shangri-La," Rynn said.

"Keep your eye out for that too, but at the moment I plan on working with what we have. Well?"

Rynn and Carpe exchanged a look but began combing the walls. I checked another section of pictures, this time a ring of birds flying over what looked like the Himalayas. No clues as to how to open the gate.

"Maybe the instructions were destroyed?" Carpe said as he checked another section on the far wall. "I mean, it doesn't look like anyone has been through here in a hundred years."

"Closer to five hundred," I told him. "Maybe more." A hiding spot? Or a secret compartment or a map to another location where they kept the instructions? I'd seen stranger things. . . . There was a trail of red bone, up above. I traced it along the wall while Rynn and Carpe continued to bicker about the best way out.

"We're not here to open a gate, elf, we're here to find the armor," Rynn said.

"Well right now the only thing in front of us *is* the gate."

I winced as my vision clouded over, just like it had before the floor had given out. If I could just see straight, let alone think straight. . . .

I frowned. Was it me, or was Carpe looking a little nonplussed too? And Rynn was watching me now in earnest, his eyes narrowed.

The supernaturals getting their panties in a bunch that the human in the room is doing a better job finding all the clues they should have picked up on already. . . .

I shook my head. Where the hell had that come from?

I wrote it off to stress mixed with lack of sleep and the fall. My vision cleared and I continued to follow the trail of red bone. It led to a small pictorial, set away from the gate with another series of images, all contained in their own circles of designs and borders. Stories, or more likely a history of things that went through the gate: what looked like people fleeing a war, carrying livestock and possessions, another showing people fleeing a famine, disease. The gate hadn't been used once by the Guge to flee disaster; it had been used for centuries, maybe longer.

And there was Jebe wearing the Lightning Armor, following a group of monks through the gate.

Jebe hadn't hidden the armor in Tsaparang—he'd hidden it in Shangri-La. That's why no one could find it, why it had seemingly disappeared off the face of the planet. The blood rushed to my head again and the fog descended, making me see an angry red when I closed my eyes.

"Even if we find the instructions, just what do you plan on doing exactly?" Rynn said to Carpe. "Blow us and all of Tsaparang up?"

"I don't know about you, but before we explore those tunnels and wake up some troll or other monster who decides elves might be tasty, I at least want the thin trace of hope that there might be another way out, which, unless you have a way up that chute, is the gate."

I shook off the fog. "Guys, hate to break this to you, but your argument is about to become a moot point." I shone the flashlight on the mural of Jebe so both could see.

Carpe crept forward to get a better look.

Rynn was still skeptical. "It still doesn't address the problem of how to open it without blowing ourselves up and leveling Tsaparang."

Begrudgingly, I had to admit he was right.

"Unless you only activated half of it," Carpe said.

"What?" I said, turning to Carpe.

"You're thinking of this as a two-dimensional doorway, but it doesn't have to be. What if there are multiple points that need to be turned on— and not necessarily in the same place or line of sight?"

I hadn't thought of it that way before. It could work . . .

"Alix?" Rynn implored. "You're not seriously considering this?"

If the armor was that way . . . "You heard the elf—look for any other images in the cave that match the gate."

Rynn clenched his jaw but didn't argue any further. The three of us set about searching the cave once more. Now . . . was that another set of pictures on the ceiling?

I shone the light up. Sure enough, dancing on the ceiling were more pink and orange elephants.

"Over here! I found another one," Carpe called out.

"I've got one too, on the ceiling," I said, before joining him. Bone inlay just like that on the wall peeked through centuries' worth of grime. I got down on all fours and started to brush it away until I uncovered a pink elephant, then an orange tiger, then a blue-and-yellow lotus flower. Carpe joined me, and we kept going until I uncovered what I was looking for—the first hint of a circular gate. I cleared more of the dirt and stood up to get a better look. The circle on the floor was as large as the one on the wall and ceiling.

Like a mirrored image of triplets. "All three need to be activated," I said. "That's what I missed before. Remember how the one in Nepal created a siphon?"

"Before or after it exploded?" Rynn asked me, arching an eyebrow.

I ignored his tone. "I'll bet there was a corresponding one in Nepal and we just missed it. Probably buried under years' worth of dirt." Or maybe it collapsed right after Texas and Michigan used it. I grabbed my water bottle of blood, but Rynn grabbed my arm and spun me around before I could reach the mural.

"Alix, think about what you are about to do. This is complete madness—and it's not like you."

More red anger—this time at the incubus, who was getting in the way. "I have a literal gun to my head to bring that armor back—and for that matter, so do you. Now move."

But he didn't. "If you can't be bothered to care for us or yourself, at least think about the people outside. What happens to them if you're wrong?"

The thrumming dimmed. Staring at Rynn, I realized he had a point. All I really had was a theory. I shook my head. If the headache would just go away . . . "Maybe you're right—" I started.

The elephants and tigers blurred together as my burgeoning headache reared its abysmal and punishing head full force.

I closed my eyes, but that didn't do a damn thing. I clutched both sides of my head and sat down. The ground—the nice, soft, and stable ground—was what I needed. . . .

Rynn's frown deepened and his grip tightened. "There's something wrong with you," he said.

I opened my eyes, and they were veiled with a red film. "Just a migraine I think. I had something like it back at the Nepal temple, just not nearly this bad." I was going to add that I just needed a moment, but another wave of pain and bright lights hit me. I stopped and just held my hand to my forehead, wishing for it to go away.

"Did she hit her head on the way down?" Carpe asked. "I hear that's quite bad for humans."

"No," Rynn said, studying me now more intently, his hands—cool where they were normally warm—gripping my chin and turning it side to side. "This is something else entirely. I'm not so sure the elves are only planning a retrieval anymore."

What was he talking about? I stopped thinking as Rynn's eyes turned blue.

Blue. There was something I was supposed to remember about that . . . something really important.

The sea of red anger descended. Shangri-La was right there in front of me; all I needed to do was open the door. The headache would go away then, I was sure of it. . . .

Rynn's bright blue eyes flared as they held mine.

I screamed and slumped back to the floor, clutching my head as the pain hit me full force. I curled up in a ball, willing the insistent thrumming to go away. Slowly but surely it receded.

In the background I vaguely heard Rynn screaming at Carpe.

"You good for nothing—you *knew* this was what they were planning."

"I swear, I didn't know! I wouldn't agree to something like this."

Planned? What had been planned? Something pulled my attention back to the mural. Not a voice exactly, but a feeling of desperation and frustration—something I could relate to. It wanted me to open it . . . calling to me, and man, was it ever hungry . . .

Or was that me? Hungry to find the lost city, where everyone else had failed. . . .

My eyes focused back on the pattern on the floor . . . and a sharpened piece of rock nearby.

That would make the headache go away. It would have to . . .

I reached for the stone piece and dragged it across my hand, not gently, like you would for a small cut, but all the way across and deep. That way, I'd be certain to get enough blood.

I watched as it pooled in my hand, then I reached out toward the bone.

I hesitated. There was something behind the thrumming. A warning . . . The headache came back full force. *That's your problem, Alix, you think things through too much of the time. Just put your hand on the mural. . . .*

Something slammed into me before my hand touched the image, knocking me to the ground. My head hit the ground, and something primal screamed at me to get back up.

It took me another second to realize it was Rynn. He rolled me over until I was staring into his blue eyes. I should be angry about that.

He shook my shoulders again, worry written over his face. "Alix, snap out of it."

Anger replaced my own bewilderment far too quickly for me to question where it came from.

"I had it," I started.

"No, you didn't. *It* had you."

The blue pushed away to red clouds, and the thrumming pull toward the doorway vanished.

I looked up at Rynn, then glanced down at the deep gash in my hand. "What the hell happened to me?"

"It's the armor," Rynn said. "That's what happened upstairs and in Nepal—it's what I felt. All this time it's been calling to you."

Son of a bitch. We knew the suit called to people, we'd just never considered the possibility . . .

"It has to be because we're so close to the portal," I said. "It's getting desperate." And if it could exert that much control from wherever the hell it was locked up in Shangri-La, what would it be able to do when people were standing there?

Rynn and Carpe exchanged a glance. "What? What are you two not telling me?"

"It's not just getting desperate. If it was, why not trick one of the countless monks or tourists to open the gate?" Carpe said.

I went cold. Oh no, not that—anything but that.

"I think the armor has chosen you as its next host," Rynn said. He shot Carpe a lethal look as he added, "And I think the elves knew it would."

Carpe held up his hands and backed away from Rynn. "Not me. I would not do that to Alix—to anyone!"

That didn't matter. None of it mattered. We had a much bigger problem. I did my best to keep my head clear, but I could already feel the darkness—wrongness—ebbing at my thoughts.

Is this what Jebe had felt? Or had he felt something worse?

"We need to get out of here now," I said, and pushed myself back up to sitting. Now that I recognized the dark thoughts coming from the armor, I at least stood a chance of holding it back. It had been so insidious, passing itself off as my own thoughts. If Rynn hadn't caught it . . . I grabbed my backpack and coaxed Captain inside.

"Why?" Carpe asked.

I gave him an even look. "Because regardless of whether or not that suit picked me, you two want to bet that now that it doesn't have me activating the portal, it can't go elsewhere to bring in reinforcements?"

Rynn swore, and Carpe got his laptop out.

Something metallic bounced down the chute. A canister pinged against the stone floor before rolling to a stop in the center of the cavern. It let out a soft puff before white opaque gas streamed out both ends. Three more canisters followed in rapid succession.

Man oh man, I hate being right at times like this.

"Down the ramp," I said. I hoped the Guge hadn't used anything that required dynamite to block off the exit . . .

"There isn't time," Carpe said. "Besides, I think they already found it. They figured out a way to flank us—I can hear the chatter on their comms."

"Rynn?" I said, the panic creeping into my voice. Between the mercenaries and the armor . . .

Rynn glanced around the cave, then made up his mind. "Get on your knees, hands behind your head," he said, and then did it himself.

"What—you can't be serious!"

"If there's anything on those computers or electronics in your bag you don't want the mercenaries or the IAA to have, elf, I strongly suggest you make it disappear."

Carpe swore. Kneeling down, he pulled out his laptop and a collection of tablets and phones. His fingers clicked faster across the keys than I would have thought possible.

I knelt down beside Rynn, cat carrier on my back and hands behind my head.

Out of the corner of my eye I saw Carpe hit the last key on his laptop before the first of the Zebras rappeled into the cave, the dangerous end of the gun first.

I swallowed. "Hi there," I said. "You wouldn't happen to be the rescue crew the Chinese sent. If you are, color me impressed."

None of the Zebras answered. Three of them detached and without a word bound both Carpe and Rynn.

Me, on the other hand . . . "What, no ties?" I asked, raising my hands.

In answer, a cloth full of chloroform was shoved in my mouth.

One of these days, I'd learn to keep it shut. This, however, was not that day.

14

ZEBRAS IN CENTRAL PARK

Time and Place? Oh hell, I have no idea

There's a saying: when you see hoofprints in Central Park, don't go looking for zebras. Yes—a zebra *could* be the culprit, but in all likelihood it's just another horse that's thrown a shoe.

The point is, don't go chasing after the exotic. Rule out the mundane first, and then worry about monsters.

At least the mercenaries who'd shoved a ball of chloroform down my throat had a sense of humor . . .

I was lying on my side—for some time, considering how my right arm and leg were going numb. And I was tied up; somewhere between the chloroform and dragging me wherever this was, the Zebras had had the brains to restrain me. I listened, but beyond the odd murmur of voices and clanging of metal—boxes maybe—I couldn't pick out anything distinct.

I craned my neck to get a better look around and winced at the disoriented protest my brain shot me. Oh my God, worst hangover ever. No wonder chloroform works so well if it does this to your head.

Besides recognizing the extent of just how incapacitated I was, I found out two other things. One, I was in a cave, and two, if Rynn, Carpe, and Captain were here, they were not being kept nearby.

My stomach churned. There was only one reason you separated prisoners . . .

As if on cue, I heard footsteps coming my way.

As far as caves went, I'd wager I was in a surface cavern. The air didn't have the stale, metallic taste that went with caves that were far underground. And though it was dark, I picked up some ambient light seeping through from outside. Rather than detract, it added a creepy veneer to the industrial LEDs the mercenaries had set up at even intervals in a circular perimeter around the cavern—at least the part I could see.

I tried to get a look around again, and this time, despite my chloroform-induced hangover, I managed to crane my neck high enough to get a good look at the ceiling. No bats. This was perfect bat habitat—which meant the surrounding area was inhospitable. Okay, so we were still in the western Tibetan mountains.

The least they could have done was get me as far away as possible from the armor.

A moment later a flashlight blinded me, and the makeshift gate keeping me locked up was rattled. I shielded my eyes as best I could and counted five mercenaries. One of them motioned for me to step out.

Considering they weren't actively trying to beat me up, I obliged.

They led me down a narrow cavern trail, me keeping my eyes on my feet so I wouldn't stumble on the uneven ground. It was a fine line, keeping my eyes down enough that the floodlights didn't blind me and not so much that I couldn't see a damn thing.

Eventually the narrow tunnel opened into a larger cavern, floodlights set at various intervals showing a small table and chairs set in the center. I didn't recognize the cavern, but I strongly suspected we were still under Tsaparang.

At least I could see. I glanced at the mercenaries behind me. One of them nodded toward the table and gestured with his gun.

Right. Sit at the table . . .

I sat down and waited. Well, if there was one benefit to all of this, the evil armor was no longer pinging my brain at every step of the way—though something told me it was saving its reserves now that it knew I was on to it.

I didn't have much more time to ponder the armor's motivations. The mercenaries guarding me all stood to attention as a man walked into the room and headed for the table. Dressed in the same black outfit as the other mercenaries, with the same white-and-black patch on the left corner pocket. He was older than the others—midforties to early fifties I guessed, tall and still muscular, with a crew cut that toed the line between blond and white. His expression didn't give anything away, but it also didn't betray any viciousness. More businessman than mercenary. Regardless, I recognized him. He'd been one of the false firemen in Vancouver.

He sat down at the table and waited for one of his men to bring him a pitcher of water and two glasses. He poured one for himself, then one for me, passing it over. I left it alone and kept my eyes on him despite the fact that I was thirsty.

"My name is Captain Williams," he said, his South African accent coming through, "and you are Alix Hiboux, also known as the Owl."

"If you say so," I said, offering a shrug.

He didn't smile exactly, but he did turn over the tablet he was carrying. "Currently you are a person of interest with the IAA. They claim you are dangerous and should be treated as a hostile."

"The IAA has a bad habit of using creative license."

He glanced up at me at that. "They also claim you are in possession of the location of Frank Caselback and Neil Chansky, the designers of World Quest who the IAA currently have hired us to obtain."

That one I didn't answer. There didn't seem much of a point.

He glanced back down at the tablet, unperturbed by my silence. "To be honest, I'm more interested in your history with vampires. Most people who run afoul of vampires, especially one of Alexander's repute, don't come out quite so alive as you have."

The research surprised me, though I did my best to hide it.

"The IAA was unable to illuminate me or my intelligence department why that might be—a failure on their part. When my clients fail to provide me with information, it makes me look."

Not knowing what the end game to this conversation was, I went with glib. "I have a strong stomach and an expansive collection of gas masks."

"Still, it's an impressive show of ingenuity. Something the IAA is not fond of in their own ranks." He made a tsking noise and sat back in his own chair, evaluating me. "Which has become their own problem, since it necessitates hiring out of their own ranks to get anything done."

"Is this the part where you coerce me to tell you what it is you want to know? Because, honestly, I'd really prefer it if we could skip to that rather than discuss the IAA's organizational failings."

"And I find it rather interesting you make no mention of your Mau cat in your success with the vampires." He turned the tablet around once again, to a photo of my cat, along with a write-up and what looked like dates beside it.

Despite my resolve not to give him anything, I leaned forward, all signs of my complacent, apathetic expression wiped from my face and replaced with a murderous look. "If this is you trying to give me incentives to play along—"

He tsked. "Oh, don't mistake my intentions," he said, turning the tablet back around. "I just wished to point out that where the IAA often misses important details, we do not." He glanced up at me again. "Nor do we throw promising assets to the wolves."

I kept quiet, not entirely sure where this was going and not wanting to rise to the bait.

Williams continued. "We are not the bad guys here. We have no interest in the IAA's political endeavors or lowering ourselves to their level of operations." He took a sip of his water. "You are accustomed to catering to the lowest common denominator—the IAA, the vampires."

"No offense, but if you're working for them, whether or not you lower yourselves to their tactics is a moot point."

Williams narrowed his eyes at me—the first show of anything but business professionalism. "We're professional mercenaries. They pay."

I braced the arms of my chair, anticipating a switch in tactics . . .

But he didn't stand up or otherwise threaten me. He simply picked up his glass of water and took another sip.

I don't know what I'd been expecting exactly—overt threats, outward violence . . . What I saw was calculation.

And a gun. Williams wasn't stupid. He'd removed one of his firearms and rested it on the table. Not exactly aimed at me but something that could very obviously be rectified if the need arose.

"Would you like to know what my predicament is?"

I didn't answer. He continued anyway. "Here is the thing. I have a contract with the IAA to retrieve two of their wayward employees. I do not know why they want them or even if the manhunt is justified, but that is neither here nor there in my line of business." His eyes were impassive. "I do have it on authority that you have also been looking for them." He slid the tablet across the table again. It was me in Nepal in the back of the orange-and-pink jeep—not a bad shot, all things considered. "And both my intelligence and the IAA believes that you are very close to finding them."

There didn't seem any point in denying it. I shrugged. "What can I say? The IAA offered me a deal to find them. One they have no intention of ever delivering on, so . . . Oh, no, wait a minute, that's not a deal, that's coercion. My mistake."

Williams sat back and smiled. "Yes. That does sound like the IAA. They are overly fond of strong-arming and coercion, which my intelligence department also says you do not respond well to. I can sympathize. Neither do I."

"You still haven't gotten to the point."

He returned to the tablet. "You were kicked out of graduate school less than four months before completing your PhD. Since then you've

managed to acquire countless supernatural and non-supernatural artifacts, survived a number of supernatural encounters. You are now considered one of the foremost experts on supernatural antiquities retrievals
in the world, even by a reluctant IAA. By all accounts you are headstrong,
argumentative, do not work well with others, and have issues with authority." He glanced up.

"*Point?*"

"Yes. You might not be the type of asset the IAA values, but you are
absolutely the kind of asset the Zebra Company hires."

I frowned. *What?* That . . . was not what I had expected. Williams
continued before I could wrap my head around the strange turn of events.

"We offer our employees incentives. Everyone is paid on salary, and
we include a percentage of contracts completed and bonuses on top of
that. We also don't force anyone into missions, and unlike the IAA, I
listen to my experts and work with people's talents and faults, not against
them. I don't believe in beating obedience into racehorses; if you want
obedience, you shouldn't be in the thoroughbred business." He smiled.
"It's why I'm still alive."

I'd be lying if I said part of me wasn't tempted. "You forget, I already
worked with a corporation. We had a disagreement and it ended up with
me almost shipped off to Siberia." I nodded at the gun still on the table.
"Somehow, I figure you guys do something worse."

I heard someone snort from back in the shadows. Williams held up
a hand. "A fair question. I would say I guarantee it, but that means little.
What I will say is that you can ask any of them," he said, gesturing toward
the mercenaries waiting in the shadows. To me he smiled. "Our work is
specialized and very dangerous. I don't lie to my employees about that.
Many people can and do die, yet many of the rest have been with me for
years, despite offers from other outfits. You can't buy that kind of loyalty."

I swallowed. A year ago, maybe even two, and I might have considered it. Goddamn. I hate it when no one is the bad guy . . . and when the
hell did I grow morals and a conscience? "Where are my friends and
cat?" It was the only answer I could muster.

I expected him to scream, yell, demand. Instead, he gathered his tablet and stood up. "Take her to the others," he said to his mercenaries as he strode across the cavern.

He was almost out of the cavern when he turned to say, "One more thing to remember, Owl, as you consider my offer. I may hate to see resources squandered like those IAA bureaucrats do, but I also eliminate threats. We are mercenaries after all."

No sooner was Williams out of sight than two of his men stepped forward to collect me. No violence, no intimidation. I don't know what weirded me out more—that the mercenaries were offering me a job or that they weren't trying to beat a location out of me.

The guards gestured for me to place my hands behind my head. I obliged, since they had all the guns. They led me to the opposite end of the cavern before heading into another darkened passage, and I noted they'd fixed night-vision goggles on. I think I caught sight of a canvas tent and an assortment of boxes, but now that we were away from the surface light and the LEDs, I couldn't be sure. Definitely heading farther away from the exit.

I heard metal clang somewhere in front of me before I was shoved inside, the metal door clanging back in place behind me—a larger and more secure cell than I'd been in. I heard the electric snap of the lock closing into place.

I reached out: bars. They'd already managed to install metal bars and make a jail cell.

I hate it when the other guys are efficient. What happened to leaving me tied up in a corner?

There was a loud meow before I felt something small brush up against my leg.

"Oh thank God you're back," I heard Carpe say. "That cat hasn't shut up."

Captain let out a series of chirps. I figured he was giving me some kind of an update, not that I understood cat. "He still hasn't shut up," I said.

"No, but at least the noises have changed."

I couldn't see, but still I felt for the lock. "Where's Rynn?" I whispered.

"They took him away about fifteen minutes ago," Carpe whispered back.

I swore. I didn't like thinking about what these guys would do to Rynn, especially since they knew he was one of the supernaturals, but there was no sense or use in letting my imagination do its worst . . . not until we saw what condition they brought him back in. I turned my attention onto the lock.

"No good" came Carpe's voice. I turned and tried to narrow in on his voice, but even though my eyes had adjusted, I still couldn't pick him out in the dim room.

"I already tried the lock," he continued. "So did your boyfriend. It's not un-pickable exactly but might as well be."

I stuck my hand out until I touched the curved alcove wall. If I had to guess, I'd say the spot they'd picked for a jail wasn't large.

"Big enough for three or four people uncomfortably," Carpe offered.

Smaller spaces meant fewer possible exits. I started toward him, making my way carefully across the uneven floor, using the wall as much as I could.

"To the left . . . and watch out for the—" Carpe started.

I stumbled and landed hard on my knees.

"Hole," Carpe finished.

I decided crawling was the smarter option until I reached a shoe. We spent a number of uncomfortable moments in silence while I managed to seat myself in the oddly shaped and small alcove cum jail cell. Unlike where I'd woken up and been questioned, this spot most definitely did have the metallic and stale smell of the caverns.

"Did they interrogate you first?" I asked as Captain continued to inspect me now that I was closer to his level.

"I . . . ah . . . no. They haven't bothered asking me anything yet, though they did take my computers. Won't find anything on them, I don't care how good their tech department is."

"Please tell me you two managed to work out an escape plan while I was out?"

"Yeah, ah, potential for escape is low—at least until we get a break. Two guards on either end at all times, no delays in shift changes, and on top of that, only three of us can see."

"Is there any good news in there?"

"Well, while we've been tied up and you've been out, the World Quest guys got back to us," Carpe said.

I frowned at him—or figured I did. It wasn't like I could see well. "I thought they took all your devices."

"I have my ways."

I sighed. From the way he caged his answer, I was almost certain I didn't want to know what those methods were—or where they were. And somehow, when it came to Michigan and Texas's demands, good news was about the last thing that popped to mind. "What did they say?"

"They gave me a meeting time. The caverns—it matches the one we were in."

Where we'd found the gate. Not that I was certain I wanted to be anywhere near it . . .

"Tell them there's a good chance we might have to raincheck. And while you're at it, see if you can get Lady Siyu an update on the mercenaries, and tell her—" What? That we were close to getting the armor? Not a chance. "That there's been a complication. Will explain later."

"I am not contacting a Naga—oomph! All right, fine," he said after I kicked him. "I'll send the message. But even if the Dragon had his own private army, which he doesn't, they'd still have to get here—"

"Just do it. You'd be surprised what the snake can do when motivated."

We both fell silent as noises and the scrape of boots against stone reached us. A moment later, the doors clanked back open. There was an exhale of breath as someone was shoved in.

I held my breath. Rynn.

The door clanged shut and the electric lock snapped back into place. I waited until the boots had retreated before whispering, "Rynn?"

"I'm fine. A little worse for wear, but they got what they wanted out of me. Mostly questions about World Quest, and what our stake was in this."

"What did you tell them?" I said.

"The truth more or less. That we were here for an artifact, but, considering your history with the IAA—"

"That if I happened to run across the dynamic duo I wasn't above taking them out from under their noses and screwing their day up?"

"Something like that. I think they bought it. They strike me as more willing to deal than coerce, even with the supernatural."

I nodded to myself more than Rynn. "I got the same impression off the one I spoke with too, Williams—or that's what he wanted me to think."

"Williams?" Rynn said, surprise in his voice. "Somehow I'm not surprised he's here himself. We've never had the displeasure of meeting, but I know his reputation."

Carpe however had a much different, fear-driven reaction. "Williams? He's behind this?"

"How do you know who he is?" Rynn asked, sounding suspicious.

"Hello? World-class digital surveillance and hacker here, remember?"

"Yet I notice you had no idea they were coming," Rynn said, the suspicion still layered in his voice.

"I'm exceptional, not omnipotent. You realize they have digital security too? An entire digital team. I mean, I still managed to get into their email, and a couple of their grunts are idiots—I mean, who streams porn on their phone while they're supposed to be on a covert mission? Worms, Trojan horses, anyone?"

"Mercenary porn-watching habits are not relevant, Carpe!" I said.

"Sort of relevant. I mean—"

"At all!"

There was an uncomfortable moment of silence that passed over us. "The point I'm trying to make is I figured out how they found us," Carpe said. "Remember the brunette woman wearing the white anorak who was harassing Hermes? Here," he said. A dim LED light went on in his hand, which he angled toward me. It wasn't a light but a small phone that fit into the palm of his hand and was flatter than anything I'd ever seen. How he'd managed to keep it from the mercenaries aside, I could see the employee shot clearly with the Zebra logo hat.

"Apparently Hermes isn't omnipotent either," Carpe said, "which strikes me as a bit ironic. Or he just figured this would keep things more entertaining. Fifty-fifty odds on that."

Somehow, I didn't think Hermes was the type. Then again, maybe watching me try to weasel my way out of a makeshift prison cell was his idea of a good time.

"And we don't know that he didn't," Carpe insisted, sounding more nervous than he had a moment before. He turned what little light there was from the phone on his face. "Seriously, Williams is bad news, even amongst the mercenaries. Alix, he hates supernaturals as much as you do—or used to," he said, shooting a surreptitious sideways glance at Rynn. "Except rather than express himself with witty quips and repartee, he expresses his distaste with violence and a wide assortment of firearms."

"He offered me a job," I said. When the two of them looked at me, I added, "I didn't take it."

Rynn shook his head. "We'll worry about Williams if it comes to that. Right now we have a much bigger problem," he said as he searched my face. I noted Carpe was also giving me a sidelong glance.

I looked between the two of them. "What? What is it you two geniuses aren't telling me?"

It was Rynn who spoke. "I don't think they just want the suit, Alix. I think the elves' plan all along was to have it possess you."

I went cold.

"There is no way that was the original plan—" Carpe started.

"Yet even you had to agree it now seems the most likely."

Carpe was still fuming, but he didn't offer any more argument.

That was what the elves had been hiding. I bet they'd even known it was in Shangri-La, which was why the World Quest time line had been ratcheted up. They hadn't wanted me to find the suit; they'd wanted to deliver me to it.

"How did they even know it would want me? The suit only finds a host it likes every few hundred years—if that."

"The archives," Rynn said. "They probably have information on every victim the suit has ever taken."

We both turned to Carpe. "I swear, I didn't know!"

"What *did* you know?" I said, not bothering to hide the venom in my own voice. "And don't even try to tell me you didn't know something."

"All I knew was that they wanted the armor," Carpe said. After a moment he dropped his gaze and begrudgingly added, "And after you retrieved the book, it was suggested you were the best person to get it—provided no one stepped on the dragon's toes this time."

I lunged at him, the LED light casting sinister shadows where my arms reached for him. I don't know what exactly I planned to do, but it involved violence. And to think I'd defended him to Rynn as my *friend*.

"And you didn't think for one moment that me knowing any of that was important?" I straddled him, pinning him down. Good thing elves didn't weigh much.

Carpe tried to block my hands as they went for his neck. "Well now it is, and so I'm telling you!"

"Alix!" Rynn said, wrapping his arms around me and dragging me off Carpe. When I was on the other side of our too-small cell he added, "That won't help us get out of here any sooner—next time the armor might not be willing to let go."

I took a deep, long breath. As if I'd needed any more incentive to get out of here . . . But Rynn was right. I could hit Carpe later.

We all heard the buzz of the cell phone, softer than a normal phone but noticeable in the close quarters.

"It's Lady Siyu," Carpe said, and handed it to me. How to broach the new predicament? Sorry, the elves planned on sending me to slaughter? You can tell them to keep their bargain and kiss my ass. . . ."

"Keep it quick," Carpe said. "I don't want the Zebras picking up the signal."

I made a face and held the phone to my ear. "Hello?" I whispered.

"Do you have the armor yet? Yes or no will suffice," Lady Siyu said.

"Ah no, but there's a complication. A big one—"

She cut me off. "Then I suggest you stop wasting time in a mercenary jail cell and find it."

"Ah yeah, a little help with that would be much appreciated."

There was a hiss. "They're humans, therefore your problem. Now find a way to deal with them or you'll be wishing you were back in that cell by the time I'm done meting out your punishment. And don't return without the armor." And with that, she hung up.

I stared at the phone then held it up to Rynn, his face illuminated by the dim LED. "Well. That went well." Oh, if she only knew what she was saying . . . then again, showing up at the Japanese Circus wearing the armor might be giving Lady Siyu her just desserts.

I handed the phone back to Carpe. "No help from her. On to plan B. We need a distraction."

I heard the intake of breath. "About that," Carpe said. "Something Lady Siyu said gave me an idea, about humans being human problems."

"What exactly do you have in mind?" Rynn asked, his voice guarded.

"Just that we do as Lady Siyu suggests—let the humans take care of our current human problem."

Rynn caught on. "Which humans that want Owl dead did you have in mind?" Rynn asked.

"Oh, I think I know exactly the ones," I said.

—⁓—

We heard the commotion outside well before the guards showed up outside our makeshift cage. Muffled, but the shouting and occasional gunfire were unmistakable.

When they did show up, they were moving quickly, and sweat was traveling down their faces. And there were only two. Two. That was even better than we'd anticipated. It had to mean the party-crashing committee Carpe leaked my location to had come in full force.

They grabbed Carpe first, as he was closest to the entrance, then made an effort to secure Rynn as well as they could with a pair of zip ties. Then, as if I was an afterthought, two guns were shoved in my face before the guards gestured toward the cavern tunnel.

"Wouldn't be having problems with the locals, now, would you?" I asked, exchanging a look with Rynn, then Carpe.

All we had to do was stick to the plan. One of the guards positioned himself behind me and shoved me forward when he figured I was watching my companions too closely. I clenched my hands.

"What's the occasion?" I asked. "And what about my cat?"

There was no answer. For one, they were professionals, but secondly, Captain was already following out of his own volition. Captain knows where his cat kibble is buttered. Still, answers weren't the point; distraction was. "You taking us out to walk the plank or whatever else you mercenaries do for fun?"

"Those are pirates, Alix," Carpe offered.

"Really don't think this is the time to split hairs," I said.

"Or give them ideas," Rynn whispered.

There was a shove from behind. "Quiet, both of you," one of the Zebras driving us said. I kept my mouth shut this time, but not because of the guard's semi-empty threats. Beyond the sparse LEDs that now lined the cavern, ambient light from outside was trickling in. We were getting near the exit—as well as the fighting, from the sound of things. Confirming my suspicion, one by one the four mercenaries guarding us began taking off their night goggles. Though, still no sign of the . . . shit!

I didn't wait for the mercenaries to shove me onto the ground—I dove and managed to take Carpe with me as four bullets struck the cavern wall where our heads were a moment before.

Jesus—those were awful close. "I thought the Chinese wanted to capture me."

Carpe shrugged. "Depends what your definition of *capture* is. From what I gather, they were pretty pissed about the terra-cotta warriors."

I flattened to the ground as another series of bullets struck overhead. The Zebras tried to line up their own shots amongst the gunfire, and we'd slipped to a much lesser priority.

"What did you tell them exactly?"

"That you were about to destroy what remained of the Kingdom of Guge in a massive explosion. Well, it worked. Didn't it?" he added as my mouth dropped open.

"You idiot. Before, they just wanted to toss me into a jail cell. Now?" I swore and ducked again as another round of bullets struck.

"If you two wouldn't mind?" Rynn whispered. "We did have something resembling a plan. I'd prefer it if we didn't let it fall apart completely."

Right. I palmed the syringe Rynn passed me. My guess was he passed Carpe one that was about the same.

The Zebras' expansive collection of pharmaceuticals might make them immune to Rynn's incubi talents, but that didn't give them the ability to watch their pockets 24/7. I watched the guard nearest me, waiting for him to be preoccupied with the Chinese again.

"Oomph!"

I glanced beside me to see one of the guards Rynn was responsible for slump over. The one nearest me turned, searching for the noise.

So much for perfect timing. I jabbed him in the leg with the needle and watched as the fast-acting sedative took effect. He crumpled to the floor.

Hunh. No alarms raised, no screaming, no shouting . . . damn, this was actually going according to plan.

The bullets were still hitting the cavern wall ahead. Since the LEDs had been shot out, I grabbed the Zebra's night goggles and fixed them to my face before peeking around the corner. I rolled back as another round of bullets struck the cavern wall dangerously close to where my head had been. I grabbed Captain by the scruff and pulled him back before he could stick himself in the line of fire.

Why was it I never had a carrier at times like this?

I handed Captain off to Carpe, neither of whom was particularly happy about the arrangement, while I crawled back to the downed Zebra to rummage through his jacket pockets.

"Not the time to loot the bad guys!" Carpe said.

I ignored him while I searched. Right pocket? No, left. There it was. I found the small mirror I was looking for, unfolded the attachment, and angled it around the edge of the cavern tunnel toward the fighting— without risking my head being shot off.

I swore under my breath as I caught sight of the black Zebra jackets tucked behind the crates, interspersed with the green, brown, and black on gray camouflage uniforms of the Chinese special forces—along with the assault rifles pointed at us.

I ducked back. "How does it look?" Rynn asked. I passed him the mirror so he could look for himself.

"That depends on what you think of the Chinese sending special ops after me. Apparently Carpe told them I was a budding antiquities *terrorist* in the making."

Rynn swore. "Your reputation precedes you. There's at least fifteen of them blocking the cavern entrance and who knows how many others lying in wait."

"What are our chances of sneaking around?" I asked.

He shook his head. "If I was on my own, maybe I could get past the ops, but I'm not arrogant enough to think I can get by the military vehicles that will be blocking all routes out, not even on a good day. We're as good as pinned." He then crouched back around the rough cavern wall as more shots were fired.

He glared at Carpe. "Next time, leave out the exploding part."

"Both of you stop it," I said, while I tried to work out something . . . anything . . .

"We could let the Chinese take us. They'd get us away from the mercenaries," Carpe started.

I shook my head though. "The IAA has ties there too. If we let the Chinese take us, it'll only be a matter of time before they hand us over to either the IAA or the mercenaries." I felt the ping in the back of my mind. I recognized it now, the armor, influencing me, sneaking into my thoughts.

Unfortunately, as much as I hated to admit it, I was pretty sure I agreed with the armor . . . or at least I sure hoped to hell it was still me thinking it was a good idea.

Regardless, I didn't see a lot of options coming my way.

"Do either of you know your way back into the caverns?" I said.

From the look on his face, Rynn figured it out first. "That's not an exit, Alix—that's a death trap."

"No, the Chinese special ops and the Zebras are our current potential death trap."

"Only if they catch us."

"Which they will if that's the only exit." I could see the indecision on Rynn's face. "Look, you can berate me when I can't get the portal open."

"If any of us are left alive." Rynn cut himself off as he pushed me and Carpe into the dirt a hairsbreadth before more bullets struck the wall above us. "What is it they say about jumping into frying pans?" Rynn asked, his expression far from happy.

"That sometimes things get real hot. Then you jump through a portal."

Rynn rolled his eyes, but he went back to watching the Chinese and mercenaries. The fight was winding down as the mercenaries retreated, leaving us to the Chinese.

Rynn held up his hand and started counting down, folding each finger carefully. When he reached five he threw something round, metal, shiny . . .

Oh shit.

"Run," he said as soon as it was out of his hands. We bolted back into the tunnels, both Carpe and I having the sense to grab the night goggles and torches from the downed mercenaries—fast—before following as fast as we could over the terrain. In my head I started counting.

"Explosives?" I whispered at Rynn, in case any mercenaries were still lying in wait. "Are you out of your mind? When the hell did I become the reasonable one and you the reckless one?"

He glanced back at me over his shoulder, not bothering to slow down, even with the uneven terrain. "You're still the reckless one. Whenever you cause an explosion you have no idea what the hell you're doing. Me? I know."

"Kettle and pots are both black."

We stopped as the cavern shuddered with the force of the grenade explosion. "Run," Rynn said again, and shoved Carpe in front of him down an offshoot on the left of the cavern past the jail cells, going next himself and pulling me behind him, Captain close on my heels.

The caverns shuddered again. I glared at Rynn. "You knew what you were doing?"

"It hasn't collapsed yet, has it?"

I swore as the aftershock continued. The hillside was not happy. "And I was trying not to level the lost kingdom!"

"Well, we can't have everything we want, now, can we?"

"And why the hell do I have to go first?" Carpe shouted back at us.

"You're the team canary," Rynn said. "You're testing the tunnels to make sure there isn't anything nasty waiting."

"Canaries die!"

"And it will be a cherished sacrifice for years to come. Now move, elf!" Rynn said, giving Carpe another shove. "The Chinese and the mercenaries won't keep themselves busy forever, and that's praying there aren't any guarding the portal."

Carpe shook his head but continued down the cavern corridor. The decline steepened quickly, and the pull in the back of my head, like a voice egging me on faster, told me we had to be getting close.

Worry about the armor once we're through, Owl—

I thought I recognized a passage up ahead, if not from my memory, then from my current dubious guide.

There was shouting and gunfire behind us as the remaining mercenaries tried to deal with the Chinese and vice versa. It might have been my imagination, but I think they were getting closer.

"That's it," I said to Carpe as I made out a fork up ahead where light escaped. "The one on the left." I pulled off my night goggles as the light brightened.

Carpe took it, and a moment later the ceiling widened as we spilled into the portal cavern.

There was a sole Zebra standing in the center, looking at us, his walkie-talkie in one hand and his gun in the other, as if he was not quite sure what to do with either.

Rynn wasn't afflicted with the same problem. He lost no time pulling out his own gun, then shot the guard.

The Zebra picked out a blue-and-red feathered dart from his chest and looked at it, then us, before falling over.

Voices were still coming through the walkie-talkie. Rynn grabbed it. After bringing it to his ear, he said, "Alix, not to rush you, but if we have any chance of escaping, you need to open that fast."

I swore and scanned the equipment that now filled the cavern. High-tech: computers, UV lasers, lights, digital cameras, monitoring equipment. "Someone's getting serious help from the IAA." Still, there was no indication which one to activate first—the mural on the floor or the mural of elephants and tigers that decorated the wall.

I crouched down and searched for clues, any clues, that the Zebras might have uncovered. There were none.

Last time, trying the wall mural on its own had been disastrous. The floor, then?

I glanced up from the patterns at Rynn. He was manning the tunnel. "You need to be sure," he warned. "A mistake could bring the entire place down."

Easier said than done. "I hate treasure puzzles," I said, more to myself than anyone else.

"That isn't true. You love treasure puzzles—you always make me leave them for you," said Carpe.

"In a video game, not in real life!" I yelled.

Carpe looked like he might say something more, but at that moment, a gas grenade dropped on the mosaic floor just outside the gate.

Rynn grabbed it and threw it back out the tunnel. He was rewarded with more shouting and screaming.

The floor or the wall? Something told me the floor was the place to start, with its lines of pink elephants and orange tigers—and if I was reading the manipulation right, so was the armor. Or it was my imagination trying to come up with a justification for an otherwise idiotic and completely unjustifiable action.

"If you're going to do something, Alix, do it now!" Rynn yelled.

I was out of time. Damn, I hoped I was right.

I took out the bottle of chicken blood and water and drew in my breath. "What do you think, Captain?"

He meowed at me, but I thought maybe, just maybe, he looked at the floor. Trial by cat. That had to be as good as any decision-making skills I had at my disposal at this point.

Time to see just how serious this suit was . . .

I sprayed the designs on the floor and waited as the blood catalyzed the mural, spreading across the floor and animating the lines of animals as if they'd come to life. I held my breath and waited, but there was no explosion.

There was the ping of metal on the stone floor.

"Hurry, Alix," Rynn called as he lobbed another gas grenade back up the tunnel.

"I have it," I said as the two murals began to intertwine, the lines of animals mixing until they were a three-dimensional work of art, no longer clear where either mural started or finished.

I shielded my eyes as there was a shot of blinding light. When I looked, the murals were gone, a mirrored portal left in its place.

"I've got it!" I called.

Rynn abandoned his post and ran for us.

Carpe glanced at me and arched a single eyebrow. "Here goes every-thing," he said, and stepped through.

Here went everything was right. . . . I grabbed Captain, who was sniffing at the portal's edges, and held my breath. Then I stepped through.

I gasped as I fell through the portal. It didn't hurt, but it rattled me, not unlike being pulled in a tire behind a speedboat over very rough water: hold on and hope you don't capsize or fall off. I tried to open my eyes but had to close them; there wasn't anything to focus on, just blurred colors and half reflections. Then, almost as quickly as it had started, it stopped. Warmth like a summer breeze brushed against my skin before I slammed into grass-covered ground beside Carpe, with Rynn in rapid succession behind us.

Captain ended up landing on his feet . . . on my back . . . because why not?

I felt more than saw him hop away. "Captain? Stay!" I tried, though I'm pretty sure it didn't come out quite that way. I lay where I was in the nice, friendly, warm grass and hoped my head would stop spinning. It wasn't like fresh-cut grass—nothing that manicured—but it smelled soft, with a warmth that shouldn't have been possible, considering the air didn't smell or feel like summer.

"Alix?" Rynn called from beside me, sounding worse for wear. There was a groan from Carpe as well, indicating he was as bad as, if not worse off than, Rynn.

I pushed myself up to my knees and blinked rapidly, trying to clear the spots from my eyes.

"Okay, I'm seeing more," I said, and tried to push myself up to standing. My head rushed and my vision clouded with the movement. Apparently disorientation wasn't the only affect the doorway had. I abandoned standing and settled for rolling over to get a look at where we'd landed.

We were on a grassy hillside inside the main town, which I thought I recognized from the game—or the parts that I could remember.

The mountains, the cool air, the sunshine, even the scent of the warm spring air—not too cold but crisp and clean, like a spring day, not the start of fall that it should be; it was all familiar, which made no sense, since I'd only seen it in a video game. Maybe I was having a stroke. That happened: your mind filled in blanks when you were having a stroke.

The grass was so warm and inviting. I figured I'd just stay there and wait for my head and stomach to clear.

Someone started to shake my foot. "Owl?" Carpe said, sounding like he was about to puke.

"Leave me alone, Carpe. Five minutes, I swear, that's all I need."

The shaking didn't stop though. "You need to look. Now. I think we have company."

I turned my head. Oh God, I thought maybe it was me who was going to throw up . . . I noticed shadows moving in the grass near my face. I braced myself and lifted my head as far as it would let me.

Shit.

Two men were standing just inside the entrance to the courtyard. They were backlit by the sunlight streaming in from outside, but still I had a good idea who they were. The cowboy hat and the disparity in height left little to the imagination.

They stepped out of the shadows until two pairs of very worn and patched hiking boots were directly in front of my face.

I glanced up, shielding my eyes from the sun—or trying to. They wore matching unhappy expressions on their familiar faces; uncanny, considering how close they mimicked their game avatars, or was that vice versa?

But that wasn't what made me want to puke all over again. It was the double-barreled shotgun that did that. The one leveled at my face.

"You just had to come through, couldn't fucking leave it alone, now, could you?" Texas said.

I lifted my head a few more inches off the warm, inviting grass. Oh, why couldn't I have gotten five minutes? "Surprise?" I said, and even managed a wave.

Texas didn't look impressed. Then again, it easily could have been the spinning in my head. I closed my eyes and laid my face back down on the warm grass. I'd take what respite I could get; I had a feeling it was going to be short.

15

SHANGRI-LA

*Noonish, guessing from the height of the sun
in the long-lost city of Shangri-La*

"I should have known," Texas said as he poked me with the barrel of his shotgun. I rolled over, but that was about as much as I could manage.

"Texas. Michigan," I said, looking up at him. "How are you boys doing? Fancy place you have here, sorry to drop in unannounced."

"You just couldn't mind your own business and meet us on our terms, oh no, you had to come barging in here."

I frowned at the barrel of the Browning. Why was he pointing a gun at me? More importantly, why did he keep poking me with it?

I glanced over at Rynn and Carpe, who were both still on the ground just outside the closed portal. Carpe groaned, and though Rynn managed to push himself up, they were still both looking dogged. Note to self: supernaturals did not handle the doorway to this place as well as humans did, which meant I was the one on diplomatic duty. Yeah, nothing could possibly go wrong from that. . . .

When Texas probed me with the gun again, I said, "Look, either shoot me or let me lie here on the warm grass in peace. Just for the love of God stop poking me."

I winced as Texas grabbed me by the collar of my jacket and pulled me to my knees. Not what I would have preferred, but at least he stopped poking me. "Hiboux, I presume?" he said. "You've got less than half a minute to convince me not to shoot you."

"Look, we didn't crash your place on purpose—we were in a bind, and it was either this, mercenaries, or the Chinese army. As much as you two can be assholes, you won as the lesser of the evils. Congratulations." We were also here for the armor, but I didn't think we needed to broach that yet.

Texas just shook his head and turned the shotgun on Rynn next. I noticed Michigan was standing a little ways back, also armed and aiming at us. I frowned, was it my imagination or was he pointing a musket at us? I also noticed the tents and boxes, not to mention the packs, surrounding the courtyard, as if Michigan and Texas were planning a trip.

"Carpe?" Texas asked, as he gestured at Rynn with the barrel, sounding not quite as certain this time. For Rynn's part, he just lifted his head and glared.

I jerked my head toward the real Carpe, who was clutching his laptop bag on the other side of Rynn, still looking green. "Try again," I said.

Texas eyed us over while Michigan stayed where he was, though I noted he was still aiming the gun less confidently than Texas. The last thing we needed was bullets flying around.

"I don't even want to know who the middle one is, to be honest," Texas said. "Son of a bitch, can you two ever take a fucking order? Like ever? Seriously. What about 'meet us' did you not understand?"

"Technically we were supposed to meet you—about now," Carpe said, pushing himself up to his forearms with some success.

Texas turned an incredulous stare on him. "After *we* opened the portal," he said.

I grimaced and looked around. "Yeah—actually, again—same difference."

Texas turned his attention and the double-barreled shotgun back on me. "Just shut up, Hiboux, will you?"

Yeah, under any other circumstance. "Look, as much as I get you want to be pissed at me, we *just* beat the mercenaries here. You're welcome."

Texas turned to Michigan. "What the hell did I say about leading the fucking pack? Didn't I say that's exactly what she'd do?"

Texas—or Frank—snorted and stormed off to the canvas lean-to, leaving Michigan with his musket on us.

Michigan didn't join Texas in his rant. "How many, and how far behind?" he asked me.

"Right behind us. Research equipment, armed teams ready to enter. If we hadn't hijacked things from right under their noses, they'd either be here or you'd be walking right into their midst. I did you a favor."

"A favor? That's rich." Texas shook his head at us from the lean-to. "You know, you try to help someone stay out of trouble . . . what about *stay the fuck away* did you not understand?" Texas yelled, the last part directed all at me.

Even though it wasn't directed at Captain, he took offense. He sat down between me and Texas and let out a loud hiss.

Texas shook his head. "Even the damn cat is crazy," he muttered.

"Okay, just everyone settle down," Michigan said. He turned to Texas. "She might actually have done us a favor," he said. "We still have time. All my research says that they'll need a couple hours before they can open it again."

"We'll have to move up the entire time line."

"And we would have had to move the entire time line up anyways! At least this way we know they're coming."

Texas swore and hit the wooden table under the lean-to with his hand. Though he still looked like he wanted to shoot us, there must have been some truth in what Michigan said, because he lowered his gun and ran his hand through his hair. "All right, Neil. Step up prep and get the barriers up with guns ready to shoot. Make sure we've got extra rounds in the packs," Texas said. With a furtive glance at us, Michigan set off at a jog for the rest of the canvas tents just outside the abandoned city square.

Extra rounds in the backpacks? Better to keep them behind the barriers . . .

"And make sure we've got the slates ready to shoot through!" Texas shouted after him. Then he turned back to us.

Okay, this was getting stupid. I clenched my fists. "Look, what were you planning exactly when the mercenaries got here? Just let them walk right through the door?"

He turned a murderous look on me. "As a matter of fact, we were planning on letting you walk right in while we walked out!"

I stared at him. "What did you plan to do? Meet us in the gate? I don't know about you, but there's no way I could hold a conversation in there—"

"There was no meeting, there was never any meeting!"

"Are you out of your minds?" I yelled before my filter could kick in.

Texas crouched down in front of me. "You wouldn't let the fuck up about helping us, so we figured we'd let you help us. We open the gate, you idiots walk in, we walk out. *That* was the plan." He shook his head at me again as he stood up, leveling his shotgun at me once again. "You just had to show up early, didn't you, Hiboux? Mess up all our plans."

The double-barreled shotgun Texas was holding was much older than I'd thought—an 1890s antique Browning . . .

"What the hell are you doing with an antique?"

Texas just laughed.

I spotted the muskets propped up against the side of the lean-to. In fact, everything here was antique, down to the crates. Even the lean-tos and tents set around the square had their canvas patched together more than once with mismatched scraps of cloth.

Those had to be eighteenth-century muskets lined up by one of the town walls, and the cannon looked like it had been taken off a nineteenth-century frigate. It was a hodgepodge collection of explorer's goods from the last three hundred years—maybe more. But if this many people had found Shangri-La?

Oh shit.

"You haven't been hiding out here at all," I said to Texas. "All this time, you've been trapped."

Texas laughed. "And now she gets it, the great Owl gets that the fabled city of Shangri-La is one big fabled sinkhole." He bared his teeth at me, eliciting another hiss from Captain. "Four years we've been trapped here. We can't leave—*no one's* left in over three hundred."

"Or at least enough people haven't come through one of those portals for it to work the other way around," Michigan said, coming back up behind Texas and carrying a large leather book under his arm. "Here," he said, handing me the book. With a wary glance at Texas and his shotgun, I started to flip through the pages. It was the journal of a climber and explorer, one George Steinback, dated from September 8, 1965, with the last entry entered on December 31, 1976.

I didn't recognize the name, but he was a self-professed archaeology hobbyist with a couple undergrad courses under his belt and an inclination to finding a lost city—or that had been the idea when he'd set out in Nepal in 1965.

"Shit, this guy was IAA," I said. Not high up but versed enough to know about the supernatural. Unfortunately, George was one for puzzles, and he'd managed to figure out how to open the portal with the help of a diary he'd found in an old box of discarded books at a university claiming to know the location of Shangri-La. His elation had turned to depression pretty fast when he'd realized he couldn't get out and no one knew where he'd gone or where to start looking.

"He was here for almost forty years before we stumbled along," Michigan said.

"And went nuts at least ten before that, if that journal he left is any indication—the pages he didn't destroy. And when George got here, he found those guys," Texas said, pointing to a collection of graves as he gestured for me to get up. I made my way to the nearest and largest of the gravestones built with stone salvaged from the temples. The stone read Col. Percy Fawcett. Him I did remember from history class. He and his entire expedition of fifteen men disappeared in the Amazon searching for a lost city as well.

I suppose if you were going to have a pocket universe, distance was the least of your concerns. Col. Percy had been well entrenched in the IAA as well. Michigan handed me a second journal, this one older and more worn.

I skimmed through the pages, but Percy's diary read just like George's—elation, concern at not finding an obvious way out, optimism, then despair. It was like the Four Stages of Learning You Were Trapped.

"They lasted about a decade trying to reactivate the gate. Then one of the team stumbled on the accounts of a British military expedition that got lost here during the India wars, who had a theory that to get out you needed to shoot enough people." I looked up at Texas from the journal. "You can imagine how things went from there," he added. "If you don't believe me, see the bullet holes for yourself." He nodded toward the pile of crates, every last one riddled with bullet holes.

The sickened feeling hit me full force . . . ten years trapped here, then someone decided to try their luck with mass murder. Fantastic.

"Not that they couldn't have survived comfortably for decades," Neil said. "Doesn't get cold here, consistent rainfall, no snow except in the mountains, and someone at some point planted crops. There's a small spattering of wildlife—bugs, yaks, rabbits. A lake."

"Haven't wanted to screw with the ecology, since we have no fucking clue how small or contained it is," Texas said.

Eat a couple yaks and the next thing you know you're overrun with plague-carrying rodents . . .

"A veritable damnable, fucking paradise," Texas said, kicking a metal can that, along with the tent canvas, had also been patched up.

I caught sight of the computer equipment. So had Carpe, who walked over to look at it. "This is years out of date," he said to Texas and Michigan as he perused it. "And it looks like you patched it all together."

"'Bout the only thing we've been able to figure out how to fix and patch into the magic of this place."

"That's how you run World Quest," I said.

"That *is* World Quest. This place," Michigan said, holding out his hands at Shangri-La, "acts as the server, not the computer. Who would have thought it, human-made magic plays nice with human-made programming."

"And don't ask us how it works," Texas said, and nodded at Michigan.

"Think a living, almost breathing, jerry-rig," Michigan said. When we all stared at him, he added, "The city decided it likes the game, so it keeps it running. And before you even ask, no, it won't work with phones—or at least I haven't figured out a way to make it work with phones or any other electronics." He held up a walkie-talkie and pointed to a pile of discarded dig equipment. "This? Those? Completely useless. The only way Shangri-La lets us communicate with the outside world is through that game."

"If the magic of this place is sentient, it has one hell of a sense of humor," Texas added.

"Why didn't you contact someone through the game? Or, I don't know, tell *someone* you were here . . ." I trailed off as Texas shook his head.

"Because it won't *let* us," Texas said.

Michigan shrugged. "Game crashes, program glitches. You name it, every time we've tried, Shangri-La stops us."

The desperate way they'd rigged the game to work with the outside world, the maps, the warnings . . . shit, they weren't kidding. They really were trapped. I glanced around at the . . . if not living, then sentient, city.

I was having a real problem lately with sentient magic things.

I didn't have a chance to ponder that one too much longer as I looked back up from the journal into the business end of Texas's shotgun.

I remembered the expedition that had gone homicidal. "Oh hell— not you two as well."

"That would only make things worse," Neil said. "Just like it did for them and the next three expeditions who stumbled into the place. People need to be *alive* in here for others to leave."

Texas lifted the safety. "And guess what? You're the first ones to have found your way through since we did."

"You were planning on tricking us into switching places with you."

"And the world-renowned antiquities thief catches on. Only took you . . . oh, ten minutes."

I raised my hands and took a step back as I did my best to try and think a way out of this. "There has got to be another way—" I started, but Texas interrupted me with a shake of his head.

"I did my best, Hiboux. We didn't want it to be you, we even tried to warn you, but what happened? You just had to come after us and bring your idiot friends. It's like the delinquents of World Quest just had to crash our front door."

"You just said you can't kill us—shit!" I dropped to the ground along with Rynn and Carpe as Texas fired a round into the lean-to behind us, adding to the collection of bullet holes. "Look, you two are making a huge mistake. Right now there is an entire company of mercenaries on their way to find you. Damn it!" I swore as another shot struck the table near my head. "I thought you said you weren't going to try and kill us!" I yelled.

"Had an awful lot of time to target practice in here. And I am not sticking around for the shit show you call archaeology."

"Where do the bullets even come from?" I shouted.

"Re-melt," Texas shouted back and lined up another round. "I can always make it a leg shot. See how well you bounce back from that. I'll give you a hint, it ain't like World Quest."

Four years locked in Shangri-La; we were not going to negotiate with these two. I cast a quick, furtive glance around for anything we could hide behind or, failing that, throw. There was the metal can Texas had kicked over and the rows of muskets . . . but Texas saw where I was looking and made a tsking noise before I could even attempt to inch in that direction.

I lifted my hands above my head. When Texas gestured for me to back away from the portal, I did—on my knees.

Carpe cleared his throat. "Um, not to be the bearer of bad news, but you both heard what they said."

I shook my head at him. Was I pissed? Sure, but I wasn't unsympathetic. If I'd been stuck here for four years with a finicky video game that had taken on its own personality traits, chances are I'd have been getting pretty desperate too. No, I wasn't going to condemn them to being trapped in here over that. "Tie them up for now," I said over my shoulder. Rynn obliged, using heavy rope he found mixed in with the supplies and fastening them to one of the tent poles, one on either side. I headed for the table where all the old books and journals that had accumulated over the years were laid out, then I started perusing the old books once more, doing my best not to pay attention to the unconscious developers.

"Alix, I hate to consider it too, but we might not have any other option."

I ignored Carpe as I went through the materials. Diaries, journals, reference books, accounts of men and supplies, some dating as far back as the 1700s. At least Neil and Frank had organized them and made their own notes. I made a point of setting them aside; I don't know if it was superstition or instincts, but I stayed as far away as possible from the jerry-rigged servers. I'd leave Carpe to deal with those, meanwhile . . .

"You forget the most important part about finding your way out of a dungeon, Carpe," I said as I picked up a journal from a pile that had *1925* written across its cover. The materials had all been organized into neat piles, with various collections of notes tucked inside—Michigan's work, if I guessed the handwriting right. It'd take me a while to go through them, but I would, provided I could fight off the armor. I could already feel it creeping at the edge of my thoughts. "There's always another way," I said, holding up the journal. "You just have to find it. Take the books on the left half of the table and start going through them," I said to Carpe. "Rynn, you start with the ones on the table over on the right. Looks mostly to be maps, but there might be notes and journals in there too. Look for anything and everything that deals with trying or failing to find a way out."

Texas shook his head once more. "Had to be you two ɛ didn't it?" He leveled the gun at my leg. "Medical supplies are the tent—a little old, but there's still some penicillin in there."

I noted Michigan was looking around, searching, about tl time I noticed that only Carpe and I were on our knees. Capt hightailed it for the crates when the shooting had started.

"Where did the blonde go?" Michigan asked.

Texas took his eyes off me to search the camp. For a moi thought he might lower the gun or waver in the direction it was p but no, he did his namesake proud.

It didn't do him any good. A dart with a bright red-and-oran not unlike a highly poisonous ornamental insect, smacked into neck. He grabbed it and managed to pull it out and look at it, tl "It had to be you two World Quest screwups," he said before h rolled back and he slumped to the ground, smacking his head on the lean-to poles.

I imagine Michigan would have had something more to say it, but he also got a neck full of one of the red darts. He didn't man pull his out before toppling over—this time onto the soft grass.

Rynn stepped out from behind the farthest patchwork tent. moment I wondered how he'd managed to keep some of his wea from our run-in with the mercenaries, but I decided that unlike Ca endless supply of electronics, Rynn had probably relieved one o Zebras of them on the way here.

Rynn checked Texas over, briefly examining the spot where he' his head on the way down. "He'll be fine except for a bruise—and a i hangover." Rynn stood. "He should wake in a couple hours."

The fact that Texas would wake up with a nasty headache shc probably not have made me feel as happy as it did.

It was Carpe who spoke first. "What do we ... ah, do with them

For a moment it occurred to me that if they'd been planning to le us here ...

I shook the thought off. I wasn't stooping to their level.

Carpe looked perplexed. "What about the armor?"

I turned to Rynn. "You okay with getting out of here and leaving the armor buried where it is?" I winced as the armor let me know its opinion of that.

"Absolutely," he said, not looking up from the stacks of papers.

As I figured it, if they didn't have me for the suit to draw in, they might never find it. I was the lynchpin, except now I knew it. "I plan on getting as far away from that thing as humanly possible," I told Carpe.

"But what about the dragon? And the Naga?"

I sorted the books and papers. "They can get used to disappointment."

That only agitated Carpe more. "But what about the supernatural war?"

I spun on him. "Not at the expense of being possessed by a malicious suit of armor." I let out my breath. "There's a point, Carpe, where everyone has to decide when the price for something is too high."

"And the elves' help just got way too expensive. We leave the armor where it is and figure a way out. We take our chances that no one else can find it without Alix to lead them."

Carpe didn't offer any more argument as he headed for the servers.

I felt the armor ping again, nicely this time, apologetically. I blocked it out and hoped I could hold out long enough. The armor didn't think so.

16

ONE HELL OF A PARADISE

Time? Late afternoon by the sun, though Shangri-La
doesn't seem to track time quite the same . . .

I leaned back in the chair and rubbed my eyes. I'd only gone through half of the pile of journals, but every last one of them had painted the same picture—and eradicated any confidence I'd ever had in my species' ability to find a nonviolent solution to a problem.

Or maybe I could chalk that up to some residual effect of the armor. But if that many people could be so easily swayed to kill each other, I wouldn't hold my breath for our collective common sense.

I picked up Col. Percy Fawcett's red journal once more—the accounts of his search for El Dorado, the same one I'd already read three times. The pages were old and yellowed but heavy enough that I could still make out all the entries, including the ones near the very end—technically and metaphorically speaking.

Well, Percy had found his lost city . . . not El Dorado but another opening to Shangri-La. He'd then spent the next decade trying to find a way out and convince the rest of his team not to kill each other. The bullet wounds and bashed-in skulls of the corpses dressed in 1925 explorer gear said just about how well that had gone.

One explorer gone missing wouldn't have dashed my optimism; it's sad, but it happens. You go venturing into some unmapped jungle or ancient ruin and there's always a chance you won't come back out. I live with that sobering thought every time I venture out. Dev, me, even someone as entrenched in the IAA as Benji. It could happen to any of us.

No, Percy hadn't sent me spiraling downward. It was all the others.

Underneath Percy's journal was another, older, dating back to 1795. That one was written in French, by a Jean-Francois de Galaup Lapérouse, whose two ships carrying 225 crew went missing shortly after leaving Botany Bay, Australia. Lots of explorers and ships went missing—hazard of the seas, even for an expert explorer and mapmaker. Lapérouse was last seen headed for the Solomon Islands in the Coral Sea just north of Australia. After hearing about a legend of a lost city, he'd decided to change course.

I wasn't going to pretend to understand how an underwater gate to Shangri-La was built in the Polynesian Islands, let alone how they activated one underwater; Lapérouse was cagey about that in his journal. What I did know was that the only trace that was ever found was a pair of severed anchors on the bottom of the ocean and I was looking at two dilapidated ships in the harbor with the names *Bousole* and *Astrolabe*.

I imagined the bodies on the boats were just as riddled with sword, knife, and musket wounds as the ones strewn around the city.

There were dozens of journals, every last one of them outlining the same thing; how explorers had stumbled onto various doorways to Shangri-La cast over the world and gotten themselves trapped in the city.

My confidence in our ability to get ourselves out of this mess, where so many others had failed, was waning. "It's like a graveyard for famous explorers in here," I said as Carpe came back into the tent.

Carpe picked up a nearby journal. "This one looks newer."

I took it back. "That's because it is. Peng Jiamu." Another famous explorer and archaeologist, this time from China, who disappeared in the desert back in 1980.

Carpe frowned. "That's not too long ago. What happened to him?"

I took the journal back before Carpe could touch the pages. "I thought that was obvious. He found Shangri-La." Carpe made a face, so I added, "He'd spent a year trying to get the door open before deciding to see just how far Shangri-La stretched. Considering no one ever heard from him again and he never came back to fill in the journal . . ."

"He might have found something—or left notes," Carpe tried.

I gestured to the snowcapped mountains that surrounded the Shangri-La valley. "Be my guest to go and find out, Carpe."

"Has anyone ever told you you're a pessimist?"

"Frequently." I pocketed Jiamu's journal. I hoped to bring that one back, since there were likely people alive who still cared—if we ever got out.

My eyes drifted over to where Texas and Michigan were still propped up under the tent. Carpe saw where my eyes landed and said, "The last thing we want to do is wake them up."

"They knew how to get out." Or at least had been on the right track.

"Yes! And apparently I need to remind you that they were about to ditch us here with that armor that has its sights set on your questionable morals—"

"*My* questionable morals?!" I said, and took a step back. Captain, sensing the change in my mood, began switching his tail around my legs prior to stalking Carpe. Carpe, not being a complete idiot, took a step back and swallowed. I continued. "You were the one all gung ho to ditch them here. What happened to elves preserving life and all that?"

"I have my weak moments, all right? And as much as I detest the idea of leaving any living thing here, them, I'm finding, I wouldn't feel so bad about."

I closed my eyes. I couldn't believe the circles Carpe was talking himself into.

"Look, maybe if we found the armor . . ." he continued. "It wants out; maybe if you get close enough to it—"

"*No,*" I said in a firmer voice than even I realized I could muster.

Carpe winced, taking another step back, and I found myself feeling guilty at the flustered look he gave me.

"Let's not get crazy desperate just yet," I said, and nodded at the World Quest duo. "Waking them in my mind is a better option than giving a sadistic magic suit of armor free reign over my thoughts."

He relented and glanced away at the table, where I'd rearranged the books. "Well, maybe if we wake them and you're really nice, they'll tell us where they rigged the explosives."

It took me a second to see where Carpe's train of logic had gone. "Okay, there is absolutely no evidence they've rigged the place—"

He turned his furious green eyes back on me. "These are the World Quest designers! Of course they've rigged the place with explosives."

I held my breath and counted to five. I was not going to win this battle—not now, not ever. "Just . . . look, why don't you help Rynn. Or better yet, find a way to dampen that suit's effects on my brain." As soon as I said it, I winced. At the mention of dampening its power and potential hold over me, the suit stuck its claws in, tugging at my own natural mental barriers. Since arriving in Shangri-La, Rynn had been trying to help me block out the armor with a makeshift mental barrier, but there was only so much he could do with his skill set of manipulating my emotions. Already the armor was making inroads, cracking my resolve and seeping into my thoughts despite the fact that I knew what to look for. Not finding a way back in, it receded, and I opened my eyes back up to Carpe, who was examining my face with a pinched expression. "Preferably before it figures out a way in my head," I said.

Carpe opened his mouth to speak, but a bang on the workbench distracted both of us. It was Rynn. He'd snuck up on us and deposited his supply bag on the table. Loudly. "Any more idea how this place works?" Rynn asked.

Thankful for the change in topic, I jumped in. "Beyond what they said?" I nodded at Texas and Michigan. "They were right about one thing: as far as anyone can tell, we're trapped." I filled him in on the gist of my findings from the journals, including how Shangri-La seemed to have a twisted taste for explorers and adventurers.

"Like a butterfly and moths to a flame," he said once I'd finished.

"What about you?" I asked him.

Rynn shook his head. "Nothing beyond what you've uncovered," he said. "I'm starting to think Shangri-La doesn't want us to leave. I'm starting to wonder if it and the armor are in cahoots."

Considering they'd been stuck together for more than seven hundred years, it wasn't all that far-fetched. I winced as another wave hit me. "Well, we need to do something fast. It's on to us, and it's doing its damnedest to figure a way back into my head."

Rynn shook his head but glanced in the direction of Michigan and Texas. "It's too adept at evading me."

"But?" I asked.

He inclined his chin at the duo. "But I agree that those two might know more than we do."

That settled it. I started for the fountain off to the side of the square, grabbing a metal bucket on my way. I had no illusions that the Zebras were sitting on their haunches. For all I knew they were opening the gate—and that was just one location. For all I knew the IAA had the rest of them and an exponential number of mercenaries on our collective tails.

I filled the bucket under the fountain and checked the water temp. Despite the warm air, the water was cold. Good.

Captain howled and jumped out of the way as water splashed out of the bucket and onto him.

When I reached Texas and Michigan, I pulled my arm back. The bucket was heavier than I'd thought.

"Try to keep it civil?" Rynn called from the lean-to.

"Yeah, something like that." I heaved the bucket over my shoulders and dumped the water over their heads.

Both of them sputtered awake with gasps from the cold as I stood there with my arms crossed. Texas was the one who made a grab for the bucket—which didn't work, since his hands and legs were tied. He did fall over though. In my current mood I couldn't say that it didn't make me feel a little warm and fuzzy inside.

Rynn came up behind me. "I told you to keep it civilized," he whispered.

"And considering they were going to ditch us here, that was civil," I whispered back.

Texas was still trying to right himself despite the restraints. "Give it a rest, you're tied up," I told him.

Texas took in his predicament—Rynn, Carpe, me. He even gave Captain a measured glare before his eyes fell back on me.

"Why you—" Texas did his best to throw himself forward again, but it didn't work well due to the restraints.

Carpe grabbed him, while Rynn restrained me before the two of us could start a brawl.

Michigan blinked the cold water out of his face, coming to slower than Texas had. Still, it didn't take him long to take in his surroundings and situation. "Frank, will you knock it off?" he said.

"With her? Seriously, you want me to back off with *her*? Name one time when she hasn't been the harbinger of disaster?"

Michigan frowned. "That's an exaggeration."

"You talk to them then. And I'll be more than happy to say I told you so."

"Okay, first—you have serious anger management issues," I said to Frank. "Second, I don't want to leave anyone here, but unlike you, I don't think beating the shit out of each other is the way to handle this. For one, we'll win." I pointed to Rynn. "He's not human and could probably take all of us including the cat, so let's attempt to talk this through."

"Why don't you untie us so we can find out?" Texas said, baring his teeth at me.

"Because I'm not an idiot!"

Texas made a show of looking around the tents and abandoned town of Shangri-La. "From where I'm standing . . ."

I clenched my fists and ignored the jibe, doing my best to keep my own temper and anger down. "We don't have time to argue. We need your help."

That earned me a snort. "In the famous words of one Byzantine Thief, you can blow—"

"Look," Michigan rushed to interrupt Texas. "It's not that I'm opposed to us working together—" Texas guffawed, and Michigan paused to shoot him a dirty look, silencing him. "But Frank has a point." He held up his bound wrists. "You haven't exactly inspired trust here."

I closed my eyes and took two deep breaths, considering carefully what to say next. "Considering you were the ones who planned to lure us here then strand us—"

"What if we told you why we're here?" Rynn interrupted.

"So you could finish burying World Quest—oomph?" Michigan silenced Frank with a jab. "I thought you said it was some noble attempt to save us from ourselves?" Frank turned his attention back on me. "Nice job, by the way."

"Partly," Rynn said. "But that was more coincidence. We were after the Electric Samurai—a powerful and dangerous suit of armor that's been hidden here for centuries." Rynn nodded at the portal a little ways away, standing inert and harmless looking. "Which if you don't help us bury will likely fall into the hands of the very mercenaries the IAA hired to hunt you down."

Another glare from Texas. "What do we care about a magic suit of armor?"

"If it gets out of here, it will be an unmitigated disaster," I said.

"And if it falls into the wrong supernatural hands, you can kiss good-bye to any hope of returning to the same world you left," Rynn added.

I thought Texas was going to deliver yet another spectacular piece of rhetoric, but Michigan beat him to it. "Wait—the armor? *That's* what you're here after? *That's* what the IAA is after?"

I exchanged a glance with Rynn and Carpe. "I think the IAA originally just wanted you two and any and all human magic associated with Shangri-La. The armor got dragged into things afterward by a third party. It's just really bad luck the two coincided." Or fantastic planning by the elves and manipulation of the IAA—though I saw no reason to bring that up now. I frowned at Michigan. "And how the hell do you know about the armor?"

He shook his head in disbelief and turned to Frank. "The Mongolian artifact mentioned by the Guge monk—the one they entombed." To me he said, "Shit, there's tons of stuff sitting here from when the silk road was going . . . right cabinet," he said, and nodded toward one of the desks. "There's a hidden drawer underneath. Red folder."

I examined the desk. Sure enough I found the latches, which sprung open the drawer. The file was tucked inside with a few other colored folders.

"I found it a year or two back," Michigan said, "and decided it was best left where it was."

Inside was an old parchment, written in the ancient Mongolian text I'd become so familiar with over the last week. I couldn't read all of it, but enough of the first few lines:

Here lies the body and dying wishes of Jebe.

It continued, and what I could piece out were bits of warnings not to disturb his rest and final entombment.

Anger rushed over me as I read. *Locked up here for centuries, Jebe deserved the tomb he rotted in.*

I shivered and pushed back against the dark thoughts—most definitely not my own. I caught Rynn watching me and gave him a shake of my head.

"Is it true?" Michigan asked. "What he says about it possessing the wearer?"

I nodded. "I don't know if it was designed that way, but it has a mind of its own now."

"And it's just as likely to kill the wearer as try to take them over," Rynn added, while Carpe kept uncharacteristically quiet.

I continued to read. Plenty mention of the danger of wearing the armor, but nothing about where it was buried. "It gets worse with each wearer—and it's sneaky about it. Given enough incentive and runway it can even reach out across the portal to find new candidates, though it's picky. Jebe didn't figure it out until it was too late."

Son of a bitch.

The only way to trick the armor, and it needs to be done now, before I can no longer hide my thoughts, is to entomb myself. Otherwise it will drive me to its next victim, of that I am certain. I do not relish my fate, but if it means this evil will cease to walk the earth, my slow death is a small price.

My mouth dropped. This was the missing piece, how Jebe had managed to imprison the suit. "Shit." I turned to Rynn and Carpe. "He didn't defeat the armor, not really—he tricked it. In the end he knew it would find another victim after he died, so he got the Guge to bury him alive." I glanced up at Michigan and Texas. "Death, destruction, swaths of bloodshed, that's all the armor lives for."

The armor tried to argue with me in the back of my thoughts, but it quickly gave up. Some truths just aren't worth trying to lie about.

"So whoever wants it is out of their fucking minds is what you're saying?" Texas said, then frowned as he caught the look Carpe, Rynn, and I exchanged.

"Someone's decided they want to stick Alix in the suit," Rynn said.

"And it seems to have warmed up to the idea. You want to know how we got the gate open? That's how. It practically led us here."

Texas snorted. "Wow. Sucks to be you, Hiboux. Good luck with that."

I took a step toward him, fists clenched. "You know what, Texas? You can go to hell."

It was Carpe who stepped between us this time. "Neither of you are helping—at all. What we need to do is get the suit and get out before the mercenaries show up."

"What we need to do is find a deeper and more obscure pit to bury it in, Carpe." I was not happy about how he kept letting that detail slip. "We can draw straws as to who gets to leave first."

"Then the others wait until the Zebras come through the portal." Rynn nodded. "That could work."

It was Texas and Michigan's turn to exchange a look. "There might be a minor problem with that," Michigan said.

"What?" When neither of them coughed up an answer fast enough, I added, "What are you two assholes not telling me?"

"The city has some strange rules about how many people enter and leave," Michigan continued. "We still haven't figured them all out yet."

I closed my eyes. "The short version," I said.

Michigan made a face. "Our numbers are hypothetical. Our gamble was to go through the same time you came in." He made a face. At least he felt bad about trying to strand us. "In theory at least three of us should be able to leave now that you're here and no one's killed anyone."

"But we're still not sure, not even if half the IAA and a private army waltzes through. As far as we can tell, the entire system broke all to hell about four hundred years ago, give or take," Frank added.

Carpe let out a breath. "Balance," he said. "I was wondering how they'd gotten around that."

We all turned to stare at him, including Frank and Neil. Carpe shifted on his feet under the scrutiny. "Ah—this place is mostly magic. It has ground," he said, and stamped his foot to make his point. "An ecosystem, even weather patterns, but it's completely contained. Not quite in a pocket universe—those eventually collapse—but in a separated stasis with all the entropy removed."

"A world without chaos," Rynn said.

Carpe made a face at Rynn but nodded. "Simplified, but, essentially, yes." He glanced up at the World Quest duo. "In order to keep this place in existence, the balance of entropy has to be carefully maintained. One person in, one person out."

Which would have worked just fine a thousand years ago when this place was the world's first major trading hub. "What happened?" I asked.

Michigan nodded toward the hills just outside the city proper. "There's a Guge graveyard just past the field on the hillside—a massive one. A disease hit the city. A bad one. Smallpox, syphilis, maybe even the plague. By the end they weren't even burying people, just leaving them in pits and throwing them in the harbor."

"The Guge," I said, and Michigan and Texas both nodded.

Well, I'd been partially right. The Guge had fled to Shangri-La, and then died en masse from a plague.

"That many people dying in a place like this—I don't even know how that would balance out," Carpe said.

"Trapping people here for the past four hundred years, that's how," Texas said.

I doubted very much it had been designed to work that way. No one plans for an entire city to up and die overnight, but where magic leads, disaster follows.

Well, that explained why no one had managed to find a way out and, in all likelihood, added to the problem with overzealous homicide. I glanced at Rynn. "Shangri-La has a warped sense of humor."

Carpe frowned at me. "I don't think it's sentient, Alix. More like a computer program. If a situation comes up that a designer doesn't specify, it still tries to do the work, even if the answer is a little . . . off."

"Right now I could care less whether this city is riding on the back of a giant pink elephant floating through space. Can we leave or not, elf?" Rynn asked.

Carpe pursed his lips. "Maybe."

"In other words, we won't know until we try." I sighed. Fantastic. I did so not want to be stuck in this place with a hundred odd mercenaries for the next ten years.

I turned to Texas and Michigan. "All right, where did they stick Jebe?" I felt elation from the armor, mixed in with ridiculous promises.

"*Don't hold your breath,*" I thought back at it. "*If being stuck in a tomb for seven hundred years pissed you off, then you really won't like me finding you.*"

The set of Texas's jaw told me how not happy he was with the direction I was going. "Chasing after a cursed suit, especially if the mercenaries are about to storm this magic mousetrap, is a lousy idea. I say we draw your straws and some of us leave now."

"Not without the armor secured and buried," Rynn said.

Texas narrowed his eyes at Rynn. "Sounds to me like it's Hiboux they want."

"*Seriously?*" I said. "What? Tie me up with a bow and leave me here for when they show up?"

Michigan cast his eyes down, but Texas met my stare. I held it. Then sighed. "Look, was I being a bit of a shit with the game? Yes, but let's face it, you left that wide open."

Carpe groaned behind me.

"But not even you two really think I deserve being handed over to the mercenaries and stuck in a homicidal magic set of armor as punishment. You might not like me, but if you really thought I deserved that, you would have banned me from World Quest years ago."

Michigan and Texas exchanged a glance, and for a moment I thought I'd gotten through to them.

Texas turned on me, eyes narrowed, teeth bared. "Oh come on, you seriously believe we're going to buy that save the world bullshit? You're a worse thief than I thought."

I sighed. Or, maybe not . . .

Rynn came to my defense. "She's telling you the truth!"

"Have you met her?"

Goddamn it. Sometimes there was no winning, no matter how hard I tried. I noticed Captain, who'd been entertaining himself looking for mice amongst the rubble, start a slow creep toward the gate. I frowned. There was an iridescent sheen to it. "Guys?" I called out, taking a generous step back.

Rynn and Texas kept arguing. "You're not even giving her a chance," Rynn continued.

"People who answer every fucking question with the choice phrases 'blow me' and 'I've got a bridge to sell you' don't deserve second chances!"

There was a distinctive ripple in it now, like when hot air meets cold. Shit. "Ah—guys," I said, louder this time, taking another step back from the gate. Captain, in a rare show of wisdom, followed my lead, clinging to the back of my legs. "I think the arguing will have to wait."

Both Texas and Rynn stopped and turned their attention on the portal. It had graduated from shimmer to reflective mirror, like a pool of water in the rain.

Texas took one look at the portal and held out his bound hands. "Untie us—*now*."

Carpe obliged, while I grabbed Captain and ran for the tents, skidding to a halt behind the crates. I didn't have my carrier anymore, so the best I could do was one of the canvas bags that had accumulated under the benches. I opened it up for him. He looked at the portal, the bag, then me, and let out a drawn-out mew.

"Yeah, I know, but it's the best I can do."

He snorted but climbed in. I fastened it to my back and set about building a barricade out of the crates I could lift.

Seeing what I was trying to do, everyone else—including Neil and Frank—scrambled back into the tent and started to help. We had the crates stacked three high when the portal snapped, a sound that echoed through the valley, followed by the scent of ozone.

The first two Zebras exited the gate into the square, guns raised. We dropped to the ground just as a round of bullets arced over the camp, striking canvas, old crates, and the grass indiscriminately—though I noted Shangri-La itself was mostly spared.

"These crates will hold up against bullets, right?" Carpe asked Rynn, his voice hopeful. In answer, one of the top crates exploded into splinters as another Zebra began firing. Lying on the ground, we peeked through the cracks to get an idea of what the hell was going on in the courtyard.

A dozen or so more Zebras had streamed through and set up a semi-circular perimeter around the gate. The gate shimmered as four more bodies passed through, three of whom I recognized: Williams, the head of the Zebras; Agent Dennings; and . . . shit. Dev.

I cringed as Williams pushed Dev forward. It wasn't a hard or cruel shove—just efficient. What about "get out of Nepal" had Dev not understood?

The fourth figure though . . . He—or she—was dressed in a dark blue robe that reminded me of something Carpe's World Quest avatar wore.

The figure pulled down the hood to survey Shangri-La, and I got a better look at what had to be an elf underneath. Like Carpe, he was thin and somewhat frail, made more so by the massive blue cloak. He was also pale—pale and sickly. He didn't conjure up the iridescence of vitality and youth. More like the pale rot that sets on living things at the end of their life, like dried wheat in a field.

Was it my imagination, or was there the faint scent of dried flowers and decaying leaves? I shivered at the imagery. The cloaked figure turned toward us, and I could have sworn weepy pink eyes fixated right on me through the box slats. Captain growled inside the canvas bag, having squeezed his head out to watch the proceedings.

"Still think the elves aren't involved?" Rynn hissed at Carpe.

"Just because *that* one is involved doesn't mean all of us are." But even through his words I could hear the uncertainty.

Rynn tried to get a better look and was rewarded with another round of gunfire striking our blockade.

"*Who?*" I asked.

"Nicodemous," Rynn said. "An elf. One I unfortunately have the acquaintance of. I doubt he's changed for the better."

I glared at Carpe, who said, "He's much higher up than me—and no, he's not the Grand Poobah elf—there's no such thing!"

Carpe was leaving something out. "Is he dangerous?" I asked. "And don't you dare lie," I added before he could get one word out.

He closed and opened his mouth again. "Not that anyone has any *proof* of," he said.

Fantastic. An elf with questionable morals and the good sense not to get caught.

Rynn had managed to maneuver himself under the table beside me, where he madly fetched equipment from his own bag as more Zebras spilled through the gate and took up various positions.

"Everything I've ever said I've hated about the elves? That one personifies it," Rynn said with more venom than I think I'd ever heard from him before.

"There has to be what? A dozen of them?" Michigan said.

"More," Rynn replied, "and that's just the Zebras."

Texas swore, but I could see the wheels churning in Michigan's head. "That'll work."

Texas frowned at him. "What will?"

"If I'm right, it means we need to get out of here sooner rather than later, preferably before they send any more through."

I frowned. "I thought more coming in is a good thing? More people in, more people out."

Michigan shook his head. "Maybe—or Shangri-La is so unstable that it decides none of us should leave. Or it just says to hell with it and collapses on itself." As if in answer, thunder sounded overhead. We all looked to see dark clouds accumulating over the snowcapped mountain range.

"That normal?"

Michigan shook his head, still staring at the storm clouds. "I've never seen a thunderstorm here."

Shit. "How long do you think it'll take for them to figure out how leaving here works?"

"More importantly, how long until they start to turn on one another," Rynn said. "I'm guessing altruism isn't a hiring factor for that bunch."

Yeah. I glanced at Williams again. Somehow I hoped it wouldn't quite come to that; he might be practical, but he wasn't evil. He was doing a job.

I ducked again as more bullets turned the tent canvas above me into Swiss cheese.

These hadn't come from the same direction . . .

I crawled on my stomach to where the tent canvas met stone and peeked underneath. Behind us, making their way through the ruins of Shangri-La's abandoned buildings, was another group of Zebras.

Rynn squeezed in beside me. "They're flanking us. They must have managed to open another gate."

I was really starting to hate the competence of these guys. And we were out of options.

I caught Michigan trying to grab something off a table. I grabbed his arm and yanked it back down none too gently before the next round of bullets could shred his fingers. "Neil, what the hell are you doing?"

"I'm not leaving my notes for them." And with that, he grabbed the nearest sets of journals and began shoving them into a canvas backpack that had been tucked under the desk.

I dropped back to the stone tiles and came face-to-face with a growling pink tiger as another round of bullets hit the crates, shattering yet another one. "Open to ideas here, people," I said.

Neil wetted his lips. "There are more portals, including the one that leads to the cave in Nepal, deeper in the city, by the temple and market districts." He jerked his chin in the direction of the overgrown city vegetation that obscured the stairs leading down. "Through there. They can't have found all of them. One should be clear."

"Anyone got a better idea?" I asked.

"Whatever we're going to do, we should do it now," Rynn said before lobbing a smoke grenade at the mercenaries to renewed rounds of shouts followed by gunfire.

There were so many of them now.

I narrowed my eyes at crates being pulled through by the Zebras under Nicodemous's direction. With IAA logos stamped on the sides. Research equipment, lots of it.

More thunder rolled overhead, and for the first time since the gate opened I heard the armor—it was laughing.

They were going to try and find the suit. Rynn, seeing where my eyes had wandered, said, "The suit doesn't do them any good if they're trapped here."

No, it didn't, but was I willing to gamble everything on that?

I couldn't, not when there was a sliver of a chance they'd uncover it.

Somehow, some way, Michigan figured out where my mind had wandered. Maybe we weren't that different. "It's in the main temple, just down the steps. It's the largest building here. You can't miss it. The tomb should be somewhere in the basement."

I nodded. That would have to do.

The armor, no longer bothering to hide its intent, laughed once again. I'd see how hard it laughed once I buried it. To Michigan I said, "Get the portal open; we'll follow as soon as we can." Or try . . .

"Down the staircase, near the harbor. There's a temple, one painted blue and yellow that has a portal around back. I think it opens somewhere in the Andes Mountains. It's remote—they shouldn't have found it yet."

It'd have to do. I nodded.

"Down the steps, past the main temple, behind the blue-and-yellow temple. We'll try to keep it open as long as we can," Michigan repeated to me.

Rynn nodded and lobbed two of our remaining smoke grenades at the mercenaries. It resulted in another round of gunfire but achieved the main goal—cover.

Michigan lost no time darting into the brush. Texas gave me one last look and shake of his head. "Goddamn it, I can't believe it—after four years we might actually get out of this hell-bound magic mousetrap." He followed after Michigan, leaving Rynn, Carpe, and me.

Carpe was staring at me, his eyes uncharacteristically wide. "Carpe, the best thing you can do now is help them get that portal open and try to keep it open."

Carpe didn't need any more prodding. He shot right through the foliage after them.

As I watched him disappear, I got the gut feeling he'd been on the verge of saying something else. I wondered about it only for a moment as I hunkered down under another volley of bullets.

"Ready to bury the Electric Samurai for good?" Rynn said, and hefted a roll of dynamite from his bag.

I watched as the mercenaries spread out, heading for the buildings.

The sooner we had the armor buried under a pile of rubble, the better. I got ready to make a break for it just as the slim, frail figure of Nicodemous stepped into the sunlight, which just made him look more sickly, his robes swallowing his thin frame. Once again I got the impression he was looking straight at me with those cruel red eyes. I felt Rynn tense beside me.

Nicodemous whistled, and the mercenaries stopped.

There was a tug at my shoulder. "Alix," Rynn said. I gave Shangri-La a last look. All that treasure . . .

I felt the cold influence of the armor, its desperation flooding my veins. But for once it wasn't trying to wrench control over me. Less concerned with my intentions now and more concerned with getting me to it, though where the change in heart came from . . .

I shook the thought out of my head as another round of coordinated bullets came our way. If it was going to cooperate now out of some last-ditch effort to escape, so be it. The enemy of my enemy . . .

"This way," I said to Rynn, and bolted for the steps that led to the temple entrance, bullets chasing our feet until we spilled through the heavy wooden doors.

As soon as we were inside, Rynn grabbed one of the massive carved doors and put his back into closing it. I followed his lead, and the two of us managed to fit the wooden slabs into the metal slots. No sooner did we have it fixed in place than the jostling from the other side started as the mercenaries tried to push their way through.

"That should hold them for an hour or so," Rynn said, backing away and checking the windows. They were high but not insurmountable.

A breeze—cooler than occurred outside—brushed against the back of my neck, followed by another round of thunder.

"Time to take a walk down a deep, dark tomb," I said to cover my own nerves more than anything else. I grabbed one of the lamps, lit it, and headed for the stairs leading down, Rynn close on my heels and Captain surveying from the bag.

Please, universe, for once don't let this one turn into an unmitigated disaster.

As I brushed a patch of cobwebs away from the narrow path in front of me, I figured that with my going rate of luck, that was a slim chance.

17

THE GUNS OF SHANGRI-LA

And this is why we can't have nice things . . .

"I could have sworn there was a passageway there a moment ago," Rynn said as we made our way back from a dead end.

"That's because there was," I told him. Like Texas and Michigan had insinuated, Shangri-La played fickle. Moving passages, disappearing doors, appearing dead ends. I checked the now-dead-ended wall. Sure enough, my chalk mark was still there. *Xs* for doors, *Os* for dead ends; this one had been marked as a door. I'd started using the shorthand as soon as we'd realized the temple was playing musical chairs.

I stopped Rynn before he could step on an inconspicuous square stone floor tile that was just a little more elevated than the others—not that any of them were exactly flush. I waved him back and knelt down, clearing the dust out of the grooves. Sure enough, it wasn't cemented in like the others.

Captain, curious and getting bored in the canvas bag, decided to stand on my back while I worked. I noted that not even he wanted to jump to the floor.

"My guess is it only takes a light touch."

"On account of the city?"

"On account of Captain not wanting to get out and wander around." He normally explored these kinds of places ahead of me, but not today. He knew something was up.

I tried to lift the tile, but it wouldn't budge. Well, if I couldn't disarm the trap . . . I searched the walls and surrounding tiles until I found what I was looking for. Three holes set into the murals—the tigers' mouths in this case. I handed Captain to Rynn and edged myself as far back from the tile as I could before laying down on the floor. When Captain and Rynn were well out of range of the tigers' mouths I reached forward, pressing my cheek into the floor, and pushed down on the tile. In quick succession, not one but six darts shot out and clattered harmlessly against the opposite wall. I tested the tile again to make sure it was inactive before retrieving one of the darts. The tip was white—a sharpened tooth. I held it up to Rynn. "Well, at least Shangri-La is thematically consistent," I said.

He took the dart and held it up to his nose. "Poisoned," he said.

"That's just the welcome mat. Wait until we get close."

"Just find the tomb so I can set the dynamite," Rynn said, crushing the dart beneath his boot.

"At least the suit isn't trying to take me over again."

"Yet. Which in my mind isn't comforting, Alix. It only means it's biding its time."

We made our way around a fallen piece of wall and found another chalk marking. This time there was a passage where there hadn't been a moment before. Not that I didn't agree with Rynn, but at the moment, the only option I saw was to continue onward and hope the city stopped playing games.

I checked the floors—no trap this time. Wonder what the tunnel held up ahead.

There was a whisper of something dark at the back of my mind. The armor wouldn't be safe here; someone would dig it out. Better to take it with me . . .

I paused for a moment and closed my eyes, pushing the thoughts out. We were burying it in here. A grave under a pile of rubble in a pocket universe—or whatever the hell this was. That wasn't negotiable.

I felt cool hands on my chin. I opened my eyes to Rynn's blue. "Speak of the devil?" Rynn asked.

I shivered as Rynn's eyes flared brighter—but I also felt the armor unwind its claws and retreat back. "I hate it when you do that," I said.

"Better than the armor taking over and convincing you to brain me over the head with a rock."

As much as I would have liked to argue I'd never go through with it, it fit in line with something the armor would try—and maybe succeed at. Instead I asked, "How did you know?"

He shrugged. "Movement. Your scent changes, so do your breathing patterns. It's nowhere near as subtle as it thinks."

I was about to comment that I didn't think the armor cared one lick about how subtle it was provided it got a chance to get back to pillaging and maiming, but a noise ahead made me pause. Rynn stopped as he heard it too; it was faint, but the echo of shifting tiles carried our way. We both stayed perfectly still and waited until Rynn broke the silence. "What do you think Shangri-La is up to?" he asked.

I shook my head. I was getting a really bad feeling. Even Captain let out a warning mew from inside my backpack. "Nothing good."

There was a shift in the stone up ahead, as if the temple was opening up another passage. I started to creep forward, angling my lamp around the tunnel so as not to miss anything.

Sure enough, a panel was sliding open, as if entirely on its own.

"Magic?" Rynn asked, keeping his voice low.

"Or mechanics of the city—wheels and pulleys." Or a combination of both. Shit.

A light escaped through the cracks as the panel continued to shift open. A light that uncannily mirrored mine. We backed up, but not in time.

"Stop!" someone shouted.

We ignored the command and kept running until two bullets struck the passageway unnervingly close to our heads.

"Can you survive a bullet to the head?" I whispered to Rynn.

He shook his head at me. "Don't know an incubus or succubus who's tried it, and I'd rather not be the first," he whispered back.

"Hands above your heads," the Zebra shouted as more footsteps filled the still-opening passage.

Without any other options, we complied. The city just had to keep screwing us . . .

"So we meet again, Hiboux," came Williams's distinct voice. I glanced over my shoulder. He was standing a few feet behind us, well out of reach, flanked on either side by his mercenaries.

Not wanting to run from bullets, I faced him. "I thought you were here to retrieve the World Quest dynamic duo."

I don't know if it was my imagination, but I could have sworn I saw Williams's expression turn dark.

"Plans have changed, I see?" I prodded. "I'm guessing one archaeology thief and an ancient and very dangerous suit of armor have been added to the list? Should have asked for more money."

"Oh, you can rest assured they are paying us for the change in directives. On your knees—both of you."

This time I didn't comply. "You've got to know by now that the IAA isn't running this pony show anymore."

"But they are signing the checks. On your knees. I won't ask again."

"Planning on shooting off our kneecaps?" I saw a plate on the floor, set just a few steps away and apart from the rest of the stone floor tiles.

"I don't need to shoot your kneecaps off to get you to kneel."

I glanced at the plate then at Rynn, hoping he got the message. I took the way he clenched his jaw as a sign he wasn't exactly thrilled with my plan but would go along.

"How about you go your way, Williams, and we'll go ours? Call it a day, no one gets shot?" I said as Rynn and I both kneeled.

Williams shook his head. "Can't let you do that, Owl."

The plate was within arm's reach. All I had to do was throw myself forward . . . But what kind of trap? I searched the walls for holes, but I couldn't find any—and the murals of baboons swinging through a jungle gave no indication what the trap might be either.

Well, beggars can't be choosers when it came to setting off ancient booby traps . . .

"Yeah, I figured you might say that." And here's to hoping I didn't get shot . . . I drew in a breath and threw myself at the plate. The tile sunk under my hand, scraping against the stone. The Zebras' guns came up as they searched for the danger—all except Williams, who kept his eyes on me.

"Oops," I said.

I'm sure Williams would have had something to say to me, but the tunnel around us started to shake. While the others searched the walls and floors, it was Williams who looked up; none of us could see the ceiling, even when everyone had their flashlights aimed up. Williams gave me one last look before whistling at his men. In rapid succession, every last one pressed themselves flat against the walls. A moment later I saw why as a stone cannonball suspended on a rope came pummeling down the center of the high-ceilinged tunnel toward us.

I swore and dove for the floor, a wisp of air stirring my hair as the cannonball passed too close for comfort. I lifted my head only to find it was coming back. I ducked my head out of the way, but one of the mercenaries wasn't nearly so lucky. I heard his gargled scream as he was pummeled down the hall.

"Now," Rynn said, and the two of us darted down the tunnel before it could return.

Oh no . . . "Rynn!" was all I managed to shout before throwing myself down as another cannonball came swinging from the other direction. Rynn shone the flashlight he'd managed to hold on to ahead. Sure enough, the entire passage was lined with cannonballs—all swinging in a homicidal arc. I also noticed that a side passage had opened up beside us. I shoved Rynn and started crawling toward it. I don't think I let out a breath until we were both in.

Then the passageway slammed shut.

"Shit." I checked the wall, but there was no trace of the doorway we'd just walked through. Maybe it was an illusion. I dug my fingers into the seams . . .

"Alix," Rynn called again, more insistently. "You might want to turn around."

Oh goddamn it, the last thing I needed was another trap. "Oh sweet Jesus," I said as I saw what was behind us.

Illuminated by Rynn's flashlight was treasure. Bowls, vases, dishes, jewelry—*lots* of it, all lined up on shelves that had been roughly carved into the walls. And not from one place either; if I had to guess, I'd say there were pieces from the medieval ends of the globe.

I stood and wiped my dusty hands on my pants in order to have something to do with them besides reaching for the treasure while Rynn examined one of the shelves—*without* touching.

"Trip wires," he said, "fixed into the back. Another trap."

Could be anything—falling ceilings, collapsing floor, more of the swinging cannonballs, a pit of lava. I shivered. Shangri-La had given up on the obvious and was setting out lures. A deadly trail of golden bread crumbs . . .

"Not even a little tempted to line your pockets?" Rynn asked.

I shook my head. "Only when it won't kill me. I think I'll just leave everything where it stands."

Rynn stopped partway down the path of deadly treasure and torqued his head. "Buzzing—magical, I think, coming from that direction." He gestured down a side corridor, then frowned. "It's thrumming, like it's tuned off key."

That sounded like the armor or Shangri-La. As far as the magic running them went, *off key* was a more generous euphemism than I would have come up with. I crept down the tunnel until I found what was reflecting the light back—not off the carved stone doors that lined the tunnel or the treasure but off a polished metal door.

I tried to check the seams, but as my fingers brushed the metal, an impatient desperation coursed through me. I pulled my fingers away. "It's definitely behind there—and the door's been sealed."

There were no inscriptions, no latches, no locks, no etchings. The copper-colored metal had been welded into the stone itself, which should have been impossible. I checked the surrounding walls. Still no indication of how to open the door.

Rynn did say he'd scented magic.

I knelt down in front of the solid metal door and breathed in deep. Mixed with dirt came the familiar tang of metal mixed with blood.

And me without my spray bottle of chicken blood . . . I searched the wall until I found a sharpened piece of stone. "Rynn, you might want to step back," I said before sliding my forearm across it until droplets of blood ran free. Rynn swore behind me.

I hoped the door didn't blow up . . . I took a deep breath, held it, and pressed my arm against the door.

The door didn't light up—not immediately. Instead the blood pooled on the metal, circling around until it formed one dark red glob, made darker still by the copper. It ran to the center and then seeped into the metal, as if the door had been porous.

"Was it supposed to do that?"

I shrugged. "Beats me—shit." I dropped to the ground as the metal door flared a brilliant red. When it didn't explode and I convinced myself I wasn't blind, I peeked at it through my fingers. Rynn was just standing there, looking at it—then frowning at me. I stood and wiped the dirt off my pants. He could frown all he wanted. He didn't have my mortality issues.

I looked at the images. Chinese characters, old ones, dating back to the Mongolian rule.

"What does it say?" Rynn asked.

"As best as I can tell? 'Here lies General Jebe and his curse for whoever dares to broach this door.' "

I took another deep breath, pressed both hands against the door, and pushed. It slid silently open, showing a darkened room.

"After you," Rynn said, aiming his flashlight inside.

It was filled with tables and chests of treasure—weapons, gold, jewels, clothes, furniture, and artwork from all over the world. And right in the center was a sarcophagus carved out of planks of hardwood and sealed together with inlaid metal that made it look like a strange broken artifact.

"That's got to be Jebe," I said.

I crouched down and checked the doorway for traps. Either Shangri-La had given up, or it had decided we deserved a reprieve.

Either way, the treasure room—or tomb—looked relatively stable. I stepped inside and picked my way around the treasure, heading straight for the sarcophagus.

The sarcophagus itself depicted a warrior who had Mongolian features and was dressed in a suit of black armor, similar to the ones I'd seen in the Guge murals. On his chest was clasped what was left of his bow. *Definitely Jebe . . .* Though the paint had long since begun to chip, I could still see the whites of his eyes, which had been left open, as if on watch eternally for intruders.

An involuntary shiver traveled down my spine. A hell of a way to go. Buried alive inside a sarcophagus to keep the armor from ever finding another victim.

I hoped I'd be that brave, but I doubted it.

I turned my attention away from Jebe's. The sarcophagus was made of pieced-together thin planks of hardwood, the cracks sealed together with molten metal. I brushed my fingers against it. Warped and twisted. Just like Jebe had said in his journal.

It hadn't been carved that way—it had split, multiple times, if the difference in metals was any indication. "Looks like it tried to break out a couple of times," I said. My fingers caught on the newer cracks that hadn't been sealed. "Looks like it's still trying."

"All the more reason to keep it locked up in here and throw away the key," Rynn said.

That I could agree with. Regardless of the danger hidden inside, I couldn't see any obvious traps in the tomb.

"I think it's safe," I called to Rynn, who was still hanging back by the doorway. As if reading my thoughts, the lanterns lining the walls—magically imbued ones, I assumed—flared on, bathing the room in an inviting, soft yellow light.

As soon as Rynn stepped over the tomb threshold though, the metal door slammed shut. Rynn tried to push it back open, but it was no use.

I abandoned the sarcophagus to see if there was some kind of inside latch to the door of the tomb. Nothing. I ran my fingers along the copper. It looked like it did before, welded into the stone. "Probably takes more blood—or there's another exit," I told him.

I don't know why, but I expected Rynn to be more upset than he was.

"This might actually work in our favor. I'd like to avoid a second run-in with the Zebras. They won't be caught off guard next time. See if you can find another exit," Rynn said.

While Rynn started setting explosives around Jebe's tomb, I began searching for another exit. I found one—a small crawl space at the back corner. Either that, or Shangri-La was back to playing its tricks.

"Found it," I called. "Though it's going to be a tight fit."

"Tight fit we can handle. We're not taking anything out of here."

Despite the fact that I couldn't tear my eyes off the sarcophagus, I agreed completely. Maybe it would stop haunting me once it was buried. It would lose hope, just like Jebe had. . . .

I stopped cold as I heard a banging sound. Rynn stopped what he was doing as well. It was coming from the sealed metal door.

Rynn was closest to the entrance. He dropped what he was doing and listened against it. "It's them."

Guess the cannonball didn't give them nearly as much trouble as I'd hoped. They couldn't get in here though, not without knowing how to activate the entrance.

The banging stopped.

But before I could breathe a sigh of relief, the entire room shuddered as explosives rocked the door.

Rynn wasn't finished setting his own explosives yet. "Nitroglycerine," Rynn called. "I need you to stall them!" Apparently there was a way to unseal magic doors . . .

"Stall them? How?"

"I don't know—talk to them?"

Talk to them? The mercenaries with guns? What exactly did he expect? *Hi, I have the suit of armor in here, but in the meantime let's play I spy?*

"*It'd all be easier if you opened the case and took me out.*"

The armor. "*Yeah, you're so not convincing me to take you out for a test drive,*" I thought back.

I grabbed one of the tables least covered in treasure and pushed it over. I found a second one and did the same. Figured it couldn't hurt to "talk" to the mercenaries from behind cover.

There was another blast from behind the door. This one left a dent. Nope, definitely not going to hold. I crouched down behind the thick table as the third and final blast blew the metal into a shredded mess.

I waited for the smoke to clear. Four Zebras came through. They were wearing gas masks, so I had no idea which one Williams was.

Rynn asked you to stall, Owl. Speaking of which, he was nowhere in sight. "Ah, hi there," I called out. "Can I help you with something?"

I was answered with a round of bullets that were surprisingly accurate at hitting the table.

"*I promise, I can get you out,*" the armor prompted again.

I glared at the sarcophagus. I won't lie, I was tempted . . . "Just because I didn't have refreshments ready is no reason to open fire!" I yelled at the mercenaries.

I ducked as they responded with more gunfire.

Well I suppose this encompassed both "talk" and "distraction" Rynn wanted in spirit . . . "Williams, you there?" I shouted. "Tell me, was it the IAA payment plan that roped you in, or did you know you were working for the elves from the start?"

One of them removed his mask. Sure enough, it was Williams. "I admire your tenacity, Owl, but you have no chance of escape—not unless there is a portal hidden in there. Why don't you and the incubus hand yourself over? I hear the IAA is still willing to negotiate."

"Was never impressed with the IAA grievances policy. Figure I'm better off taking my chances with the ancient booby traps."

He didn't look angry—more disappointed. "Do the sensible thing. You won't get a better deal."

"You'd be amazed how many times people tell me that, but it seems like my life turned around when I stopped doing the sensible thing."

Williams might have said something else, but at that moment, a sizzling ball of cloth—silk, maybe—sailed over my head and landed in the doorway.

I took that as the signal to get away from the entrance. I dove for the treasure. There were shouts behind me, and I could have sworn I heard bullets striking loose treasure and stone tiles equally.

The gunfire was interrupted only by the explosion. My ears rang as the entire temple shook. I looked in time to see the doorway collapse, blocking off the entrance, the mercenaries on the other side.

My ears were useless, which is why I didn't hear Rynn calling for me—not until he was directly behind me, pulling at my arm.

I let him help me up. Where was Captain? I found him cowering at the bottom of the canvas. I glanced back at the entrance, the metal door now reduced to layers of rubble. "Think it'll keep them out?"

"Provided there isn't another entrance? Yes."

We bolted for the tunnel.

"*You're making a big mistake,*" the armour pleaded.

"*Yeah, well you can fuck off.*"

I crawled into the tunnel, Rynn behind me. Ten meters in I spotted light up ahead—sunlight. I sped up my inelegant shimmy until I reached an overgrown pathway. Rynn spilled out behind me.

"Quick, help me set the next two," he said, and hefted the dynamite in his hands, as if weighing it against the tunnel. "If I'm right, two more should collapse the entire tunnel."

I hesitated. *Should.* What if the mercenaries and IAA wouldn't dig it out?

"The smartest thing we can do is get away. There's too many of them."

I knew he was right, but I couldn't shake the feeling that I was leaving the job half-assed done.

Rynn set the explosions—two rolls of dynamite wrapped in silk, which he threw into the tunnel. "Run," he said.

I didn't need to be told twice—my ears were still recuperating. We bolted through the brush until we found steps, then headed downward into the city proper. I spotted the yellow-and-blue temple Michigan had instructed us to run for. I hoped to hell they'd gotten out—and that Carpe had kept the gate open.

We ducked behind a set of statues to avoid a pair of mercenaries patrolling the market, then bolted for the temple, jumping the stone fence and landing in a garden overcome with weeds. Michigan was standing at the edge of the courtyard, his back to us. The gate wasn't open.

I started for him, when Rynn stopped me. "Why isn't he moving? And where are the other two?" Rynn whispered.

He was right. The hairs along the back of my neck prickled. Something didn't feel right.

Captain let out a low growl.

I was about to bolt—until I saw Carpe.

"Was that who you were growling for?" I whispered to my cat, who had crawled out of his bag and was perched on my shoulder, watching the clearing, his ears set flat back.

Man, at times like this did I ever wish he could talk. Carpe was searching the foliage and spaces between the buildings. He was looking for us—or someone . . .

Go to Carpe, or sneak around?

A scuffle on the other side of the clearing, which was hidden by foliage, stopped me moving. None other than Dev shot out.

He looked ragged, panicked, as he searched the courtyard. His hands were bound behind his back. "Run, Owl, it's a trap!" Dev shouted before two Zebras caught up and pinned him to the ground.

"Let's get the hell out of here now, Rynn—"

I didn't get the chance to finish my sentence. A safety clicked off behind my ear and the cold barrel of a gun pushed into the base of my skull.

I started scanning the ground for a rock—anything I could use.

"I wouldn't do that if I were you, Hiboux," the familiar voice of Dennings said behind me. "The incubus might survive a gunshot, but I assure you, you won't—and he won't be able to put you back together this time."

There were smart things that went through my head, like striking up a conversation with my newest captor, or trying to gain a better position. Hell, even collapsing in a heap on the ground would have been a better idea.

But I couldn't pull my eyes off Carpe as he stood there in the courtyard, mere feet away as the Zebras filtered out of the brush around him.

Son of a bitch. He'd done it again. Despite everything he'd said, he'd gone and screwed us over again. Only this time he'd betrayed us. It was like having a knife turned in my gut. Sense went out the window.

Before Dennings could do anything, I ran for him. "You no-good, lousy excuse of an elf," I snarled.

He looked shocked, then sheepish at my outburst. "It was to save the world. I'm sorry, I didn't think it would be you—"

He didn't get a chance to finish before I slammed into him, knocking him to the ground.

Carpe hit the ground—hard. I didn't waste any time straddling him and getting my hands around his throat. "Alix, I had no choice! It's for the better good—oomph."

"What did you do?" I shouted as I struck his face, which he had the sense to block.

One of the Zebras finally reacted and delivered a nasty shot to my kidney.

I doubled over. Contrary to popular opinion, that's about all you can do when someone hits a kidney hard enough. I rolled over on my side. Oh, I was going to be feeling that for the next few weeks. That and my ears . . .

"*I told you things would go badly. You had your chance to do it your way. Now we'll be trying mine,*" the suit keened in my head as Carpe scrambled out of my reach.

The mercenaries, a dozen or so, were all pointing guns at me now. I raised my hands and put them both on the back of my head before turning around.

Someone dragged Dev over and deposited him beside me, looking much worse for wear than when I'd last seen him. Rynn followed, though Michigan was nowhere to be seen. "Dev. How you holding up?"

He inclined his head. "Still wishing I'd ditched Nepal a few hours earlier. You?"

"Something like that."

"Well, well. What do we have here? Finally, the dragon's thief," the owner of the dry, reedy voice said, stepping out of the blue-and-yellow temple. Nicodemous. This time his hood was lowered. "Allow me to introduce myself and clear up any imminent misunderstandings," the elf said, approaching me. "I'm Nicodemous. Leader of the council of elves."

"I'd say it was a pleasure to make your acquaintance, but I'd be lying through my teeth." I winced as Dennings pressed the barrel of her gun into my back.

Unperturbed, Nicodemous crouched down in front of me. I held my breath against the scent of decaying leaves and trees that emanated off him. "I'm the one you've been chasing after that suit for."

"You can't have Owl, Nicodemous. I won't let you take her," Rynn said, not making any effort to veil his hostility.

Nicodemous turned his red eyes slowly to Rynn, regarding him, then back on me. "You're here because I decided I'd rather have you in my sights for the next while."

"He means he's going to try and screw us over." Rynn bared his teeth as he spat the words at the elf.

Nicodemous seemed to find that entertaining more than anything else. "Oh, on the contrary. I've already reported to the dragon that our terms have been met. Rest assured our representatives are entering into an agreement with Mr. Kurosawa and his Naga as we speak."

"*Fantastic*. Then untie the ropes and let us go," Rynn said, and held out his hands, which had been bound.

Instead of addressing Rynn's question, the elf smiled, and I got the first glimpse of his teeth. They were tinged pink, the gums a bright red, as if eternally bleeding. "The dragon and Naga never specified they required either of you back," Nicodemous said to me as he examined my expression. "The elves never work on assumptions. A lesson the dragon will be wise to learn."

Well, now I knew how the elves expected to stick me in the suit. They'd planned on trapping me before I ever made it back to the Japanese Casino.

"I thought you said they could go," Carpe said from the spot by the wall where he'd retreated. A blossoming fat lip took the edge off my anger at the fact he was still standing. He made a point of skirting around me— and Captain. Captain gave him a warning growl, then threw a deeper one at Nicodemous.

Nicodemous looked less than thrilled—with my cat or Carpe, but Carpe plowed on."Once you had the armor, you said you'd let all of us go—that was the agreement."

"Why you sneaky, no-good—" I started to stand, but Dennings buckled my knees with a well-aimed kick.

Nicodemous shrugged. "That was your ideal outcome, though as circumstances have changed, I am no longer able to let all of them go. If it makes you feel better, most of them will go free. Eventually." Funny, he didn't look the least bit put out by that fact.

"Most of them?" Carpe said, clenching his fists. "Fine, take me then."

"Not you, you self-centered idiot," Rynn said. "He needs a body. Maybe a few, isn't that right?" he added. If looks could kill . . .

Nicodemous glanced at Rynn, and his carefully schooled expression fell for a moment. "I remember you being more agreeable, Rynn. And asking fewer questions."

"I used to hold elves in higher esteem."

I glanced around. Dev, Rynn, Captain—there were too many of us to do something reckless and stupid, and Michigan and Texas were nowhere to be seen. Damn it—I really didn't want to end up the newly damned Electric Samurai. Despite what the armor seemed to think, I was a thief. I'd make a lousy warlord. . . .

"Look, there's no reason to keep all of them," I said. "If it's me you want, then leave them here and take me."

"Alix, no—" Rynn shouted. He tried to break the mercenaries' grip, but it was no use. They only hit him, again. That made Nicodemous laugh.

"If things had worked out differently, I would have been considering your generous offer, Owl. However, circumstances have taken an unexpected turn, so we'll be taking a different approach. May I call you Alix? Owl is such a . . . strange name."

"I'd actually prefer it if you didn't say that much to me at all, to be honest. Especially since you plan on sticking me in that cursed metal death trap."

He tilted his neck to the side, reminding me of a long-necked bird, something Carpe had done on occasion. "Well, we can't always have what we want. And who says I want you for the . . . *Electric Samurai*," he said, stumbling over the foreign words.

"Either you elves are more arrogant than Rynn said, or you just couldn't be bothered to do your research. The suit decides who wears it," I told him.

"Mmmm. I suppose it does have a history of being obtuse when it comes to satiating its hunger for violence and blood." He glanced over his shoulder at Rynn then, his red eyes catching the sunlight like sickly jewels, unlike the rest of his pale self, which seemed to suck the light away. "But who said I was going to let the suit decide anything? I'm not accustomed to letting inanimate objects dictate the terms of use, despite how animated they've become."

I felt the first pang of uncertainty from the armor.

Texas and Michigan . . . that must have been why they weren't here. "You want to stick someone else in the suit? Fine, but do you really want to go out on a limb and say two archaeology school dropouts are going to satiate whatever sick and twisted mind-meld blood lust preferences the Electric Samurai has? The suit's had six hundred years' worth of explorers paraded in front of it, and not once has it lowered its standards. You think you can convince it to take one of those two?"

Rynn, seeing my logic—that there was more than the elf to rattle in the immediate vicinity—jumped in. "You only have four humans, Nicodemous. After the armor burns through them, the only humans you'll have left are the mercenaries. Somehow I doubt those mercenaries are going to volunteer to step in the suit. Williams's men don't strike me as idiots. They *do* strike me as types who settle workplace disputes with flash bang grenades and bullets."

A few of the Zebras glanced between each other and Nicodemous, readjusting their firearms. They trusted the elf about as much as I did.

"I remember you having fewer opinions, Rynn" was all Nicodemous said in reply as he turned and headed back for the center of the small square. "You're right. None of the specimens here are ideal, including the mercenaries." He fixed his red gaze on me. "And it does seem to rather like you. Though for the life of me I can't fathom why."

It was probably the suit, but the idea of putting on the armor and frying Dennings and Nicodemous—and maybe Carpe—was growing on me.

"Let them go and I'll volunteer, no tricks. Promise." Hell, the suit already loved me; I throw punches, pick bar fights, and tell every supernatural I come across to fuck off.

But Rynn was less than impressed with my plan to get everyone out of harm's way. "You can't have Alix," Rynn said again. "Whatever scheme you have planned, Nicodemous, I won't let you take her."

Nicodemous didn't seem to take Rynn's threat seriously, but the mercenaries did. The ones flanking Rynn readjusted, and one hit him in the back of the head with a gun.

"And what exactly do you plan to do about it?" Nicodemous asked him.

"You know me, I have a reputation for being resourceful."

Nicodemous nodded, as if he'd expected such an answer. "Yes, you do. A frightening reputation, all things considered. If we wanted the girl, you wouldn't be able to do much about it." He turned those red eyes back on me, the polite expression replaced with a cold one. "As it happens, I don't want the girl."

We all stared at Nicodemous, but it was Rynn who looked the most wary.

"No. The council of elves is not about to stick a thief into the Storm Armor. We need a warrior—one of unparalleled character, one not corrupted by thieving and selfish tendencies."

I went cold as I processed his words. But no—that wasn't possible . . . "It won't work—it wants me," I said, my voice thinner than it had been a moment before.

"Normally that would be the case." Nicodemous held up a worn leather book, one I recognized. How could I not? It was the same one I'd retrieved for Carpe a few short months back. The spell book.

All this time, they'd never wanted me to put the armor on. They'd wanted Rynn.

Worse, I'd led him right to them—and the suit.

I wasn't the only one who was hit hard by that revelation. I felt the armor's surprise, which fast morphed to outrage and anger. My expression must have betrayed me, because the next thing I knew Nicodemous was smiling, his pink teeth looking unnaturally sharklike in his pale face.

As one of the mercenaries produced a syringe and pressed the tip into Rynn's neck, I strained against Dennings, but she wouldn't let go.

Rynn managed to knock out one of the mercenaries restraining him, but the narcotic they'd used was fast acting. He stumbled as he reached for a still-standing mercenary, who wisely kept his distance. Dennings, figuring the damage was done, released me. I ran for Rynn, hoping to hell I got a bright idea real fast.

Rynn grabbed my shoulders in an attempt to stay on his feet, but the drugs had hold. He sunk to his knees. "Alix, it won't work," he said. "The suit doesn't want me, not when you're this close. The plan is doomed to fail. He just doesn't know it yet." He tried to say something else to me but his eyes rolled up, then shut.

Two Zebras towed his unconscious body back to the stairs and up, toward the temple.

It was madness. I wasn't the only one who thought so.

"You can't put him in the suit!" Carpe started. "It's disastrous for supernaturals. The suit is made for humans—it's human magic."

Nicodemous barely glanced at Carpe as he followed where his prize was dragged. "You played your part well, Carpe. You'll be rewarded." It was a dismissal.

Carpe didn't take the hint. Fists clenched, he tried to follow Nicodemous but was blocked by a mercenary. He looked so strange, his slight frame against the much larger Zebra. It was pathetic. "You promised!" he shouted after Nicodemous.

That made Nicodemous pause.

"If we got you the suit, you'd find someone else—besides Alix," Carpe screamed.

"And so I did," Nicodemous said. "We're elves, Carpe. We trick everyone, and if you're only learning that lesson now, then I've done you a favor." And with that, Rynn, Nicodemous, and a guard of mercenaries left.

Leaving us with the rest of the Zebras. And Dennings.

I looked at her over my shoulder. She was smiling in a way that in my experience usually precedes grievous bodily harm. "Is this where the IAA reinstates me as an archaeologist?" I asked.

Her smile was made vicious against her severe hair and lawyerly black suit. "Should have taken our deal from the start, Hiboux. And now it's going to cost you."

Captain hissed at Dennings as she hit me over the head with the butt of her gun. My head hit the tiles while my eyes were still open, and the very last thing I saw before everything faded to black was Rynn disappearing up the steps of Shangri-La.

18

THEIR WICKED, WICKED WAYS

Time? Evening if the dark sky is any indication
Shangri-La

I felt my face. Oh, man. I seriously needed to stop letting people hit me over the head. Brain damage started to happen after enough of those, didn't it?

No bruises, no broken bones, no blindfold or eyes swollen shut . . . at least they were professionals and above beating me to a pulp. Well, except for the throbbing pain in my head from being hit. Dennings was going to pay for that if I ever got a chance.

Funny the things you remember after someone knocks you out. It was the scent of pine mixed with rotting autumn leaves that stayed with me as the wave of nausea crested. And the nightmare replaying over and over of an unconscious Rynn being dragged off.

Okay, Owl. Time to open your eyes . . . Oh the light hurt, though the dark storm clouds that had moved in overhead dampened the effect. A peel of thunder rolled through Shangri-La, shaking the ground right to its core. Not a good sign.

From my spot lying on the floor, I took stock of my new surroundings. I was still in the courtyard with a skeleton crew of Zebras—three that I could see, probably four. Dev and Texas were tied up beside me. I was also tied up, but no one had thought to stick me upright. Dennings's work, I was guessing.

Captain was stuck in a sturdy metal cage sitting in the corner with a large rock holding it in place. Captain didn't like stationary carriers. He preferred ones he could knock over—made it easier to roll them across the floor when it suited him.

I wondered which unlucky mercenary lost fingers getting him in there.

There was no sign of Michigan, or Dennings, or Carpe, for that matter. That I could live with.

"How's it feel to be back in ropes?" Texas said.

I managed to push myself up to a sitting position despite my hands being bound behind my back. First problem solved—now for the next hundred. "How long was I out?"

"An hour, give or take," Texas said as another roll of thunder ran through Shangri-La, followed by lightning this time. "And as to the weather?" He glanced up. "In six years all I've ever seen is a mild rainstorm. Even then the sun still shone through."

Carpe and Neil both said the balance was already screwed to high heaven. Where did they take them? "Neil and Rynn?" I asked.

It was Dev who answered this time. "To the temple—the one you and your friend came out of." After a pause he added, "We've been hearing blasts from inside—and feeling the aftershocks."

Probably to get the suit out. I just hoped that we'd managed to bury it better than they'd anticipated.

"Why would they take Neil?" Texas asked me.

I chose my answer carefully. "Most likely they wanted someone who was familiar with Shangri-La and the magic running this place." There was of course another reason: the spell they planned to use to force the armor on Rynn needed a human blood sacrifice . . . or something worse, though I chose not to say that.

Texas took it better than I expected. "A little early for the IAA suits to be involving themselves, isn't it? I always thought they showed up after the damage was done."

"They've graduated from cleanup crews to offensive on account of them getting caught with their pants down a little too much as of late, I imagine." We all fell silent as one of the Zebras did another pass. From the two black eyes Texas was sporting, I was guessing that was the incentive.

"This turned into one hell of a clusterfuck," Texas said once they passed.

"Welcome to the modern world of archaeology," Dev said.

While they glared at the mercenaries, I took stock of what we had— or, more accurately, didn't have. They'd taken what few weapons and equipment we'd had. I watched the mercenaries as they finished their round of the courtyard.

Sometimes the best way to get some forward motion is to throw a stick . . . and as far as I could see, that was the only break I was going to get.

"Hey!" I shouted. Texas swore.

"Are you out of your mind?" Dev hissed.

I ignored both of them. The two Zebras exchanged a dark glance between themselves. "Yeah, I'm talking to you. How 'bout some water over here? Or service."

Either they suspected me of something or couldn't believe I was that much of an idiot. A little bit of column A, a little bit of column B, I imagined. Either way, they headed over.

"Quiet," one of the mercenaries said with a much thicker Afrikaans accent than Williams.

I did no such thing. "Get me a water—no, make that a beer and then we'll talk about me shutting up." I made a show of glancing up at the sky. "Wouldn't mind an umbrella here either. Think we're due for rain?"

"I'm being serious," the mercenary said, giving my thigh a rough kick. He was visibly upset now that his bluster and threats weren't having the expected or desired effect.

"So am I. About a beer. Go get it." *Come on, you know you want to lose your temper. I'm an asshole, I'm demanding and have no respect for your gun or authority. Teach me a lesson—just do something stupid. I'm all tied up; how much harder could it get?*

For a moment I thought the mercenary might come closer, might take me on, might let himself make a mistake . . .

"That's enough." Williams stepped out of the foliage. The mercenary I'd been baiting looked like he might argue, but Williams added, "Fall back to checking the perimeter. Relieve Malcolm, he's been sitting on a dock for four hours."

The mercenary nodded and without even a glance at me disappeared from sight down the trail. After a nod from Williams, the other two followed. Williams then stood in front of me, arms crossed.

"No offense meant, but I figured it was going to take you a few more hours to crawl out of those tunnels," I said.

Williams only smiled. "Are you trying to start a brawl?"

"What can I say? Inaction offends me."

He made a tsking noise. "I had a lieutenant like you a few years back."

"Let me guess. You fired him?"

"Didn't have to. Ended up dead all on his own."

I shouldn't have smiled back—I knew it was a bad idea. Williams wasn't a twenty-something underling with a temper and something to prove. "And I'm betting having the supernaturals running free isn't going to be nearly as good for business as you think it'll be."

Williams gave me a casual shrug. "I have it on good authority that most of the time, not even the elves can predict the outcome of their own clandestine machinations. And make no doubt about it—I'm as disposable as you are to the lot of them at the best of times, though there's one thing I've got going for me that you don't."

"And what's that?" I asked.

Williams crouched down to my level. "I carry a big stick. I've done you a favor keeping you here with my men."

I didn't bother arguing. He probably had; Dennings and anyone from the IAA would have had far worse for me in store. Instead I said, "No one does favors for free."

Williams stood back up and nodded. "No, they don't. On that we're agreed."

I watched him leave and two more guards returned to take up position. Williams's message was loud and clear. *Stop screwing around. I'm watching you, and I'm not stupid.*

"Well, that went about as well as anything you do goes," Texas offered.

I would have told him to shut it—my pounding headache and ears really didn't need it, but something else caught my attention. At first I thought it was a bird, except for the fact that it was sticking out of a wooden door. It was a dart . . . and there was another one on the courtyard tiles. I was certain they hadn't been there a moment before.

I watched one fall out of the air close to the mercenary's feet. He stepped down and picked it up, looking at it before another one dropped and lodged in his neck. He toppled over, and about five darts later, the other two in sight fell as well.

Normally I'd be happy about a rescue—any rescue—except I knew who had to be behind it.

Carpe stepped into the clearing, watching me, wary. Captain let out a low growl that made Carpe jump as he edged by the cage.

"Speak of the devil," Texas murmured.

Carpe stopped a few feet away from us—nowhere near close enough for us to lynch him while we were still tied up. I held my breath and schooled my face to neutral until he came over and began to untie my hands.

"I knocked the other one out already," he said. "We have about five minutes or so before they'll be expected to check in," he said.

As soon as the ropes restraining my hands were gone, I leaped at him, knocking him to the ground.

"Hey!"

"Son of a bitch," I said. "All this time you *knew* what they were planning."

"Not everything! And all I did was make a deal—"

"And look where that got us!? You *idiot*."

He managed to loosen my hand. I pinned his neck with my forearm instead.

"It's not that simple, Owl. It's one person against saving the world. I can't put one person over the greater good like that—it goes against everything we believe!"

The greater good. I wondered how many people through history had said just that. "That's just it, Carpe—a world where people toss each other over for the greater good isn't the kind of world I want to live in."

"Just listen to me, will you?" he said as I tried to punch him. "I think I know what they're planning to do with Rynn and how."

I loosened my grip. "You've got three seconds."

"Three? Fuck me, three—"

"*Two*."

"Fine. They plan on making Rynn the Electric Samurai because he was one of their best warriors before he told them to fuck off. They've wanted him back ever since but haven't been able to do anything until now. Take away his free will and make him the Electric Samurai, under their control. Alix, there was nothing you could have done. They've been planning this for years, and when you found the spell book, it gave them the means. World Quest provided the opportunity."

"Did you know? When you made me go after that spell book?" I slammed his head against the stone tiles. A roll of thunder rumbled overhead and I smelled rain on the air.

"I swear I didn't know! Now will you stop hitting me?"

Would I stop hitting him? After he betrayed and delivered Rynn to a band of real monsters? Not a chance. But Texas stopped me, wrapping his bound hands over my head and dragging me off. "You can beat an apology out of him later. *After* we're all the hell out of here," he said, holding up his still-bound hands.

He was right. I let go of Carpe and watched him scramble back up. Captain must have disagreed, because he let out a cross between a growl and a meow. "Don't for a second think this is over, Carpe. You should have told us."

Carpe frowned. "Could have, should have, didn't . . ." Carpe set about untying Texas, and I helped Dev. "Look, we need a distraction. A big one," Carpe said. "They have them in the temple, and it's well guarded."

"How the hell do you expect us to lure away a band of mercenaries? That's not a plan, Carpe. Not even remotely!" I finished with Dev and opened the latch to Captain's cage. He lost no time darting into the foliage, where he could hide and watch.

"I have an idea."

We all turned to look at Texas. "You need something big, that's going to force them all to do something—give them a bit of a scare?" He nodded toward the other side of the courtyard. There was a statue on each corner—a dragon, a dog, a monster I couldn't immediately identify. Closest to us there was a stone tiger. The temple district was littered with them . . . "Are those what I think they are?"

"Reason we never set up camp here. No one with half a brain did. Didn't want to trigger one accidently."

Golems were an interesting category of magical device. Popular up until the Middle Ages, they'd been used to guard treasure and people, but as far as magical constructs went, they were simple. They might be able to move, but the commands were literally set in stone. There was no improvisation. If you made it to chase intruders, it would chase anyone it wasn't programmed to ignore . . . which occasionally meant the house cat or the hapless owner. "I've had bad luck with golems."

"You know how to set one off then?" he said, not bothering to hide his optimism.

I crawled over to the nearest unconscious mercenary and removed his gun. I was familiar with the mechanism if not the gun itself. "Yeah, more or less." Before anyone had a chance to argue, I aimed and fired at the dragon.

Texas grabbed the gun from me before I could fire at the second golem.

"You said activate it!"

"Yeah, I figured by turning on the bindings! Just what the hell kind of archaeology school did you go to? 'Hold my beer and watch this'?"

"*Guys*," Dev said.

We turned as the dragon golem shuddered, moving its first few inches in centuries. Its eyes sparked like glowing red embers, and it fixed them on me.

"Run," I said.

I took the gun from Texas and fired at the other three golems before dropping the weapon and running for the path after Carpe, Texas, and Dev—the same way the mercenaries had gone. "Head for the temple," I said. With any luck, the golems would view mercenaries carrying weapons as larger threats than we were.

As we ran, I could hear them catching up, their stone feet hitting the ancient steps in rapid succession. Of course they were gaining. But I could also hear the mercenaries up ahead. I caught sight of the temple entrance, guarded. The mercenaries saw us now—they were pointing and scrambling, but whether from us or the golems . . .

Time to remove ourselves from the line of sight.

Captain shot ahead of us and veered off the trail into the foliage.

"Follow my cat," I said, and plunged into the foliage after Captain. Turns out it was less an outcrop and more a steep hillside blanketed with fallen leaves—years' worth. My feet shot out from under me and I started to slide down. I heard Carpe, Dev, and Texas follow suit. I also heard gunfire behind us, the roar of a golem, and, more importantly, no large stone objects hitting the hillside.

The slide Captain had found wound its way down until it reached a flat clearing. The chaos and screams stayed above us.

Captain was waiting for us, licking his paws as the others slid to a stop beside me. "Your cat is an asshole," Texas said.

I got up and checked the area around us. A smooth, unnatural wall was half overgrown with foliage. I brushed some of the vines aside. It was the temple—the bottom of it. "Jackpot," I said. All we had to do was find a different entrance. They wouldn't even know we were inside.

There was a rumble of thunder, followed closely by a sheet of lightning. The ground shook in the start of an earthquake.

"It's getting worse," Texas said.

"They must have opened the gates again and let more people in. I told them not to, that it would affect the balance," Carpe offered. He glanced up at the sky, a nervous look on his face. "For all we know, Shangri-La is about to implode with all the new activity."

Like a time bomb sitting on a rickety shelf without a timer.

I ran my hand through my hair. Thankfully, the armor had laid off the prompts so I could think. Probably had its own immediate fate to worry about.

"I don't think the mercenaries have uncovered the portal in the temple courtyard," Texas said. "They got us before we got close, and like I said, it's hidden."

I nodded. If we were gone, there was no reason to leave guards. Not with the golems at any rate.

"And what's to stop them from following us?" Dev argued. "Besides, they all lead to the middle of nowhere. Implode here or starve or freeze on the other side. Unless one of you has a cell phone shoved up your a—"

"We might have an alternative," Texas said, "but we'll need to get access to the computers. I might be able to get a message out through World Quest. Nothing substantial, mind you, but considering how busy Shangri-La is playing with the mercenaries and fucking up its own weather patterns, it shouldn't be watching the game."

If it worked, we could have someone waiting on the other side of the gate. . . .

"Okay, new plan," I said, and pointed to Texas. "You and Carpe deal with the computers. Dev, you come with me, and we'll see if we can find Rynn and Neil before the elves and IAA do something stupid. After that we'll meet at the gate. Whoever gets there first opens it and goes through. No questions or waiting."

Dev swore, but he didn't argue.

Carpe, on the other hand . . . "I should come with you—" he started, then trailed off at the expression on my face.

"You know World Quest, you'll be more help there." I didn't add that Carpe had done enough.

Carpe wasn't about to let up though. His features twisted back into a frown.

"I'm sorry," he tried again. "But I was trying to do what was right—"

I spun on him, my voice barely civil. "Listen up and listen good, Carpe. I will *never* trust you again as long as I live."

He stared at me for a long second, then fell silent.

"Who do we contact?" Texas asked me.

"Ever wrangle vampires?" I asked.

Texas frowned at me. "Anyone ever tell you, you are one messed-up chick?"

"All the time."

I felt the first snowflake land on my nose. I held out my hand. More large snowflakes fell, collecting on the ground around us.

"Gimme the contact info," Texas said. "And hurry up. I don't think this place is going to hold up much longer."

I checked the bag I'd grabbed before running from the golems; it had belonged to a Zebra. There was a light, along with some other somewhat useful tools. The grenades were what I focused on. Next was Captain, who was swishing his tail by my feet. "You go with them," I said, pointing to Texas. Captain snorted at me.

"There'll be vampires." That had him perk up—one of the few words he understood. He was listening, and regarding Texas less as an adversary and more as a potential means to chasing vampires. I picked him up and handed him to Texas. "You'll need him to strike fear into vampires on the other side. That, and he'll keep Carpe from misbehaving." For once Texas didn't argue.

I checked the grenades before swinging the stolen bag over my shoulder. I wouldn't feel bad about trapping anyone in a tomb this time,

Dennings and Nicodemous included. "Let's hope we all don't die," I said, and with that we set off.

—⟋⟍—

"Are you sure this is the right one?" Dev whispered from behind.

Mostly, I thought. Though I had to agree, it was awfully narrow—and dusty. I shook my head. Just the city trying to throw me off. "I'm positive it's this way."

"Then crawl faster, will you? I'm getting claustrophobic back here, and there are bugs," Dev said, though his voice was muffled by the flashlight carried between his teeth.

There weren't any bugs—that was Dev's imagination—but still I picked up the pace. No saying what Shangri-La was up to. "Just keep your eye out for traps, and keep that flashlight on the stone."

"I am."

"No you're not, you're lighting up half the tunnel looking for bugs." And that was when I saw an exit up ahead, about twenty feet or so.

Dev swore and grabbed my foot. The flashlight went out. A second later I saw why—a group of Zebras passed by the entrance. One even shone a flashlight down, but we were too far back.

I kept silent until they passed. We crawled faster this time, hoping to beat them before they returned.

"Good ears," I whispered—or hoped I did. Mine had yet to recover from the dynamite.

"Speaking of ears, I don't hear any more blasting."

Meaning they more than likely had gotten back into the tomb and had the suit.

We reached the end of the tunnel and crawled out into a proper passageway. One we could stand in. It didn't look familiar, but that was fine. All we needed to do was get to the center. We had to almost be there.

We heard a noise up ahead, and both of us made our way slowly toward it, until we found a ledge. We were on a balcony above a temple auditorium, and below, at the front, was Nicodemous, with Rynn on a temple slab.

All they needed was a pit full of lava.

"I hate it when life reflects movies," Dev offered. "If anyone starts ripping out hearts, I'm leaving."

"I'll be right behind you." Beside them was a standing sarcophagus . . . in two hollowed pieces. I spotted the desiccated body, skin and old cloth clinging to the bones like parchment. That had to be Jebe, discarded in a useless heap on the floor. But if that was the case, then where was the armor?

My heart sunk, stealing what little hope I'd mustered with it. Rynn wasn't dressed in his black clothes. Instead, he had been dressed in black metal and leather plated armor, the very same style that would have been worn by Jebe. Small lightning bolts decorating the leather and metal flickered in the lamplight. That sealed it. Rynn was already wearing the Electric Samurai armor. I held on to the last trace of hope coursing through my blood, telling me I wasn't too late.

I spotted Neil being held off on the far side of the platform, on the other side of the sarcophagus. Two elves had him on his knees, but he was still alive—though from the bruise on his face and the slump to his shoulders, he was worse for wear. And there was Williams, standing off to the side as well—smart of the man—along with more elves; three to be exact, though not pale like Nicodemous. They looked more like Carpe, though older. The scent of dried, decaying leaves and pine mixed with incense reached us.

All we needed to do was get down there. Rynn had to be close to waking up, unless they'd kept drugging him. All we needed was a distraction . . .

"Where's the IAA woman?" Dev said, frowning.

Before I could answer, the telltale click of a gun sounded behind us. I swore and turned.

Dennings. Of course she'd be crawling around the temple like the rat she was . . .

"I had a hunch you might try and crash the party," she said. "Was that your idea, the golems? Or just the city trying to kill everyone?"

I didn't bother answering. Instead nodding toward the spectacle below. "You're IAA. You can't possibly think any of that is a good idea—" She made a tsking sound and I fell silent.

I expected threats. Instead she said, "You're getting a better deal than most. Any other graduate student in your place would consider themselves lucky."

"I'm not a graduate student anymore."

"Not according to our agreement with the elves," she smiled. It wasn't friendly. "You've already been reenrolled. Repayment for past wrongs done. We won't even go after your friends," she said, turning the gun on Dev. "Including Nadya and Benjamin. See? We can be generous."

"I'm not taking the deal." *Think, Owl.* I searched for loose rocks . . . maybe I could shove her off the ledge.

In answer, a rumble coursed through the temple and the ground shook.

Dennings's eyes went wide and she dropped the gun, trying to steady herself. Then she fell over. Dev was standing behind her, a palm-sized rock in his hand.

"Ever since they found me in Nepal, I've wanted to do that."

I wrote it off to Karma. People tended to get theirs. Eventually.

"Let's get Rynn and get the hell out of here while the place is still standing," I said, and ran back to the ledge. Nicodemous and the elves were still presiding over Rynn. I looked for something to throw, but Dev's rock wouldn't do anything from this distance. I ran back to Dennings and grabbed her gun. I took the safety off and aimed for the floor below.

"Since when do you use guns?"

"I don't," I said, and fired. The bullet didn't hit anything useful, but it made a lot of noise.

Our entrance earned a momentary glance from Nicodemous. I

looked straight into his pale red eyes. "Hi!" I shouted. "Hear you've got a supernatural party for me to crash."

Nicodemous's mouth twisted into a snarl, exposing his pink teeth. And there, in his hands, was the spell book. The one Carpe had made me fetch all those months ago.

"*Come on, just look at me—look at me, Rynn.*"

"He's not moving," Dev said.

"I know that!" I'd hoped Rynn would be conscious enough to use our distraction and meet us partway. Which meant I needed a bigger distraction . . .

"Alix," Dev said. I glanced back down to where Nicodemous and the elves were chanting. Sure enough, the black suit was now glowing an angry, disruptive red in response. It really didn't want to be there. I was hoping to oblige it—at least halfway. I'd worry about that when we got there. I felt the suit pinging me, demanding I get it out of its predicament.

"*Get in line,*" I told it.

"Keep her from the ceremony," Nicodemous said, then got back to his incantation from the book. The other elves began to secure the final pieces of the armor on Rynn.

The remaining mercenaries began to move our way. I fished a grenade and gun out of the bag I'd stolen and handed them both to Dev. "Lead them up the stairs—toss the grenade down once you're up top. And stay ahead—they know what they're doing."

"What the hell are you planning on doing?"

I didn't answer, in turn giving Dev a shove. "Just make sure you lead them away—and keep running until you reach the gate."

The volume of the chanting increased. Rynn stirred on the bench below, and his eyes opened as a red mist surrounded him and the armor. They found me and were burning blue. "Alix, run!" he shouted.

Now that Rynn was struggling against the restraints, Nicodemous stepped up his pace. Rynn screamed as the angry red mist glowed and flared around him.

I aimed Dennings's gun and fired it at the elf. It went high—I was a lousy shot from this distance. I needed to get closer. I started down the narrow stone staircase to the temple floor, taking the steps two and three at a time, pausing only as the temple shuddered. Must have been Dev dropping the grenade. Hopefully the mercenaries wouldn't be getting back anytime soon.

I raced down the steps as fast as I could. The three elves rushed forward to meet me. I hesitated aiming the gun—shooting at Nicodemous was one thing, but firing at someone's chest? I spotted a loose stone off to the side of one of the steps, and quickly found holes in the wall. There were an awful lot of them.

One, two—when the three elves were all in range, I jumped for the step and ducked. White-tipped darts shot out of the wall and lodged in their sides. A moment later they collapsed. Apparently elves were one supernatural with no immunity to poison.

Now all I needed to do was get close enough to hit Nicodemous—

But Nicodemous had vanished from the temple floor. I cautiously approached the slab and Rynn's prone form.

My heart bottomed out, and I heard myself yell as I ran for the slab. Rynn was wearing the armor, but it had changed, warped itself. Like all the other reincarnations, it had molded itself into something that fit the times. Now it resembled the Kevlar armor I'd seen the mercenaries wearing. It fit like bike gear. It was simple and modernized, with nothing ornate to give its true identity away except for a small, silver lightning bolt etched over his heart. It was magic—I could feel the air tingling around me with static electricity—but it wouldn't draw attention outside, not even on a street corner.

I couldn't stop myself; maybe I wasn't too late.

"Rynn?" I said, shaking his arm.

He opened his eyes and blinked, as if trying to clear a bad headache.

"Rynn?" I couldn't believe it: he looked okay, not bloodthirsty, not crazy . . .

His eyes cleared as he looked around the temple. He fixed his gaze on me and frowned. It was cold—and blank. "Rynn, it's me," I tried. "Are you okay? Can you get up?"

He frowned down to where I was holding his arm. I let go and he sat up, still fixated on me with his gray eyes, darker than I remembered them.

"Alix," he said, as if testing out a foreign word. He swung his feet down, and the leather boots the armor had decided to form touched softly on the ground.

I took a step back in spite of myself. It was Rynn—the same movements, the same features and expressions. I mean, he recognized me, obviously, but there was something in the way he watched me, as if trying to place me.

His nostrils flared, as if he was scenting the air around him. He was still staring at me, but his features took on a vexed expression. "It's an interesting sensation," he said. "I can feel your emotions, like a jumble, stronger than before. Theirs too," he added, nodding at the elves and Neil, whose body had been left on the ground.

Rynn took a step toward me, but his motions reminded me more of a predatory cat than the person I knew.

"I can feel everything you feel," he continued. "All those strange, mixed emotions tumbling over themselves—relief, fear, anger in there settled underneath all those layers. Even love." He looked away from me. "I remember them. All of them—it's like a signature imprinted on me. The funny thing is, I don't care anymore. I used to, I know I did." His expression hardened as he looked back at me. "What did you do to me?"

I shook my head. "I didn't do anything, Rynn. It's the armor—and the elves. They did—"

But he shook his head, and I saw the first glimpse of anger—something that was usually foreign on Rynn's face. He never showed anger, not like that. "Not that. Before. What did you do to me, Alix? Why do I remember caring?"

There are a few moments in my life about which I can remember everything, every detail, clearly. Most of them aren't very nice: being kicked out of grad school, beaten up by vampires, cursed by an artifact, losing Captain. Then there are a couple of really clear good moments—most of them with Rynn and Nadya.

This was definitely the worst.

"I swear I didn't do anything to you. It's the suit. You can tell I'm telling the truth."

"Or you *think* you are," he said, and his lip twisted up in the start of a snarl. I wracked my brain for what I'd read in Jebe's journal—anything that could explain this . . .

But there was nothing. I started to back away. Slowly.

It couldn't just be that he was supernatural . . .

I turned to Nicodemous. "What did you do to him?" I said, still backing away from Rynn.

Nicodemous was focused on Rynn though. "We made some alterations while binding him to the suit. He was always unpredictable—difficult to control. Now he won't be."

Rynn was still watching me, as if trying to remember something, grasping for a thought or faded memory on the edge of his mind, just out of reach.

Finally he turned his attention on the elves and Nicodemous. "Her," he said, nodding at me. "Who is she?"

The first glimpse of uncertainty crossed Nicodemous's face. "No one. Leave her. I gave you a direct order."

Rynn ignored the order. "She doesn't strike me as no one," he said.

I clenched my fists. His voice was strained, but I could hear the thin layer of doubt in it. Rynn was in there somewhere—he had to be. If we could just get the suit off him . . .

"There is an adjustment," Nicodemous continued. "All will be explained, and your misgivings will fade in time." There was condescension in Nicodemous's voice, so sure was he the spell had worked. Here was the thing. Magic like that never worked out the way you supposed it would.

The gun felt heavy in my hand as I watched Nicodemous cross the temple floor toward Rynn. I'd never killed anyone before, but if there was ever a time to cross that line in the sand . . .

I lifted my arm. It was shaking. I clicked off the safety and aimed.

Someone stopped me. It was Dev. He took the gun out of my hands. "You can thank me later," he said, then nodded at Rynn and added, "look at his hand."

I spotted it. A knife. Thin and black . . . I remembered one of the things Williams had said about the elves: that even the elves never knew what their plans would bring.

Nicodemous stood up straighter and placed his hands behind his back—the consummate politician stance, I suppose.

Rynn looked at me once more over his shoulder and his eyes narrowed, as if he was trying to remember something—or trying to decide. Whatever it was, Nicodemous didn't like it. "I gave you an order. Leave the girl alone," Nicodemous said.

That got Rynn's attention. He began to calmly walk over to the elf.

Nicodemous relaxed. "That's more like it. I have things for you to do. You needn't waste time on her or any of them." He sounded more annoyed than concerned. He simply stood there and watched as Rynn approached.

Some of the mercenaries had returned, and they were all watching Rynn as well, not certain what to do. "Quick—go get Michigan," I said to Dev.

"And you think I'll follow? That I'll listen to you?" Rynn said to Nicodemous, his mouth curling up at the corners.

"Because I made you. You're bound to the elves to do our bidding. This time you can't leave."

Rynn seemed to regard him. Nicodemous might have missed it, but Rynn in his current state didn't strike me as anyone's servant.

But Nicodemous either didn't see what I did or didn't deign it a threat, even as Rynn drew the black knife back.

The knife slid into Nicodemous's chest. The elf's eyes went wide and he gasped, but even though his body arched, I don't know if he realized what had happened. Not until he looked down at the blade sticking out of his chest and the blood pooling around him. It seemed to dawn on him as he looked back up—right into Rynn's snarling face.

"I might not know what I feel for her, but I *do* remember how much I hate elves. *That* hasn't changed one bit," Rynn said, and drove the knife deeper into Nicodemous's chest before taking it out and sliding it across the elf's neck.

I still wasn't certain Nicodemous realized what had happened even as he collapsed to the floor—dead.

It was Karma of a sort—bloody, rendered Karma.

I started to call out, but Dev clamped a hand over my mouth and dragged me off the platform and out of Rynn's line of sight. With him was Neil, looking drained but alive. "What are you doing?" I snarled at Dev once I got his hand free.

"Preventing you from getting his attention and getting us both killed." He nodded back to the platform above us.

Rynn was focused on the other elves now, still lying prone on the steps. The mercenaries were oddly frozen. Rynn glanced back up at us, but for now the elves were winning his attention. He dragged them back to the altar.

The ground shook, stronger than it had before, loosening rocks above . . . all that magic in one place, then a death, and supernatural blood . . . shit.

Michigan went white. "We need to get out of here—now," he said.

He was right; as much as it pained me, we started to run back up the steps.

We were halfway up the steps before Rynn called out. "Alix?" His voice echoed off the temple walls.

I stopped and turned, slowly.

The mercenaries started to reassemble around him.

Dev grabbed my arm and tried to steer me away. "Come on, we have to leave now—before he decides to get rid of you the same way he just did Nicodemous."

But I had to give it one last try. "Rynn, the elves did something to you. You need to take the armor off."

He just stood there and stared at me, on the verge of taking another step.

"Just . . . will you say something?" I shouted, hoping I'd somehow managed to get through. He had to be in there still, somewhere.

He shook his head. "Something made me head back this way, but for the life of me I can't remember what it was." He turned away, back toward the mercenaries. They didn't attack; they fell in line.

He was using his power, a lot of power. More than I'd ever seen him use before. Son of a bitch, he was compelling all of them.

If I could keep breaking his attention . . . "Rynn, don't walk away from me!"

He crossed the floor and was up the steps faster than I would have thought possible. His gloved hand wrapped around my throat. I wanted to struggle, tried to, but I couldn't move. Rynn had frozen me in place.

He studied my face. "To be completely honest, I can't tell if I loved or hated you," he said, his eyes narrowing, cruel, calculating. "I think it might have been a bit of both." He brought his face close enough to mine that I could smell him. His scent had changed to something darker, more sinister. "I'll warn you once, Alix. *Stay out of my way.*"

He let go, and I fell to the ground as he strode back to the mercenaries.

I let Rynn walk away. I'd failed. Completely. When it actually mattered, I'd still managed to screw up.

Arms reached under my shoulder as Dev and Michigan both helped me up. "We need to get out of here before he compels us to jump off a fucking cliff," Dev whispered.

I made myself move, following them blindly until I remembered something. "The book!" I broke their grips and raced back to the platform as the temple shook again. If the book had gotten Rynn into the suit, maybe there was something in there that could get him out.

I skidded to a halt by Nicodemous's dead body, the red blood collecting in a pool around him, smelling even more like death and decay. I hesitated only for a moment before prying the text from his dead hands, none too gently. I tucked the book into my bag and ran back up the steps, catching up to Neil and Dev as they reached the tunnel out. As we crawled in, yelling from outside reached us. I wasn't sure if Rynn was compelling more mercenaries or just making the ones he had compelled shoot the ones he hadn't.

We spilled out of the temple as the entirety of Shangri-La shook to its core. There was a thick layer of heavy snow on the ground now, and the sky was filled with pitch-black clouds, the lanterns hanging from the buildings the only light to see by. We ducked behind a building as screams drew closer and a group of IAA suits bolted past, chased by the tiger golem.

Won't lie. Hard to feel bad about that one. It was a shame Dennings wasn't with them.

"This way," Neil said, and set off at a breakneck pace up the hillside steps. We followed. I just hoped to hell the gate was still open—or functioning . . .

We were so set on reaching the gate that we didn't notice Williams and what remained of his band—which included those who hadn't been in the temple or hadn't been maimed by golems—until we ran into them. We all skidded to a halt, staring at each other. A few of his men pulled guns.

"No offense, but I really don't think this is the time or place to be shooting each other," I said.

Williams nodded. The guns went down. They weren't bad people. Another time, another place . . . "Make sure you get your men out soon—before the IAA and the elves. There's a problem with numbers. Not everyone will be able to leave," I said.

Williams gave me a wary nod.

"We're even now," I said.

Williams smiled. "I suppose we are."

And with that, we went our opposite ways.

Between dodging golems and IAA, it took us longer than we would have liked to reach the portal. Texas and Carpe were still there. "I thought I told you two to open it."

"Fuck off, Hiboux. We decided to wait." Texas didn't say anything else, but gave Michigan a nod.

I would have yelled more, but the wind had picked up and waves were breaking the ships in the harbor into pieces. In the distance, a temple crumbled to the ground, and Shangri-La shook. Captain found me and huddled by my feet.

"They've opened another gate," Carpe yelled.

Rynn—he must have opened it. "Then get the gate open!" I just hoped we could still leave . . .

The ground shook again, and I heard screams as a temple toppled across the square. If it kept up, we had minutes at most.

Texas cut his hand and dropped the blood on the three diagrams—the one on the floor, then the temple, and then the courtyard wall. The gate shimmered—and wavered—and for a moment I thought it might collapse. But it shuddered into existence. We all stared at each other. Who got to go first?

"Michigan, Texas, Dev, Captain, Carpe, then me," I said. Why Carpe before me? Because as much as it pained me to do it, I'd been in charge of this disaster. I watched as Michigan and then Texas and then Dev went through the gate. I set Captain down and pushed him toward it. He sat on his haunches and looked at me as if I was an idiot. All of Shangri-La shook, and to my horror, the blue-and-yellow temple started to crack. Lousy, no-good cat. I scooped him up and held him out to Carpe. "You take him through," I said.

But he didn't take Captain. Instead, he took hold of my shoulders.

"What the hell?" I snarled.

"I told you I was sorry!" he shouted at me over the wind and thunder, and gave me a shove, sending me through.

And that was the last thing I heard from him before Captain and

I hit the ground on the other side. I waited, but Carpe didn't follow. My nerves were so raw from everything that had just happened that I didn't know how I felt in that moment—about anything—except completely numb all the way down to my bones. All I managed to do was push myself up on my knees before puking up the entirety of my stomach.

—⁓—

We were stuck on a mountaintop. Definitely the Andes, though whatever civilization this had been had long been lost. We waited a day. It was cold, but I had to admit I welcomed the numbing effect it had—on my body and my emotions.

I welcomed the numbness, because otherwise I felt empty without Rynn. I kept going over and over how I could have made it down to the platform faster . . . what I could have done differently . . . how I hadn't seen it coming from the beginning . . .

After all the times Rynn had saved me, the times he'd been there for me . . . At the end of the day, when it had counted, when it had been my turn, I'd come up completely short.

I didn't know if I could ever forgive myself for that, even if I managed to fix things. I spent a lot of time wondering how much the suit had taken over his thoughts, and how much had been the spell the elves had used.

"*Stay out of my way.*" That had been the last thing he'd said to me.

Hell would freeze over before that happened. If there was anything of him left, anything at all, I'd find a way to get him out.

When I wasn't dwelling on Rynn and my own failures, Carpe also invaded my thoughts. I was also glad for the numbness, because all my last exchange with Carpe did was confuse me.

Goddamned stupid elf.

Considering we hadn't had an exact location for the gate beyond—assorted ruins in the Andes—I was surprised when a helicopter circled us in the early evening. More so when it landed and a heavily reinforced cat carrier, four bottles of water, and four gas masks were tossed out toward us. Peace offerings, vampire style.

"May I offer you a ride?" a thick French accent shouted down at us.

I wrangled Captain into the carrier—no small feat—and got him subdued to a low growl before stepping onboard.

Alexander went so far as to offer me a hand. I pulled myself in. "Just keep to your side of the helicopter, Alexander."

"I believe this is the start of a wonderful friendship."

I knew I should be civil, but I couldn't bring myself to do it. "Stuff it."

We rode most of the way in silence, until Dev finally asked, "What do we do now?"

I shrugged. "My advice? Lay low, stay far away from the IAA, and run if a dragon offers you a job. "

Dev made a noncommittal shrug and turned his attention back to the others. I was staring at a laptop I'd reluctantly borrowed from Alexander. Getting back into my email outweighed my indignation at having to talk to a vampire.

A few messages from Lady Siyu—which I ignored—and one from Nadya.

It was simple, straightforward, and had the dire undertones that lack of details often gave.

Come to Tokyo as soon as you can.

Looked like I was headed for Japan.

I watched the night world pass by outside. As an afterthought, and searching for something to do, I opened my phone and messaged Lady Siyu.

Things just got a hell of a lot worse. I hope you're happy. And I'm keeping my cat.

For once I didn't get a response. I counted that as a good thing.

Somehow I figured this had just gotten a lot bigger than just Mr. Kurosawa and Lady Siyu's war with the other supernaturals . . . and I had the unsettling feeling that Rynn had just become the center of it.

Captain stopped his growling and gave me a forlorn mew, as if sensing where my thoughts had gone.

"You said it, Captain," I told him.

I'm Alix Hiboux, antiquities thief for hire, specializing in the supernatural. I need to save the world from my cursed supernatural boyfriend.

As Texas was so fond of saying, *"Sucks to be you, Hiboux."*

Epilogue

Tokyo, Space Station Deluxe

I stood outside Space Station Deluxe, Nadya's bar, for longer than I needed to. The place was deserted—not just closed, but deserted. As if the street no longer existed.

I only knew of one supernatural who could do that.

I pushed the door open and let Captain run ahead before stepping inside. He hugged the walls, as if he knew there was something out of the ordinary and we should have our hackles up.

The lights were off, all except the red night-light, something both Nadya and Rynn had installed four or five months ago in each of their bars. Nadya's in red, Rynn's in blue. Seemed like an awfully long time ago now.

Nothing jumped out at me, so I headed to the back. The red tinge was giving me an unsettling feeling.

"Nadya?" I whispered. "Nadya?"

I heard sound in the back—where her office was. The door was ajar. I held my breath and pushed it open.

Nadya was sitting there behind her desk, waiting. Captain mewed and wasted no time jumping up on her lap. "Jesus, do you have to keep all the lights off like that? You nearly gave me a heart attack."

"Necessary. Come with me," she said, and closed the door to her office before waving me toward the back of the club—farther away from the lights.

"What's going on? And why the cloak-and-dagger?" I asked, though I already had my suspicions.

"You'll see" was all she said.

"No offense, Nadya, but I've had a lifetime's worth of surprises this last week between the IAA, the elves, Rynn, and now this . . ." I trailed off as I spotted the lit cigarette in the back of the bar. At first I could only tell that he was male from his silhouette, but then I glimpsed the tattoo winding up his face as the cigarette once again burned bright.

Oricho.

I clenched my fists but held my tongue. This was the supernatural who only a few months before had tried to take down Mr. Kurosawa and wipe out every supernatural creature in Vegas, including Rynn. I'd briefly counted him as a friend. And told him never to cross my path again.

Oricho stood, and the lights flared on, illuminating the back corner of the bar. Now I was certain why there were no other people hanging around. Oricho could do that. He was that powerful. And dangerous.

"Well, I see the dragon and the snake didn't eat you," I said.

He smiled. There was a gaping wound on his neck, half covered by the high collar of his jacket. "Likewise. I would say it is a pleasure, but I suspect from your expression you do not share my sentiments." He bowed his head.

"I'm pretty damn sure I said I never wanted to see you again. Ever."

He nodded again, but the slight smile—not vindictive or mocking, but sad—remained.

"And I apologize for not following your request."

I was starting to wish I'd remembered to grab Nadya's baseball bat. Not that it would have done any good besides making me feel a little more secure from having something violent in my hands. "What do you want?"

Oricho inclined his head. "Due to recent events, you are at a disadvantage. The time has come where I believe I can help. And I owe you a favor, which I intend to repay."

The question always arises with supernaturals: what the hell happens after repayment?

I pushed that thought aside. I didn't think Oricho would kill me right now—he'd have done it already.

"How do you think you can possibly help me?"

He arched a single eyebrow, and the tattoo of the dragon winding down his neck moved, possibly a trick of the lights—or not.

"Because I know what has befallen Rynn. And I can help."

There are moments in life when the things you swore you'd never do come into direct opposition with the things you promised you would do . . . I'd been running into a lot of that lately. Tell Oricho to fuck off, or find out if he really could help me get Rynn back from whatever the elves had done to him?

I glanced over at Nadya, and she inclined her head.

"All right," I said to Oricho. "Say I'm willing to take you on a sign of faith. How? Rynn's the Electric Samurai now, and Nicodemous did something to him and the armor with magic. We don't even know what Rynn wants—"

"He is driven by the corrupted armor and bent to its will, however warped the elf has made it and him," Oricho said. "Its purpose is to rain war and destruction on the world. Rynn *will* become the warlord the elves wanted, but he will be outside of their control."

"You still haven't told me how you can help."

"I cannot." Oricho paused to take a drag from his cigarette, savoring the smoke before turning his black eyes back on me. "But I know the ones who can. They call themselves the Tiger Thieves."

Acknowledgments

As always, thanks go out to Steve Kwan, Leanne Tremblay, Tristan Brand, and Mary Gilbert, who read each and every Owl installment. Their encouragement keeps the series going.

I also have to thank my agent, Carolyn Forde, who picked the original *Owl and the Japanese Circus* manuscript out of the slush pile; my editor, Adam Wilson, who makes Owl that much better and puts up with me; and Brendan May for his encouragement and handling logistics at S&S Canada. There are many other people who have mentored and encouraged me in my writing career—thank you all!

Finally, there is one nonhuman without whom this series would never have been written, and that is my cat, Captain Flash, on whom the character Captain is absolutely based.